Black Halo
THE WITCH & THE GUARDIAN

A. S. ARAMIRU

Author email: ASAramiru@gmail.com
Author web site: https://www.Aramiru.com

Published by Shadywood Lane Publishing in 2014

ISBN-13: 978-0-9862004-1-0

Cover art by D. Elling. Artist web site:

https://www.facebook.com/people/Diana-Elling/100006265306067

a Special Thanks

To my friends and my family who've helped me get even this far. When the time comes, I'll help you all chase after your foolish dreams.

Prologue
a Recorder's Search

"Kalin?" the Witch called to her redheaded follower. He turned his head towards her as he gently held her hand.

Master Raina,

It's hard to imagine the world of before. Before magic, the Great Calamity, and the Witch. What remains of the past provides us with only glimpses, but never the whole story.

From the ashes, we were left with only children's tales passed on from generation to generation regarding the fate of the Old World. We've all heard it at least once in our childhood from either our parents or grandparents. With the passing of time and shifting narrators, the tale naturally shed the light of its truth and garnished itself with embroideries. I am, of course, referring to the tale of the Witch and the Guardian.

Even with the variations it has seen through the cycles of storytellers across the world, the core of the tale remains the same. It always begins with the time of the Old World when men built the world with just their hands. And then one day, without warning, the Light appeared. A mysterious light that could be seen no matter where a person may be. And with it came magic and the Witch.

"If things were not the way they were, where do you think we would be?" The Witch looked out to the vast ocean with a cold gaze. At the end of the horizon, the Light.

The tale is never clear on why the Witch started her war against humanity. Some iterations say that the Light gave birth to the Witch to carry out its will, believing that the Light and the Witch were both a judgment from the gods who ran out of patience for mankind's arrogance and foolishness. Some variations say that the Witch was just a bitter woman who was granted enough power from the Light to spread her anguish throughout the world. And then there are those that simply claim the Witch to be a creation of pure evil that came as the shadow to the Light.

The Witch's follower couldn't find an immediate answer to such a question out of the blue.

No matter who the storyteller, one fact remains the same: the Witch is always the enemy of mankind. Even during the infancy of magic, it was said that she wielded unimaginable powers which dwarfed even the greatest of man's inventions.

Beyond the children's tale, whispers among those wiser of what truly happened say that the Witch planned to do this with a device of catastrophic powers—the device that ushered in the Great Calamity and, with it, the end of the Old World: the artifact only known as the Black Halo.

"Probably somewhere with less fire, less blood, and less of all of this," the follower replied.

No one's certain on the specifics of its powers, but the magnitude of it is clear from the ruins of the past. If the Witch had had her way, there would have been nothing left. Despite that, the tale of the Witch and the Guardian is that of courage and preservation. The tale ends with a brave hero who challenged the Witch in a grand and desperate battle for the fate of the world. Before the Witch could realize her dream, her blood soaked the hero's blade and she fell unfulfilled. The people may have faced the Great Calamity, but at the end they had rebuilt their civilization with the newfound gift of magic.

It is the duty of the Guild of Recorders to preserve as much as we can of the history and passing times for the future. It is our duty to prevent losing the world once again. Perhaps it is due to my youth, but as a member of the guild I cannot help but continue pursuing my curiosity on this tale that I was told of as a child.

"But I'd like to think that at least somewhere, at some time, we would have met."

PART 1

Chapter 1
A DREAM OF THE WORLD'S END

She never called for the sandman, but he came for her anyway. To most, this might not be a notable event, but for Kiara it always was. When she awoke from the uninvited slumber, her body was drenched in sweat and her eyes were moist with tears. Her dorm room was still brightly lit with the light she hadn't turn off and she was lying on the floor beside the bed that she couldn't reach in time. Kiara grabbed onto the bed sheets and pulled herself up. She sat on the bed, burying her head into her hands. Her hands trembled. And her eyes forgot to blink.

Breathe in. Breathe out.

It wasn't the first time she had had an episode after a dream nor did she expect it to be her last. But these dreams were always more vivid and memorable than the ordinary ones.

Breathe in. Breathe out. Breathe in. Breathe out.

She glanced at her novelty cat clock on the wall, and the cat mocked her with a stupid grin on its face as it playfully swung its tail left and right. He told her it was almost twenty minutes after midnight. She had been dreaming for a few hours. It was already long past lights out, and it was unlikely that anyone was still awake. The polite thing to do would be to wait 'till tomorrow before she alarmed the Director. The reserved thing to do would be to just shut her eyes once more, but this time go to sleep by her choice.

Breathe in. Breathe out. BREATHE IN. BREATHE OUT. BREATHEIN. BREATHEOUT.

But the visions were relentless. The room became smaller and smaller as the clicks from the vile cat grew louder and louder.

Click. Click. Click. Click. Click. Click.

She had to go.

The light from Kiara's room lit the dark hallway as her door violently swung open. Kiara walked briskly, restraining herself from sprinting or stomping. As she breezed through the hallway, the lamps between the doors of her dorm-mates dimly lit and acknowledged her presence even though the dorm-mates themselves were deeply asleep. The remnants of her *dream* refused to leave her mind.

The Witch stood before a colossal gate at the peak of a grand white stair-case. The gate slowly opened, and the blinding light from beyond flooded the room. The Witch stepped into the light, and the gate closed behind her.

Kiara reached the stairs that led to the lounge below. The lounge, lit only by the fireplace left burning through the night, was bright enough to reveal the piano and the pool table with the balls neatly organized inside the wooden triangle. Someone had forgotten to put away the blankets on the sofas in front of the television.

"One of your oracles is up and frantic, Nancy." A man with a lingering accent reported to his boss through the telephone. There were watchful eyes all around the facility and this man was in the room center of them all. He had his legs up on the tables where the monitors revealed all that the watchful eyes could see. One hand resting behind his head and the other on the phone, he watched as Kiara descended the stairs too hastily and recklessly. Her feet tangled at the last couple of steps and she finished her descent downstairs by falling. Her landing didn't go unnoticed by those sleeping in the rooms nearby but they dismissed it quickly and returned to slumber.

The aged man tried to hold his laughter, but it managed to squeeze past through his clenched teeth.

"Which one, Yuri?" The female voice on the other end of the call was sharp and agitated.

"It's the one that sees forwards and not backwards," Yuri replied no less playfully than before as he scratched on his rough five o'clock shadow. He knew he was probably the only person who can get away with such behavior given that he had known her since she was a child as her father's friend. He liked to exercise the privilege whenever he could.

"You should get to her soon, Nancy. She's in such a hurry she decided to fly down the stairs." The call ended without a reply. Yuri placed the phone down on the table and united the freed hand with his other hand behind his head as he continued to amuse himself watching the frantic girl.

After some moaning and groaning, Kiara dragged her body to the bathroom. As she opened the bathroom door, chilly air scented with lemons and oranges escaped from the darkness. Heaters were off. Power conservation was in place for the night. Her body gave a quick shiver as her bare feet touched the cool tiles. The wall adjacent to the door was dimly lit with the soft light from the touch screen pad. She placed her finger over the **ON** icon and the subsequent burst of light made her cringe. The whirl of the heaters coming on, and its gentle warm breeze immediately filled the room. The rows of sinks, bathroom stalls, and the shower booths revealed themselves with the light. These were all luxuries to help them forget how far they were from their homes. The bathroom seemed larger without other girls going through their morning and evening routines. The quietness felt strangely lonely this evening.

Her breathing had calmed down but her heartbeat still echoed through the empty bathroom. Kiara placed her hands under the faucet and it let loose a flow of clean cold water. For a little while, she simply let the water slip through her fingers. The visions of the *dream* were still clear. She cupped her hands to catch the cool water and splashed it across her face.

Some time has passed since the Witch entered the gate. Kiara knew as if the dream had whispered it to her. She now stood in various parts of the world and saw firsthand the world being tested for its survival. Mother Nature violently struggled as if she battled for her life. Earth split across the globe, gusts of wind swept across civilization, endless rain drowned all those that couldn't fly, and rocks and fire rained from the sky to bury all that was remaining.

Mankind retaliated against Mother Nature with wars and drew blood from one another to survive. Dead bodies blanketed the streets. Children that were left without families and left with blood in their eyes chose to continue their parents' war.

Civilizations decayed into anarchy, and Mother Nature never forgot to remind mankind how small it was. For every scar that mankind gave her, she eviscerated them with all of her wrath. Even beasts, familiar and foreign, rose against mankind to save their place in the crumbling world. A miasma of death blanketed whatever was left. The world as it was once known was no more. No more since the Witch entered the Light.

Warm tears mixed with the cool water drizzled down Kiara's face. She looked toward the blinded windows in dreadful anticipation. Even if she couldn't see *it*, she knew it was there. Kiara left the bathroom and headed for the padded doors that led outside. The doors were always a bit heavy, but especially during night when it was windy. She put her shoulder against the door and pushed. Chilly and dried up wind of the desert greeted her outside.

It was there. Over the horizon of the night sky was a thin line of light piercing skywards. She walked further and further away from the building and closer and closer to the Light. It's been there since all *this* began. It was a silent but constant reminder to the world that change will come. No that the world *already* had changed. Kiara's legs crumpled and she fell to her knees, her eyes still attached to the Light. Somewhere in the world *she* could also be watching the Light—planning to make what Kiara saw in her *dream* come true.

"Kiara?" a gentle, familiar voice called out to her from behind.

She turned her head to find Ms. Jones behind her. Ms. Jones was still dressed in her lavish office attire and had her arms crossed to fight the chilly desert evening. Her eyes permeated with concern.

"I was told by security you were out here. What's the matter?" Ms. Jones carefully asked as she approached closer. Ms. Jones crouched down and placed her hand on Kiara's shoulder. The Director's warmth slowly dissipated Kiara's anxiety but stirred her longing for someone to let her know that everything will be alright. Kiara's tears ran freely down her eyes as she embraced Ms. Jones. The Director gently patted the crying child's back

"What's wrong?" Ms. Jones asked once more.

"It's the Witch, Ms. Jones," the Oracle-That-Sees-Forward answered through her tears. "I think she's going to do something horrible. I think she'll be the end of us all."

Ms. Jones looked beyond the crying teen's shoulders and saw the Light piercing the skies with the unanswered questions it held. She wondered what value the answers may have. Until then, Nancy regarded the Light as a puzzle for a bored mind to ponder about. The Witch, the Light, and the Gifted were all probably part of a grander scheme, but Nancy's aim was to simply find her place within that vast plan. But her instincts were never silent and whispered to her that her greater ambitions were going receive their calling. Her instincts told her that today was the day her curiosity will grow into something more.

"There, there…" Nancy gently patted Kiara on the back. "We won't let that happen, Kiara. That's why we're here." The Director gave a small kiss on her student's forehead.

"Tell me more, Kiara. What did you exactly see?" Nancy asked as she embraced the oracle tightly against her chest. Her eyes were set on the Light as the child spoke softly in her ears of the dream of the world's end.

INTERLUDE I
COMING OF AGE

"Mom?! Mom!" Kalin's shouts were loud enough to echo.

From the loft, Kalin went down the stairs to his family's florist shop. The various perfumes of the flowers and plants tickled his nose as they always did. He found his mother near the exit of the store tucked into a thick winter jacket and a wool beanie she had knitted. She had a small mail carrier bag strapped across her chest and was busy gathering the picket signs.

"You're going out again? For those freaks?" Kalin grumpily asked.

He didn't have a particular reason to dislike the "freaks" other than that he worried about his mother. Hostility from their community was growing each day ever since Kalin's mother announced her support of those weirdos.

"First, the politically correct term we are apparently using is to refer to them as the 'Gifted.' If you're up to feeling a bit silly, you may call them wizards. Second, though they may be wizards, the Gifted are still people, Kalin," his mother spoke sternly but with tenderness. She knew it wasn't an easy thing for her son to understand, and she understood that he was worried for her. "Maybe someday you'll understand, hun. I imagine your father would be out there with me too if he was still around." She finally managed to gather all the picket signs and carried them over her shoulder, holding them steady with one arm. With her free hand, the mother ruffled her son's hair.

Kalin shooed his mother's hand away. His father wasn't a hero or led a particularly interesting life, but everyone who knew him told Kalin that his father was a good man. Illness took him away while Kalin was still a toddler. After he passed away, it was just Kalin and his mother and the flower shop. They were the only family each other had left.

Every time she mentioned his father, Kalin felt frustrated and guilty. Perhaps it was because he felt he couldn't take some of the burden off of his mother or perhaps it was because it seemed like he was the burden itself. Each time she mentioned him, Kalin could still see the twinkle in her eyes of a woman who still hadn't been able to let go of her long gone other half.

"The church people don't seem to like it when you go, Mom. They looked pretty angry at us last time," Kalin gave his final complaint to fight for his mother's stay.

"Kalin, sometimes people let their fear and anger get the better of them." She looked at her son who didn't seem too happy with the answer. "It's during these times that we have to remember"—Kalin's mother poked at her son's head—"we have this"—she poked at her son's heart—"...and that!"

"No, mom! There are people out there hunting down other people who support those freaks! And, yeah, those *Gifted* murdered people. I don't think it's naive to overlook something like that! Are you saying that doctor deserved to be killed by that Witch? Don't you remember all those stories on the news? All the people crying for the doctor?" Kalin retorted.

"We can't judge an entire group of people on few bad eggs. I know you already know this, my stubborn, stubborn son."

"But, mom!"

Kalin's mom set aside the signs and embraced her son into her arms. The nervousness in the son's heart lingered but his anger subsided in his mother's hug.

"I know you're worried, kiddo. Sometimes it's difficult and dangerous to do the right thing. Sometimes the right thing may seem like the wrong thing to do—even more so as we get older. But if all the good people hid from doing what's right, what kind world would we leave behind tomorrow?"

Kalin still didn't look satisfied.

"I have to be both your mom and your dad. I want you to know that your parents were people that didn't just talk about doing the right things, but actually did them. And I want you to think of me as a"—the mother paused for a moment and grinned—"badass." She gave him a peck on the forehead. "And you'll have to live with that." She squeezed his cheek and gave him a smile.

"At least let me go with you," Kalin grumbled.

"Nope. School night. Just tell your mum, that you love so much, that you love her and ask her to come home safe." His mother stood and gathered up her signs again. Kalin wanted tell his mom that he *did* think of her as a 'badass'. That he was proud of her. The words tickled at his throat but never made it out.

"If you say you'll pick me up a burger on the way home." Kalin crossed his arms.

"You should be sleeping by the time I get back, you pig." His mother rummaged in her pockets for her keys.

"You have no power here when you're not home." Kalin smirked.

"Only if you give me a kiss." His mother puckered her lips and closed her eyes.

Kalin reluctantly gave her a peck on the cheek, and it was enough for his mother to be satisfied with her small victory.

"I'll lock up. But don't forget to turn off the lights before you go to sleep, alright?" His mother asked with half of her already out the door.

"I won't sleep 'till I get my burger," the son replied as he headed for the stairs.

"I really don't know from which gene pool made you so stubborn." She locked the door behind her and walked out into the dark empty street of a cold winter night. The street was lightly covered white with snow. The sedan left behind by her late husband was parked right in front of her shop. The warmth from the store made the sudden chill hard to bear. She hurriedly packed the picket signs and her bag into the back of her car. Her face was already numb from the cold wind.

As she closed the door of her car and headed towards the driver's side, she saw a group of three men coming her way.

A different layer of chill than the cold of winter jolted down her spine.

Instinctive fear telling her to *go*.

Run.

She jumped into her car and attempted to start it. The engine didn't turn over. The front window was iced. She couldn't see them but she could hear their footsteps crunching into the snow as the crunches grew louder and louder. She turned on the headlights and fruitlessly tried to turn the engine again.

Don't be stupid. She told herself. Calm down. You're being paranoid. Following the guidance of her inner voice, she turned to her glove box for the ice scraper. When did the crunches stop?

Knock. Knock. Knock.

A dark metal object tapped on her window. The man pressed his forehead on the icy glass and the blurred image of a face hidden behind a black ski mask was all she could see.

"Hello," the man called out to her almost playfully as Kalin's mother immediately went to lock the doors. They made the distinctive click to let her know that they were already locked.

She could tell even with the iced up windows that the men had surrounded her car. She hoped at this point that they were only here for her.

Knock. KNOCK. KNOCK.

It was obvious at this point the object was a gun.

"What do you want?!" She shouted out the car as she hysterically searched her bag for her phone. The mother wondered whether to call the police first or her son.

"Open the door."

She tried to start the car only to fail again as she dialed away on her phone.

"Open the door," The man requested again as calmly as before.

"I'm calling the cops!" She threatened.

Kalin had just cracked open his textbook in his room when he heard the commotion outside. As he approached his bedroom window that overlooked the main road, a loud bang echoed through the neighborhood followed by the sound of car alarms from the street. Kalin rushed over to the window and looked outside. He saw a group of men surrounding his mother's car and felt a chill wash over his body that made his stomach turn.

"That's what all of you witch-lovers get." It was followed by a similar bang as before, and his mother's car brightly lit up for a short moment before descending back into darkness.

Kalin felt his innards twist and sink as he screamed for his mother. He stumbled down the stairs frantically and dashed out of the front door of his flower shop. One of the men threw a dirty glass bottle into the car that engulfed it in flames.

The three masked men stared at the terrified boy.

"Your mother got what she deserved, boy," The one who threw the bottle said. "And you're going to end up the same if you follow in her footsteps."

After giving Kalin their warning, the three men fled. One of the men looked back to check the spectacle only to see instead what he thought had to have been his eyes playing tricks. The boy was in the air with bluish streams jetting from his body and coming at him with astonishing speed. Kalin landed on the man and they tumbled on the snowy street.

Kalin yelled and screamed nigh incomprehensible words as he beat on the man. Some blows felt about as strong as what a young teen could muster. Some blows, those that jetted similar streams from earlier, landed harder than anything the man had experienced in his life.

The man's two accomplices saw their friend in trouble and ran back to help. They could hear the sirens rapidly approaching. Kalin didn't notice the two men until they kicked him across the face and stomped him to the ground. They helped their friend up and began to flee again but stopped when they realized their friend wasn't with them. The two looked behind to find their companion stomping the boy. Kicking to satisfy his anger.

"We got to go!" one of them yelled.

Just a little more, the man thought as his foot rose up into the air and landed hard again on Kalin.

The two partners in crime grabbed the man by his arms and dragged him away as he cursed at the boy. They had to drag him until the sirens grew loud enough with their lights beginning to turn the white snow red and blue brought him back to his sense enough to run on his own.

Some neighbors and bystanders slowly came out from their hiding and witnessed the burning vehicle and a boy beaten to a pulp laying in the streets. Kalin turned onto his back and drowned in the night sky. The taste of blood filled his mouth and his body hurt from all over. But the void he was feeling inside—a tear—was the only thing he could feel. In the sky, he could see the stars and the Light. Snow began to fall again as he coughed up blood.

Sirens and lights of red and blue quickly flooded the scene. The three men were eventually captured and were found to be part of their victim's church. All three admitted to their actions and went on to testify that they were proud of what they had done. They claimed they were simply stopping a disease from spreading across the world.

The victim's son disappeared a few months after the incident.

...There are no clear records of when and where the Witch and her follower met. There are no clear indicators of who he was, what he did, and what he was to her. The only thing clear seems to be that when the Witch first arrived, she was alone. But during some point she met a companion who'd follow her until the end of her life...

Chapter 2
THE REDHEAD

A quaint little coffee shop.

It was one of many a person could find in the city. Small enough to still seem snug with its single early-bird customer, the cafe decorated from top to bottom with 'personality' to save itself from becoming what they considered to be lifeless coffee shop chains. There were pictures of past visitors, vinyl hanging like paintings—some of which even the young customer recognized—and a bulletin board for the local bands to advertise their garage shows. Instead of the usual easy listening jazz, this little shop decided a little grunge was better fitting with the morning caffeine.

The lone customer waited for his order as he listened to the cafe's unique choice of music. The flashy intro of the news program on the TV caught his attention. His head snugly tucked into the hood of his leather jacket, he turned his attention from the music to the television on the wall.

"Make no mistake," A plump man, aged and molded by a long career of being dissatisfied and irate, spoke with authority and confidence. "We are at war. It's a war not with our people but with this sudden but very drastic change. With change, we have to adapt. That is the law of nature—adapt to survive. The people have the right to be protected and to feel safe in their homes in this great nation of ours. We aren't talking about imprisoning men and women out of prejudice. We are talking about simply containing these men and women—who, mind you, possess a catastrophic potential to harm us—in the name of security of our nation. Joining our discussion today is the host of a popular news commentary show, The Independent Voice, Erol Acar."

The image on the screen split in two. One side of screen still showed the original man with his ginger comb over, and the other side showed a new, tan skinned man who was younger in comparison with a square jaw and a comparably fuller set of black hair.

"Thanks for joining us on The Point, Mr. Acar. It's a pleasure," said the host.

"Thanks for having me, Mr. O'Connor," Mr. Acar answered politely.

"Please, call me Brian. So the topic today: is what we are doing with those wizards and the witches—the Gifted—morally wrong?"

"Uh... well, Brian, first of all, I have to say, I think you're losing touch with humanity." The host's eyebrows slightly furrowed at Mr. Acar's remark. "At war, Brian? We are at war? You say it's against 'change,' but those 'changes' are people! Our own people! The Gifted are our citizens! Not to mention most of the Gifted we discovered so far are mostly children and teens!"

"Children who can blow up buildings, Erol! Children who can and have killed people."

"Not all 'gifts' have been inherently hostile! Like that boy a year or so ago who simply... disappeared... teleported away from his bullies! And even if a child or a person had a dangerous 'gift' it doesn't mean they'll use it to harm others! You and the government are asking people to preemptively judge a person guilty and dangerous before they did anything wrong!"

"Sure, but we don't let children carry guns..."

"Guns aren't part of their being! You're teaching the people to be scared and to fear these people who need our help and understanding!"

"Because the cost of simply waiting and letting something happen is too traumatic, Erol!" Mr. O'Connor slammed his desk in outburst. "It's not a preemptive strike at the Gifted. It's simply a precautionary measure. I'm not asking these Gifted to be publicly executed like in some of those other countries. I—we—are simply asking for some sort of containment! And do I need to remind..."

"There are new studies being done that acquiring 'gift' may not necessarily be a predisposed condition," Mr. Acar, heated by the conversation, didn't let the host finish. "But that anyone can acquire these abilities. Some even suggest that you can learn these abilities on your own. Should all of us then be taken in as a precautionary measure by those private military companies?"

"Alright, we're getting a bit off the topic here, but you know what? I'm going to address this. Those private military companies work for the government and for us—the people—Erol! For you, for me, and for our friends and families! We can't expect our military to step in on this matter! They have their own jobs and duties to fulfill. And we certainly can't expect our police officers to be able handle potentially walking, living, breathing weapons of mass destruction! We've already seen the results of that. We need specialists and those with matching fire power. And YES! Anyone who decides to become part of those Gifted should be dealt with the same way!"

"That's just ridiculous, you're allowing..."

"We didn't start the war, Erol! They did! Do I have to remind you what happened?" The host pointed his finger in emphasis to each of his statement, and now it lingered in the air as he waited for his guest to answer so that he may pounce again.

"No. You don't have to do that. As I was saying…" Mr. Acar fought to finish his point.

"No, I am going to remind you. Two years ago… almost three years now, that Light appeared out of nowhere. We don't know what it is, where it's from, and why it's here. Just look out your window and it's there like an eyesore. On the day that thing appeared, so did the Gifted. The first one to introduce us to the rest of them was the Witch! The Witch everyone's looking for one who's now even considered an international terrorist by many governments. What did she do? Erol? What did she do that day?" Mr. O'Connor waited for Mr. Acar to answer with a smug smirk.

"Brian, let me finish what I was trying…"

"She MURDERED a well-respected doctor in his home. That's the first act done by the Gifted in this world and a very fitting act to let us know what was to come. She's now popping up all over the world terrorizing it with her red-haired lemming…"

"Terrorizing? Really? Name one thing that could be considered a terrorist act. I can name a few where you can say 'reckless' and 'questionable' but 'terrorizing'?" This time Mr. Acar interrupted.

"She attacked our own military!"

"Sources from people who were actually there reported…"

"And who knows what she's doing in those other countries. Is she a spy? Is she a gun for hire? Is she a walking bomb trained by our enemies? Ignorantly meddling in foreign affairs has a tremendous impact around the world. It's simply irresponsible and dangerous!"

"…a few rotten apples shouldn't…"

"Hey, your orders are ready," the part-timer at the coffee shop tried to get the attention of her lone customer.

"A few rotten apples?" Mr. O'Connor interrupted yet again. "These few rotten apples are popping up everywhere now. They're even organizing. They have demonstrated that they are a tremendous threat to us regular people. These so-called few rotten apples went off in schools, offices, courts, and even out in the middle of the street in downtown. And people died, Erol. They didn't even have a chance. We already even have a suspected Gifted serial killer they call… what do they call him… 'The Invisible Man'? And like I said before—there are even groups of them now. Banding together to do god knows what. There are rumors about these bands that are evolving even from just being gangs to selling their 'gifts' for use to the highest bidder. That rumored group called the Wolves or something like that is one of those. It's birth of a living, breathing black market for new types of weapons that the world has never seen before. Except this time, the weapons themselves get paid. Who knows what they'll do next! Who can protect us from them? You, Mr. Acar?"

"Can I talk now?"

"Go ahead," Mr. O'Connor smugly gave permission.

"I recognize there are few of the Gifted out there, like the Witch, who should be brought to justice. And they are, without a doubt, making the world a harder place for the other Gifted and us. But we have to remember, no matter what, that the Gifted are still people like you and me. In fact, if the new studies prove to be correct, any of us can be the Gifted. The Gifted may not even be that Gifted. What you are arguing for is to allow our government to unofficially establish a police state through the private military, and to treat people like criminals regardless of whether or not they've committed a crime. We can't let fear rule us like they want us to. It is during the times of greatest fear that we must remember to be brave enough to do the right thing."

"Yes, yes. Very touchy, Mr. Acar. We'll be back with the sentimental Mr. Acar after these commercials." The host looked at the camera and smiled. An outro melody begins to play as the camera zoomed out.

"World's gone mad," A girl's voice said, bringing the lone customer back to the real world.

Startled, he quickly turned away from the TV to the register, and found the brunette waitress resting her chin on the palm of her hand. She was looking straight at him with a grin and sparkling eyes. She blinked in quick succession as a response when the customer finally recognizing her existence. In front of her were two paper cups fixed with lids and fitted in a drink carrier to accompany a small box.

"I've never actually seen any Gifted yet myself. At least, not with my own eyes." She lifted her chin off of her hand while maintaining eye contact. "I tried to get your attention before, but you seemed really into it so I thought I'd just let you be." She had a wide, amused smile on her face. "That'll be 8.75," she said, reaching out with an open palm to the customer revealing her heavily tattooed arm. She watched as the boy searched his pockets for his wallet. Even though she, herself, was only a sophomore working through college, he seemed even younger than her. Probably just a high school student or maybe he was a freshman in college. He was about as tall, maybe slightly taller, than average for a guy around his age. His hood scrunched his long, obviously dyed red hair that hid most of his facial features, but she thought his revealed milky skin harmonized well with his hair like strawberries and cream. She figured he was probably another fan of the local music scene or perhaps one of many who wanted to stand out against the norms of the society.

"Here's a ten." The customer dropped a couple of bills onto her hand. "Keep the change." He gave a small smile to return hers, and packed the box carefully into his backpack. Once the package was secured, he grabbed his hot drinks and headed for the door.

"Come back soon!" she shouted after the customer as the bell over the door jingled with his departure.

Although it was still only the eve of winter, even the gentlest of winds were frigid and piercing. The skies were gray and without mercy from the sun. People passed through the busy street huddled into their winter coats and paced briskly to their destinations. The cups weren't marked. The redhead sniffed at the drinks to find the one that didn't have the sweet oozing scent of chocolate; if he found the one with the dry but rich and nutty aroma of freshly brewed black coffee, then he would have found his beverage. He was lucky. The first cup passed his sniff test, though it smelled a little burnt.

He took a moment to let the warm drink heat him up. A small award for the long journey he had made. It's was a long walk to the city and it wouldn't be any shorter going back. The winter season easily excavated memories buried deep beneath as if the soil never hardened. Maybe the memories just weren't buried deep enough.

It'd been almost two years since he went off on his journey. Two years since his new life began, and his old life started to fade away. As time passed, the distance between the two moments of his lives grew further and further apart. The old times seemed more imagined now than a one he lived through. Only the artifacts of past memories reminded him that they were all very real.

A police car.

The sirens and lights of the law enforcement drove away the nostalgia and brought the boy back to the present. How ironic that something so key to his old life now snapped him back to reality. It reminded him that his old life was over, and he was in the present. He turned away as much as he could from the flashing vehicle. Once the car turned a corner, the redhead put his coffee back into its holder and hastily went on his way. It didn't feel right that he enjoyed the drink by himself as someone was waiting for him. Kalin felt a slight guilt brewing inside.

Chapter 3
SERENDIPITY

Landris stared blankly out the window. It'd been a long time since he
had been downtown full of people. A while since he sat in a restaurant about to eat a mediocre breakfast that'd taste surprisingly as bad
in any of its sister restaurants across the country. The theme of the
chain was 'retro,' and its idea of 'retro' was a jukebox, neon lights, and
checkered floors. He looked at his two companions who had been giddy since their plane ride. They chatted about doing things they probably knew they didn't have time to do on this trip, and of the things
they missed that they would long for again when the trip ended. He
didn't feel as excited as these two. Frankly, he was bored. When was
the highlight of this trip going to happen?

"So what will it be guys?"

He ignored the middle-aged waitress who he guessed probably
had had too much fun in high school and now couldn't afford to do
better than work in a second-rate chain restaurant. Her dark brown
hair that was obsessively curled and her bright red lipstick made her
look like she was either dressed to the restaurants theme, or she woke
up that morning and decided that she'd dress like a relic.

"I'll have the pancakes with scrambled eggs and hash browns!"
The female companion cheerfully answered. Landris always thought
Sarah was too much of a looker to be hanging around with her friend
Julian. She had brunette hair curled in lusciously soft waves, an egg-
shaped face, and a smile that'd even turn drunkards to gentlemen.
Julian, on the other hand, was scrawny with dirty blond hair, and no
signs of a single muscle in his body. To make matters worse, he followed her around like a puppy and like so, he was probably going to
order—

"I'll have the same please," said Julian with a smile.

Yep. Just as he had guessed.

Sarah, Julian's 'best friend', was a sweetheart. She was hot, if
Landris may be frank, and she probably could have gone through
her entire life with just her looks. To her credit, she managed to also
develop a personality and respectable intelligence. Meanwhile, Julian
was just *that kid* always in the background who was too timid for his
own good. They claimed they were childhood friends, and Landris
figured Julian probably knew he was lucky to even have that. Julian

got plenty of attention from other boys and men when he walked around with his brunette princess. Though, Landris also figured Julian will probably never have the guts to actually spark something between them.

"Can't decide on your own food, Julian?" Landris asked with a smirk. It was a need for Landris to push Julian around. He wanted to get the toxin of weakness out of Julian.

"Don't be a jerk, Landris. Julian can order whatever he wants!" The princess came to rescue her wimpy prince. Her voice was stern, but never had a hint of venom—always like a mother scolding a child.

Landris simply smiled in response to Sarah and glanced at Julian drowning in its implications. Sarah was a nice girl, no complaints there; she was both a pleasure to be with and to look at. She just needed better taste in men. Whether he seemed interested or not, Sarah also seemingly went out of her way to include him in various activities. Small things like that both Landris and Julian noticed.

"Oh, and where's the older gentleman who came with you guys?" the waitress asked, seeing that the only trace left of the man was a bag beside Landris.

"He's in the restroom. What did Mr. Jung want again?" Sarah looked to Julian and Landris for answers.

"Breakfast," Landris replied.

Ignoring the smart-ass, Sarah furtively placed the tip of her ring and pinky finger on Julian's hand.

"Right," Sarah recalled. "He'll have the steak omelet with hash browns on the side please. He also said he'd like to get his coffee topped off"—The waitress jotted down the order on her notepad with a pen—"...and an orange juice for the table please," Sarah finished her order.

"Hun? How about you?" the waitress asked Landris with a friendly smile. She caught herself staring at the boy. Ash blond hair with emerald green eyes. His body permeated athleticism even beneath the layers of cloth, and his face had sharp and chiseled facial features as if the boy was a movie star of the golden age. These qualities of Landris were one of the few reasons why he was favored to be the poster boy for Director Jones' new project. The only detractions were his mouth and attitude that went against his Prince Charming looks.

"I'm good," Landris answered curtly. "I'm probably better off not eating here anyways."

"Landris..." Sarah paused for a moment before deciding it wasn't worth pursuing the rudeness of the latter part of Landris's statement. "You have to eat something. You haven't eaten anything since we left." The mother Sarah scolded and gave Landris exactly what he wanted from her. Right on cue, Julian flashed him a look filled with jealousy. It didn't go missed by Landris.

"Well," Landris began, leaning closer towards Sarah. "What would you suggest then?"

"Well," Sarah replied, leaning closer towards Landris. "I suggest breakfast."

Landris and Sarah exchanged sarcastic smiles.

"I'll have whatever they're having," Landris told the waitress. The waitress scribbled down the last order and told the group it'd be fifteen to twenty minutes before going about her way. As she walked towards the kitchen to submit the order, she passed by the older gentleman that came with the group. He was a bulky middle-aged man whose prominent cheekbones made him seem younger than he probably was. Short hair combed with enough gel to shine, thick eyebrows that were always furrowed, and he walked with the pride of a soldier's march.

"Did you guys order me the omelet?" The man asked as he sat beside Landris and rejoined the group.

"Yes, sir!" Sarah cheerfully answered. Mr. Jung appreciated Sarah over the other two kids he had to babysit just for her brightness. The waitress returned with a glass pitcher full of OJ and poured four glasses for each person in the party.

"Can I see it again?" Landris reached out his hand to Mr. Jung as he sipped on his juice.

"How about a 'please'?" Mr. Jung suggested. The two stared at each other for a short while, both refusing to stand down.

"Please," Landris gave in. It was Mr. Jung's tablet after all. Mr. Jung dug into his bag and handed the boy what he wanted. Without showing much gratitude, Landris turned on the device and found the image right away.

It was a rare image, albeit a very blurry one, of the Witch and her red-headed friend. They were spotted in the war-torn desert country seemingly helping a few civilians from certain death. The picture showed a group of men, women, and children facing a ragtag group of gunmen masked with clothes and scarves with the barrels of their weapons aimed at the people. Standing between them was the Witch and her crimson-haired friend. The quality of the image was blurry at best, but it was the image that became the controversial evidence for those who advocated the falsehood of the Witch's notoriety and advanced the movement to stop scrutinizing those who are "Gifted'. Meanwhile, it also became one of many evidence against the Witch for her apparent lawlessness and disregard for sovereignty. There were rumors that all of the gunmen were killed.

Unsurprisingly, the image of a dainty girl standing up to men armed with some of man's most trusted lethal weapons added fuel to the fire for those who already feared the incalculable potential of the Gifted.

"Is it true that she stopped a tank before, Mr. Jung?" Julian asked as he organized the sugar packets at the end of their table by their colors.

"The official word from the military and the intelligence agencies are, 'no comment.'" Mr. Jung peeked over at his tablet Landris was holding. "...but our inside sources say—yes, a few of them apparently."

"I don't get it. What's her 'gift'?" Julian looked at Sarah who simply shook her head and then turned to Landris. "I don't think even you could stop a tank, Landris." His words went completely ignored by Landris who was still glued to the tablet.

"Let me see that again too, Landris." Sarah reached out for the tablet, and Landris handed it over to her without a fuss.

"She looks even younger than us. How can a tiny girl like that be so frightening?" Sarah marveled as she zoomed in on the blurry picture in a futile attempt to get a closer look at the Witch's facial features. She dragged around the zoomed picture until she stumbled onto the Witch's right hand that was raised straight from her chest. A solid black band dangled from the Witch's wrist that seemed like a common and cheap accessory anyone could find at department stores. Sarah owned a pink one herself. The insignificant item made the Witch seem even more like a regular girl to Sarah.

"Well..." Landris cringed as Julian took on his 'professor' tone that he unknowingly adapted whenever he shared his vast knowledge. "There are a lot of countries out there that still use child soldiers, and children are so malleable that they sometimes make even better killers than adults do. They can do things adults wouldn't and couldn't imagine, doing them without giving it a single thought. So, seeing that, it's all possible that the Witch could be a terrorist."

"I guess," said Sarah as she now zoomed in on the witch's friend. "Her redheaded friend looks more like our age. He looks cute. Wonder why he follows her around so much." Sarah smiled and gave a playful look to Julian. "Do you think they're a couple?"

"Maybe they're related?" Julian offered his own theory while suddenly feeling a bit sheepish at Sarah's smile.

"Maybe he's just stupid or nuts," Landris answered. "How can you tell if he's 'cute' anyways from that picture?"

Sarah shrugged.

"You have weird taste in men, Sarah," Julian joined in.

As the kids chattered, Mr. Jung thought over how he ended up here with these kids. To him, all this was still just madness—the Witch, these kids, and Nancy Jones with her programs. How could these kids and others like them hold the world hostage to their whim.

"So, basically... you want me to babysit." He recalled his meeting from day before.

Mr. Jung had a slight accent whenever he spoke, but it was so minute that only the most petty would point it out. A middle-aged man, his body had seen better years. The only things remaining of his bravado days in the military were his poor excuse for a civilian haircut that was always gelled to a shine and combed to make it seem even shorter, and the trainings ingrained in his mind and body that even showed with how he walked.

He sat across from the mahogany desk of the director, Nancy Jones. Her desk, with a cup of fresh tea on it like any other time he saw Director Jones in her office, was placed in front of a wide panel window that oversaw this entire facility of the Silver Aegis Private Security Firm. The grand office room was elegantly decorated and furnished from top to bottom with exuding tastefulness. Mr. Jung never was very artistic, but even he felt a bit of awe for the extravagance of the room — it was rich yet lacked overtness, and all while still being grand.

"Ma'am?" Mr. Jung tried to get Nancy's attention away from her tablet and focused back on him.

"You were former special forces in your country with high commendations," Nancy recited off of her tablet. It was exactly what Mr. Jung wrote in his application to the company. "That's quite impressive. Not to mention you also spent a little time as an intelligence agent after your military career." This time, Nancy didn't recite from her tablet. She looked right at Mr. Jung and studied him. Unlike before, the details of his time in the intelligence community weren't reported in his application. To be precise, no one should know. Mr. Jung kept his poker face.

"Father of two children with a son of age fifteen and a daughter of age twelve. Tough time for parents, I imagine. Going through the trouble of moving to a new country for this job, I'm assuming was for their benefit?" said Nancy with a gentle smile.

"Yes, but what does any of this have to do with anything?" He and his family had been researched. It wasn't the cleanest feeling in the world, but she was his boss and his meal ticket. Before the timing was too late, he added, "Ma'am?"

"I'd guess you are a better father than a patriot," Nancy continued. "...the money and the opportunities here were too good to shy away from. *But there are some blanks here that I'm curious about.*"

Caving in to his hunger, Landris walked to the front counter of the restaurant where he saw they had a basket of complimentary hard candies for their customers. He popped one into his mouth and pocketed another for dessert.

Mr. Jung maintained his deadpan expression as he listened to the director. On the surface, Director Jones was a woman that he'd wish his daughter to be like when she grew up. Nancy took the time to present herself properly. She was dressed well in clothing that was obviously luxurious but subtle with opulence much like her furniture, and she carried herself even better than she was dressed. Her golden hair was always perfectly kempt and glowed with radiance, her clothing were always perfectly washed, ironed, and fitted, and she walked in confident strides with perfect posture. Neither newly rich nor petulantly rich, she was groomed into her class and naturally exuded her status. Young and powerful, and as elegant as she was intelligent, Nancy's presence demanded respect. For the lesser few, simply being around her made them feel inadequate and uncomfortable.

"What did you do initially before you came here? There's a couple of years here you had off after you quit the intelligence work."

"Money wasn't good in the government job. I wanted a better life for my two kids, so I took on a business opportunity my friend offered. It failed. So, I came here. Are we going somewhere with this?" The usual calm manner of speech by Mr. Jung was slightly littered with snappiness. Nancy left the tablet on her desk and walked towards the giant panel window that made her office into a watchtower. The sun was shining down on Facility Zero, a small part of the Silver Aegis that also happened to be one of its most important division. From her watchtower, she oversaw the training courses, the armory filled with vehicles and weapons, the rows of trucks bringing in new supplies, and the school and dormitories that were the very purpose of the entire facility. Even as they spoke, there were students being groomed by the Silver Aegis to become leaders of the coming new age. She responded to Mr. Jung as she observed her empire ticking like gears in a clock.

Nancy spoke gently, "When my father started this company, it was just him and a few friends he met from the service. He knew that the world would always need guns, and guns free from a leash would be more beneficial and appreciated in this world than the ones that were simply used as the government's exclamation mark," Nancy spoke with her eyes on her father's legacy. "His work, Silver Aegis, is now the world leader in private security and became one of the most profitable businesses in the world. We have more than twenty facilities placed around the world equipped with gear and technology that can match the military and even some that the military is too cheap to use for their own personnel. On our best days we are the only ones able to provide protection to those the military can't seem to find the motivation to help."

Mr. Jung raised an eyebrow.

"We have more than a hundred thousand successful operations and currently employed in twenty-four different nations for fifty-three different operations. A few of those operations technically don't exist. Right here, Facility Zero, is one such place. Do you have any idea how much it costs to keep an operation of this size off the record?" Nancy seemed proud and amused as her eyes smoldered with ambition.

Ms. Jones finally turned away from the windows and made eye contact with Mr. Jung. The light shining from the windows outlined her body with light. *If one didn't know better, some might say she seemed angelic.*

Landris sat back down in the booth. He handed a candy to each person, and all but Mr. Jung who was deep in thought thanked him. Julian and Sarah continued their conversation as Landris looked out the window.

"But the costs are worth it because all else that we have doesn't compare to what we have here—the students in that academy. Those kids in there will not only be the world's future, but our future. The Gifted marks the end of an old era and the beginning of a new one. The world will never be the same."

Mr. Jung knew about the vague purposes of the facility. Other than the top people and instructors, most of the staff rarely got to see the kids studying, training and exercising their 'gifts.' Even so close, the Gifted were a bit of tall tale.

"So yes, it's a babysitting job. But you're babysitting the company's most valuable assets; especially, the boy who will be the company's face for our new project. If things work out, we will also be getting our hands on the world's most notorious Gifted."

"The Witch." Mr. Jung crossed his arms. It was his way of relaxing a little. "How credible is the info that she'll be in that city on that day?"

"Certain enough to dispatch the students with a chaperone. Though sadly even with such a tip, going myself is a risk we cannot take yet."

"Is the 'face of the project' you're speaking about that delinquent, Landris?"

Nancy was well aware of Mr. Jung's distaste for Landris.

"He has rough edges but he's been making progress. Landris is still a teen and still has much to grow. But he has more than proven himself with his capabilities and his abilities are the type to draw admiration from people. His stubbornness combined with his ambitions will get him to places. He will do what other will not—he'll be a leader."

"He's a delinquent. A punk. There are also pretty troubling rumors of his past." Jung expected a response from Nancy with that last statement, but his boss remained collected—always wearing a mask with a gentle smile. "I think you see too much in him and I can't say I understand why."

"Think of him what you will, Mr. Jung. But there are many other agencies and governments looking to acquire these Gifted children, and your job is to watch over three that we have."

"Why not just send some of us out instead of using the Gifted?"

"If she were any other Gifted, yes, we'd handle it between us. However, this is the Witch we are dealing with..."

"...and you don't really think we can handle her," Mr. Jung finished Nancy's sentence for her. He figured she probably wasn't wrong.

"In so many words, yes." Nancy took a sip of her tea. "Besides, I think it'd be great for the students to get some experience outside the facility, and they'll help even out the odds. I'm also going on a hunch that she'll be more cooperative with other Gifted than with just us."

"If you say so, ma'am. Alright, so what can these kids do exactly?"

"The exact details are confidential for now. But the students we've selected to accompany Landris are the ones we thought would be the perfect complement to him and to this assignment. They know their roles, your job is to simply make sure they stay out of trouble and have supervision."

"When are we leaving?" Mr. Jung asked. He decided not to press further for an answer.

"Tonight. The students are already getting packed and expecting you."

"Here's your order!"

The smell of eggs and buttermilk pancakes stole Mr. Jung from his flashback. He saw Sarah and Julian's eyes glimmered with glee when the plates landed in front of them. Curiously, Landris eyes were glued to the window.

"Landris? Your food is here," Sarah said with matching excitement in her eyes as Julian.

"Look," Landris said, pointing out the window. "The redhead."

Landris's words drew everyone around the table to look out the window at the city street. Across the street on the sidewalk was a young man carrying a bag and a drink carrier with what seemed to be two coffees. His long crimson hair peeked out from the black hood of his leather jacket.

Landris leapt out from his seat before Mr. Jung could give any instructions. Guided only by his gut feelings, Landris rushed out the door to chase after the red-haired boy.

Chapter 4
THE CHASE

Landris stalked after the hooded boy with all the care and attention of a proper predator, though part of him wished to simply ambush the man and be done with it. He moved through the crowds while maintaining what he thought to be the perfect distance from the red-head—close enough to keep his heart beating with excitement, but far enough to keep the prey deaf to it.

To Julian and Sarah, Landris's movements seemed unnaturally skillful. He seemed to know the exact moment to change his pace and know exactly how to incorporate the oncoming traffic of pedestrians as part of his camouflage. Though, his talent in espionage wasn't too surprising as Landris always seemed to excel during the training and athletics back at the facility. His talent seemed near uncanny and un-reachable to most of the other students.

"Do you think that's really him?" Julian jogged up next to Landris. Sarah quickly followed after her friend.

"Don't know. Seems like it," Landris whispered his reply back without turning his attention away. He was completely in tune with his target.

"Maybe instead of stalking the guy, we can try to talk to him," Sarah suggested. The two boys responded by giving her a dumb-founded look.

"He might not be—" Sarah let out a defeated sigh. "...never mind."

Red light.

Landris shortened his stride as he saw the hooded man stop at the red cross-walk sign. Julian and Sarah stopped with Landris, and the three clumped up together as if they were enjoying a chat. Landris peeked at his prey and had a funny feeling that the man was peeking back at them. But it was difficult to tell with that hood shrouding most of his head.

Green light.

"Should one of us wait for Mr. Jung?" Sarah asked as the group began picking up the pace after the redhead.

"Is he still at the diner?" Julian looked back at the restaurant which was, by now, the size of a small toy. Mr. Jung was on his phone catching up behind them at a steady pace. He nodded to them to go on.

The redhead knows, Landris instincts warned him. *Doesn't it make sense for someone who's with the most wanted person in the world to develop some sort of extraordinary perception for this sort of thing?*

The redheaded boy led the Silver Aegis students further and further away into the outskirts of the city. More and more abandoned buildings and less and less people filled the streets.

He's either flushing us out or—Landris's heart beat slightly faster with the next thought—*...he's leading us to her.*

"He's sure confident, isn't he," Julian whispered to Sarah as they trailed a few steps behind Landris.

"Suppose that's why he's the leader," Sarah replied with a hint of respect in her speech.

The graying sky was fitting for the silent and desolate emptiness of the outskirts. The bustling signs of life that the city had died, and only the occasional whispers of the autumn wind accompanied the footsteps of the few who remained. The students and their instructor continued their slow and gradually more obvious pursuit.

The redhead suddenly turned off the main sidewalk and slipped into an alleyway between some buildings.

Landris tossed aside the subtlety and ran after the man. Julian, Sarah and Mr. Jung followed after the two.

By the time Landris turned into the alleyway, all there was were traces of what he guessed to be the redhead's 'gift'. Blue streams of energy lingered in the air, dancing lazily before fading like smoke. Landris looked up. The redhead looked down at him from the top of the building. His hood had fallen down from the jump revealing his iconic crimson hair. The redheaded teen looked startled. He had guessed that someone was after him, but he didn't expect to be right. The drinks the redhead had carried with him had spilled from the leap. He inspected the drinks before deciding to keep them. After returning the hood to its proper place, he walked away.

Landris tightened his legs. Beneath his jeans, the veins of his legs began to glow in luminescent light.

"Lan—Landris!" Julian managed to catch up moments before Landris's leap. His shaking voice and legs hadn't caught up to him until that moment. Face to face with the Witch's friend, Julian's nerves struck without a warning. Even when he grasped why he was shaking, Julian still couldn't manage to keep himself steady.

Landris completed the jump, soaring into the air and landing on the top of the building right about where the redhead stood. Sarah and Mr. Jung arrived at the alleyway only to hear Landris land on the rooftop above them.

"Go," Mr. Jung instructed his other student without missing a beat. "Julian, Go!"

Julian looked at Mr. Jung helplessly and decided to hide his trembling hands by clenching them to a fist.

"Julian…" Sarah called out to him with a worried look. Her look gutted Julian and the shame of his cowardice acted as courage.

He looked above and saw Landris's broad back standing tall about to confront *the redhead*. The one chosen by the Witch to serve her.

"Are you alright?" Sarah asked as she gently placed both of her hands around Julian's shoulders and studied his face. Whatever look was on his face wasn't the face Julian wanted to show Sarah. "You don't have to go, Julian. Landris can take care of this."

Clenched fist. Clenched teeth. Julian disappeared before Sarah's eyes.

Chapter 5
SEEING RED

...According to the records, the Magic of the past seemed entirely different than the way it is today. It is speculated that it is due to the streams of aether itself were not yet fully developed in the world, and the human species' bodies were not yet ready to accept them naturally. Instead, each individual's bodies reacted to the aether differently. Those whose bodies were predisposed to react to certain types of aether reacted to them by acquiring certain specific talents of Magic even without the need to manipulate and conform the streams...

The redheaded teen stood at the center of the rooftop when he heard the noise behind him. He cringed at his suspicion of what the noise could be and let out a sigh of frustration when it was proven correct as he turned to find his stalker. It was bad as he could have asked for. He wasn't just any curious stalker, he was a fellow Gifted.

Countless particles of light gathered in an instant and formed Julian next to Landris. Julian looked below and saw Sarah looking up at him with worried eyes. It was a look that he didn't want to receive from Sarah. He turned to the redhead and decided to face him as Landris would.

"What are you guys?" the redheaded teen asked with a voice just loud enough to be heard across the distance that separated him and his chasers.

Julian unconsciously glanced at Landris for his guidance—his lead.

"We're Gifted like you!" Landris yelled back. "We just want to talk!"

"Are you with Emily?!" the redhead asked. The hint of puzzlement on his pursuer's face confirmed to the redhead his suspicion that his stalkers were definitely unwelcome solicitors.

Sarah looked up at her two friends, uncertain how she could join them. Mr. Jung, on the phone requesting for assistance, inspected the main streets. A few pedestrians who noticed the boy leaping to the rooftops were already on their phones. She guessed, some were calling the police while others filmed the event.

"So, talk!" the redhead demanded.

"Like this? I'm pretty sure it'd be best for all of us to find somewhere away from the public eyes! That tomato-red hair of yours is pretty eye-catching." Landris wanted to say 'an eyesore.'

"Or, it sounds like it'd be best for all of us if we just go our separate ways!" the redheaded teen raised his voice slightly.

"Look!" Landris paused for a moment, looking for the friendly tone to his voice. "We are a group of Gifted who are looking for more of us to band together. To provide a safe place for all of us. Even for you and your friend!" This scenario was annoying; it would be simpler, quicker, and more satisfying for him to simply rush the redheaded ingrate and drag him back with them.

"No, thanks!" the redhead curtly replied and turned around. He had figured they might have had an idea who he was, but the confirmation gave him no reason to stay.

It was time for Julian to step out of Landris's shadow. The only way for him to grow was for him to take the steps forward. Pushed by the urge to prove himself, Julian appeared next to the redhead and grabbed onto his arm. His eyes met with the redhead's eyes. Julian quickly realized he wasn't ready to meet the eyes of someone who was willing to fight for his life.

"W-wait." Julian felt as if those words were squeezed out of a pinhole.

"Your legs are shaking," the redhead calmly spoke, realizing the boy to be not much of a threat. "Perhaps whatever you guys are doing, you're not suited for it." The teen snatched his arm away from Julian's grasp and began to walk away. Julian's face contorted with shame and frustration with himself—especially at the slight relief he felt inside.

Landris moved next to Julian, and they watched the redhead leap across to the adjacent building. His body jetted off streams of blue light and confirmed to Landris what he saw earlier was indeed that boy's 'gift'. Though even at this point, he was uncertain what the specifics of it were. The unknown was strangely exhilarating and made his heart pound. Landris felt awakened as if he knew that the redhead wouldn't disappoint him as his prey. The small smile on Landris face startled Julian and made him further realize that they were of different breed.

"Julian," Landris called out to his frozen stiff companion. The better option than chasing after the man himself depended on his lackluster comrade.

"Julian!" Landris raised his voice and finally grasped Julian's attention. "You want to make up for what you did right here?"

Julian felt twisted inside. What was it that made him and Landris so dissimilar? Were they truly just built differently? He always thought, at the very least, he would be able to find courage and talent during the times when they counted. That when the call to action came, he would rise to it.

"You're the one who's going to have to fix this, Julian." Landris placed one hand on Julian's shoulder. His hands were large compared to Julian's bony shoulders, and the hand felt like a mantle had been placed protectively upon his shoulders. Julian hated the comfort it gave him.

"You have to go after him because it's going to be a mess if I do," Landris spoke softly but sternly. Julian responded simply by nodding.

"I'll go look for somewhere private where you can bring him. You got your phone on you?" Landris began inspecting the buildings that surrounded them.

It took a bit for Julian to process what Landris was asking. Once he realized it, he looked at Landris with widened eyes.

"Y-yeah, b-but," Julian tried to explain why what Landris was asking would be unreasonable. Perhaps even impossible.

"Alright, I'll call you once I find the place." Landris ignored Julian's protests to force the boy into action.

"Landris, I don't think this is a good idea. You know that I can't..."

"Julian!" Landris raised his voice. "We have no time for this. It's time to man up. Your time to prove yourself, alright?" Landris stared right into Julian's eyes. His eyes pierced through Julian's straw exterior and shaking heart. Julian simply nodded. For the first time, he felt a genuine respect for Landris and even the sense that he was their leader.

"Sarah isn't going to be with a baby forever," Landris said as he turned away.

Dick.

Julian looked over yonder at the adjacent building the redhead had gone to, and disappeared from where he stood.

Landris jumped off the rooftop back down to the alleyway below.

"Landris, what's going on? What about Julian?" Sarah tried to grab Landris who briskly walked past her and Mr. Jung.

***

Julian stood on the edge of the adjacent building's rooftop and looked down below at the alleyway. His teleportation was nearly silent, and it didn't alert the redhead walking through. The Witch's lackey headed the main street. Sirens were wailing from afar and closing in.

"Seriously?" The redhead muttered as Julian appeared few feet in front of him.

Julian's stomach twisted as he worked his mouth, but nothing came out. His mind was frozen. Were they about to fight? Was he about to be murdered? What would Landris do?

What would Landris do? Really?

The redhead began to walk towards Julian.

"I thought I was pretty clear. Just let me through," the teen spoke as he approached the scrawnier and the younger looking one of the two stalkers.

"Look…" Julian's lips quivered. "Just... just come with us."

"No," The Witch's friend replied. "And you should rethink being a part of any groups with the Gifted. That usually means trouble."

As the redhead walked past him, Julian grabbed the man's arm again. A position that was far too familiar to both of them now.

"Let go," the Witch's friend spoke. He had also heard the sirens and was running out of patience.

Feeling as if the redhead was looking down on him like Landris would, Julian threw a punch and landed it squarely on the boy's face. The blow didn't seem to do much more than make him very irritated. For a moment, they stared at one another in silence as the redhead contemplated his next action.

The sirens.

The redhead, streams jetting from his body, grabbed a hold of Julian and tossed him towards one end of the alleyway. Julian helplessly flailed his arms and legs until he hit the wall and slid to the ground. The Witch's friend turned the other way and ran with the streams still emanating from his body. He was fast; perhaps even as fast as Landris. Julian quickly came up with an idea that he knew he may regret. The phone vibrated in Julian's pocket. Ignoring the list of consequences growing in his mind, he teleported once more.

Julian appeared as close as he could to the redhead. Close enough that at his speed, the redheaded teen wouldn't be able to stop in time. His plan in near completion, Julian braced himself with the little time he had. The collision with the redhead sent Julian flying into countless particles as he immediately teleported again.

The sheepish stalker's howl of pain came from behind the redhead and before he realized what had happened. The particles gathered behind him in an instant and carried Julian through with all of the momentum from the collision. The two collided again and they tumbled onto the ground. Luckily for Julian, he was on top. Realizing his plan had worked Julian smiled through the pain.

Writhing in pain, Julian quickly took out his vibrating phone from his pocket and turned it on.

"Hey, we're ready. You got him?" Julian heard Landris's voice through his phone, and latched onto the redhead's jacket tightly with one hand and held his phone with the other.

Although teleporting with inanimate objects was tested to be as natural for Julian as traveling by himself, when it came to living things it proved to be far more difficult. The success rate was currently about twenty percent. Out of five attempts, failures resulted in anywhere from Julian and the test subject failing to appear at the designated location, Julian and the test subject appearing in separate locations, and the final failure that resulted in Julian refusing to do anymore testing which resulted in the test subject ending up at the end of the teleportation much differently than how it had started. It was a result traumatizing enough that Director Jones allowed Julian to stop as well.

Julian stared at his phone. Landris had called him in a video call and presented Julian the empty room. With a heavy breath and a grunt, Julian spoke to the Witch's friend, "Just so you know, I'm really sorry if we..."

And Julian and the redhead dispersed into countless particles.

INTERLUDE II
THE HOMELESS &
THE RUNAWAY

A cold, empty night. The better part of the city had already turned in long ago, and the void was filled only by vagabonds and stragglers. The noises of the day were reduced to mere rustles from hungry cats probing the trash, and the swoosh of straggling cars hurriedly making their way home. In an empty playground lit only by the flickering lampposts that should have been fixed long ago, a lone girl sat on the swings. For her, the darkness and the silence of the night were more comforting than the bright and bustling light of day. She felt safer without the people. Without their judging eyes. Without their noisy mouths. Without their mysteries. In the night's shroud, she didn't feel naked and vulnerable.

She looked up, her head tilting skyward only by its weight. The skies were painted black and were studded with the shining glitter of luminous stars. The girl tried to count them all with her sunken eyes. As she counted, the tips of her naked feet gently brushed back and forth over the beauty bark that covered the playground. Although she spent most nights under the veil of the night sky, it was still hard to believe how many stars there were twinkling above. Counting them calmed her mind and gave solace through the sleepless nights. For her, slumber was short and sparse. Rest only came when her desperate body forced her into sleep out of survival, and the sleep was dreamless when they were good. But most of the time, her slumbers were nightmares reincarnated from the chaos she struggled with her mind while she was awake.

Beyond the horizon, the night's endless black sea was split by the pillar of white light piercing the skies. The Light was another tool for her restless mind to find some sort of peace. Some nights she'd stare off into the Light and buried her mind in its womb. It was there when she returned. It was there for her to go to. Though she doesn't know how to go there, by what means to get there, or by when she needs to get there by. Even the reasons were now unclear. But an imperative calling in her heart urged her to go. A mission in her life; a promise from her past.

She looked down. The black band that appeared with her and the Light dangled on her wrist—always teasingly slipping out of her dainty hand. It was cold as ice. Even on the hottest days, it would be frigid and it was thin like a sheet of glass. But despite how thin it was, it felt tougher than the hardest of rocks.

It was her only possession and her only companion. Somewhere deep within her among the bodies of buried memories was a small kindle of memories that tried to remind her of its significance. An echo of the past that she wanted to—*needed* to remember. Or perhaps those were all just her imaginations.

Three young boys, drifters and wanderers of the empty city, watched the girl since she began counting the stars. With the shriveled hearts of scavengers and a foolish confidence deriving only from their number, the boys believed they were rulers of night. Behind a corner, shrouded by the night's shadows, they amused themselves observing their prey. She was dressed in a jacket, which seemed to be a secondhand of a secondhand; a homeless man probably donned it until he saw a girl who seemed in need of charity even more than he did. Beneath the thin, shabby jacket, she donned a ruffled one piece dress that was barely excusable as clothing and seemed more fitting as rags. Its color was tarnished to such oblivion that one could hardly believe that it was once cloud white. Her tiny feet were filthy with dirt, mud, and god-knows-whatever-else she picked up on her barefoot journey, her face as pale as the moon, her hair pitch-black as the unlit night, and both littered with traces of her long and directionless journey. She was small. She was weak. She was alone.

The girl's skin tightened, and her hair rose when she heard the flurry of footsteps coming her way. Without hesitation, she rose from her seat on the swing and began to flee away from the encroaching steps. Her body and mind were still fatigued. Her legs wobbled and she felt as if she could be carried away by the wind. She forced herself to flee as frantically as she could. She didn't want to be a bother to anyone or even be a person of the faintest interest.

"Hey, you!" a voice pitched in that awkward range of a young boy transitioning into a young man called out to her. "Hold on a moment!"

Her heart beat violently, and her face was crushed with terror. Her eyes didn't blink and kept themselves set on the outskirts of the playground. The exit. Just a little more. She heard the boys behind her trying to mute their laughter. As she wobbled faster, the boys gave a short and easy chase. The young drifters surrounded the dainty vagrant. They walked slowly to match the girl's pace. The girl's determination remained unshaken by the boys who surrounded her as she headed towards somewhere away from them.

"Going home?" The same voice from before now bluntly mocked her. It was a boy with a fresh buzz cut. The thin patches on his head and the baby sprouts of hair growing above his upper lip suggested he was a dirty blond. He wasn't big, but plump, and squarely built. His face was scrunched together as if someone had squeezed the face of a ball of dough, and the dough was decorated with red spots of adolescence. Standing next to the homeless girl, he felt as if he was twice as big than he actually was.

The rest of his gang consisted of a short boy with curly ginger hair, freckles and metal braces that laced over his teeth, and a boy with skin the color of sand with thick black hair and even thicker eyebrows. He was the tallest of them all. The two laughed at their leader's every remark.

"Are you a hooker?" The ginger boy asked. "Ma said any homeless girls running around are just hookers and no good addicts. Can I pay you for some *services*?"

The girl kept walking, whimpering a bit from fear. The boys laughed.

"Oh my god, she's like a small dog," The sandy boy remarked through his giggles. "I feel so bad for her. Hey, are you hungry?" He reached into his pocket and threw a piece of gum at the girl. She paid no attention to it as it bounced off her jacket. The girl ignored the boys and only focused on the edge of the playground that was getting closer and closer.

"Didn't anyone teach you it's rude to not to listen when people talk to you?" The buzz cut boy pulled her back and threw her onto the ground. "Maybe if you weren't so rude, your parents would have kept you around…" The boy finished his sentence with a kick. The girl felt the air in her lungs erupt through her mouth, and the pain echoed fruitlessly as her mind and body were already long numb to the sensation. Her eyes stopped blinking and any twinkle of life was gone.

The boys ooo'ed and cackled.

"Jeez, son, how can you kick a girl?" The sandy boy laughed. "Didn't yo daddy teach you not to lay your hands on women?"

"Hey, hey, what if she's that Witch everyone's talking about on TV?" The ginger boy masked his fear with a jovial tone.

"The Witch?" The buzz cut boy scoffed. "If she is the Witch, then she deserves to be kicked around a lil', doesn't she? And my daddy didn't say nothin' about laying hands on worthless garbage like her!" The buzz cut boy kicked her again and then stomped on her.

"Dirtyin' up the streets and takin' our money!" He stomped on her and then kicked her. "They're filthy, man. Filthy! Get a job! Do some-thin' with your life! Stop leechin' off of us people who're doin' some-thin'!"

The only reaction from the girl was the sound of life escaping through her mouth in small grunts. After his short beating, the buzz boy poked her around a little bit with the toes of his shoe. Even through her thin jacket and one-piece dress, he could feel the bony body. The girl had barely any meat on her. He smiled satisfyingly realizing that his blows were probably very painful.

"Yeah! My daddy didn't say nothin' about worthless people like her either!" The ginger boy said as he mimicked the buzz boy by kicking the girl even more. His kicks were awkward and weak—especially compared to the previous attacker. He was the shortest of the bunch and his voice squeaked as if he was the youngest.

"You don't have a daddy, Frankie," The sandy boy remarked, looking the ginger boy dead in the eye.

"Shut up! Ass!" The ginger boy took his frustration out by kicking the girl across her face. A tear on her lip warmed her face with blood. He was swiftly smacked across the back of his head with such force by the buzz boy that he fell to the ground beside the girl.

"Don't touch her face, you idiot!" The buzz boy yelled. "What are you, an animal?" He looked the ginger boy squarely in the eye who looked confused and barely holding back the tears.

The buzz boy knelt down near the girl's face and inspected the damage.

"Hey…" the buzz boy gently slapped her face. "Hey, are you the Witch? Maybe we're doing the world more than a favor right now. Maybe we're about to be heroes." He brushed her hair aside and was for a moment startled. There was blood on her perky lips. Dirt and small cuts on her white cheeks. But her eyes. Her eyes were wide open, yet dead. She didn't have a scintilla of anger, fear, or sorrow. The eyes were simply there, witnessing.

"Why you starin' at her, Johnny? You falling in love?" the sandy boy teased.

"Shut up, retard." The buzz boy studied the girl closer. If they weren't so dead, her eyes would have been entrancing. Her lips were shaped perfectly as if someone sculpted them on her. Her smooth face with its innocent features made Johnny blush. He flipped the girl over, and as if she suddenly awakened, the girl began to struggle violently. She violently flailed her arms and kicked her legs as much as she could with Johnny's weight on top of her.

"Whoa, whoa! What are you doing Johnny?" the ginger boy spoke in shock.

"Shut up. You and Manny just watch to see if anyone's coming," Johnny spoke with his eyes glowing something grotesque and putrid.

"Hey… are you serious? Johnny? You're crazy!" Manny sounded more excited than shocked.

As Johnny leaned in closer, the girl slapped him across the face. It was weak. It was pathetic. At the same time it was eye opening and degrading—especially with his boys laughing at him. He returned her slap with a proper rage-filled slap. Her arms and legs stopped flailing and her body stilled as if she was dead. The signs of life from her eyes were extinguished yet again.

Johnny's lips quivered as he leaned in closer again for his first kiss. Manny yelping like a kicked dog abruptly interrupted Johnny's sacred moment. Before Johnny could complain, he felt a violent tug on his shirt. Without a moment to think, he was flung away from the girl. Johnny looked up and saw a boy near his age standing over him. His eyes were that of an angered beast, and his face was inhumanly distorted with anger. Johnny was staring at a real lion—an actual carnivore about to devour his meal.

Johnny tried to stand, but the beast pounced on top of him. Without giving Johnny even a chance to whimper the first syllable of his plea, the beast's fist buried itself into the bully's face.

"You…!" the beast spoke as his other fist buried into Johnny's face.

"…Sick!..." Back to the original fist.

"…Cowardly!.." The other fist again.

"…Piece of…!" The right.

"…Garbage!..." The left.

With a roar, the beast wailed on with just brutality on Johnny's face until his blood mulched into a nice cushion. Once the beast was done, Johnny stared silently at the beast with tears drizzling from his eyes. Defeated and petrified with the fear that even breathing too loudly would earn him more beatings. The beast, still on top of Johnny, now turned his attention to the rest of Johnny's posse. Manny and Frankie had been frozen with their eyes bearing the horror. They weren't sure if they were breathing through the entire frenzy. Without protest, they frantically stumbled to their feet and fled hysterically from the scene.

"Get out of here." The beast dismounted from the buzz boy and stood over him. "If I see you doing things like this again, I'll bury you." The beast inspected his battered hands. The adrenaline-induced numbness was diminishing. His hands were a bloody pulp, bruised, and torn, but not all of the blood was his. He stared down Johnny as the boy struggled to stand. With a battered face that his mother might not even recognize, Johnny glimpsed at the beast before limping away from the playground without a single word or complaint.

With buzz boy leaving, the boy checked up on the girl.

"Are you okay?" The boy crouched beside the girl. Her eyes were glued to the skies and he looked up along with her to see what she was seeing. Stars. Countless stars that filled the skies. He glimpsed back at her and his heart sunk at how void of life her eyes were.

"Hey," the boy tried again, clearing his throat. "Are you alright?

They're gone now." He reached his hand out to gently nudge her shoulders. As the boy's battered hand closed in on the girl life came back into her eyes. It startled the boy. She let out a scream and scurried away from the boy. That startled him even more. She hid under a big metal slide, hugging her legs close, and buried her head into them.

"Geez!" the boy chuckled as he studied his hand. "Ow! I guess I wouldn't want to be touched by these hands either…" The boy looked at the girl whose head was still buried into her legs.

"Promise you won't tell," the boy said with a smile to his audience of one who paid no attention to him. He stared at his hands and concentrated. A stream of energy engulfed his hands as if every particle of his skin was becoming part of the stream itself. He wondered if this was smart. It wouldn't be too surprising for her to turn against him knowing now that he was a Gifted. She could probably also find herself someone who'd pay her well for the information. His hands slowly began to repair themselves, knitting together the torn flesh and even 'burning' away the mess of blood on them into streams.

"Ta-da~!" The boy looked up at the girl and wiggled all of his fresh fingers. To his surprise, she was looking his way. Her eyes were opened as wide as they could be, and her hand stretched as far it could with her trembling palm facing him. Startled, the boy lost his balance and fell backwards only to be saved from his tumble by a wall.

A wall?

There should be nothing but an empty space behind him. The boy quickly looked back to find the buzz boy standing behind him with a brick in his hand frozen in motion from striking down.

The boy looked at the girl. It was her doing. She was a Gifted like him.

"You… frea…ks!" Johnny, with much effort, barely managed to squeeze out those words through his teeth. The girl closed her palm into a fist, and the brick in Johnny's hand spilled down his arm as dust.

The rescuer now the rescued met eye-to-eye with his could-have-been-assailant in amazement.

"Wow," he gently admired. "This is pretty cool." As he poked at Johnny who was clearly annoyed by the gesture, the boy started to recall the things he heard of the most famous Gifted of them all. The pieces and hints of her that he had heard on the news and during his travels. His guts told him he had found her but his head refused to believe those pieces and hints put together painted a young, homeless girl.

"You really shouldn't have come back, man." The boy clenched his hand into a fist. "I think you earned yourself another beating." His fist cut through the air and stopped right before it made contact on Johnny's face. Fresh tears began to drizzle down Johnny's eyes and his pants darkened.

"No sense in it, is there?" The boy turned his head to the girl. "Can you let him go?"

She seemed surprised and uncertain. But she nodded and lowered her hand. As the hold on Johnny's body released, Johnny collapsed onto the ground. He quickly studied the hand that held the brick and then analyzed the damage on his pants.

"You should run," the boy said.

Johnny fled on all fours until he eventually found himself on his two feet at the edge of the playground. He took a glance at the boy and a glance at the girl then walked away, cursing under his breath as he left.

"You freaks will have what's coming!" Johnny turned back once he had reached the exit to the playground and spoke just loud enough to be barely considered a shout.

"Maybe I *should* have smacked him once more," the boy spoke light-heartedly as he watched the bully walk away with his tail between his legs. He turned to the girl with a smile and said, "But given what people think about us with these 'gifts,' I thought we ought to be a little more generous than others. My mom always did say to be the bigger man." The girl's head was buried in her legs once again; except, this time he noticed she was furtively peeking out at him. The boy shook out his shaggy dark hair for the little bits of brick dust that got sprinkled in from earlier.

"Thanks by the way," the boy said. "We should get out of here. It's especially not safe for people like 'us.'" He squinted to find her peeking eye in the darkness. As their eyes met, she hid it away behind her legs. The boy walked gingerly towards the girl and sat just barely a hands reach away from her. She flinched a little bit, but there weren't any screams or fleeing.

Progress?

"Hey," The boy spoke softly as he would to a young child. "Did you hear me? It's not safe at night—especially for someone tiny as you. They might come back. Maybe with even more people now that he knows we're couple of freaks."

No response. Not even a budge. She reminded the boy of a hedgehog rolled up into a ball, hiding away from the scary world. He poked at the ball with his finger. Her body was cold, stiff, and *thin*.

The boy searched his bag and pulled out a small, white paper bag.

"You've got to be starving," the boy said as he pulled out a white, powdered, jelly donut from the paper bag. "Here," he said as he wiggled the donut in front of the girl. She gave it no real attention.

"It's really good," the boy said as he tore the donut in two and put the half of it in his mouth. He wasn't exactly sure why he thought doing this would help to entice her to eat it as well other than that he saw it on TV and movies. But perhaps because of the smell of the donut's sweet nectar, the sight of its glistening jelly under the moonlight, or simply from having to witness someone devour a meal with an empty stomach, the girl's eyes twinkled as she quietly and secretly observed the boy. The boy carefully offered her the remaining half of the donut and she cautiously accepted with slightly trembling hands. She first sniffed the soft and powdery bread with certain amount of discretion. Her eyes widened and she sniffed the bread again with a bit more excitement. It wasn't long before she finally decided to lick the jelly. A lick quickly turned to two and the two turned into a bite after bite until the donut was no more.

"Why didn't you stop them if you could do what you did back there?" The boy worryingly asked as he watched the girl finish the donut. As he had expected she didn't give him an answer and he quietly watched her licking the red goo off her fingers. After she was done the girl stared at the boy as if she wanted to say something. Her lips moved ever so slightly as if she had said something to him before she went back into her cocoon again.

"Well, I'm gonna go then. You're on your own, alright?" The boy stood up and began to walk slowly away from the girl. He peeked back to check if there was any response from the hedgehog.

There wasn't.

He almost made it out of the playground until he realized his actions were futile and made a U-turn back to her. She peeked at the footsteps coming back to her. The girl observed as the boy tossed aside his backpack and took his jacket off. The boy was stripped to his thin, plain white t-shirt. The season was getting warmer, but lacking a jacket made him realize it was still formidably chilly during the night. When he turned her way, the girl hid away once more. She felt his jacket softly caress her. The boy then took off his shoes and his socks. He stuffed his socks into his shoes and placed them by her feet.

"A girl should be wearing shoes," the boy remarked. "And I swear those socks are clean. They're a new pair I just got."

After he gave the girl the gifts, the boy gave her a comfortable distance before finding a place to sit. He hugged his legs much like her but for warmth. Shivering slightly, he buried his head into his legs. The boy constantly reminded himself that he was a sentry for the evening and he was not to fall asleep. The girl, however, unlike the boy watchman, slipped into slumber after the violent incident took the last ounce of energy out of her.

He stayed awake for hours until the black night sky waned to a lighter purple from the rising sun. His young mind relented to fatigue for what he figured to be half-an-hour, or perhaps three-quarters-of-an-hour of slumber. When he opened his eyes, he noticed the jacket he gave the girl was no longer blanketing her. Instead, the jacket blanketed him.

"Thanks," he quietly muttered uncertain if she was still awake. The girl carefully poked her head above her legs. They stared awkwardly in silence for a short moment.

"My name is Kalin," the boy introduced himself. "Want to go get some breakfast? I'm starving." He wasn't really that hungry, but he felt the need to feed the girl. "I can pay for us." Kalin stood and gave his body a morning stretch before he offered his hand to the girl. The girl stared at the boy with her eyes filled mostly with curiosity and still slightly with intimidation. Ever so carefully, her gauntly hand reached out for his. When her hand softly landed into his, he gently enclosed his hand around hers.

For her, the small gesture was a paramount reminder.

A reminder of how much warmth there was supposed to be when you touch another person. Even though his hand and her hand were both frigid from the night, warmth ignited within her as his hand wrapped around hers.

"Ruby."

Her voice was so soft that it sounded like a gentle wind passing by. "My name is Ruby."

The revelation made the smile on the boy's face even wider. With Ruby's hand in his, Kalin led them out into the daylight.

Chapter 6
NEGOTIATION

"Die!" Julian felt the air and the light change and hoped that he finished his sentence at the proper place.

Landris looked up as Julian's voice cried out above him to see him and the redhead emerging from countless particles of light closer to the ceiling than the floor. Gravity did its work and yanked the two down. Luckily for Julian, the red-haired friend of the Witch served well to break his fall; although at this point, Julian was simply glad he was able to finish his sentence in one piece at the right place. A small abandoned office, a wave of dust from the fall and the distant sirens celebrated Julian's success.

"Whoa! You actually pulled it off," Landris remarked in genuine surprise with a grin.

Dick.

As Julian tried to stand to defend his honor, he found his celebration was short lived. The injury he sustained from his rumble with the redhead pierced his senses. He cried in agony and fell next to the red-haired boy and gasped for air.

"I think I broke a rib," Julian muttered with a groan. He looked up to Landris who seemed uninterested in either him or the redhead. Instead, Landris fiddled on his phone for a little while until he eventually placed it into his pocket. Once done with his precious phone, Landris approached Julian and the captured prey. He noticed the streams gathering around the redhead's arms.

"Julian!" Landris's cry was too late. The redhead sprang up and grabbed on to Julian, throwing him at Landris. He dispersed into countless particles as Landris ran through him. A thud and groan of Julian behind him, Landris ran after the redhead who ran for the door.

"Don't make things messier than it has to be," Mr. Jung greeted the redhead at the other side of the door for the redhead, gun drawn and pointing at the redhead's chest.

Seeing the boy frozen in his tracks didn't stop Landris. The veins in his arms glowing, he grabbed the redhead and launched him into the air. He could hear Mr. Jung yelling at him. Probably telling him to stop. He didn't care. The redhead smashed into the ceiling and fell to the ground. As he tried to pick himself off from the ground, Landris stomped down on the boy and pegged him to the floor.

"Come on, try that thing of yours again," Landris challenged the redhead and he accepted. The stream gathered around his arms again, and the redhead tried to lift Landris off of him. Futile attempt. Landris crushed him further into the ground with his foot.

"Guess I'm stronger," Landris smirked.

"That's enough, Landris!" Mr. Jung yelled as he holstered his gun. He closed the door behind him. It was an old abandoned office building. Four-stories high, they were in a room that probably served as the conference room.

"Landris!" Sarah came into the room after Mr. Jung. She noticed Julian curled up at the other end of the room. "Oh god!" She ran after her childhood friend and knelt next to him.

"Are you okay?" Sarah asked her friend writhing in pain. Obviously, he wasn't okay. He wasn't okay at all. The sharp pain screaming from his rib didn't help his already exhausted state. He felt nauseated. The teleportation had drained him.

"I'm alright." Julian forced a smile and topped it off with a thumbs-up. His face was drenched in sweat. "Look," He spoke weakly. "I did it!" Julian pointed at his redheaded trophy under Landris's feet.

"Yea, you did." Sarah placed her hand on Julian's cheek. His heart skipped a beat as his face froze with a dumb expression. "Good job. Rest now." Sarah smiled for her friend.

"Get off of me!" The redhead growled.

"Landris, enough! This has gone too far. We've started this whole thing wrong." Sarah walked towards Landris after giving her coat to Julian. She placed her hand on Landris's shoulder. "We came here to talk. Not fight."

"It's too late for that now. He doesn't want to talk," Landris contested. "Isn't that right, tomato-head? Kind of a dumb idea to dye your head red when you're one of the most wanted men in the world, isn't it?"

The tomato-head grunted, desperately trying to free himself but to no avail.

"We're sorry that it came to this." Mr. Jung crouched down to speak with the Witch's young companion. "If you can cooperate with us it doesn't have to be this way."

"My name is Sarah Starr," Sarah spoke to the boy. "That's Julian." She pointed at her childhood friend. "This is Mr. Jung." She pointed at Mr. Jung. "The jerk is Landris." She didn't need to point. "The three of us are Gifted like you. Despite how it may seem right now, we don't want to cause you any harm or any more trouble. We just want to chat."

Silence engulfed the room as they waited for the redhead's answer.

"Sure," The redheaded boy replied almost too complacently for Landris's comfort.

Sarah looked at Landris with demanding eyes. *Get. That. Foot. Off.*

"Landris," Mr. Jung spoke sternly.

"Landris." Sarah almost sounded irritated.

Reluctantly, Landris lifted his foot, and the Witch's friend slowly picked himself up. He dusted off his clothes, stretched his back, and then he checked his bag. The goods were ruined. A sigh. He took a moment to consider darting for the door but figured it'd be déjà vu. With no better options, he turned around and faced his kidnappers. He gave Landris the middle finger before taking a seat on the floor.

"So? What do you guys want from me?" The redhead asked in resignation.

The Silver Aegis crew looked at one another to see who should strike up the conversation first.

"Well," Sarah volunteered. She crouched in front of the redhead. "What's your name?"

"Bob," the redhead soberly answered.

"*Bob?*" Sarah was a bit amused by what seemed to be a blatantly false answer though she wasn't entirely sure if the name was indeed a pseudonym.

"Bob," 'Bob' assured Sarah once more with a deadpan expression.

"Bob," Sarah confirmed.

"This is just load of..." Before Landris could finish his remark, he was cut off with an angry look by Sarah and Mr. Jung.

"Nice to meet you, Bob," Sarah reached out for a handshake. 'Bob' obliged as he forced a half-hearted smile to match Sarah's. However, unlike Sarah's smile his oozed with snideness and bitterness.

Contact.

The redheaded boy, 'Bob' stood in a small cafe waiting for an order as he watched the television.

The visions go back further.

Bob got off the bus in the downtown.

Even further.

Bob is walking towards a bus stop at the outskirts of the city. The sky is barely beginning to blue from the morning sun.

Further.

Deep in the woods outside the city. The sky just began to bloom purple from the advent morning. Over the horizon beyond the trees, Bob saw the sun beginning to poke out its head behind the city far off in the distance. He looked back and waved good bye to a girl.

The girl.

The girl is barely visible. Long black hair. Tiny. Young. She's waving good-bye.

The Witch.

"See you soon," she says because she doesn't like saying good bye. "See you soon..."

"Kalin." As Sarah murmured the name, 'Bob' quickly retracted his hand. He was startled and felt betrayed—disgusted.

"That's some invasive 'gift' you got there, lady," the-redhead-formerly-known-as-Bob said.

"I'm sorry." Sarah shook her head and snapped herself out of the visions. Was it really *her*? "I'm really sorry."

"What did you see, Sarah?" Mr. Jung asked. Even Landris and Julian at the other side of the room turned their attention to the Oracle-Who-Sees-Backwards.

"Sometimes, it just...just happens without me intending to do so. I'm... I'm really sorry." Sarah looked at Kalin who still looked distrusting of her. "But you're really him. And that..." Sarah paused for a moment. "That was really her."

"I don't know what you think you saw—"

"...it was the Witch in the woods. You're her mysterious friend." Sarah didn't give Kalin a chance to even deny it. "The Witch." Finding the treasure excited Sarah but realizing the implications turned the excitement to uncertainty and fear.

The sound of sirens echoed from afar.

"Sarah! Get away from him," Julian cried from where he still laid slumped against the wall.

Mr. Jung stood up and reached into his pocket for his phone.

"I already let them know of our location," Landris said. Mr. Jung was a bit surprised, but felt comforted that Landris wasn't just all bullheaded.

"That's good," said Mr. Jung. "Apparently the *other guys* got a whiff that the Witch was in town."

Landris turned his head to Mr. Jung and raised an eyebrow.

"Y'know," Landris said. "I'm kind of surprised this guy was actually him. I thought maybe he was one of the many Witch and her friend wannabes."

Mr. Jung looked at Landris, uncertain what to think.

"So... what's your 'gift'? Mind reading?" the redhead asked Sarah.

"Not exactly. It's more like... I can see through the memories that you have. Kind of like watching a movie—except, more intense. Much more intense," Sarah answered with her eyes glued to the ground as if she could still see the images before her eyes. When she raised her head, she saw the Witch's friend staring—glaring—at her. He was studying her, and Sarah almost missed the smirk he had on before. They stared at one another, uncertain of what to do next.

"Look, Kalin," Sarah began, filling in the silence. "We can get you and the Wi—your friend to safety. A haven of sort for us Gifted."

"I'm guessing you guys are not the people I was supposed to meet. What are you guys?"

"Have you heard of the Silver Aegis?" Mr. Jung asked.

"The private military company?" Kalin sounded a bit surprised and startled.

"Private *security firm*," Mr. Jung corrected.

"We are students from the Silver Aegis' program for the Gifted." Sarah took over again. "We were sent here by our director to offer you what she provided for us."

"An offer?"

"An offer of protection and guidance. As I said before, a haven. You guy's won't have to run from the world anymore." Sarah almost felt proud and happy to tell them of the offer.

"What's it to her?"

"What?" Sarah was slightly taken back, though she quickly realized herself that it was a fair question.

"Nothing!" She replied adamantly. "I know that's hard to believe, but Director Jones wants to help all the Gifted out there during these chaotic times. She believes that we are the next step for the world, but the world just isn't ready for it yet. She wants to provide all the Gifted out there a safe place where they can learn and hone their new found talents. To show the world that these 'gifts,' especially with the theory now that anyone can acquire them, can be used to make the world a better place. A world we could have never imagined before. A *revolution*."

"A revolution, huh?" Kalin wasn't interested in revolutionizing anything. "Let's say I know the Witch. How could this Director Jones protect the world's most wanted person?"

"If you knew the Witch." Sarah decided to play along. "You can let her know that Director Jones is an influential and a caring woman. She'll find ways to push the world to accept us and even the two of you. Until then, we have a secluded place that's far from the world's eyes and judgment."

"Even for criminals?"

The sirens echoed from afar but was drawing closer.

"Damn!" Mr. Jung placed himself on the wall next to the windows and took a peek. Luckily there were still blinds attached to the windows. "Where's our back up?"

"Director Jones believes that you and your friend deserve the fair chance of at least being heard. And we know that not all of the fame she has is from a bad place. Especially among some of the Gifted." Sarah thought for a second before she spoke again. "Knowing the people she gets support from, I don't think it's that outrageous to believe she might not be who most of the world says she is."

"You really believe that?" Kalin asked.

"I'd like to. The world is a messed up place right now. I just know that all of us there at the facility are better off now than we were before. We just want to offer you the same." Sarah paused for a moment as she tried to find the words to describe what the facility meant for her and her friends. She thought of a word, and even in the somewhat chilly, abandoned office space that they were in, the word warmed her heart. "We want to offer you a home."

"You say home but that's a pretty hefty promise. Look, I'm sure you mean well, but whatever is hunting the Witch at least have pure and clean intentions. It's the honest ones—the nice ones—that are the scariest behind their masks." Kalin stood up. Landris took a step towards Kalin.

"Please. The Director is a good woman. She's even supporting us and our families while we're gone." Sarah stood up with Kalin.

"So she bought you guys?" Kalin gave a judging look.

"No! We all chose! The whole world is afraid and against us. She gave us shelter and a chance to feel safe and normal! For us to at least learn what's going on with ourselves. Sure, it'd be great if we could just march down the street and live with our families. That's the dream!" Sarah calmed down and lowered her voice. "But it's a fantasy for most of us. Especially once you've been exposed."

The sirens were loud enough to fill the room.

"What is going on here?!" Mr. Jung exclaimed. "We have to get moving. Now."

"Mr. Jung?" Sarah turned her attention to Mr. Jung who set his bag on the ground and began sorting through its contents.

"Someone help Julian up. It won't be long until *they* are here as well." Mr. Jung snatched up his phone again.

"How'd they find us so fast?" Landris asked, peeking out the window.

"Something's not right here." Mr. Jung placed his phone against his ear and held it in place with his shoulder as he continued rummaging through the bag. He pulled out two different cases.

Sarah helped Julian up and guided him over to the rest of their group. Kalin walked over to the windows at the other end of the wall where Landris crouched, already peeking out of them. Multiple cop cars, sirens wailing and flashing lights, were parked in front of the building.

"This is Jung. We are in trouble; the police are here which means *they'll* be here soon. What's the situation with the pickup?" Mr. Jung spoke as he opened both cases and began assembling various metal components.

"*They*," Landris began as he walked away from the windows. "Are already here."

Kalin watched multiple black vans drive up next to the police vehicles. On the side of the vans was a familiar sign that read, 'the McKinley Securities.' As soon as the vehicle came to a stop, groups of men armed with rifles and fitted with vests and various gear exited the vehicles.

"We're done," Julian chuckled in disbelief.

"We'll figure it out, Julian." Sarah attended to her friend and helped him walked over to the rest of the group. Julian found relief in Sarah but cursed himself in his mind for instinctively missing the chance at showing fortitude.

"Alright." Mr. Jung hung up the phone.

"What'd they say?" Landris asked.

"First things first." Mr. Jung stood up and revealed the finished product made from the components in the cases he had taken out from his bag.

"Mr. Jung, wait!" Sarah was in disbelief at what she saw.

Kalin turned around to find himself in a familiar position again with Mr. Jung. He pointed at him with a weapon that very closely resembled a gun, though slightly bigger than the average handheld.

"Mr. Jung!" Before Sarah's voice finished and before Kalin could speak in his defense, Mr. Jung pulled the trigger.

Sirens flooded the streets outside.

Chapter 7
MOMENTS BEFORE THE BREACH - ONE

Mr. Morris pushed through the waves of flashing lights and the ocean of uniformed officers and the McKinley Security Firm's agents. Mr. Morris, formerly known as Captain James Morris, was a respected and well-known member of the McKinley Security Firm with his renowned service in the military. It was said that he was known to have loved and respected the military life, and it was a surprise to those who knew him to hear that he had left of his own volition rather than being forced to retire due to being too old and decrepit to even stand. He was specifically asked by Mr. McKinley himself to fly across the country after receiving a tip that the Witch might be in this city. With Mr. McKinley's blessing, he was assigned to be the team leader for all operations within the city. No one had any complaints. Though nearly falling off his prime, the wrinkles in his face didn't show age, but rather experience. His hair was shaved just as he had it in the military until very recently when he decided to grow a small patch of Mohawk at his younger girlfriend's insistence for a more casual look.

McKinley agents were dressed in black and fitted with armor and padding from head to toe. They stood out even among the uniformed officers of the city. It wasn't a common sight for the police to see these government employed mercenaries, and it wasn't an easy feeling for them to know that they were essentially outgunned. The agents knew very well of their superseding authority and superior firepower and stood proudly in the midst of the nervous officers. Many of them dismissed the officers' existence, deeming them unworthy of their attention.

McKinley's forces on the scene were sixty-three men strong—nine members per van of the total seven vans that arrived. Each squad had a squad leader who was a notch above in pay grade and had the duty of babysitting the men. Many of them had lost a lot of the discipline from their times within the military now that they were in their new, less restrictive and much better paying jobs. Above the squad leaders was the team leader. The squads waited for their orders from Morris.

Team leader Morris made his way in front of his men. Standing next to him was his partner he specifically requested from Mr. McKinley, Damon Henderson. Mr. Henderson and Mr. Morris had worked together since the early days of Mr. Morris' career at the McKinley Security Firm, and the two had developed a respectable friendship. Mr. Henderson was a muscular man whose impressive physique made his already tall height seem taller than it actually was. But despite his intimidating physique, he was an easygoing man and often served to smooth the coarse edges of Mr. Morris. Mr. Henderson quickly devoured the leftover packed lunch that he couldn't finish in time. Mr. Morris raised an eyebrow to which Mr. Henderson simply shrugged.

Mr. Morris saw the excitement in the eyes of his men. The excitement wasn't for the job itself. No, Mr. Morris knew that most of them were more excited about the giant payday the mission would prove to be if the Witch was indeed present, and the fame that'd come by putting a bullet in her head.

"Alright, settle down and listen up!" Mr. Morris' rough voice echoed through the McKinley agents' earpieces. Even through the ruckus that surrounded them, they heard him clearly.

He began with the standard reminder that the operation was taking place within the city and to act with discretion. That even though this was their operation, each men should remember that this city is under protection by its police. There were rules, laws, and etiquettes that they still had to follow.

"Remember to put a muzzle on those guns unless you're about to get your heads blown off," Mr. Morris said. "Last thing McKinley needs is another spanking from the government boys up top. If you want your paychecks, I suggest keeping our boss in good graces."

Mr. Morris turned to Mr. Henderson. "Henderson, take a couple of the sharpshooters we have and give us eyes from that building across..."

"Hey! Hey!" an older man with salt and pepper hair yelled from behind the rows of the McKinley's men and interrupted Mr. Morris. He was a rangy old man dressed in a cheap suit probably from the local department store whose only real impressive feature about him was his height and mustache. If it wasn't for the badge shining from his belt and his lack of being intimidated by having a group of heavily armed men glaring at him for his interruption, Mr. Morris would have figured he was your run-of-the-mill friendly aging neighbor who collected stamps and talked long hours about his uneventful fishing trip.

"...Henderson, get to your post with your men. You'll be Alpha. I'll deal with the police. Jason, Carlos, and Ryan, your squads are Bravo, Charlie, and Delta, respectively. Jason, cover the back, and the rest of you squads are with me in front. We'll breach when I give the go."

More often than not, meeting with the local law enforcement was a stressful matter. Mr. Morris understood the necessity of working with them and preached its importance, but at the same time, he shared the similar sentiment with the rest of his men that their jobs would be easier without them. Sometimes it was due to their sheer incompetence in dealing with the Gifted. Sometimes it was due to the corruption within the force that drove them to pursue these cases with only praises in mind. But generally, it was the annoying ego competition of the two forces comparing the sizes of their manhood. However on rare occasions, there were certain types of police officers that he appreciated but also made his work even more difficult: the good ones.

"Yes, officer?" Mr. Morris approached the senior man. The police formed a parameter around the McKinley vans, and officers crowded the area like civilians witnessing a crime scene. They were nervous and yet excited for the show. The old man looked at his men with a little bit of disdain.

"Detective Sergeant Tony Fowler." The detective offered his calloused hand.

"James Morris of McKinley Security Firm." The two men exchanged a quick but firm handshake.

"You guys got here pretty quick, Mr. Morris. It seems that none of us from the department called you guys, but you have a whole army here ready to tear that building apart. Is there something we should know and a reason why we weren't informed in our own city?"

To even the most jaded police officers, Tony Fowler was not only respected but admired. He was one of the few referred to as 'natural police.' One of those guys who joined the force believing that he'd do good for the society and found himself not only good at the job but also kept his vision for the job alive.

"We received a last minute tip," Mr. Morris somewhat lied. "That there's potentially a highly dangerous group of Gifted in there right now. There wasn't much time. We apologize for not informing the city's finest but given the circumstances we hope you all understand."

"On what kind of 'tip' do you think there are 'potentially high dangerous group of Gifteds in there? From the looks of things it might as well be the Witch in there!"

"That's classified information," Mr. Morris answered coldly and with authority.

"Classified, right." The detective thought for a moment. He scratched his head and played with his chin as he tried to digest Mr. Morris' answer. "That's a load of crap, James." Detective Fowler got closer to James than the McKinley Security officer was comfortable with. "Classified. So what? Are we just supposed to just sit here and watch you boys gung-ho around in OUR city? I don't care if you guys were hired by the federal government! I know the things McKinley tried to sweep under the rug ever since this whole fiasco started! I'm not going to just sit here and watch people—CHILDREN—get murdered in my city!"

Mr. Morris thought for a moment. His attention drifted away from Detective Fowler as he noticed the thin light piercing the skies over the horizon. The Light was as devoted as ever to its role as a constant reminder to mankind of the chaos that came with it.

"So what?" Mr. Morris replied as coldly as before, turning his attention back to Detective Fowler.

"I'm sorry?"

"So what, Detective Sergeant Fowler? You boys want to take over then? You want to go in there and take care of this? Look at your boys right now. Half of them are giddy for a show and rest of them looks so lost, like they just got spat out of their mother's wombs. How many cases dealing with the Gifted have you guys dealt with? How many?"

The detective couldn't answer. He looked at his officers admiring the armada of the private military company and chattering amongst themselves about what could unfold in a matter of moments and their opinions about the Gifted.

"We are under government contract to do what we do because we are the only ones who *can* do what we do. I'm speaking to you out of courtesy right now—out of my respect for all those who choose to wear that badge. But we don't need your permission. We are above you."

"..."

"These people! These 'children'! Are walking bombs, detective!"

Walking bombs. Fowler wasn't sure how he felt about having propaganda being spat at his face. Was he offended? Disgusted? Or was he simply too green regarding the Gifted.

"I've lost one of my men just couple of weeks ago," Morris continued. "A boy, probably no more than 7 or 8, started cutting him up by just waving his fingers around. Can you even imagine that? We've lost total of 23 men just this year dealing with these children, these people. We are being paid to be the guinea pigs, detective. To be the front lines of experiencing what these Gifted can do for the benefit of the rest of you. At least, let us be fodders in peace."

Detective Fowler silently chewed on the reality check.

"...if there's a dead body at the end of this, you can be damn sure that we are taking this over. Even if that means the government coming down on us. You can be sure of that, Mr. Morris." Detective Fowler nearly gritted his teeth as he relented.

"You do that, detective. The commotion seems to have already attracted the media scavengers so just keep them off the premise." Mr. Morris turned away from the detective and waved his hand to signal his men. He looked behind him and found Henderson on top of the building across the street.

"No body bags, Morris! You hear me?! Not a single one!" The detective gave his final words before waving at his own men to secure the perimeter.

Mr. Morris didn't acknowledge the detective and kept walking. He didn't want dead bodies; no one wanted to simply kill these Gifted. Well, perhaps not 'no one,' but he couldn't imagine killing children being easy to anyone who was still sane. But people forget. If these kids had guns in their hands, they wouldn't. If they had guns, at least people would know what they were capable of. And as people like Fowler would say, the Gifted were people like them. Only, they were people just like them that could snap after a bad day. Or just one day when their boredom and curiosity got the best of them. He and his men at least had the right to protect themselves and had the duty to protect the people from this great unknown.

"Where's my air support," Mr. Morris spoke into his ear piece.

Morris, I think we got the real deal here. It looks as if someone punched through the metal door in the back to get in and there's... Carlos reported from the back entrance.

Sir, there's smoke, the voice of one of his other men interrupted the conversation.

"Smoke?"

From the open crevices of the building smoke began to leak out, and all of its windows slowly began to fog with thick smoke.

"Resourceful bunch, aren't they?" Mr. Morris signaled the men with the battering ram to come to the door. "Keep your eyes open and minds sharp. No one fires without my permission unless fired upon. Remember, they're worth more alive than dead, especially if it's *her* who's in there." Mr. Morris gave the sign to signal:

Breach

Chapter 8
MOMENTS BEFORE THE BREACH - TWO

The gunfire was unimpressive. No louder than a balloon pop and certainly not loud enough that anyone outside the room could have heard the noise. The redhead checked the slight stinging pain right above his left breast and found a small dart.

A tranquilizer.

He wanted to speak and curse Mr. Jung but before words could come out, his vision went dark and he collapsed onto the floor.

"A prototype for Silver Aegis agents. It's non-lethal but enough to put a horse to sleep. I had hoped that he'd be more cooperative, though I didn't really expect it." Mr. Jung looked at Sarah and Julian who still seemed stunned and shaken from the unfolded events. "Get a grip," Mr. Jung said. "We have to be quick. They'll be breaching soon."

Mr. Jung turned his attention to Julian who still seemed sick as a dog.

"Julian, are you going to be alright or do we have to leave you behind?" Mr. Jung figured putting Julian in survival mode would give him some pep. He then turned to Landris who seemed not at all fazed by the current events and simply marveled at one of the darts from the case. Mr. Jung could somewhat see what Director Jones saw in the troubled boy.

"Landris, I think it's up to you to help Julian, Sarah, and the boy there to the rendezvous point." Mr. Jung checked his phone. "They'll meet you guys at point A, the alleyway a couple of blocks down from where the cafe was. The crew there should take care of you guys from that point."

"I know. I got this," Landris replied apathetically, more concerned about the dart he was observing.

"Just in case…" Mr. Jung reached into his bag and tossed Landris a couple of plastic restraints for the redhead. Afterwards, Mr. Jung packed up the rest of the goods into his backpack, but not before taking out a few canisters the size of an adult's fist.

"Remember that you guys are not even supposed to exist yet so don't get caught." Mr. Jung strapped on the pack. "And especially don't let that boy get in the hands of the McKinley Securities. Do you guys remember what to do if you get caught?"

"Yes. Don't say anything, don't do anything, and just wait for Director Jones," Sarah recited the procedure instructed to them before they left.

"And if I'm the only one who got caught," Julian interjected. "I just find the right time to teleport away."

"You're good at running," Landris remarked with a smirk. Julian could only glare as a response.

"Great. I'm going to buy you guys some time." Mr. Jung placed as many canisters as he could in his pockets and some around his belt strap.

"Mr. Jung?" Sarah called out for Mr. Jung who hastily headed for the doors with the tranquilizer pistol still in hand.

"Don't worry about me and go. Head for the roof. Landris, leap over the buildings as fast as you can with Sarah and the redhead. And Julian?" Mr. Jung turned and faced Julian.

"Don't worry about me. I'm good at 'running away.' Worst case scenario, they can leave me behind, and I'll get away on my own," Julian, still looking sickly, tried to assure Mr. Jung with a smile and a nod. The pain from his rib was nauseating, and he was still drained from his earlier struggle with the Witch's friend. He tried his best to not let any of that hold him down; especially if Sarah's safety depended on it.

With that shaky assurance, Mr. Jung headed out the door. They were in a four story building. Each floor was connected by an elevator and two fire-exit stairways on both ends of each floor. The first floor was a simple lobby with only the elevators and entrances to the stairways. Second, third, and fourth were offices stories. Each of them had a hallway with doors for different offices, storages, and etc. Landris had chosen a meeting room inside one of the bigger office spaces on the third floor.

Given that, Mr. Jung's goals were simple. Flood the stairways with smoke, then each floor as he worked his way down to the first floor. Hopefully that'd be enough to slow down the breach for the kids to escape.

"Let's get moving guys." Sarah looked at Landris who was looking at the redhead with an amused smile on his face.

"No way," Julian exclaimed as he watched the redhead slowly pick himself up. Perhaps the stories of the Witch and her friend being inhuman were true after all.

"You guys are..." he spoke groggily, though it was apparent that he was gaining his strength back. "...garbage."

"But how? Are you alright?" Sarah walked over to the redhead to help him stand. He pushed her away. She was nonetheless relieved to see that he seemed unharmed.

"It's that 'gift' of yours, isn't it?" Landris asked.

"Wouldn't you like to know?" the redhead answered. His body still wasn't fully responsive yet. He dragged his body to the windows and took a peek outside. It wasn't supposed to be such a complicated day.

"Once we are out of this building, I'm off." The redhead offered his hand for a temporary alliance.

"If you help us get all the way to the checkpoint, I promise we won't pursue you further," Landris offered.

"And I'm supposed to just take your word for it? Rooftop. We are done there."

"Fine," Landris compromised. "...Then just do me a favor and make sure these guys get to the rooftop. I'll catch up, but there's something I have to do."

"Wait, what?" the red-haired boy protested.

"Yeah, Landris. What?" Julian protested with the redhead.

"I'm not going to leave Jung out there by himself if we don't have to." Landris was already walking towards door. "I'll catch up. Do I have your word that you'll get them up there?"

"You can't be serious." The redhead looked at Sarah and the exasperated Julian.

"If you let anything happen to these two, I promise I'll make it my life's mission to hunt you and your friend down." With that last warning, Landris stormed out of the room.

The redhead wasted no time.

"Come on," the redhead said as he approached Julian. "Get on my back." He crouched down in front of Julian. "Hurry!"

"No way, man! Take Sarah!" Julian glanced at Sarah with embarrassment.

"Julian, just do it." at Sarah's insistence, Julian begrudgingly climbed onto the redhead's back, trying his hardest to ignore the pain from his rib.

Breach

Chapter 9
THE BREACH

The shattering noise as the battering ram destroyed the main doors echoed from the floors below.

"I'll be moving fast. Try to keep up, Sarah." The redhead ran out the door with Julian on his back and Sarah trailing behind.

"The stairway is the first door on the right outside the office," Sarah told the redhead, recalling her way through the building.

The stairway was already beginning to fill up with smoke, and the stairs below them were drowning in it. From what it seemed, Mr. Jung and Landris succeeded.

The redhead and Sarah begin climbing up the stairs. The smoke teased their lungs and eyes, and the three coughed and tried to ignore their watering eyes as they made their ascent. The coughs were especially painful for Julian.

Streams from his legs helped the redhead to climb the stairs even with Julian on his back. Periodically he looked back to check on Sarah. She was determined to not be the one to hold them back.

A gunshot.

The loud blast echoed through the stairway and a barrage of more gunfire immediately followed after.

"What's going on down there?" The confidence in Sarah's face swiftly washed away with the noise.

"Keep moving!" The redhead hastened his pace. As they neared the roof exit, they heard loud roars of machinery from above. The Witch's redheaded friend recognized the noise immediately. He hesitated for a second in front of the exit.

"Is that...?" Julian whimpered from the redhead's back.

"Yeah," the redhead quickly answered.

The swarming footsteps of the McKinley troops grew louder and louder. The muffled sound of the men was becoming clearer, and they could begin to make out what they were saying. Staying within the building or heading back down wasn't an option anymore. The redhead looked at Sarah, and she seemed to understand their pigeon-holed predicament. Their only chance awaited beyond the door. She gave him a nod in affirmation. The redhead kicked the door open with the aid of his streams, and the door flew across onto the rooftop and skipped over the pavement. The smoke began to vent out through the gaping chasm of outdoors.

Through the smoke, the three walked out into the daylight. Their worst fears confirmed as they were immediately bombarded with instructions from the helicopters that hovered over them. The redhead noticed the men on the rooftops of the building across. They looked down the scopes of their large rifles with their cross-hairs on the redhead's chest. A few men from the helicopter propelled down onto the rooftop and decorated the Witch's friend, Sarah, and Julian with red dots from the laser sights of their guns.

Chapter 10
NO WAY OUT

Two males and a female on top of the roof, Morris. One of the males has red hair like the description for the Witch's friend. The female, though, doesn't fit the Witch's description, Henderson patched through Morris' earpiece.

"Cooper and Thomas, stay down there and secure that body before the cops see it. Holland, if you don't have a convincing story of what happened down there, you can be damn sure you're finished. The rest of you to the roof on the double," Morris patched in.

Landris walked towards Sarah, Julian, and the redhead. He kept his head held high for his audience and looked at the noisy helicopters in annoyance.

"Don't move!" A voice commanded from the McKinley's men surrounding them. All of them were dressed in black with armored vests, rifles, and various other items attached to their uniform. With their heads and faces covered with helmets and masks, they all looked like factory produced soldiers. Landris looked down on them. Their confidence came from the shells and the guns they hid behind. They were afraid. They feared them.

"So much for counting on you, redhead," Landris spoke somewhat jokingly as he joined the three.

"Got them to the roof, didn't I?" the redhead responded. "Hope you guys have a better escape plan."

"Landris!" Sarah tugged on Landris's shoulders. "What happened down there? Where's Mr. Jung?"

"Put me down," Julian said to the redhead. "I can stand."

The redhead obliged and gently set Julian down who managed to stand, though he still looked quite sickly.

"Landris?" Sarah called out to Landris again when he didn't give an answer. Landris looked at Sarah but didn't say anything. The silence was enough of an answer for Sarah and Julian for their remaining zeal to crumble.

"Sorry," the Witch's friend told the two.

The four heard roaring footsteps from the entrance to the stairway behind them. More of the McKinley's armed men flushed out onto the roof top. A rough-faced man with a humble, shaved mohawk slowly approached the four. He stopped at a comfortable distance.

"My name is James Morris," the man introduced himself. The men who just arrived join the group that propelled down from the helicopter and formed a semi-circle in front of the four. Now all the guns pointed at them and the man with the mohawk.

"We are from the McKinley Security Firm under government orders." Morris began to walk around the four until he faced them with the rest of his men. "And the government has asked us to take care of the Gifted menace. That'd be you guys." Morris pointed at the four. "None of us here wants to hurt you. So please. Let's make the process easier for all of us and come with us peacefully."

"What about Mr. Jung!" Sarah asked with fierce eyes. Landris gave her a frustrated glance at revealing Mr. Jung's name.

"The lesson there, little miss," Mr. Morris spoke calmly. "...Is to know when to fight and when to surrender."

"Landris, what do we do?" Julian asked.

"The situation is already ugly, but trust me it can always get uglier. It all depends on you guys. Let's be wise and make the right choices, yes?" Mr. Morris crossed his arms and waited for their answer.

The four remained silent. Half of the eyes were filled with uncertainty while the other half seemed to be calculating all of their options.

From afar, in the woods outside the city, a girl sat in the sky as if the air was solid ground. Higher than the tallest tree in the woods, she looked for her friend through the small monocle formed by her curled fingertip touching the tip of her thumb.

"Come on, we don't have all day." Mr. Morris grew impatient. He turned his attention to the redhead. "Hey, you there! Redhead! Shouldn't really have a hair like that when you're one of the most wanted men in the world, yeah? Where's your friend?"

The red-haired boy resented his remark. He had enough people pointing out his hair today. Landris couldn't help but smirk.

"The *Witch*?" Mr. Morris clarified. The redhead decided to maintain on not answering.

"So what's the plan?" the redhead asked Landris.

"Didn't you hear? Our orders were to give ourselves up if we got to this point," Landris answered.

"Good for you guys. What about me?"

"I guess that depends on whether or not you decide to join up with us." Landris gave the redhead a smug smile. The boy replied back with a smile of its kind.

"Henderson, it doesn't seem like they're going to cooperate. Let's end this right here. Your men have your shots?" Morris whispered into his ear piece.

Tranquilizers are loaded and we have a clear shot on the targets. Just waiting on your go. Henderson and his men watched the events through the scopes of their rifles.

"Get the redhead and the blondie first," Mr. Morris responded.

Her long search finally proved successful. She found her friend. Even though he was far, far away, she saw his red hair through her handmade monocle like a red dot on a map. Her glee was short lived as she saw the trouble he was in. Though she had been told to stay in the woods, she felt her friend needed her by his side. The girl stood up and descended from the sky as if she was climbing down an invisible staircase.

"I think I could make a run for it," the redhead said.

"I wouldn't recommend it," Landris commented.

"Don't think I have much of a choice here."

"Don't think you got what it takes to get out of here," Landris criticized. "Look, if you try to run, those trigger happy idiots will probably shoot us all."

The redhead didn't respond. Landris was probably right. Running didn't seem like an option anymore.

"Last chance, kids!" Mr. Morris yelled. "Either cooperate or we'll take you guys in by force. Be smart!"

The girl concentrated on where she saw her redheaded friend. Once she felt her concentration find its intended target, she focused on the second matter of casting her spell. She couldn't explain in words exactly what she did while casting her spells. It was a feeling—an instinct. She pointed her pale finger to the ground like a wand and drew a large arch over her head as far as her arm could reach and back down to the ground. Within the little arch she drew, she crisscrossed from one point of the arch to the other until it resembled a shattered mosaic. Then with all of her other concentrations still intact, she concentrated on her palm and placed it on the 'surface' of the arch and began to push.

"Alright! We give..." Landris paused before finishing his sentence. Were his eyes playing tricks?

Boss, I think they're doing something.

Anyone else seeing that right now?

If we're going to do something, we should do it now!

"Henderson, prepare to take the..." If it weren't for his men storming up in his earpiece, Mr. Morris would have thought his eyes were playing tricks on him. Even when he realized his eyes were fine, it didn't help explain what he was witnessing. It looked as if the air itself was beginning to crack like glass.

Boss? Henderson's finger teased the trigger.

"Are you seeing this, Julian?" Sarah asked.

"Ye...yeah" Julian answered.

The three Silver Aegis students watched in awe as the cracks begin to rumble. They seemed as if they were struggling to tear away from one another or struggling to stay intact.

"That idiot," the redhead grumbled under his breath.

Push. PUSH. PUSH!

The pieces of the mosaic door scattered and dangled in the air as if still attached to their original place by a thread. Each piece contained the plane and the view they once represented. From where the pieces scattered, a small girl in an innocent and humble one piece dress that matched her long raven hair, walked out from a forest onto the rooftop in the city. A band of black steel dangled on her wrist.

Chapter 11
AN UNEXPECTED GUEST

Anderson didn't know what came over him. Perhaps it was from all the stories about her from the news. But when she appeared, he knew as probably everyone else did as well, that the tiny little girl was *her*. He didn't exactly understand what he had witnessed, but he knew it had to be her. And it was only at the day's end, Anderson realized her eyes and his only met out of pure coincidence. But at that moment, he felt their eyes met because he was going to be her next victim. He would tell his friends and coworkers that her eyes were that of the devil. Though in the privacy of his mind, Anderson remembered her eyes as hauntingly normal and appealing like any other girls' eyes. He was simply standing at the wrong place at the wrong time.

He didn't even feel his own hand squeeze on the trigger. Only when his gun roared and began to spit out its bullets, Anderson realized he was shooting. Soon as the first shot was heard, others joined in until there was an orchestra of gunfire.

"NO!" the redhead and Mr. Morris cried out at the same time.

But the bullets were already in the air, faster than the cries of their voices. Just moments before reaching the Witch at about an arm's length away from her, the bullets exploded into fine steel dust. The explosion of dust stayed still in the air as if time itself had stopped for them.

The girl's eyes were widened with surprise. Her heart was beating as if she ran down the stairway again. She let out a sigh of relief and turned away from the men with guns. She knew her friend was just on the other side of the portal and that he might not be very happy that she came here. Although given the circumstances, she figured she'd escape the scolding.

Kalin?

She looked behind the portal and saw her redheaded friend. He, as expected, didn't seem too happy to see her. She went behind the portal again. The shattered pieces danced in the air. After finding her courage, she scurried to Kalin, and grabbed onto his hand. She pulled on his hand to let him know that they should leave. Kalin wasn't very happy to see her, but he knew the resentment was towards himself and not her. She gave him her puppy-eye look that she did anytime she thought he was mad at her.

"Thanks for coming," Kalin muttered under his breath. "I'm sorry that you had to come." The girl gave him a bright smile and shook her head. As she led Kalin towards the portal, the girl stopped and looked behind her. She let go of his hand and ran towards Landris. He towered over the tiny girl. When she looked up, he looked down at her with menacing eyes. Landris had no ill intentions but his resting face had a natural frown. She quickly looked away and stared at the ground, but the girl still grabbed his hand.

The girl then turned her attention to Sarah. Sarah was lovely and reminded her of the princesses in the stories she enjoyed. The girl looked at Sarah with admiring eyes and grabbed on to her hand as well.

"Come," the girl said gently to Sarah as she even more gently tugged on her hand. She then looked at Julian and nodded for him to come as well. Julian, dumbfounded, simply nodded back. Sarah waved her friend over and held his hand.

"Wait, wait!" Kalin protested.

"They have to come," the girl said. Kalin glanced over at McKinley's men and relented. He didn't know what these kids from Silver Aegis were planning, but it wasn't good for any of them to stay.

Boss? Orders? Henderson asked Morris.

"Take aim. All sights on *that* girl," Morris quietly gave his orders, although somewhere deep inside he believed there was nothing they could do at this point to stop the girl.

Holding Landris's and Sarah's hands, the girl walked back to Kalin. With a wide smile, she gave Kalin a nod.

"Excuse me, little miss, you're not thinking of just leaving are you?" Mr. Morris called out to the group.

The girl looked at Morris for a moment. She looked uncomfortable. She *was* uncomfortable. Without saying a word, she continued leading her redheaded friend and her newly found friends towards the portal.

"Take the shot, Henderson." As soon as Mr. Morris' words left his tongue, Henderson and his fellow sharpshooters pulled their triggers. The tranquilizer darts pierced through the air like the bullets from before. And like the bullet, they scattered into dust before they reached their target.

Julian looked in amazement at the portal. Across the small door the girl came from was a forest. They could smell and feel the air of the woods as they approached closer. Giving into his curiosity, Julian slowly reached out to touch one of the dangling pieces of the shattered shards. His finger went through them as if they were still what they were before shattering.

One step away from the portal, the girl felt the hesitance from the people she was leading. She looked at each of them curiously with worry. The girl let go of the hands she held and walked through the portal first. On the other side, she gestured them to come across.

"Come! Come!" She said.

"Come on. All you have to do is step across," Kalin said as he stepped over.

Sarah was hesitant for a second until her eyes met with the girl. The girl waved her over with such childlike innocence that Sarah could only respond with a defeated smile. As she took her first step across, Sarah immediately felt the change of air and a chill run through her spine as dirt crushed under her feet. From the smog of the city to the breeze of the forest. From concrete to dirt. She was in the woods. She looked around in amazement and was tempted to cross again just to cross back.

"Julian, this is amazing! Come on!" She waved at her friend. Not wanting to lose to Julian, Landris crossed over first. Julian followed after. Landris acted as if the whole trick made no impression on him. Julian, seeing another form of teleportation of sorts, couldn't help but admire and envy the spell.

Meanwhile, Mr. Morris and his men watched helplessly. As soon as the last of them crossed over, he heard a swarm of men storming out from the entrance to the stairway.

"Freeze!" Detective Fowler yelled with his gun drawn. Behind him were squads of heavily armed and armored police officers that mirrored the McKinley's own agents. With their guns drawn and pointed at the McKinley's forces, they formed their own semi-circle on the other side of the portal. Though their guns were still holding their aim, the officers couldn't help but be astonished at the sorcery before their eyes. It was the first time most of them have seen a 'gift' in action. McKinley's men raised their guns.

Mr. Morris looked around in quiet disbelief at the mess that was made. How did it come to this? He looked at the portal again and saw the girl who had caused everything to go wrong. She was waving goodbye. Not tauntingly, but sincerely waving goodbye. He couldn't help but give a small and quick single wave back to the tiny girl. And as if that was the sign for her to disappear, all the shattered pieces of the dimension immediately found their natural place. For a moment they could still see the creases of the fragments but they quickly mended themselves. At the exact moment the door closed, all the dust that were frozen in space blew away with the wind as if the laws of physics turned back on for them.

Mr. Morris let out a big sigh.

"Are you guys dense? Lower your guns," Mr. Morris ordered.

"We're not here to kill cops."

All of McKinley's forces obliged their leader's command. Mr. Morris looked behind him and saw Henderson and his men were surrounded by police as well.

"Drop your guns!" Detective Fowler screamed as him and the police officers came back to their senses after being mesmerized by the Witch's trick.

Mr. Morris nodded at his men who then placed their guns on the ground. Detective Fowler and his officers approached the disarmed McKinley agents and began to apprehend them, while the detective moved to handcuff Mr. Morris himself.

"Didn't I say no dead bodies, Mr. Morris?" Detective Fowler asked.

"You do realize you can't arrest any of us, right?" Mr. Morris reminded Detective Fowler.

"I'm well aware, Mr. Morris," the detective answered. "But I wanted the satisfaction for me and my officers of at least knowing what it feels like to put you and your men in handcuffs and for you and your men to at least get a taste of what it feels like to take the walk of shame. And…" The detective led Mr. Morris near the edge of the roof. From below Mr. Morris saw the entire major media outlet in a frenzy. At the sight of Mr. Morris and Detective Fowler, all of their cameras turned towards them.

"We sure as hell can't touch you guys," Detective Fowler snarled into Mr. Morris' ear. "But I'm sure they'll do a good job bringing you down."

From a building afar, a girl tucked away in a beaten bomber jacket watched the entire affair unfold with her obnoxiously large binoculars. They were uncomfortably large, but they allowed her to have the closest thing to front row seats for the event. Her phone rang from her pocket with the loud and offensive music she set as her ringtone.

"Yeah?" she answered with a devilish grin.

"Did you see all that?" a male voice asked.

"Yep," she answered while watching through the binoculars as McKinley's men were escorted off the rooftop by the police.

"I guess he was the real deal," the voice said.

She set aside the binoculars and cracked open a can of soda that she had brought with her for the show. The soda was finished in one gulp, and she let out a satisfying sigh of relief as she crushed the can with her hand and tossed it over her shoulder. Holding the phone between her ear and shoulder, she then dug into her pockets for her pack of cigarettes and spanked the pack a few times before fishing a stick out with her mouth.

"I can't believe you got to see her with your own eyes! I'm jealous!" a different voice, that of a young girl, pitched in. Even when she was excited, she sounded sleepy.

"Mmhmmm," the girl responded with a cigarette pinched between her lips, and flicked her index finger against her thumb. The tip of her finger lit with a ball of flame, and she used the fire to light her cigarette. Once the flame served its purpose, she wagged the fire away.

"What now?" the original voice asked.

"Plan B," the girl answered while taking a deep breath of her smoke. She brushed aside her long blond hair over her shoulders and took out her aviator glasses from her pockets. It felt right at home over her eyes.

"What Plan B, Emily?" the voice asked.

"Da, what Plan B, Em?" the young girl's voice pitched in again.

"The Plan B I just came up with." The girl hung up and dropped the phone back into her pocket. She took another dose of the smoke again as she stared at the distant and now the empty rooftop.

✳✳✳

"Kalin!"

In the woods somewhere outside the city, a girl celebrated her friend's safe return. She wrapped herself around his arm and hugged it tightly.

"You shouldn't have come, stupid. I told you to wait for me here," Kalin told the girl.

"But, but, but!" The girl tried to find words to justify herself. She always had trouble with words. "You were gone for a long time! I was worried!"

"And those guys," the redhead pointed at the three students from Silver Aegis as he spoke. "...are not our friends."

"But, but..." The girl tried again to find more words for more justifications. "They were in trouble! Guns!"

"Yeah, but..."

"I think you should thank her for saving your hide, redhead," Landris interrupted. The redhead gave Landris the stink-eye.

"Ours too." Sarah approached the girl.

"Sarah, wait." Julian tried to stop his friend.

The girl slid ever so slightly behind the redhead but watched Sarah with curious eyes.

"Thank you very much." Sarah had to bend a little bit to meet the girl at her eye level. "My name is Sarah," she offered her hand and a smile. It was just a bit hard for Sarah to put on that smile with all that was going on in the back of her mind of what had transpired so far that day. But she focused on the warmth of the small hand that grabbed onto hers just moments before.

Seeing Sarah's smile, the girl quickly grabbed Sarah's hand. She couldn't see it, but she could feel her redheaded friend putting on his face of disapproval behind her. He worried for her.

"My name is Lily!" With a sunshine smile, the Witch shook Sarah's hand.

END OF PART ONE

PART TWO

BREAKFAST AT PATTI'S

"You guys are up early this morning, ain't ya?"

In three weeks, Patti would have been working at this 24-hour diner for ten years. Working graveyard shifts introduced her to many colorful characters who roamed through the wee hours of the morning, but even as a veteran, it still made her cringe anytime she saw kids five in the morning for breakfast. Especially when they were dirty like they've been living on the streets. It didn't help that one was a girl and the other was a boy.

"Table for two, please," the boy asked. Patti forced a smile and the boy smiled back. The girl's eyes were glued to the floor as if there was a picture show playing just for her below. The waitress led the two to an empty table towards the back of the restaurant. The boy held the girl's hand and led her to the table.

"You alright, sweetheart?" Patti asked the girl, not trying very hard to mask her concern about the boy. The girl nodded slowly. The boy seemed busy looking through the menu.

"Well, my name's Patti." She pointed at her glossy name tag. "Just holler if you're ready to order!" As Patti left the two, she asked herself whether or not to alert the authorities. She looked at the table again. The boy didn't seem so bad and the girl looked like she needed something to eat. Patti herself had a colorful childhood—what good could come from calling the authorities. Maybe she'd be shoving her nose where it didn't belong. Her life was complicated enough without the extra hassle.

Though he ate irregularly, Kalin had the freedom to eat anytime he wanted to. He was a spoiled runaway. His mother's life insurance had given him enough to be more than comfortable, and in that sense, he was more of a vagabond than a runaway. He tried to keep his eyes on the menu as he flipped through all the breakfast options.

The Breakfast Extravaganza was 12.99 but it was piled with eggs, bacon, pancakes, hash-browns, sausages, and came with toast. It was a bit more expensive than he would have liked to spend.

She's the Witch. Kalin felt his grip on the menu tighten as the thought flashed across his mind. The unjustifiable blame he had against the Witch for his mother's death still burned inside.

I mean, she's gotta be the Witch, right? Kalin peeked over the menu and saw her staring at the unopened menu.

He had to be sneaky when trying to catch a glimpse of her. She seemed shy, and it made him feel as if he was harassing her just by looking at her.

How can *she* be the Witch though? He would have thought that she'd at least have shoes.

Only two pancakes and bacon? The kids' menu had some of the cheaper stuff, but Kalin wasn't sure if it'd fill him up. It was only 3.99, but that's some small kid they were trying feed.

Even though she looked like she hadn't had a shower in weeks, the Witch was kind of cute.

The omelets were probably filling, but they were 9.99... *Wait, what? What*

Outside was a still-dark sky that was turning a brighter blue by the minute, and a few early birds were already filling the streets. Her menu still wasn't open. Did she not want to eat? Or even be here perhaps? Was she worried that she'd be a burden? But she had to be hungry. From the way she the donut before it seemed like she hadn't had a decent meal in a while.

Kalin stared at the girl for a while longer than he intended as he tried to sort through her mysteries and his own feelings. Thankfully, the Witch seemed too preoccupied with the outside world to notice his stare, but Kalin decided to not be too brazen and followed her gaze out the window.

The Light. Of course they could see it from here too. Was she looking at that?

Kalin went through a bit of metamorphosis with his relationship with the Light. When they first met, Kalin felt a bit disturbed. Then it turned to a violent disgust after that incident during a certain winter, until it finally settled into a bittersweet numbness as it is now. He wondered what her relationship with it was.

"Hey," Kalin called out to her. She didn't seem to hear him. "Ruby?" he called out to her again.

This time she quickly spun her head around like a startled deer. Bewildered, she blinked with wide, sorrowful eyes.

"We should order soon." Kalin opened up her menu to the breakfast section while Ruby looked at the colorful pictures and words describing the 'world famous' breakfasts of the restaurant. Her face brightened up a little bit. She seemed amused by the pictures.

"You should be hungry. My treat today. Count yourself lucky; I don't treat often." Kalin tried to ease the awkward tension between the two, but it didn't seem very effective. Ruby looked up at Kalin's statement and vehemently shook her head.

"I'm okay." Those were her first words since they walked over from the playground. The words seemed like they were struggling to coming out.

"Well, too bad. I already said I would, and my mom taught me that a man never goes back on his word. Never. So order anything you want." Kalin lifted the menu and hid his face behind it. Why was he blushing?

Ruby cringed and looked at the menu again.

"…water."

"What?" Kalin asked.

Startled, Ruby quickly fixed her answer.

"Water, *please.*"

"Geez!" Kalin was startled himself. "I didn't mean 'what' like that. I meant like 'what' as in 'what? I didn't hear you very well.' Your parents must have been pretty strict, huh?" Kalin looked over the empty tables in search of Patti. She was standing by the kitchen, chatting with the cooks and flipping through the channels of the TV. Something about a plane crash, some sort of an infomercial, and then an early morning news talk show type of thing that she finally decided to settle on.

"Patti!" Kalin called out. Patti walked through the near barren diner to her young customers.

"Ready to order?" She asked as she pulled out a notepad and her pen.

"Yeah, two Breakfast Extravaganzas, please." Kalin ordered without.

Pattie raised an eyebrow. "Anything else? Something to drink?"

"Water, please."

✳✳✳

The two sat in awkward silence until their orders arrived. Both looked out the window watching the sky gradually turn lighter blue and watched the streets come to life filled with the headlights of cars and pedestrians. Kalin thought about breaking the silence, but in the end he thought perhaps the silence was better than a pointless conversation. In some sense, the silence and watching the world outside tick away was soothing after the night they had.

The silence was broken as Patti sat down two large plates piled with a gluttonous amount of food. They both looked at Patti as if she was Santa Claus. Ruby was excited to see the colorful picture she saw on the menu come to life.

"Orange juice. It's on the house," Patti said as she sat down a great glass jug of orange juice marbled with perspiration.

"I can pay for it," Kalin insisted.

"It's alright, kid. We just had too much OJ around. You just treat this little lady right. Enjoy your breakfast!" Patti gave Kalin a pat on the shoulder and went on her way.

Ruby looked down at her plate of food and then looked at Kalin and back down at her food. Kalin poured Ruby a glass of the orange juice. Ruby watched Kalin pour the juice and then watched Kalin pour himself an orange juice.

"Don't worry and just eat," Kalin said as he reached for the syrup at the end of the table for his pancakes. Ruby was mesmerized as she watched shiny and thick ooze pour over the fluffy and golden brown pancakes. Kalin cut and forked a slice of pancake and stuffed it in his mouth. It wasn't until he started chewing that he noticed Ruby's plate remained untouched and the girl was simply staring at him.

"Here." Kalin poured some syrup over Ruby's pancakes. "Eat!"

Ruby grabbed a fork and a knife and approached the pancakes with caution. She then worked on her pancakes by clumsily mimicking Kalin. The boy thought about helping her but thought perhaps it'd be best to let her practice on her own. Though to her credit, she seemed to pick it up quickly as the breakfast went on.

"So, Ruby..." After finishing his pancakes and now cutting the sausages with his fork, Kalin thought it might be a good time as any to ask some important questions. "Where are you from?"

Kalin looked up when he didn't hear an answer. Ruby had a giddy smile on her face as she poured syrup over her sausage.

He didn't realize it, but watching the girl douse her food with syrup put a smile on his face as well.

"Huh, so you have a sweet tooth," Kalin said. Ruby cut the syrup drenched sausage—as Kalin did—with her fork and ate it with glee. After finding the syrup and sausage combination to be more than satisfying, Ruby decided to pour syrup over her hash browns.

"That's kind of weird," Kalin remarked as he watched Ruby scoop up the syrup drenched hash browns. The results of her test gave Ruby the confidence to pour syrup all over her food on the plate. Lots and lots of syrup.

"Okay, I think that's enough syrup." Kalin felt sick just from witnessing the gooey horror. Ruby stared at the syrup dispenser, and Kalin didn't need to be a psychic to figure what she was planning next. As soon as she opened her mouth, Kalin took the syrup from her hands.

"Yep, no more syrup for you." Kalin noticed a hint of disappointment in Ruby's face. "So, now we know you have a serious sweet tooth. Which also explains why you liked the donut so much." Her eyes seemed to brighten up at the mention of 'donut' as she munched more on the goopy pile of hash browns.

"So, Ms. Syrup, where are you from? Why are you wondering the streets at night?"

Ruby seemed reluctant to answer. Not even the syrup seemed to be cheering her up anymore. Kalin wondered if these questions were worth asking or even his place to ask. He debated with himself during the silence on what to do.

"I don't know," Ruby quietly spoke.

"You don't know?" Kalin carefully asked. Ruby simply shook her head.

"Where's your home? What about your parents? I'm sure they're looking for you."

"I think so too," Ruby answered. "I want to see them."

"Are you lost?"

Ruby nodded.

"When was the last time you saw them?"

"Long ago."

She looked at her puddle of syrup and swashed the contents back and forth.

"I want them to know that I'm okay," Ruby finally spoke.

"That's it?"

Ruby nodded. She stared at the black band on her wrist.

"There are so many people in the world. Billions." Kalin lowered his voice. "...and you're the Witch..."

Ruby flinched at that word.

He felt guilty for having said it. It was stupid.

"... The whole world is after you." Kalin didn't fail to notice that Ruby seemed sensitive to the fact that she was known as the Witch. "But you're not gonna let that stop you, are ya?"

Ruby shook her head.

Kalin looked out the window. He needed a moment to think. The world outside was now full with people starting their days and writing another page of their lives. How many different tales were being written just today? Most probably written without the consent of their subjects for stories the subjects didn't plan for or even want. Of the billions of stories, there was a story being written right in front of him of a girl branded the Witch who was hunted by the world. Of a lost child looking for her parents and dreaming her way home. And of a runaway who happened to run into such a girl. Choices.

"Alright, you done with your food?" Kalin asked. The question startled Ruby, but she nodded.

"Let's go," Kalin said. "We've got a long journey ahead of us, I think."

Ruby seemed confused.

"Let's go find your parents! Come on!" Kalin set down a couple of bills to cover the meal and pay a generous tip for Patti. He reached over and grabbed Ruby by her hand.

"Let's go!" He insisted. Ruby let Kalin take her out of her seat and out of the restaurant. He yelled thanks and goodbye to Patti as he left.

Outside, crisp and chilled morning air greeted them. Kalin took a deep breath and let it out.

"Why?" Ruby asked.

Kalin found himself stumped for a moment. He didn't exactly know how to answer.

"Because I don't have anything better to do," Kalin began his explanation poorly. "And it seems like you're not what people seem to think you are." A little better. "And you seem like you need a friend."

"Friend?"

"Yep! Come on before we go anywhere though. I—we—have to visit my mom." Kalin offered his hand and the still confused Ruby accepted it. As they took the first few steps of their long journey ahead, Ruby realized she couldn't remember the last time she felt any comfort walking in the daylight.

Chapter 12
AFTERMATH

Mr. McKinley grumbled angrily as he stomped away from the beach to his winter getaway. A red button-up islander shirt sized heftily enough for even a man of his size, designer swimming trunks and sunglasses, all topped off with a straw hat. All of these items should have been a warning to others that business was the last thing Mr. McKinley wanted on his mind. On a long overdue vacation with his wife and children—a son and a daughter—Mr. McKinley was at his estate in the islands, and he expected to be able to shut his brain off regarding work. However, even from the start of this forced vacation, Mr. McKinley knew very well that he'd not be able to relax. How could he with the chance to have *her* in his grasp?

And when a member of his securities team handed him his phone and whispered into his ear of James Morris' botched run-in with the notorious Witch, Mr. McKinley's worst fears were realized. His vacation had ended after 32 hours of being away from his office. With his phone clenched to the breaking point in his hand, Mr. McKinley hastily made his way back from the beach into his vacation home. His staff and security who heard the news made way for Mr. McKinley's bulldozer march, and those who didn't were smart enough to judge from his fiery eyes and the way his eyebrows squeezed tightly enough to meet at the nose of his sunglasses or his flaring nostrils that created waves on his flaming mustache as a good sign to stand aside.

Before he stepped into his office, Mr. McKinley shooed away his security and only gave permission to his personal secretary to enter with him. His vacation house office wasn't large, but it also wasn't humble enough to be considered small. He had basically all he needed for an office: an expensive desk, an expensive computer, an expensive TV, an expensive bookshelf filled with various expensive books, and a window large enough that it gave him the entire view of the beach outside. Mr. McKinley looked out the window and saw his family. He caught his wife looking back at him with a concerned look mixed with disappointment. Thankfully, his kids were too busy with the sand and the tides to care much for their father leaving for business as usual. This was his second wife and second set of children. She was about a decade and a half younger than he was, and he liked her enough to try harder than he did with his first wife. Liked her enough to let her convince him to come to this vacation when he very well knew he shouldn't.

"James." Mr. McKinley put the phone up to his ear and turned on the TV.

James cleared his throat. Mr. McKinley could hear over the phone the commotion of sirens and people scattering about. They were probably the onlookers, the police, the hyena media scavenging, and his employees trying to contain the situation. "Yes, sir," Mr. Morris replied.

"I had hoped at least if something were to happen, we could keep it quiet." Mr. McKinley flipped through the major news channels and saw his company being branded everything from a mistake to a travesty to the nation. He turned the TV off. "Now explain to me exactly what happened. And James?"

Mr. McKinley grabbed the monitor of his computer and threw it against the wall. The ruckus startled the staff outside while Ms. Kerry took note to order a new monitor for the vacation home's office.

"This has put me in a very, very bad mood, James." Mr. McKinley let out a deep sigh.

"Right, of course, sir." Mr. Morris rolled his eyes.

"Get with the explanation."

"Yes, sir. We arrived at the scene shortly after the police arrived. It seemed like the tip we received was on the money about the Witch being in the area."

"James, my dear James," Mr. McKinley interrupted. He took a moment of pause. His voice oozed with unalloyed anger. "Let's start with the dead body."

"Right. When we breached the building, the perpetrators had flooded the floors with smoke."

"Smoke bombs?"

"They were military grade smoke grenades."

"Go on."

"Visibility was basically zero. We heard some commotion and followed our ears to one of the two stairways to find the body on the ground. He was alive at this point and someone who was with him was heading up the stairs."

"So how did that body end up with bullets in its chest?"

"Holland stayed with the John Doe while the rest of us chased after the runner up the stairs. We heard the gunshots as we were about passing the second floor of the building. Holland claims that the John Doe pulled a weapon on him and he fired out of self-defense."

"You believe him?"

"There were a couples of guns found with the John Doe. One with tranquilizers and the other with live ammunition. But no, sir, there's something odd about the whole thing. Hopefully during interrogation we can figure this out. We've detained Holland for now and put him in the car."

"How did you let those *vultures* in the media get all over this?" Mr. McKinley emphasized the word with snarling distaste.

"An overzealous detective who had too much of our mess, sir."

Mr. McKinley groaned and massaged the bridge of his nose with his fingers.

"The government," Mr. McKinley continued. "Is going to be asking a lot of questions and will possibly be asking a lot from us to make good with what happened today. We might lose our cut of the pie because of this. You're certain it was her?"

"Yes, sir. The Witch was definitely there."

"Damn! Only if we at least had her…" Mr. McKinley's eyes suddenly sparked with dreaded realization. "James."

"Yes, sir?" Morris felt a tap on his shoulder as Henderson handed him a note.

"Who was the John Doe?"

"I just received the info, sir." Mr. Morris read off from the note. "It's David Jung. David Jung of Silver Aegis Securities."

Mr. Morris heard through the phone Mr. McKinley screaming profanities and what he guessed to be Mr. McKinley slamming on his desk with his fist. It was followed by pained groan that Mr. McKinley tried to hide under his breath. Then there was silence until broken by a small chuckle.

"Little Nancy's all grown up now, isn't she," Mr. McKinley muttered to himself as he pulled out a bottle of whiskey from his desk and poured himself a glass.

"Sir?"

"You said there were other Gifted that left with the Witch?"

"Yes, sir."

"Right. Of course. That's another theory confirmed." Mr. McKinley took a sip of his whiskey. "Mr. Morris…" he paused for a moment. "David Jung was the man who gave us the tip on the Witch."

A phone rang.

The secretary dug into her pocket for her phone and excused herself from the room.

"Come back immediately. If Nancy wants a war, we'll give her one. We'll take the Witch."

"Understood, sir."

Mr. McKinley hung up the phone and finished his glass of whiskey. He looked back at the window and watched his family enjoy the vacation that had been robbed from him. Even though he didn't want to be here, it'd have been nice to enjoy it. He poured himself another glass.

The secretary walked back into the room quietly.

"Mr. McKinley?" she asked carefully.

"We are going to war, Amanda," Mr. McKinley said as he watched his son build something with the sand. "We're going to get our hands on the Witch even if it means risking everything."

"Sir, given the current circumstances I believe it'd be best if we take a different approach to this matter. I mean who is the Witch to make it worth such a risk?" Amanda stood next to her boss.

"I could give less than a rat's ass *who* the Witch is. It's *what* she is. What we made her to be. She's the key to winning this game. And the one who can save us from the place Nancy just sent us to." Mr. McKinley finished his drink. At the horizon was the Light, a phenomenon that fascinated many others, but Mr. McKinley didn't really care much for it.

"Then you might be interested, sir, in the phone call we just received."

Mr. McKinley turned away from the windows and faced his secretary.

"A girl claiming to be part of the Wolf Pack."

"The *Wolf Pack*?" Mr. McKinley felt a bit silly saying their corny little name out loud.

"Apparently so. She says their services may be in our interest."

"The *Wolf Pack*, huh?" A wide grin stretched over Mr. McKinley's face. "Perhaps little luck's on our side now. Set us up with a meeting at the earliest date possible. Make sure she goes through a *thorough* check. I'll be flying back to the headquarters tonight."

"Yes, sir." Amanda quietly closed the doors behind her as she left.

Vacation was indeed over for Mr. McKinley. He liked his new family. His son James, the eight year old who was as stubborn as he was, and his daughter Danielle, the eleven year old who already resembled a lot of her mother. And his 'trophy' wife Michelle, who caught her husband still looking out the window watching them. Mr. McKinley gave her a hesitant wave. She didn't wave back. Her eyes were dead with disappointment with only a slight spark of anger as she knew that their vacation will be missing their father and husband again. But what enraged her more was that they both knew Mr. McKinley was returning to his real marriage and leaving the mistress behind.

***

Detective Fowler took a swig from his traveling mug as he

watched the McKinley's crew packing up. His coffee was cold. The media folks were still making lot of ruckus as each of them finalized their reports for the evening news. Perhaps this would even be discussed on *The Point* later that evening. He knew that he jeopardized his position with the higher ups for what he had done, but the faces of the McKinley's men whose zeal had been crushed out of them gave him a small sense of victory. And all the names he was being called by them was the cherry on top. The dead body that wasn't swept under the rug and was instead being carried away by the ambulance was definitely a victory. The detective's eyes met with Morris' who didn't seem too happy with his phone call. Fowler smiled and raised his coffee mug as a toast.

Henderson had just finished telling all the reporters the same answer for all their questions.

'No comment.'

He dug into his pockets for a candy bar he had saved since lunch. As he took his first bite, Henderson found Mr. Morris who was standing in the middle of all the chaos with a phone in his hand and mouth slanted as he chewed on his thoughts.

"What now, Jimmy? What did the boss-man say?" Henderson asked as he took another bite from his candy bar.

For a moment, Morris didn't seem to notice Henderson. Then he stared at Henderson without words as if he was still trying to decide what to do.

"For now, take charge and make sure none of the guys do anything stupid, and then just pack it up and head back to base," Mr. Morris finally said.

"What are you gonna do?"

"I have to make another phone call." Mr. Morris walked away from Henderson to find some privacy. Henderson shrugged and finished his candy bar before organizing a swift retreat for the McKinley's men.

Mr. Morris managed to sneak away from the media and head a couple of blocks down and into an empty alley. He placed the phone in his hand into his pocket and dug out a separate phone. He dialed a complex series of numbers before it began to ring.

"This is agent Daniel Graham," Mr. Morris said once someone picked up on the other end.

"Connect me to Director Hamilton right away. Tell him it's an emergency."

Chapter 13
PAPER CRANES

The birds chirped, and the gentle breeze conducted the leaves into a symphony. It was hard to believe that just moments ago the air was filled with the noise of cars and smog. These woods, though so near human civilization, was virtually untainted by men. That is, until a certain girl and her redheaded friend stumbled into these lands, and brought along three others through a magic gateway from the city into the woods.

Sarah shook Lily's hand.

"Well, nice to meet you, Lily!" They smiled at one another without words as their hands continued to go up and down.

"And Kalin, I suppose we should formally introduce ourselves." Sarah glanced at the redhead brooding behind the Witch. Lily seemed to be enjoying the hand shaking exercise.

"There's no need for us to—"

"Who's that?" Lily pointed with her free hand at Julian.

"That's my dear friend, Julian. He's very nice," Sarah replied with a smile.

Julian waved weakly through the pain.

Lily waved energetically back and then stared at Landris who she felt too afraid to point at.

"That handsome fellow is Landris. He's nicer than he looks." Sarah caught Lily's look.

Lily waved energetically to Landris who did not wave back— though truthfully he was a bit tempted to.

"This is Kalin!" Lily said enthusiastically as she pointed at her redheaded friend.

Kalin buried his face into the palm of his hand.

"Hi, Kalin." Sarah waved at him with her free hand.

"You can let go of her hand now," Kalin told Lily.

"But her hand is so soft and warm!" Lily stopped the shaking, but still held on to Sarah's hand. Sarah was relieved as her arms were growing tired. "And she looks like a princess!"

"Why, thank you! You're a doll yourself!" Sarah felt as if she was with a little niece or a little sister only to be quickly reminded in the back of her mind that the girl was the Witch.

Kalin grumbled under his breath something along the lines that

Lily was an idiot, and Lily stuck her tongue out as a response even though she couldn't exactly hear his words.

"I don't think the Witch has seen too many girls. Don't balloon up her ego," Landris said.

"Jerk!" Sarah snapped back at Landris but without enmity.

"Hey!" Julian protested, still pressing his hand against his rib. Crying out loudly made a sharp pain echo throughout his body.

"What?" Landris turned to Julian expecting the boy to squirm.

"Sarah's a good-looking girl," Julian responded in the way Landris had expected.

"Thanks, Julian!" Sarah smiled. "This is why we are friends for life!"

Julian knew without looking that there was a giant, smug grin on Landris's face.

Although the girls had broken through the borders and found instant peace, the boys still remained hesitant. Lily, holding on to Sarah's hand, looked back at her grumpy, redheaded friend and waved him to come. Sarah followed Lily's lead and waved her two friends to join her. Kalin walked behind Lily and crossed his arms. He was a bodyguard—not an ambassador.

"Anyways," Landris said. "I'm going to call Director Jones and let her know what's going on. Hope we get some signal out here." Landris turned away from the group.

"You're not calling anyone," Kalin warned.

"Pretty sure I am, tomato-head. But you can try to stop me if you want to eat some more dirt. Tomatoes do need it to grow." Landris paid no attention to the tomato-head and pulled out his phone from his pocket.

"Why don't we see if I can or can't?" Kalin's hands flared up with the streams.

"Just hold on, Landris!" Sarah looked back at her blond friend.

"Seriously, Sarah?" Landris reluctantly obliged.

"Lily." Sarah looked down at the girl holding her hand. Lily eyes were full of concern and confusion. "We came to the city in hopes of finding you because we want to help you."

Lily obviously liked Sarah, but her eyes told Sarah that the girl still wasn't convinced. It held doubts and fear in them.

"Listen," Sarah spoke softly. "It's been a crazy day…" Mr. Jung's face flashed by Sarah's mind and left it blank momentarily. Her voice quivered ever so briefly when she continued to speak. "Director Jones just wants us and you two to not have to go through these kinds of days anymore."

Lily caught the moment of anguish in Sarah and looked at her worryingly.

"And just from meeting you and speaking with you even just this much," Sarah continued. "I think all those things people say about you may be wrong. And that's why even more so now than before, I think you should come with us. We will keep you and your friend safe. Give you two a home."

"A home?" Lily stared at Sarah like a stray kitten trying to decide whether or not to let the random stranger pet her. *A home.* She thought.

Lily turned her head towards Kalin. "I think she's a good person."

"You tend to think just about everyone's a 'good' person," Kalin replied.

Lily gave Kalin an apologetic smile.

"Lily?" Kalin asked trying to decipher the meaning of the smile.

The Witch raised her free arm parallel to the ground. Landris, Julian, and Kalin felt their bodies gently lift off from the ground.

"Lily, wait!" Kalin protested.

"Whoa! Whoa! Whoa!" Julian kicked his feet in the air.

Landris tried to fight the Witch's will but quickly discovered how futile it was.

The three were gently but swiftly carried closer to Lily and Sarah. They remained floating in the air. Surprised and slightly worried, Sarah looked at her companions.

The girl shut her eyes and let out a small sigh of breath. From the dirt of the ground, the green of leaves and plants, and from the trunks of the great trees, dots of green light began to spore out of them. Freckles of green in the sky, like emerald fireflies, filled the air and surrounded them.

The witch took a small gasp of air and let out a small sigh of breath again. She whispered quietly that only the air around her mouth could hear, and the ground began to rumble. The gentle breeze around them seemed to sing around them in the echoes of a windy language.

Sarah and Landris glanced at one another. She gave him a nod of confidence to trust the girl.

"It'll be okay," Lily spoke to Sarah as if she had noticed despite her eyes still being closed. "Don't be afraid."

The glowing emerald dots of the forest began to whiz around them in a wild fury. They seeped into the ground and the trees nearest to them. The ground rumbled harsher than before. Loud cracks and the rustle of leaves filled the air.

From the ground roots of the grand trees erected and slithered towards the group. Countless snake like roots surrounded them and began to entangle with one another until they trapped the group in a dome.

Darkness.

"Li-Lily?" Sarah whispered, gently squeezing the girl's hand.

Lily gently squeezed Sarah's hand back.

From one end of the dome, the roots cracked open and the daylight shone through. The ground rumbled again and more roots revealed themselves. Lily lifted herself and Sarah off the ground. The roots slithered above the dirt until they covered the ground entirely. Lily released her magic over herself and the rest of the group and they landed softly onto the newly formed floor.

"Wow," Julian breathed, looking around the dome. The shelter was tall enough to give everyone a comfortable head space except Landris who barely had enough for comfort. But the size was large enough for all of them to snugly share.

"This is incredible, Lily! You're amazing!" Sarah said looking at Lily. Their eyes met only for a second before Lily quickly turned away. Her pale face ripened red.

"I just learned it recently," Lily said quietly.

"Lily, you forgot the fire..." Before Kalin finished his sentence, Lily waved her hands. Kalin gestured to the group to take a step back from the center of the dome they were standing near. In the center of the dome the roots cleared out of the way. Lily pointed her finger at the dirt, and when she raised her finger, a chunk of dirt lifted off and formed a hole. She directed the pile of dirt out the gap of the dome.

Lily cleared her throat. "Eh-hem! Fighting is not allowed in the house!" Lily announced.

"Lily..." Kalin let out a sigh and walked a short distance away from the group. Lily let go of Sarah's hand and walked over to Kalin.

"If you really think it's wrong, I'll do what you think is best," Lily spoke softly. "But I really, really think Landris, Julian, and Sarah are good people."

Kalin looked at the three. Julian sat and rested his back against the root-wall. He took deep breaths trying to deal with the pain. Sarah walked over and knelt by him. Landris stood with his arms crossed and watched his two comrades.

"And I think they can help me with what I have to do," Lily spoke just as softly as before. She stared at the ground not wanting to see if Kalin was angry or not.

"*We*," Kalin corrected as he gently grabbed Lily's hand while still watching the Silver Aegis students. Holding his hand always comforted Lily. "What *we* have to do," Kalin emphasized.

Lily couldn't hide her joy. As they walked over to Sarah and Julian, Lily had a wide smile on her face.

"Let me take a look," Kalin said as he knelt by Julian and placed his hand over the broken rib.

"What are you doing?" Julian asked.

"Don't worry," Kalin said as his hand began to stream. However, instead of drifting off in the air, the streams seemed to be absorbed through Julian's body.

"Come on!" Lily said as she reached for Sarah's hand again. "Can I show you my things, Sarah?"

Sarah looked back at Julian, who nodded her to go. She was curious and yet ever so slightly nervous of what sort of collection that the Witch might have. Her fears, however, were mostly doused by certain sense of warm comfort that Lily gave her thus far.

"Kalin will help him be better! I promise!" Lily said as she dragged Sarah to the other end of the dome. The walls of the other dome opened up again and a root slithered in and dropped a small backpack. After the delivery, the walls closed off again. The two sat around the bag as Lily began to unzip and reveal its contents.

"You." Kalin looked behind him at Landris. "If you're going to make that phone call, do it next to me!"

Landris shrugged and landed his bottom next to Kalin and Julian. He pulled out his phone and began to dial the number for Director Jones.

✳✳✳

"And this is a necklace Mr. Curtina gave me after I helped him from his sinking boat!"

A necklace with a beaded chain and a carved wooden turtle as an ornament.

Lily pulled from her backpack an assortment of items one after the other as Sarah tried to keep up with the Witch's pace. Though it was amusing, the large mess of knickknacks was becoming understandably tiring.

"I don't wear it because it makes my neck itchy! This is a ring Mr. Hashimi gave me after I helped him and his family. It's too big for me, so I keep in here."

An old tarnished silver ring.

"This is a cookie a boy gave me after I helped him get his balloon. Kalin got mad about that."

A common brand of cookie. The size of an adult's palm, and two per pack.

"Why was he mad?" Sarah asked.

"Well…" Lily seemed a bit shy from sharing. "It probably wasn't a good idea to climb the sky in the middle of the city."

Sarah chuckled. At this point, the story didn't surprise her much.

"But he was crying!" Lily defended herself.

"I'm sure you made him very happy," Sarah comforted Lily. "Why didn't you eat the cookie?"

The Witch seemed embarrassed.

"Memories," she sheepishly confessed.

"Memories?"

"Memories." Lily nodded.

"Well that's sweet." Sarah grabbed Lily's hand. Lily seemed happy about the gesture. Something about such small gestures bringing such a smile to the girl made Sarah feel an uneasy joy and slight pity for her. "What about this bracelet you always wear?" Sarah asked as she turned her attention to the black band on Lily's wrist.

The Witch seemed hesitant. "It was something given to me by someone someplace far away." Lily seemed to find it difficult to explain her answer. Sarah decided to move on from the topic.

"What more do you have?" Sarah pointed at the bag.

"Well…" Lily pulled out a small diary. "This is my journal! Kalin said it'd help me with my writing because my handwriting is terrible. And he said it'd be good because I like to remember things." Lily gave a sly smile to Sarah. "I don't let him read it though."

"Of course!" Sarah smiled back.

Lily pulled out a sketchbook with thick black covers.

"This is my picture book…"

"Oh, you draw?"

Lily didn't seem to hear her as she rummaged deeper into her bag that at this point seemed bottomless to Sarah.

"Ooooooh," Lily exclaimed. She pulled out few colorful but small stacks of folding papers encased in clear plastic. "I got these from a girl I found feeding a kitten. She was wearing a really pretty dress. I couldn't understand what she was saying, and she couldn't understand what I was saying, but we ended up playing together the whole day! She gave me these at the end as a present!" Lily cringed for a moment. "Kalin was also mad that day. He had no idea where I was."

"Oh, wow! I have a few of these back in my room!" Sarah took one of the cases and held it out, "These are folding papers, Lily! You can make really fun things with these."

Lily looked at Sarah with curious eyes.

"May I?" Sarah asked.

Lily nodded.

Sarah unpacked one of the cases and took out a paper. It was small enough to fit inside even Lily's palm. One side of it was bright pink with patterns of flowers while the other was plain white.

"I can make cranes, fish, frogs, a hat, a bunny…" Sarah listed her capabilities with a little bit of pride.

"Can you make a butterfly? That'd be so pretty!" Lily requested.

Sarah stared at Lily blankly for a moment.

"Let's make a crane!" Sarah suggested.

"Okay!" Lily agreed.

"They say," Sarah spoke as she made her folds. "If you fold one thousand paper cranes, your wish will come true."

"Really?"

"Sure!" Sarah chuckled again. Paper cranes were Sarah's specialty. She was done in few moments and presented Lily with a perfect paper crane. As Sarah offered the crane to Lily, the Witch put her hands together for Sarah to place it on.

"It's so pretty!" Lily said as she marveled at the craft in her hand. "Can you teach me? I want to fold a thousand of them!"

"Sure," Sarah said, handing Lily one of the papers and grabbing herself another one. "You have a wish you want to have come true, huh?"

They folded about two or three when Landris waved Sarah to take the call from Director Jones.

Chapter 14
THE PHONE CALL

Near an unspectacular city was a large military base that served as a home for military personnel and their families. Guarded behind the gates of this installation was a large but a simple building that served as the headquarters for the nation's security and intelligence operations. It was covered in dark-tinted windows that reflected its clandestine nature and resembled a giant box made of dark glass. Near the top edges of this box, behind one of the many dark-tinted windows, was the office of William Hamilton, the director of all operations that existed and those said to not exist carried out by those who worked in this simple building.

"It's agent Graham, sir."

"I've been expecting your call, Daniel. What the hell happened out there?"

"One of these idiots from the McKinley's killed someone. I don't think it was an 'accident.' I think it was a hit. They were paid off. Given the person who died, I'm guessing it was Nancy Jones who hired them."

"Who was he?"

"Do you know a David Jung of the Silver Aegis?"

"David Jung?" Director stood from his seat and held his tongue from letting out a curse. "Can't say that I do."

"You should have someone look into him because it seems like he's been leaking information from the Silver Aegis to the McKinley's. But I'm guessing based on what happened today, the McKinley's might be done dealing with the Gifted. At least on government orders."

"We'll see about that." Director Hamilton sat back down into his seat and rested his forehead into his hand. "What about the Witch?"

"It was her alright. We almost had the redheaded boy and a few other Gifted until she showed up. We were outmatched. I can believe all those crazy stories about her now."

"I want a full report regarding what you saw today, Daniel. Did you say there were other Gifted?"

"Yes, sir. I don't know if they were with the Witch or not, but they all left together through some sort of a… 'portal'… opened up by her."

"A *portal*?" Director Hamilton chuckled. "Of course. A portal."

"Sir, I think it's time to shutdown the McKinley's. He was going off the deep end about what happened today, talking about starting a war with Nancy Jones."

"A war? What do you mean war?"

"I'm not certain yet. I'm supposed to be returning the headquarters to find out."

Director Hamilton paused for a moment and sorted through all the options.

"Let him do whatever he wants, but just keep me posted, Daniel."

"Sir?"

"It's possible that those other Gifted you saw today were part of the rumored secret project by the Silver Aegis. If that's true, worst case scenario is that Nancy Jones now has an army of Gifted and the Witch. The Witch is the symbol of all the fear and resentment in the people around the world today for the recent *changes*. By having her, Nancy has the world's favor. And if that should belong to anyone, it should belong to the government—to our nation. We sure as hell paid for it."

"But sir, what does the McKinley's have to do with…"

"Let them fight among themselves. Let them dirty their own hands. It will give us a reason to step in and show them who's really running the show. Your job, Daniel, is to keep us informed so that we may coordinate our next moves correctly. We'll fuel the fire if we need to."

Mr. Morris sat in silence for a moment.

"Daniel?"

"Understood. Sir. I better be going."

"Keep up the good work."

The call ended without a reply from Mr. Morris. Director Hamilton leaned back into the cushions of his chair and pondered the game being played. After much thought, he reached for his phone yet again.

Chapter 15
THE WITCH'S DEMANDS

"Landris," Nancy answered the phone in her office. Yuri sat on the couch enjoying a hot black coffee with cookies while reading news articles on his tablet. "What happened?"

"There was a problem with the assignment."

"Obviously. Where are you right now?"

"Nancy, er, Director Jones, before that, there's something I want to talk about."

"I'm guessing it's about *him*?"

Landris peeked over to Kalin and Julian.

"Wow, the pain... it's actually getting better," Julian said with Kalin's hand still infusing his body with the stream. "What is this thing?"

"Just be quiet and let me concentrate. In a few more minutes you should be as good as new." Kalin's forehead was starting to bead with sweat.

They seemed preoccupied.

"Yeah, it's about *him*. You know it's about *him*," Landris whispered as he turned his head away from Kalin and Julian.

"Honestly, what did you think was going to happen?" Nancy's voice was calm and collected as always. It almost sounded friendly.

"What?" Landris felt a bit dumbfounded. He wasn't sure if he found himself dumb for asking or surprised by his sister's cold nonchalance.

"What. Did. You. Think. Was. Going. To. Happen?"

"I..."

"Get a grip. It's done." Nancy's tone chided Landris like a misbehaving child.

"Don't toy with me, Nancy. Not with me," Landris spoke with a bite, but he wondered if he sounded whiny or seemed like a child.

"*Toy* with you? Do you think I'll steer you wrong, Landris?"

"No... But..." Nancy's firm voice made Landris squirm.

"Do you or do you not trust me, Landris?"

"I..." Landris paused for a moment. "I trust you."

"Then just follow me. I'll take you to the top. I'll take all of us to the top."

"Yeah."

"Now, compose yourself. Regain that nasty attitude of yours. You're not alone right?"

"Yeah." Landris looked back at Kalin and Julian. At the other side of the dome, he could see Sarah and Lily were looking through some knickknacks. Sarah glanced up at him.

"We're with the Witch."

"Really? My, my, what an interesting turn of events. I'm assuming this isn't a hostage call for ransom." Nancy's voice reverted back to her regular friendly, egoistic tone.

"No. She actually saved us from those McKinley idiots. Even though her friend is a bit of a dick…"

Kalin raised an eyebrow.

"…she seems to want to work with us."

"How is she like?"

"Kind of nice. Kind of weird."

Kalin raised an eyebrow.

"How are the others?"

"Julian got injured while having a tiff with the Witch's friend. But the tomato-head… err.. 'Kalin' is using his 'gift' to fix him up it seems."

Nancy made a mental note of Kalin's 'gift.'

"Is he badly injured?"

"I'm guessing a cracked rib."

"What of Sarah?"

"You should talk to her actually; the Witch seemed to have taken a liking with her. Sarah!" Landris waved at Sarah to come over. She whispered to Lily and left her with her knickknacks as she made her way over to Landris. He handed her the phone.

"Hello? Director Jones?"

"Yes, Ms. Starr. How are you doing?" Nancy's voice was comparably softer and warmer than when she was speaking to Landris.

"I… um… I," Sarah's voice quivered.

"Ms. Starr?" Ms. Jones worryingly asked.

"I'm really sorry, Direct Jones." Sarah's eyes welled up with tears. "What happened with Mr. Jung, I'm really sorry."

"It's…" Nancy cleared her throat. Her own voice began to shake a bit. "It's alright Sarah. What happened was tragic, and we will get to the bottom of it. But you have to stay strong, alright?"

"Yes, Director." Sarah wiped away the tears from her eyes. Lily looked from afar, worried for her new friend.

"Thank you, Sarah. How's Mr. Caldwell?"

"Julian was hurt, but he is now being treated by Kalin."

"I'm assuming Kalin is the Witch's friend? The one who made a puzzling choice of dying his hair red?"

"Yes."

Kalin's nose tickled, almost as if he had to sneeze.

"How's the Witch? Landris told me that she is willing to come with us?"

"Yes, it seems like it. Her name's Lily. She's a sweetheart, Ms. Jones. I really think people may have been wrong about her."

Nancy smirked.

"Is that so? That sounds wonderful! Would it be alright for me to speak with her?"

"Yes! Of course! Lily!" Sarah gave Lily a little smile and waved her to come over. Lily jogged over to Sarah who placed the phone on the Witch's small hands. The Witch seemed a bit awkward with the device. She inspected the phone for a bit and had a slight twinkle of marvel in her eyes as she put it against her ear.

Kalin realized his little friend was about to speak with the director of Silver Aegis. "Give me a sec," he told Julian as he picked himself up and wiped the sweat off of his forehead with his arm. He came to stand beside Lily.

Lily had placed the phone to her ear but did not speak. Her anticipation was building to hear something.

"Hello?" Nancy finally broke the awkward silence.

"Hello," Lily replied.

"Hello, Ms. Lily. I am Director Jones of Silver Aegis. How are you? Actually, first and foremost, I'd like to thank you for helping my precious students out of a tight spot today." Nancy tried to sound as bright and welcoming as possible.

"I am Lily, and I am doing well. How are you?" Lily asked.

"I'm fantastic," Nancy replied.

"Okay," Lily said.

There was an awkward silence.

"Yes, I, well..." Nancy was caught off-guard. She cleared her throat once more. "I understand you want to come with us?" She was surprised at herself for stumbling on words. When was the last time that she stumbled with words?

"No," Lily replied, looking up at the uneasy Kalin.

"No?" Nancy answered Lily's reply with a slight sting. She was again surprised at herself for losing her composure. This girl had a way of getting under her skin.

"I mean, yes, but there are things that we have to do before we go, an-and we were wondering if you could help us with that, Miss Director Jones..." Lily voice shriveled as her sentence continued. Kalin tried to be confident for his friend, but on the inside he wanted to bury his face into his hand and groan.

"Miss Jones or Director Jones would be fine, dear," Nancy said endearingly. "Sarah didn't mention to me there were things you needed to do! What could those be?" Truthfully, Nancy was a bit nervous to hear what tasks the Witch had to do. Even while realizing that most of Witch's notoriety was fabricated, it didn't mean the enigma that surrounded her was any less real. But then again, given her conversation with Lily thus far, Nancy thought she'd only be slightly surprised if the Witch asked her to take them to an amusement park as her demand.

"We..." It was now Lily who had to clear her throat. She took a deep breath. "We want to find my parents!" The words nearly erupted out of Lily's mouth.

"I'm sorry." Nancy was thrown back. "What was that?"

"Kalin"—Lily looked up at Kalin—"and I want to find my parents, and we can't go with you until we do. I'm sorry."

"No need to be sorry. I'm sure we can manage that." The task intrigued Nancy. The parents of the Witch? If she can procure the Witch's origins, all of her secrets might be hers to keep. "What are their names?"

"I don't know..."

"When did you last see them?"

"Long ago..."

"Where was the last place you saw them?"

"We had ice cream..."

"At...?"

"I don't remember..." the Witch sounded as if she was about to cry. "I'm sorry."

"Well, you certainly have a difficult task on your hands." Nancy was tempted to ask how the Witch ended up with the murdered doctor. But she decided against it. "I'll do all that I can to help you, Lily."

"Really?"

"Yes," Nancy chuckled. "Really."

"Thank you so much, Miss Direc... Miss Jones! You are as kind as Sarah said!"

"Well, I'll try my best, Lily." Nancy grabbed the pen from her desk and started looping it around her fingers. "Were there other things you had to do?"

"Yes."

"Well, what is it, dear? Don't be shy."

"There's somewhere Kalin and I must go."

"Where would that be?" The pen in Nancy's hand stopped its circus around her hand. It was now pressed between her index finger and her thumb to the point. Nancy's heart was excited. Her instincts told her the Witch's destination before Lily even spoke of it.

"The..." Lily's lips tightened for a moment and her tongue hesitated. Kalin placed his hand on her shoulders. "...the Light."

Nancy's eyes widened and her lips stretched widely.

"The Light?" Nancy tried to sound astounded. "My, my. You mean *the* Light? Now why would you ever want to go there?"

Lily was silent.

"Oh, dear. You're just a bundle of secrets aren't you? Such daunting quests for such a sweet girl." The pen in Nancy's hand was looping through her fingers again.

"I'm sorry," Lily said.

"You say 'sorry' far too much, child. It's a word too precious to be used so lightly. I'll look forward to hearing the answer to why you want to venture to the Light, but for now, we'll forget about it and help you find your parents first."

"Really?" Lily's face brightened.

"Yes, really! And given our circumstances, the quicker, the better, yes?"

"Yes!"

"And I really can't convince you two to come with us while you wait for us to find your parents? It may make things easier."

Uncertain, Lily looked up to Kalin again. He looked back down at her and gave her a smile of confidence and squeezed his hand on her shoulder gently.

"No..." Lily replied.

"Alright, I understand. Would you be so kind, dear, and hand the phone back to Sarah?"

"Okay!" Lily handed the phone back to Sarah and grabbed Kalin's hand. She hopped in place with his hand in hers.

"She said yes!" Lily cried as if she was celebrating a successful proposal.

"Director Jones?" Sarah answered the phone as she watched the giddy Witch in amusement.

"The Witch has asked us to find her parents, and I think we will need your help."

"I understand."

"And if you can, Sarah..." Nancy's tone became slightly more stern. "Please also try to find us any other significant information regarding Lily so that we may be able to help her better."

"I..."

"Sarah, I know it's a lot to ask, but this is a special case we are dealing with. You and I may be able to truly help this girl."

"Yes ma'am."

"Thank you, Sarah. Can you hand over the phone to Landris?"

Sarah handed the phone back to Landris whose eyes were shut as he rested his back against the vine-wall.

"Yeah?" Landris answered.

"You should be proud. You all have outdone yourselves. Just keep an eye out on the Witch and her friend, and keep me informed at all times."

"Yeah."

"And…" Nancy thought through her words for a moment. "I'm really glad you're alright. I was worried."

"Yeah." Landris hung up the phone. Lily had already dragged Sarah back to her little corner with her backpack. Kalin had gone back to attending Julian who appeared a bit hurt that Director Jones hadn't asked to speak with him.

A bittersweet feeling lingered within Landris as he placed the phone into his pocket. He didn't quite understand why such an emotion remained with him as he pondered what could happen in the days ahead.

Stomach grumble.

"Hey," Landris grumbled. "Is there anything to eat around here?"

***

"Apparently," Yuri spoke as soon as Nancy appeared to be done with the phone. "There's a pretty credible rumor that the near extinction of a certain... *behemoth* criminal family was due to our little *Wild Card*." He put his tablet by his side, sipped on his coffee and munched on a cookie.

"You're still calling *her* that?" Nancy said as she joined Yuri across the table and grabbed herself a cookie.

"I think it's the perfect description for her." Yuri grinned, walking over to the small pantry to take out a cup for Nancy.

"Well, it seems that we have what you called the *Trump Card*. Or, at least, we are really close to it." Nancy regretted a bit in taking part in Yuri's tacky comparisons.

Yuri looked a touch surprised but mostly impressed. He poured Nancy some coffee before he poured himself his second cup.

"Well, well, well," Yuri said. "It seems all the pieces are falling into place just as you wanted. Congratulations. Though I still think you should be more concerned about the Wild Card." Yuri spoke smugly, charmed that Nancy took part in his little games.

"I'm not ignoring her existence, but I don't see the reason to be concerned." Nancy took a sip of her coffee.

"You are something special, Nancy. No doubt about that." From Yuri's tone, Nancy could tell there was an incoming criticism. "But don't forget that there are others out there who may be just as good as

118

you."

Nancy shrugged. She didn't appreciate being told elementary facts of life like a child, but she listened to the old man politely. "I'll worry about it when I need to worry about it. With the Witch almost in our grasp, I think we're going to win this game," Nancy said as she reached for the last cookie only to be denied by Yuri's swift hand.

Nancy gave Yuri a quick glare that made even Yuri flinch a little. He broke the cookie and offered her half, but she shooed it away.

A phone rang.

Yuri checked his pockets and pulled out a phone. Wrong phone, wrong pocket. He checked his other coat pocket and pulled out the ringing phone, but when he saw the number, he handed it to Nancy instead.

"What do you call him in this little game?" Nancy asked with a smirk.

"The Jack of Spades," Yuri answered with a smile.

Chapter 16
FULL CIRCLE

"Nancy?" Director Hamilton spoke solemnly.

"Yes, Bill. It's been a while. How have you been?" Nancy jovially asked.

"Fine."

"How's Marissa?"

"She's doing well."

"And you're son—Eric, was it?"

"He's fine. So are Connor and Carissa. You want to ask about my in-laws too?"

"My, my, Bill." Nancy smirked at Yuri who amusedly watched and pieced the conversation together from across the coffee table. "You sound like you're in a sour mood."

Always with the 'my, my's, Director Hamilton thought as he lit up a cigar and poured himself another glass of his amber alcohol. "I guess you could say that, Nancy. What happened out there today?"

"Out where today?" Nancy checked her nails. She considered perhaps getting a manicure soon.

"Stop. Just stop, Nancy." Hamilton held his tongue from saying harsher words.

"The Witch is my hands now, and Mr. Ahn has been dealt with by me," Nancy spoke while still inspecting her nails—a light salmon pink might be a good color. It'd be graceful and polite. "...or should we keep referring to him as Mr. Jung?"

Director Hamilton took a moment to regain his composure. He didn't want to reveal to Nancy the extent of his surprise at her blatant confession.

"I think you forget, Nancy," Mr. Hamilton spoke quietly but threateningly. "No matter how clandestine, you are currently employed by our government."

"But of course, Director Hamilton," Nancy quickly replied. "How could we ever afford to have a place like Facility Zero without the government's support."

"What you did today was beyond reckless. Were circumstances any different, I'd be putting you down myself."

"What I did today was dirtying my hands for this country and for you, Bill. To do what you couldn't do."

"What?" Director Hamilton was flabbergasted and didn't realize his cigar was missing the ashtray.

"Now, let's not pretend that either of us are so naive and innocent or plain stupid." Nancy sipped on her cup of coffee. "Must I explain myself?"

"Yes, I think you must, Nancy."

"Let's begin with Mr. Jung or Mr. Ahn."

"I'm assuming you found out that he's been a double-agent in your company for the McKinley's. But that doesn't give you permission to kill a man."

"And I'm assuming that you either forgot or were simply compelled to not let me know that Mr. Ahn wasn't working for either us or McKinley."

Director Hamilton remained silent.

"He was sent by the International Security Council in united efforts by other nations to make sure that our nation was not making developments with the new elements in the world that'll further set us apart from them. They were frightened, and they had every reason to be frightened."

"How did you find this out?"

"Money knows no loyalty but it can sure buy a lot of it. No matter what country or position that loyalty may be coming from."

"You're reach is impressive, as always. But I hope you understand that obviously, I was urged not to reveal Ahn's position as a sign of cooperation with the rest of the world."

Nancy enjoyed forcing the great Bill Hamilton make excuses.

"Don't worry, Bill, I understand. I just did what you couldn't do to save yourself and our nation from the trouble."

"You didn't like the world's eyes watching us."

"Yes, no need for them to know what we are up to—especially when we are so close to the Witch. If they were so concerned, they might consider doing some of the work themselves or be better at having us do all the dirty work."

Hamilton chuckled. "They never even did try to stop us."

"And by having the McKinley's take care of Jung, it was the perfect way to give you an excuse to cancel their contract and sign us up in their place. You can play dumb on knowing Jung's assassination and the pressure from the world government would be the perfect last straw. We can keep the activities that belong in the shadows in the shadows while still keeping a face people can trust now in the front. This will make things cleaner and smoother for everyone."

"This sounds like it was more motivated by business than patriotism at this point, Nancy."

"If you want to believe that, sure. That's fine, Bill. But either way, the end result for *you* seems to be the same."

"I…"

"I did *you* a favor."

Nancy Jones made Bill Hamilton at loss of his words again. As much as he hated to admit it, Nancy made the director feel diminished into something weak and minuscule. "What of the Witch?" he finally asked. "Do you have her in custody?"

"Perhaps. Perhaps not."

Yuri chuckled as he listened to Nancy teasing the man in charge of the nation's securities and secrets.

"Nancy!" Director Hamilton slammed on his desk.

"*Excuse me*, Bill. I'm not one of your goons that you can yell and order around."

"You are under government orders—MY orders."

"And who do you think enticed the government to start this project in the first place, Bill? To have you in charge of this whole operation?"

"What?"

"Listen, Bill. I'm not your enemy here. We are allies. Our goals and methods may be different, but that doesn't mean that we can't help each other achieve what the other wants. Play it smart, Bill. I'm giving you another chance." Nancy hung up the phone.

Half of a second went before Bill threw his phone across the room. He watched it shatter as it hit the ground and regretted his loss of temper immediately. After a deep sigh, Bill stood by his windows and rose up the blinds. He needed a break. The office was stale, and it wouldn't be too long before he felt choked and nauseated by it. It wasn't a spectacular view, but it was a view. The mundane view of the parking lot, the spots of trees, and the other facilities and buildings that filled the base gave him a sort of peace. And beyond the horizon, the Light.

The Light.

Director Hamilton lowered the blinds and crashed back into his seat. He massaged his temples with his finger and thumb.

The room was stale.

***

Yuri chuckled as he pulled out a cigar from his pocket. "With this one, Nancy, you might be overestimating his depth and intellect as a man." The glare Nancy shot him was enough for him to reconsider and put the cigar away.

"Hopefully, he'll at least be smart enough to know what's best for him," Nancy said as she rested her head against the sofa. She shut her eyes. She couldn't remember if she had slept the night before.

"You and your brother are something else," Yuri said with smile. "You guys are willing to do what others dare not. I'm proud of you both and yet a bit sad that your lives had to—ah, what's the word—scar you so much to be this way."

"You're an oddly sentimental person, Mr. Ivanov."

Yuri laughed.

"My ambition is for our family to be the greatest that it can be—a name that'll remain in the history books. But I'll be satisfied with leaving behind a better future for my brother. I mean, who else is left to take care of him?"

"I hope Landris can appreciate all that you've done for him," Yuri said.

"It would be nice, but even if he doesn't, I'll still be doing what I must as his older sister. Landris has the potential to do great things; he just needs the proper platform. If I can be that platform to take him to the top, what more could I ask for?"

Yuri chuckled.

"How's your mother doing these days?" Yuri carefully and sincerely asked.

Nancy didn't answer. She shut her eyes and allowed her mind to rest, though it would only be a brief rest.

INTERLUDE IV
CLOAK & DAGGER

"I spoke with mother. She was wondering why you haven't called her for so long."

As he left Sarah and Julian behind with the redhead, Landris recalled the meeting he had with Nancy. He spoke with her after she had debriefed Mr. Jung regarding their assignment.

"What'd you say? How is she?" Landris asked. His tone was a mixture of annoyance, hyper-sensitivity, and a dash of worry.

McKinley boys could breach at any moment; he didn't have much time. Landris saved time from making his way down the stairs by simply leaping from the top to the bottom. The smoke was already filling up the stairways.

"I told her you were busy, but you'll call her soon. Don't make me into a liar to our mother, Landris. If you really want to know how she's doing, give her a call." Nancy leaned closer to Landris and gave him that older-sister-scolding-her-little-brother look.
"I'll get around to it," Landris coldly and quickly replied.
"She seems as fine as she could be in her state," Nancy told her brother what he wanted to know but couldn't get himself to ask. "Landris, if you want to blame yourself on what happened..."

First floor.
Mr. Jung hid behind the turn that split the lobbies from the stairways. He peeked past the corner and observed the crowd of the McKinley's men smothered by the red and blue lights of the police behind them. Among the crowd, Mr. Jung recognized the man with the shaved mohawk talking to an older man he assumed to be police.
James Morris.
The infamous right hand man for Mr. McKinley when it came to dealing with the Gifted. Mr. McKinley must have decided he wasn't going to pull any punches after the tip he received of the Witch being present. Mr. Jung guessed seeing Silver Aegis make their move solidified the tip he gave to Mr. McKinley. Given Mr. McKinley's all-out effort, it was probably impossible for him and the Silver Aegis stu-

dents to make their getaway. That was fine. It'd be one way to hinder or perhaps even shut down Nancy Jones and her insane plots while being able to naturally absorb himself into the McKinley's company to watch over them afterwards. Even if they somehow found a way to get away, it'd give Mr. Jung—Mr. Ahn—more time to study up on Nancy's facility and plans.

Time was running out. Mr. Ahn still had his part to play as Mr. Jung. He set the smoke bomb right around where he stood, and the smoke filled up the small hallway and the lobby within minutes.

Stomps coming from the stairways.

Someone was coming after him. The smoke from the canister hissed and began to fill the room with white smoke.

"...you can go right ahead; blame yourself. I'll be the last person who's going to lie to you and say that you were faultless in what happened that night."

Landris looked away from his sister. She was right, and he knew she was right. He tormented himself every day in order to not repeat the same mistake of that evening again. Something about hearing it out loud, however, had an unbearable sting that he wouldn't be able to give himself.

"But"—Nancy's fierce eyes cooled off—"never let it keep you down. Use it to become stronger. Learning how to fail is one of the most essential lessons for life. A man who only punishes himself for his past mistakes just extends his failures. But a man who uses his past mistakes to grow turns them into success." She sounded more like a sister—a mother—than a director.

"Is that all you called me for?" Landris asked after reflecting on his sister's words for a bit. "Thanks for letting me know mom's well, and thanks for the therapy. Can I go now?" The topic of that night and his mother wasn't something he felt like he could ever be comfortable with.

"No, Landris. There's one more thing I wanted to talk to you about. A concern of mine that should only stay between the two of us..." Nancy glanced at the large man sitting by the coffee table. He was studying the label on the back of a bag of chips. "... and Yuri." Her voice dropped to a near whisper as she revealed the secrets and bittersweet revelations. "It's about Jung."

Mr. Jung aimed his pistol at the door to the stairways. When the pursuer swung open the door, he'd have a surprise for him.

Another thump of his pursuer landing at the base of stairway.

The handle of the door clicking as it turned.

The door swinging open.

Landris.

"Landris?" Mr. Jung aimed the gun between Landris's eyes. Smoke had almost filled the room, and James Morris had just finished his conversation with Detective Fowler. The pursuer and the pursued stared at one another in silence.

"What are you doing here?! What about the redhead? Where's Sarah and Julian?!" Mr. Jung had to restrain himself from screaming those words at Landris.

"It's fine. They're taken care of. The ketchup-head and I made a deal," Landris calmly explained.

"You did WHAT?!" Mr. Jung had to try harder to restrain himself from screaming. "For what?!"

"To make sure that you're alright!" Landris responded with frustration.

Smoke had now nearly filled the room. There was enough of it now for it to force its way into Mr. Jung and Landris's eyes and throats. Mr. Jung tugged hard on Landris's shirt to signal him that they should head back up. When they reopened the door to the stairways, smoke flushed out into the hallway like dumping water into the ocean.

"Whether the Witch is there or not doesn't matter. We'll solve both problems at once," Nancy told Landris.

Landris grabbed Mr. Jung from behind. His arm crossed under Jung's arm and around his head while the other arm ripped away the gun in Jung's hand. He fought to free himself from Landris's grip but proved powerless to the brute strength of Landris's 'gift.'

"Landris! Have you lost your mind?!" Jung shouted as he struggled.

The sound of the building door being shattered by the battering ram thundered through the hallways.

"We won't let anyone take away our future and our dreams, or to make a mockery for all the sacrifices we've made. Can you do your part to protect us, Landris?" Nancy wasn't pleading but asking Landris for reassurance.

"Director Jones sends her regards, Jung." Landris gripped tighter.

"You know the answer to that already, Nancy."

"Never did like you very much, Jung." Landris dug into his pocket for one of the tranquilizer dart he swiped from earlier. "Then again, maybe I have a sixth sense for traitors."

"Wait, Landris! Just…"

Jung let out a small howl of pain as Landris shoved the dart into his neck. After the chemicals began to flow into Jung's bloodstream, Landris pulled the dart out of his neck and crushed it into dust before throwing the debris across the room.

"What was that?" Mr. Morris leading his teams through the smoke filled building heard the faint echoes of Landris and Jung's struggle.

This ain't no homemade smoke bomb. This is definitely military grade. Look how thick it is. Rodriguez's voice patched through Mr. Morris' earpiece.

Can't see even two steps in front of me. Gallagher this time.

"Take extra caution. These guys obviously aren't just ordinary freaks off the street," Morris warned his teams.

As he felt Jung's body become more and more limp, Landris dropped his body onto the ground. His body slumped beside his gun which had fallen earlier.

"Power... to change... the world..." Jung muttered the words with a shaky smirk, his consciousness drifting away from him. "...but learning.... to be... dogs..."

"A dog?" Landris smirked as he walked away left Jung to be devoured by the smoke and to be scavenged by the McKinley's. "We are all dogs to someone."

It wasn't long before the McKinley's men arrived by the smoke filled stairway. Morris opened the door and found the stairway filled with smoke as he had expected.

Really? More smoke? These guys are getting on my nerves.

There's someone heading up the stairs!

"Hey! You! FREEZE!"

Landris disappeared into the smoke as he ignored Mr. Morris' orders and hastily leaped up the stairs.

"Henderson, there's one heading up! Let me know when you get visual!" Mr. Morris paged his partner on the roof.

Aye, aye. Choppers are here. Henderson responded.

"Morris! There's someone here! He looks unconscious!" Holland yelled.

"Stay on him! The rest of you, with me!" Morris yelled as he chased after the mystery man.

Got it boss. Holland responded.

As Landris leaped up the stairs, the McKinley forces slowly worked their way chasing after him.

"GUN!" Holland yelled loud enough to cut through the smoke.

A gunshot.

The screaming noise of the firearm froze everyone in the stairways. Landris stood still briefly before bracing himself to make his way up the stairs again.

More gunshots in succession.

Detective Fowler, outside the building, heard the shots and slammed on the roof of his car, letting out a stream of curse words.

"What was that, Holland?!" Morris yelled into his ear piece.

* Two males and a female on top of the roof, Morris. One of the males has red hair like the description for the Witch's friend. The female, though, doesn't fit the Witch's description.* Henderson's update forced Morris to move on for now.

"Cooper and Thomas, stay down there and secure that body before the cops see it. Holland, if you don't have a convincing story of what happened down there you can be damn sure you're finished. The rest of you, to the roof on the double!" Morris patched in.

Landris heard the roaring behemoth above as he approached the door to the rooftop. Without hesitation, he walked out onto the rooftop, and the light of the outside world greeted him. As the smoke cleared from his vision, Landris saw the three familiar faces looking back at him. Crowds of gunmen from the rooftop of the building across welcomed him with red dots scattered all over his chest.

Chapter 17
BREAKING BREAD

No one heard when Landris called for food. Kalin was busy with Julian's recovery, and Sarah and Lily were folding more papers into cranes.

"I can't even really feel it anymore," Julian said. "Thanks, man. I feel like I have more energy now too!"

"Good." Kalin wiped off the sweat from his forehead with his arm. He stood and stretched his back. The feeling of his back straightening after crouching for so long was near euphoric. Landris tapped on his shoulders.

"So how do you guys get food around here?" Landris asked.

Kalin gave Landris an annoyed look, and then looked over at Sarah and Lily who were chatting and giggling as they folded papers. He was starving as well; fixing up a broken rib was hard work.

"Come on." Kalin gestured to Landris. "Let's go find some dry wood before it gets too dark. It'll be cold at night."

"You stay put and rest up," Landris told Julian. "You'll be less useless that way."

"Shut up," Julian picked himself up. "I'm helping out. It's the least I can do."

It took the boys only a short while to gather enough firewood for the night. When they returned, it seemed as if the girls hadn't even realized they had left.

Kalin dumped the wood into the pit at the center, and the other boys followed after him.

"Lily, dinner time!" Kalin called out to his friend who was earnestly folding a paper.

"Okay." Lily wanted to get the last fold just right. Sarah watched over her as she folded another one of her own.

Curious and intrigued, Landris walked over to stand by Lily and Sarah and watched the Witch fold cranes. From the piles of cranes between them, it was easy to tell which were Lily's and which Sarah's were.

"You're terrible at this," Landris remarked.

Lily spun around and gave Landris an angry look.

"I'm getting better!" Lily protested.

"She's getting better!" Sarah echoed.

"Lily, come on. We're starving!" Kalin insisted.

"Okay, just a second." Lily finished the crane she had been working on after a couple more folds. She smiled proudly and placed it by the rest of her cranes. "That's fourteen! Only..." Lily looked at her fingers and looked up in the air as if there was a board she was writing the equations on. "Nine-hundred and eighty-six to go!"

Lily grabbed the thick sketch book and gleefully made her way to the pit. Kalin had pulled out his matches from his own bag and tried to light the woods in the pit.

The fire ignited and the whole hut was instantly illuminated with the orange hue of the flame. It gradually filled the hut with warm air.

With a wave of her finger, Lily directed the vines to open a small gap above their heads for the smoke to escape.

"What do you want to eat?" Lily asked as she waved around her sketch book. The black band around her wrist dangled about as her arms waved back and forth.

Sarah, Landris and Julian shared a puzzled look with one another.

"Sit," Kalin told the three. "Lily, pass around the book."

The five huddled around the pit, and Lily gave the book to Sarah. Landris and Julian huddled around Sarah to see what was within the book. As the thick cover turned over, the first page revealed a photo like image of a hamburger still in its wrapping.

"Whoa, is this just printed on here?" Julian said as he scratched on the picture. Landris took the book from Sarah and started flipping through the pages.

Pasta, French fries, steak, cake, fish, rolls, various sodas, candies... Page after page of different images of food and drinks filled the book.

"So you want us to just choose from one of these?" Landris asked.

"Yep!" Lily replied.

Wanting to test the Witch, Landris pointed at one of the hamburgers and then flipped through the pages and pointed at a soda. The Witch reached her hand out to Landris and gestured for the book, and Landris obliged and set it on her hands. With the book in hand, Lily placed her palm over the picture of the burger first. She closed her eyes and concentrated for a brief moment. A small amount of streams gathered and gave a short, small burst under the Witch's hand as she lifted it away from the page. The paper no longer had the image of the hamburger printed on it, but an actual hamburger sitting atop as if it had simply popped out. Lily handed the burger to Landris. It was warm as if it had just been grilled and wrapped. Julian and Sarah watched in awe.

"Is this the one?" Lily flipped through the pages and found the soda Landris asked for. Landris unwrapped the burger and inspected it.

"Lambris?" Lily called out to Landris again.

"It's Landris. And yeah, that's the one." Landris took a bite. It was a real burger.

After the same process as before, Lily popped out from the page a soda and handed it to Landris. It was cold—very cold—as if it had just been taken out of the fridge. Landris cracked opened the can and took a swig.

"Oh, I want to try next!" Julian exclaimed. Lily smiled and handed him the book. He pointed to a slice of pizza and soda, and as she did for Landris, Lily popped them out of the page.

"Nice!" Julian cried as he bit into his pizza.

"May I?" Sarah asked Julian for the book, and found herself a sandwich and a bottle of juice. Lily happily obliged and handed Sarah her dinner.

"This is amazing. Thank you so much, Lily!" Sarah said as she realized how hungry she had been after the first bite.

"So." Landris crumpled the wrapper as he finished his burger. "I guess by now we shouldn't be surprised and just assume you're the Witch and this is just 'magic'… but how did you do this exactly?"

"We go to town once in a while and buy a bunch of food. Then Lily puts them in her book." Kalin selected a basket of fish and chips.

"Yep!" Lily said as she popped out Kalin's dinner.

"Thanks." Kalin took his lightly steaming meal.

Lily flipped through the pages to look for her own dinner.

"How do you put them in the book?" Landris asked as he crushed his empty can of soda.

"Like this," Without looking up Lily waved her fingers and lifted the can off of Landris's hand. The crushed can gently floated to Lily's hand as she flipped to an empty page of the sketch book. After placing the can on top of the page, Lily placed her hand over it. With a little concentration and effort, the can's structure became ethereal, similar to Kalin's streams, while mostly retaining the shape of a can. Lily pushed down into the page and when she lifted her hand the photo image of the can was on the paper.

"Neat," Julian remarked as he worked on his pizza.

"You really make me feel like maybe all this is magic after all," Sarah said, her hand frozen holding her sandwich since Lily started her magic show.

Landris gave a light scoff. "I guess you really are the real deal. A bona fide Witch."

Only Sarah and Kalin caught Lily's frown at Landris's remark, but her frown quickly dissipated at the page with a slice of cake.

"No," Kalin said as he took a chunk off of a golden fried fish with his mouth. "Eat some real food."

Lily seemed disappointed until she landed on the page with the same sandwich that Sarah was having.

"Besides," Kalin said as he stood and walked over to his backpack. "I got you something from the city."

"Really?!" Lily seemed ecstatic as she took a bite of her sandwich. She wondered if tomatoes would ever not taste so funny to her.

Inside Kalin's bag was the box he picked up at the coffee shop earlier that morning. It was a bit squished. He carefully opened the top of the box and found the four jelly-filled donuts unified into messy goo.

"Dessert—all for you." Kalin placed the box next to Lily. "It's your favorite. Sorry about the mess. But you can somewhat thank my run-in with those bundles of joy over there."

"Sorry about that," Julian apologized.

"Thanks Kalin!" Lily hugged Kalin's arm.

"Aww, that's sweet of you, Kalin," Sarah remarked. "You must be so happy to have such a caring friend, Lily!"

"Kalin's the best!" Lily said. Kalin felt heat rushing over his face and put his head down to hide any of its signs. They probably couldn't tell with the orange glow from the campfire anyway.

Lily separated the mess of donuts back into four pieces. She walked over to Sarah and handed her a piece.

"Oh no! Lily!" Sarah denied the gift. "I couldn't! I feel bad enough we ruined your gift!"

Lily frowned and raised her lower lip over her upper lip. Her lips formed an upside-down U, and she insisted by dangling the donut in front Sarah.

"Well, thank you, Lily. You're very kind," Sarah relented.

Lily then gave another piece to Julian. He accepted simply with a smile.

"Thanks," Landris said as he accepted his piece.

Kalin considered stopping her seeing that he intended those to be for her and not the goons who were sent to capture them, but he realized his efforts would be futile. This is who she was.

Lily took the final fourth piece and tore it in messy halves of gooey jelly and pastry. She handed the half to Kalin.

"No, Lily. I'm full," Kalin denied.

"How can I have some if you don't?" Lily asked.

An awkward silence ensued as the three Silver Aegis watched the Witch and awaited her friend's response.

"Alright, thanks." Kalin took his piece and shoved it in his mouth. With her friend fed, Lily allowed herself to begin working on hers. With drops of jelly around her lips, Lily seemed satisfied.

"I like these," Lily said as she took her last bite.

"So are you guys like—" Before Landris could finish his sentence,

Sarah tapped Landris with her foot.

"Eh hem!" Sarah exaggeratedly cleared her throat. "Thank you very much for your hospitality. You two are both very kind."

Lily smiled, and Kalin silently worked on his meal. As the five worked on finishing their meals, Julian spoke up.

"So," Julian thought through his words, unknowingly taking on his professor tone once again, "We are like… inside the trees care or something, right? How do they feel about us burning wood inside them?"

Landris let out a groan, and the five finished their meal in serene silence.

✳✳✳

The night fell in the woods. Cold winds gently breezed outside the hut, and the crackling of fire filled the atmosphere. Kalin spat out the water he was gurgling after brushing his teeth, looking beyond the horizon at the glittering city lights. The all-tall buildings lit up as if stars had fallen from the skies, and behind the city was the Light as always. Kalin had gone through a series of feelings about the Light and found his temperament towards it to change sporadically. Today, he didn't care much for it. Mildly annoying, but mostly neutral. Landris was standing near the edge of the cliff and seemed to be looking at the Light himself. Kalin wondered what Landris's feelings were towards it, but before he wondered for too long, he turned to head back into the hut.

"Did you brush your teeth?" Kalin asked Lily as he crawled back into the hut. Julian was fast asleep, and Sarah and Lily were back to folding more paper cranes. She was getting better at folding them.

"Yes," Lily answered, focused on her paper crane. Kalin looked at Sarah.

"Yes, she did. We did it together. Thank you for the toothbrushes, by the way," Sarah answered.

He looked around the hut. It seemed the garbage had been taken care of by Lily as well. There were pages in the sketch book dedicated for garbage. They waited until they were in the city to throw them away.

"Where's Landris?" Sarah asked.

"He said he'll take the first shift of watch. I'll take over after him," Kalin said.

"Is it okay if I lay down, Sarah?" Lily asked as she worked on another crane.

"Yeah, sure, Lily." Sarah moved her hands to allow Lily to use her legs as a pillow. "You think that's necessary?" Sarah asked Kalin.

"Can't hurt to be careful," Kalin said as he put away his toothbrush. "She's going to fall asleep, by the way. Like, immediately."

"What?" Sarah looked down and Lily's eyes were closed, her half-folded crane resting on her chest. "Wow, she falls asleep quick."

"One of her many talents," Kalin said as took off his jacket and put it on Lily. "You can wake her up if you want."

"I think I'll be alright." Sarah rested her back on the hut. "I think I can sleep like this. I mean, aww, just look at her. How could I wake her up?"

Kalin watched Sarah as she gently brushed away Lily's raven hair covering her face.

"Is she always this friendly to everyone?" Sarah asked.

"I guess. She also tends to prefer girls over boys," Kalin answered. He sat down next to Sarah and rested his back against the vine walls.

"Haha, well that seems normal."

"She seems to particularly like you though." Kalin shut his eyes. He was tired.

"She's a sweet girl. How old is she?"

Kalin shrugged. "I'm not entirely sure. She doesn't really know either."

"How did you guys meet?" Sarah asked as she fixed the coat Kalin had put on Lily.

Kalin seemed hesitant to answer. He thought through how to share the information and contemplated whether or not he should share it.

"We ran into each other at a playground a couple of years ago," Kalin said as he let out a yawn.

"I see. You guys must have had a tough journey. I can't understand how a girl like her became known as the Witch. You don't seem to be such a bad person either." Sarah turned her head and smiled at Kalin only to find that the boy seemed to have been fallen asleep as well.

It was an exhausting day for everyone. That was no exception for Sarah. The cozy warm air by the campfire that filled the hut made it easy for her to doze off not long after Kalin and Lily.

A couple of hours into her sleep, Sarah was awakened by the fidgeting girl on her leg. She struggled to open her groggy eyes to find Lily suffering from a nightmare. Lily had tossed off the jacket on her, and her face were wrinkled with suffering. Sarah reached for Lily's shoulder to wake her.

Chapter 18
A NIGHTMARE

The glow from the fire was gone. It was dark and the salty scent of the ocean filled the air. Rhythmic clashes of tides crashing in and washing out softly filled the room. Sarah knew she wasn't in the woods anymore, but didn't recognize where she was. Under her feet were no longer the vines but a rug. Above her head a ceiling and a fan.

A door slammed.

The sound echoed throughout the house. Her head snapped to the side at the noise, her eyes wide. Her body had frozen in place, paralyzed into merely staring off into the darkness.

A loud screech. Then a slam again.

"I'm in her dream," Sarah whispered to herself.

A loud screech. Then a slam again.

Correction, not just a dream, Sarah realized, she was in Lily's nightmare. She was an unwanted extra in Lily's personal horror film. Sarah had lost control of her 'gift' again. But was it her, or was it Lily that made her lose control this time?

A loud screech, then a slam. The thundering noise was disturbing enough with the darkness, but the silence in between made it impossible for Sarah to get used to it.

She looked around for clues to where she was. She 'spawned' behind a leather sofa. Across from the sofa was a television in a large cabinet filled with movies and exotic knickknacks. Some of the knickknacks had fallen to the ground. The living room was gently lit from the glass panel that took up most of the wall, revealing the dark blue night ocean view outside.

A loud screech, then a slam.

The TV cabinet and the sofa were separated by a coffee table with various magazines thrown about. The house was a mess as if someone had ran around purposefully scattering everything. There was a picture left standing on the cabinet through the rampage. In the photo was a man dressed in a snow jacket on top of a snowy peak raising his arm in victory. Something tickled at the back of her mind as she studied the man. Sarah held the picture frame with her hand and stared at his face, searching her memories for who he was.

A loud screech, then a slam.

The disturbing noise jolted Sarah each time it finished its pattern. *Dr. Cowan.*

Sarah remembered as if the noise jolted her memories as well.

Dr. Bradley Cowan.

The very doctor who had been murdered by the Witch—by Lily.
Sarah carefully set the picture back down onto the cabinet. She wanted to leave, but she wanted to know even more. Perhaps, Sarah thought, exploring the nightmare may shed some light on who Lily was. And, perhaps, whatever she may uncover may give Lily some justification to the murder she supposedly committed—the murder that made her the Witch.
As her eyes grew more and more accustomed to the darkness, Sarah was able to make out more of what made the home. Sarah passed the plants and the paintings, the bookshelves filled with various kinds of books, and then the marble dining table with a candle centerpiece and a bottle of wine.

A loud screech, then a slam. Sarah was getting closer to its source.

Down a small hallway, she passed the wide open bathroom door, a shut door, and through the room with its door slightly ajar. The hallway had an indescribable stench that tainted the ocean scent and filled the air throughout the rest of the house. In the bedroom there was a grand bed, another TV, and a small coffee table with a book and more pictures of Dr. Cowan and his travels. The noise that had been disturbing Sarah came from the door that led to the patio. It had sprung open, and the wind took rein of its functions.
Sarah went out onto the patio and looked into the dark waves. The tide had come in high, nearly just below the patio. She could taste the

saltiness in the water through her nose and the cool moist wind as it brushed past her face. Surrounding her were other homes built in a similar style to the doctor's home to make the most of their water-front. Sarah vaguely recognized the neighborhood from the news stories about Dr. Cowan's murder. From off in the distance, she could see the flickering glint of light as a train passed through the trees and made its way around the bend. The train's horns roared, and Sarah felt it rumble as it passed by the neighborhood. Without a doubt, this was the same home Dr. Cowan had been murdered in by the Witch. But why was Lily here? A chill went up Sarah's spine as another detail from Dr. Cowan's case sparked in her mind.

This house shouldn't be here. Sarah realized. Part of the Witch— Lily's—deed was that the house itself 'destroyed' with the doctor. Why did Lily bring it back in her dream?

Sarah closed the patio door behind her. She made sure to close it tightly to prevent the nerve-wrecking sound echoing throughout the house again. The house was much quieter now, and in some sense only more unnerving. As Sarah left the bedroom, past the open bath-room door, and the shut door again, odd noises stopped her in her tracks.

She heard a faint mumbling and the familiar noise of… fire? No, more specifically, *sizzles.* Like something was burning. Sarah wasn't certain if those noises just came to be or if they were there the whole time. She turned around towards the noise, and approached the shut door. The closer and closer she got, the louder and louder the noises grew. Sarah's hands trembled as it reached for the door handle. Part of her valiantly encouraged her to discover what was beyond the door, but another part of her desperately begged her to plant her feet into the ground. Clenching the handle tightly, Sarah pressed her ear against the door.

"…'m s…ry…"

Lily! Sarah immediately recognized her voice. The sizzles made Sarah's imagination run wild with the worst possible outcome. She swung the door open and it revealed a long stairway down. Unbear-able amounts of the indescribable stench she had smelled before gusted out from the abyss below. Sarah covered her nose with both of her hands, but nothing could stop the stench permeating through her fingers. She froze in her tracks and tried to keep her stomach from turning. There was a menacing orange hue illuminating the bottom half of the stairway. The raucous noises and the sheer light of it made Sarah imagine bellies of hell before she even had the chance to see it.

"Lily!" Sarah cried out as she held her nose. She forgot that within the minds she entered with her 'gift,' she was merely a ghost—an invisible spectator. One hand still covering her nose and the other gliding along the stairway handle, Sarah descended down the stairs in a hurry.

"I'm sorry. I'm sorry. I'm sorry." Lily's voice was louder and clearer now.

At the bottom of the stairs on the concrete floor, Lily was on her knees in front of the large flame.

"I'm sorry, I'm really sorry, I'm sorry." Lily's tone was that of a dying animal.

Sarah gasped and felt every cell of her body harden to stone when she saw the flame. She wanted to either cry out to Lily or scream, but her throat couldn't find the strength. Her legs never felt heavier. The flame was a person. It stood in front of Lily, burning. The body was charred and the hair had long been burnt off. From its crusted face and where its eyes should be, Sarah could tell it was looking down at Lily. It just stood there, staring at the girl who was profusely apologizing it.

Stomach turned. Vomit surged. Sarah gave everything she had to hold it down.

"I'm sorry. And I'm sorry that all I can do is to say I'm sorry," Lily spoke through her tears. "I'm sorry, Jade. I'm sorry. You don't have to forgive me, but please know that I'm sorry."

'Jade' didn't respond. She stood there in flames and simply glared at Lily. Sarah took a gasp of air. She had forgotten to breathe.

Lily spun around, her head snapping back towards Sarah. Their eyes met. Startled, Sarah stumbled backwards until she realized that no one could see her in their dreams. She was a ghost, she reminded herself—an invisible bystander. Lily stood to her feet with her eyes still glued in Sarah's direction.

"Sarah?" Lily murmured quietly in disbelief.

"Li-Lily?" Sarah replied back also in disbelief.

"Why are you here?" Lily's already moist face was drenched again in tears. She had been violated. She didn't want anyone else to witness her sin—her greatest regret and shame.

***

Sarah opened her eyes to find Lily back on her lap. The air was crisp and aromatic of moist leaves and dirt. The violent sizzles of *Jade* were replaced by the soothing cracklings of the campfire. Lily's eyes were wide open and staring back at Sarah. Tears drizzled down the side of her pale cheeks.

"Lily…" Sarah wasn't sure if she should hold Lily or apologize to her—or both.

Lily picked herself up from Sarah's lap and rubbed the tears off of her eyes with the palm of her hands. She looked around, looking for *him*.

"Lily?" Sarah asked worryingly. "Lily, I didn't mean to, I'm so sorry. Are you alright?"

Lily paid no attention to Sarah. It wasn't out of spite, she just wanted to see her best friend. Lily crawled over to Kalin who was still sleeping next to Sarah. She sat next to her friend and rested her head on his arm. Landris crawled into the hut to find a distressed Sarah.

"What's up?" Landris asked. His eyes were baggy.

"Lily?" Kalin slowly awoke from his slumber. "What's wrong, Lily?" Kalin asked, reading his friend's face. He then looked at Sarah hoping for an explanation.

"She had a bad dream, I...?" Sarah tried to put into words what had happened and what she saw.

"She has those once in a while. Though these days, it's been quite frequent," Kalin said as he worriedly studied his friend. Lily eyes were shut and she seemed to be ignoring everyone else in the hut.

"Nightmares? Did you see it?" Landris walked over to Sarah and quietly whispered to her.

"Yeah..." Sarah glanced at Lily. "Just... yeah."

Landris raised an eyebrow. "You alright?"

Sarah looked somewhat surprised for Landris's concern. She must have been visibly shaken.

"Yes, I'm alright. I'm worried about her though." Sarah and Landris watched Kalin and Lily gently embracing one another like a parent and child or an older brother and younger sister. Kalin consoled her with a soft voice that only she could hear.

Landris checked his pockets to see if *it* was still there. He walked over to Lily and tapped her on her shoulder, and she looked back with eyes glistening with moisture and wide with tentative curiosity. Landris reached out and gestured with his hand to demand hers. When Lily reached out with her hand, he placed into her hand *it* and clasped her hand for her. After giving his gift to Lily, Landris left the hut again. He did a little stretch and let out a big yawn as he watched the city over the horizon still brightly lit even through the night.

Lily opened her hand to find a piece of candy.

Chapter 19
THE ONE-WHO-SEES-FORWARD

Kiara woke up from another one of her uninvited slumbers, but this time with an unexpected calm. The sandman had been polite enough to wait until she was in her bed this time. She stared at her ceiling without any sense of time. The dream she had had was one that she always knew she'd inevitably have someday. She just didn't expect it so soon.

A single tear drizzled down her cheeks. She hadn't really felt sad enough for that tear to make sense, and she certainly didn't feel the need to cry. As she wiped off the enigmatic tear, she got out of bed. Tussled blanket neatly folded. Pillows organized in a clean pile at the head of the bed.

Much like usual, the memories of her dream were stuck on replay, but there was neither thought nor emotions behind it. Just images passing through her head over and over. Over and over. With her bed organized, Kiara checked the time. It was 7:15 am, still in time for breakfast.

Kiara went to the mess hall and got herself a couple of pancakes, a scoop of scrambled eggs, an apple, and a glass of orange juice as she always did. And then as always, she was pleasantly surprised how great the meals were in the facility.

There were a total of thirteen Gifted children in the facility with news of about four more expected students on the way and a little over a hundred staff to keep the facility running. The staff usually ate and generally did their day-to-day chores separately from the Gifted as Mr. Jones thought it'd make the children feel more comfortable. Though lunch and dinner varied, most of the Gifted gathered in the mess hall for the breakfast time except for a few usual absentees. Kiara could see the ones who were usually there in the morning all doing their usual morning routines and hanging out with their usual crowds.

Gus and Maria sat together, chatting through their language barrier. Gus spoke little but listened keenly to Maria speak. Everyone thought the two were a couple, though they never established themselves as one. Similarly, Sarah and Julian were also part of the same age group as Gus and Maria, and yet everyone assumed they were just good friends. Kiara secretly wished Julian and Sarah to become an item.

As Kiara passed the less-than-ambiguous couple, she found another group working through their language barrier to hold a conversation. Shannon and the twins, Jing Hwang and Jing Fung, or the new names they've adopted, "Jamie" and "Jean." Kiara never really had a chance to get to know Jamie and Jean as they kept very much to themselves. She initially thought the two sisters were shy but realized their seemingly timid nature may simply be due to the language barrier as the twin seemed to have a lot talk about between themselves in their native tongue.

Shannon, on the other hand, was someone Kiara wanted to get to know better due to her obvious intelligence, charismatic individuality, and political activeness. Also having the older sister vibe, Shannon reminded Kiara of Sarah. However, though on paper Shannon seemed very much like Sarah, it didn't take much interaction to realize Shannon and Sarah's souls were from two different worlds. Although Kiara had an easier time getting close to Sarah, there always seemed to be a sort of a wall that Shannon and Kiara put up for one another.

Relationships, Kiara thought, *were more complicated than they needed to be.*

Finally Kiara reached her lonely table. Nada wasn't at breakfast again. Kiara usually ate with Sarah, Julian, and Nada, but with Sarah and Julian gone, Nada was the only company she could expect for her meals. But it seemed Nada had stayed up too late reading her books again and was going to miss breakfast.

Not even in her teens yet, Nada was the youngest but any sense of her youth dissipated as soon as anyone had a conversation with her. Her maturity, intellect, and the air of authority around her earned her respect with her elders and even from those who found the prideful and stern youth annoying. Kiara could have used her company this morning. She'd never tell her of the dreams or the plans she had in mind, but Kiara thought perhaps Nada could have enlightened her in some way. Give her guidance. A clear direction. Before she took her leap of faith by meeting the final member of her breakfast club.

It was hard to seriously consider him as a member as he usually skipped breakfast except on very rare occasions. But it was him who she wanted—needed—to see today. Kiara knew he wasn't asleep. Like always, he was probably just doing his own thing in his room.

After returning her dishes to the kitchen staff, Kiara picked up a new tray and filled the plate with a new set of the breakfast meal. She headed out to the dorms across the courtyard. For those who were used to the site, Facility Zero truly felt more like a small sanctuary in the middle of the desert than a research lab. The dorm was co-ed, but it was generally frowned upon for a boy and a girl to be in a room together, and it was strictly forbidden during after hours. Each cadet received their own room.

Up the stairs. Down the hall. The room right before the room next to hers was her destination. It belonged to her friend that Kiara so needed to see right now.

On her first try of knocking, there was no answer. She could hear the sound of a video playing in the room. On her second try of knocking, there was still no answer.

He's probably ignoring them, she concluded.

On the third try, she added this time around, "It's me, Kiara," and the noise of the video in the background abruptly stopped.

A rustle in the room was followed by scampering steps toward the door. Then the steps themselves were followed by a moment of quick pause before the door swung open.

"Kiara!" The boy smiled brightly, his golden hair obviously hastily brought back into shape from a bed head.

"Howard!" Kiara tried to reflect Howard's brightness.

"What brings you to my humble abode so early in the morning?" Howard asked as he masterfully hid the butterflies in his stomach.

Kiara replied by gesturing with the tray full of food.

"Oh geez!" Howard opened the door wider and waved her in. "You didn't have to do that!" As always, he had his brown leather gloves on.

Entering Howard's room was always like entering a magical toy shop. There were models, figures, replicas of scenes from famous movies, and whatever else spawned out from Howard's imagination. Weapons and armors—all dulled in accordance to Director Jones' rules or some reduced to a pint-sized imitation from their rightful stature in order to fit in the room—filled the shelves and every corners of Howard's room. Some even dangled in the air, hanging from the ceiling.

"It looks liked you added more to your collection," Kiara observed, awed at the sight as she walked further into the room towards his cluttered table where she could set the tray down.

"Can you tell?" Howard chuckled as he tried to clear the mess.

On his table were various art books from movies, cartoons, and games, as well as his own sketchbooks and papers filled with his designs. Next to his laptop (which had an old movie with spaceships, aliens, and such paused at the arrival of Kiara) was a snowball-sized aluminum sphere that was inside a glass case for viewing, but not touching.

"You came a long way from being able to make just that." Kiara looked at Howard and smiled as she set down the tray.

"Yeah." Howard quickly looked away to whatever direction Kiara wasn't in as his pale face reddened.

She found his timid nature somewhat endearing. Kiara wondered if knowing the boy's affection and ignoring it for her favor made her a bad person.

"What are you working on right now?" Kiara asked, looking at the pieces, all very detailed and seemingly with each their own purpose, cluttered on his desk.

Howard pointed at his laptop which was still paused on the spaceship. "I was trying to make a replica of that for Julian. And"—Howard pointed at the pieces of armor consisting of gauntlets and greaves in his room—"also working on an experiment with Gus."

"For his birthday? And does Director Jones know of this experiment?"

"No, it seemed like he was a big fan of the film, so I thought I'd just do something nice. And No."

"I see." Kiara composed herself. She could ask for this. He would do it. As manipulative as it was, she knew he would do it for *her*. "Can I sit here?" She pointed at the bed.

"Of course!" Howard nodded and quickly swiped the bed with his gloved hands to prepare it for Kiara.

"Howard," Kiara whispered submissively, almost whimpering as the images of her dreams flashed through her head again. "I was hoping you could make me something."

"Sure thing!" Howard seemed happy that Kiara would give him a task. And luckily for him, it was a task he was rightfully confident in. "I can make just about anything! They don't call me the Inventor for nothing!" Howard sat next to Kiara. "What is it?" He asked, brimming with confidence.

"A gun." Kiara didn't hesitate nor stutter. Once her mind was made and her heart assured, her sight was clear.

"A what?" Howard's smile of confidence turned into a smile of disbelief.

"A gun, Howard. There's something I must do. Someone I must stop. Even if it means I have to kill that person."

Howard shifted and immediately stood, looking over her. He crossed his arms and tried to read her face and understand her motives. "Kiara," he finally spoke after a moment of silence. "I'm only even considering this because you're my friend and I know of your 'gift.' Did you see something in one of your dreams?"

Kiara patted the seat next to her on the bed, and Howard obliged, sitting back down next to her and leaning in close to listen to the tales of Kiara's dreams. Her dreams of the Witch. Her dreams of the oncoming calamity. And her latest dream foretelling her death. She then proceeded to convince Howard of her self-imposed task to save the world, or at least die fighting knowing that she had tried. After a long, tug-of-war discussion between moralities and consequences, the Inventor wrote her up a list. A list of ingredients they'd need to gather in order for him to build her what she needed. An end to the Witch and the nightmares.

Chapter 20
WOLF IN BOOTS

Emily rested her head against the soft fuzz of her bomber jacket's collar while she twirled her long golden hair with her finger. The black roots were beginning to show, but she grew to like the blond and black contrast. Sitting alone at one end of the long meeting table in the conference room of the McKinley Security Firm, Emily had made herself comfortable. Reclining back on the leather chair, she stretched out her legs and rested her feet on the table with her boots still on. Black leather boots with yellow shoe strings, she wore the boot for just about any occasion. It was probably an audacious move on her part to rest her veteran boots on the table that was probably as expensive as a car, but frankly, Emily didn't care. Straight across from her, she could see her reflection on the over-sized TV screen. It was probably for conferencing, but she humored herself imagining that they probably just used it to sit here and watch movies and the what-not. Yep. She was bored. She really wished they let her keep her phone.

Many pairs of eyes turned to her as soon as Emily Wolf stepped into the grand McKinley Security Firm headquarters. She was a skinny young blond girl, taller than average though not by much, hiding her green eyes behind aviator sunglass which was currently in its case tucked away in her jacket pocket after being told they were not allowed to be worn within the facility. She walked confidently in her army jeans and leather boots while she was among men and women who were old enough to be her parents with a few having experience in wars as part of their curriculum vitae. But she seemed undeterred with her confident grin. She wore an oversized t-shirt with an old rock band logo beneath the worn-out, slightly too big for her bomber jacket, and she stood out among all the suits and ties of the McKinley staff.

The staff whispered among themselves trying to guess the mystery girl's identity. Some thought by her sheer bravado that she was an illegitimate daughter of Mr. McKinley himself and was here to collect some sort of payment. Some even ventured into darker theories that she was someone of a more intimate relationship. Though no one else seemed to know for certain who Emily was, all the security checks and secretaries seemed to know to let her through and guide her to the private conference room used only by the most exclusive meetings with Mr. McKinley himself.

But it had been too long, and boredom always made her bad habits itch. Emily stopped playing with her hair and instinctively reached into her pocket for her carton of cigarettes. She stopped. Noah forced her to promise that she would only smoke just once a day—a tall order since she was coming down from a carton a day. So was it worth it right now to smoke? It was already two in the afternoon, and she did have a long drive back to the airport. If the meeting went well, she might want a celebratory smoke. And then she was probably going to have dinner on the plane, so she wouldn't have to worry about a savory and filling meal tempting her. She was thinking too much. She didn't like it when she caught herself over thinking things.

Oh.

Emily was surprised to see that the carton was already in her hand.

She spanked the carton to pack it all in. Then she opened the top and tapped one out enough for her to fish it out with her pink lips. She stuffed the carton back into her jacket and relaxed into the chair as she rested her feet on the table again. She rolled the cigarette around inside her lips. She wanted to savor the taste and drag out the experience before it even started.

This IS a nasty addiction. Just light it. Look at me, I'm pathetic. She thought to herself.

Emily raised her index finger and the tip ignited with a flame long enough to resemble a safety-removed lighter. She approached the cigarette in her lips to the fire. The satisfaction of the initial inhale nearly sent shocks to her body. She felt disgusted with herself, but after the exhale, she immediately went for another inhale. The second was never as good as the first. She arched her head back and puffed out a donut. The door behind her opened with a scurry of footsteps.

Timing. Emily thought to herself. Her arch-nemesis.

"Aren't you a little young to be smoking, miss?" Mr. McKinley asked condescendingly with a sly smile as he briskly walked past her. He had chubby legs carrying his even chubbier stomach, and he had with him a briefcase. He was followed by four men in suits that she assumed to be his guards. Two men stood behind Mr. McKinley as he sat down across from her at the meeting table, and the other two men stood behind Emily.

"You are aware you invited me for a merc job, right?" Emily took another deep inhale of her delicious smoke and casually blew it out towards Mr. McKinley. To Mr. McKinley's surprise, the smoke made it all the way across the table and scattered around his face. He kept his dignity, letting out only a gentle cough, but it didn't help with Emily's lips stretching into a cocky smile.

"Well, nevertheless. No smoking is allowed in here. Rules are rules, Ms. Wolf; Even I abide by them," Mr. McKinley said as he unloaded the contents of his briefcase. The man standing behind Emily took Mr. McKinley's words as a cue to drop in front of her a crystal ashtray from one of the drawers in the room. He was a mountain of a man with sandy skin and deeply black, never-go-bald hair. In a room full of glazed-eyed guards, his sharp and stern look caught Emily's attention.

"Thank you, Faran." Mr. McKinley appreciated his guard's ability to take a hint.

Assuming Mr. McKinley was using his own people as guards, Emily figured these guys were some sort of ex-commando, Special Forces types. The best of the best to guard the head honcho.

'Faran' tapped twice on the ashtray firmly enough to let Emily know it was no longer a request but a command.

She looked Faran in his eyes and smiled. It wasn't in Emily's nature to be coerced, but this *was* a business meeting, and it'd be better for her to be on her best behavior.

Maintaining eye contact, Emily obliged Faran by slowly pulling the cigarette out of her mouth and rubbing it out with her tongue.

Faran raised an eyebrow.

Still smiling, Emily tossed away the dead cigarette into the ashtray. Emily caught one of the bodyguards across smiling and sent him a wink. "You can take this away now" — Emily firmly tapped twice on the ashtray — "Faran."

Faran didn't complain. He removed the ashtray from the table and dumped its contents in the trash. Once he was done, Faran returned to standing behind Emily.

"So... I noticed the fire on your finger as I walked in. Is that your..." Mr. McKinley searched for the right words, "...'gift'? Power to control fire?" He asked unenthusiastically.

"I think they call it pyrokinesis."

That was the word Mr. McKinley was searching for. "Yes, that."

"Nope," Emily answered.

"Oh?" Mr. McKinley was surprised. He had heard about people with more than one 'gift,' but he had never seen one himself.

Emily tapped on her head. "I've been told I have a pretty good head on my shoulders." Emily gestured her hands to present her legs that were still resting on the table. "And I get compliments for my legs a lot."

Mr. McKinley was not amused.

"And I'm pretty good at what I do," Emily finished with a smug smile.

Faran gently shook his head.

"Could you put your feet down?" Mr. McKinley asked, and Emily obliged.

"So." Mr. McKinley took some folders out of his briefcase. "We found it was pretty difficult to unearth any substantial background on your life story, Ms. Wolf. Surprising, to say the least, in this day and age—either you just appeared out of thin air, or you have some very resourceful and talented people covering your tracks." Mr. McKinley scratched his slightly balding head. Emily had the look of a proud mother on her face.

"So how does a 20-year old girl end up with a group of Gifted that's rising to become the new superstars of the world's underbellies?"

"Some kids come up with the next brilliant website, some kids come up with the next platinum record, and I guess some kids just become really good at forming a successful guns-for-hire business."

"You guys are supposedly already a sort of myth—legend, shall we say—among the Gifted. You *are* twenty, correct? It's what I have on the files, but it's more of a guess."

"More-or-less. If it'd ease your mind, I am old enough buy my own smokes," Emily lied.

Mr. McKinley smirked. "Quite an impressive resume," he continued. "Not to mention the only group of Gifted organized enough and talented enough for serious people to even consider hiring for serious kinds of jobs. You guys have been busy, the *Wolfgang?*"

"*Wolf Pack*. I think *Wolfgang* is a rap group. I personally prefer Emily and the Wolf Pack, but the crew had some slight problems with that."

"I can imagine," said Mr. McKinley of the McKinley Security Firm. "You and your pack have been sighted all over the world. The jobs that we know of includes taking out insurgents and terrorist cells in various countries, and making some of the notorious Gifted and Gifted groups disappear. There are probably a lot more jobs that we don't and won't ever hear about. Rumors say you guys took out a sizable organized crime family that was causing such havoc, not even the law enforcement could touch them."

"No," Emily said. "That last thing wasn't us."

"Oh?" Mr. McKinley seemed a little disappointed, though he was somewhat glad that such an extravagant story wasn't true.

"That was just me," Emily said.

"What?"

"I did that one by myself. It was personal; they pissed me off." Emily leaned in a bit. "Look, we follow the money as long as it doesn't make us feel too dirty at the end. During our off time, we're usually hunting down criminals and troublemakers and what not.

Just trying to make the world a better place."

"Very noble of you." Mr. McKinley made some notes in his files. "Rumor has it you guys are the ones who deserve the credit for the disappearance of the notorious 'Boogeyman Killer'" — Emily tried to hold in her sudden burst of laughter. She always thought that the 'Boogeyman Killer' had to be the worst name for any killer in history — "that had everyone too afraid to come out, day or night?"

"Anyone who was a criminal posing as an innocent citizen, maybe."

"Maybe you know something that we don't know, but anyone crazy like that, I'm sure, was a menace to anyone who wanted to live their lives righteously and safely. How did you manage to catch him? Or was it her? I'd think only a woman would be careful and thorough enough to be such a perfect assassin. They say that no matter who the person was or where they were, she'd be able to get them. Hence the 'Boogeyman'" — Emily let out a small guffaw — "...Killer.' She had to be a Gifted, but fascinating nonetheless," Mr. McKinley continued with only slight interruption.

"That'd be sharing trade secrets, Mr. McKinley," Emily replied, her legs itching to just rest on the table again. "We didn't build up to where we are by giving away our secrets. I'm sure you didn't either."

"Fair enough."

"Let's get to it, Mr. McKinley. You're a busy man and I'm a busy girl. What's the job?"

"Yes, of course." Mr. McKinley closed his briefcase and set it down on the ground. The files were still scattered in front of him. He planted his elbow on top of the files, then locked his fingers and rested his chin on top of his hands. "We have intel that Ms. Nancy Jones, CEO of the Silver Aegis Securities, has a private facility holding onto several children who are Gifted."

Emily raised an eyebrow.

"Your job, Ms. Wolf," Mr. McKinley continued. "Would be to support our raid of that facility."

"Alright, so who's contracting you for this?"

"That's classified information."

"Because carrying out this kind of operation doesn't exactly seem legal in this country, and I don't think government employed mercenaries should be doing those sorts of things." Emily smiled innocently.

This time Mr. McKinley raised an eyebrow. Emily still had that grin on her, but now it was if she had something over Mr. McKinley. She was sort of correct.

"Given the special circumstances, we were given permission to carry out this operation," Mr. McKinley lied. "I assure you that there will be no blow-back on you and your 'Wolf Pack' for your part in this. Nevertheless, it'll be an evening that never happened. We'll sign a contract and pay you and your crew well enough to insure that."

"Sure, but I'm still not sure if this would be the right job for us."

"The money's *real*."

"Uh-huh, but we are also risking becoming national criminals. You see, we want to be the vigilante-you-want-to-hate-but-kind-of-love kind of group, not the hey-everyone-we-hate-you-and-we-don't-care-if-you-hate-us kind of terrorist-group. But if there were something more of interest to risk that…" Emily leaned in a little bit and gave Mr. McKinley a look. She knew. Or at least, she heard something.

"There's an extra benefit for you guys if you go."

"Go on."

"A little birdy told me that the Wolf Pack was also looking for the elusive Witch. It wasn't too difficult to tell seeing as how you and your friends show up at a lot of the locations where the Witch had been sighted."

"Mmhmm." Emily tapped her fingers on the table in a wave pattern.

"Our intel told us that the Witch is currently with Ms. Nancy Jones."

"So the rumors were true."

"But we can't hand you the Witch, if that's what you were hoping."

"That's fine. We just want some time with her."

"I suppose we can arrange that."

"Guarantee it. Put it in our contract."

"I mean, alright." Mr. McKinley chuckled. "Pretty thorough, aren't you. What do you want with her?"

"That, again, would be a trade secret, Mr. McKinley. Nothing too dangerous, I promise you." Emily pulled out a small notepad from her pocket and a pen. She scribbled something down and raised it in the air. When nothing happened, she started to shake it in the air.

"Come on, Faran!" said Emily, flustered when Faran couldn't take a hint. Faran looked at Mr. McKinley who insisted with a nod that he oblige to Ms. Wolf. Faran snatched the paper from Emily's hand and walked it over to Mr. McKinley.

"What is this?"

"The price."

"The rumor has it that you are not shy with your prices." Mr. McKinley opened up the paper. "And they were not kidding. This is quite the bold price. I had other numbers in my mind."

"The world is only small for those who can't think big, Mr.

McKinley. There's short supply of Gifted let alone ones organized and experienced like us. Plus, we are damn good at what we do, and you know what they say: If you are good at something... don't do it for free."

"Done. But I expect nothing less than exceptional at this price. Not to mention discretion."

"I'm sure you won't be disappointed. Including me, there will be three others."

"Only the four of you?" Mr. McKinley was clearly flustered.

"Without disclosing any actual numbers, the Wolf Pack isn't as big as some people think. I only choose best of the best that I can find and, more importantly, those I can trust. I assure you, four of us will be more than enough." The tone of Emily's voice changed with this statement, reassuring Mr. McKinley. It was confident as always, but with the serenity and sincerity of a leader and businesswoman.

"Alright," Mr. McKinley said, swayed by Emily's demeanor.

"I also expect that our expenses, equipment, travel fees, and grub will be provided for?" Emily asked with a smile as she morphed back into her former self.

Mr. McKinley just nodded without a word. He had almost expected to hear those words at this point. At Mr. McKinley's consent, Emily stood and walked over to her new employer and offered her hand for a handshake. Surprised and bewildered, it took a moment for Mr. McKinley to grab Emily's hand.

"Good to be workin' with you, Mr. McKinley!" said Emily.

Mr. McKinley couldn't remember the last time he had felt uncomfortable with women, but Emily had completely swayed him with her quirky charisma and confidence.

"Yes, I look forward to working with you, Ms. Wolf," replied Mr. McKinley, hiding his surprise at the strength of Emily's grip. "We'll have the papers ready by tomorrow. Let's drink to our partnership." Mr. McKinley gestured at one of the guards, and they produced from a cabinet a bottle of liquor and two crystal glasses on a silver tray. Mr. McKinley poured both glasses with the bronze liquid.

Emily took her aviators out of the case and donned them. Both of them felt at home.

"Mr. McKinley," Emily began as she rummaged through her pockets for her cigarette. "I'm pretty sure it's illegal to offer underage girls alcohol. Sorta creepy too." She held the carton of cigarettes in one hand and grabbed the glass of liquor with another. She downed the glass with one tilt of her head. The liquor burned and glided down her throat. Emily knew when a drink wasn't cheap. She let out a loud sigh of satisfaction.

"Thanks for the drink," Emily said as she spanked the cigarette box. She headed for the door as she fished another stick out with her lips to feed her 'disgusting' addiction. Since the last one was cut short, in her mind, Emily wasn't cheating her promise to Noah. Her finger ignited with a flame again, and she lit her cigarette before she opened the door. As she took in that delicious first inhale, a thin ringing in her ears made her snap her head back to the group. She caught a glimpse of Faran glaring at her, and the cigarette in her lips exploded like an overenthusiastic party popper.

Mr. McKinley immediately turned his head to Faran surprised at his subordinate and yet a bit proud.

Emily's face and her cherished jacket were a mess of ash and tobacco. She spat out the remnants of the cigarette in her mouth as she checked her eyebrows to see if they were all there. Her face felt dirty, but her eyebrows were safe and sound.

"That was unnecessary," Emily said to Faran who had an ever so slight smirk on his face. She kept her temper down and lit her index finger with a humbly-sized fire. "I have a lighter of my own."

"No smoking, remember, Ms. Wolf?" Faran spoke sternly. Perhaps there was a slight playfulness in there, but no one was certain.

"What? No crystal ashtrays now that y'all don't have to impress me anymore?"

"Just reminding you that these gifts don't make us special, Ms. Wolf. They are a disease."

"That's enough Faran." Mr. McKinley reached into his pocket for his leather wallet as he walked over to Emily. "Allow me to compensate you for the mess."

"Please, now you're offending me." Emily shooed away the wallet as she spanked out another cigarette (the last one didn't counter either). Mr. McKinley snapped his finger and pointed at Faran then Emily. Faran pulled out a handkerchief from his pocket and walked it over to Emily as she lit a fresh stick.

Faran tried to hand his handkerchief to Emily as she exhaled a big stream of smoke.

"Maybe you're sick," Emily said as she ignored Faran's offer. "But I'm not. Then again, maybe I'm just not self-aware." She ignored the handkerchief. Shades on, smoke in her lips and a new job in her pocket, Emily left the conference room. It must have been less than half an hour, but to those in the room, it felt much longer.

"Get James Morris on the line," Mr. McKinley said as he returned to his seat. "And Faran, that was very unlike you. You can do whatever you want with her after we get what we want out of her. But until then, behave."

"Yes, sir. I apologize sir," Faran replied as he folded the handkerchief and placed it back into his pocket.

"But maybe it was good to remind her of her place. That the world is full of people much scarier than her." Mr. McKinley scratched his chin as he pondered his current circumstances. Emily Wolf would be put to good use for the company, and this would help the McKinley Security Firm to even the score with the Silver Aegis Securities—with Nancy Jones. And she was, perhaps, the only way for Mr. McKinley to save his company in the predicament Nancy Jones had put him in.

***

Outside the McKinley facilities, Emily sat in her rental car with the window down. She was enjoying the remaining half of her cigarette. She dialed a number on her phone, and it rang long enough for Emily to think that the person on the other side wasn't going to pick up.

"Da?" A girl with an accent weakly answered.

"Olivia, it's Emily."

"I know."

"Is the line secure?"

"Mmhmm," The girl replied with the same amount of energy and enthusiasm she answered the call with. Emily heard keyboard typing over the phone.

"Did you spend the night in front of the computer again?"

"…" The girl remained silent, and the sound of the keyboard typing stopped. Emily chuckled as she exhaled her smoke.

"At least eat something, will ya? The *fish* bit. We got the job."

"Mmhmm."

"Tell Noah and Norah to get ready. Plan B is a go. And also tell Leon."

"Da."

"And we are going to need to contact your prince charming."

Emily could imagine Olivia's groggy eyes, glowing by the hue of the computer screen, lighting up with life. "Gabriel's busy. He doesn't want to be bothered," Olivia had a little more pep and personality in her voice than before. She scratched her head through her messy blue bed hair and stretched her arms and back.

"Well, tell the 'Boogeyman' to get un-busy because it's time for him to pay his dues. The job's the big one."

"You mean…?"

"Yeah."

"Alright."

"Call me when everyone's there. And, seriously, eat something once you're done, Olivia Kulikova. I'm serious."

"Yes ma'am." Olivia hung up on the assumption that was the last of it. She had a habit of doing that. Back at the studio the Wolf Pack used as their headquarters, Olivia sat in front of multiple computers screens. Her skin pale and her hair a colorful mess (this month was mix of blue and pink), the only light that lit up her features was the faint glow coming off of her monitors. She typed away like a virtuoso pianist on her keyboard to assemble the members of the Wolf Pack.

"Was that Emily?" A man playing with a toddler on the other side of the room asked.

"Mmhmm."

"What she say?" The man lifted his baby daughter in the air and gave her a kiss on her forehead.

"Plan B is a go. She says she wants you for it, Leon. I need to call *him,*" Olivia began to fix her hair for her phone call. *She might even take a shower.*

Leon let out triumphant laughter.

"Plan B is a go, eh?" Leon put his child down. "Amazing. Just amazing. I wonder if all of them know—Nancy, McKinley, and the Witch—that they're all playing on palm of her hands."

Olivia hurried into the shower.

Chapter 21
SEARCHING FOR WHAT'S...

The next morning began with breakfast in a similar fashion to the previous night's dinner. Julian awoke feeling rejuvenated and as good as new. He found Sarah sleeping near Lily, and Lily sleeping by the side of her redheaded friend. Landris crawled into the hut, and from the look on his face, Julian wondered if he had been awake the whole night.

"Why didn't you wake me?" Kalin asked sleepily as he sat up, woken by the noise of Landris crawling in.

Landris let out a big yawn. "Figured waking you up would wake up the Witch. Imagine the fuss she would have made. No need for that. Besides, figured it'd even us out for you taking care of that wuss's rib." Landris collapsed near the fire pit. He stared up at the roof, looking at the lightening blue sky of morning through the smoke hole Lily had opened the night before. Not too long afterwards, his eyes shut themselves and he fell into a sleep.

It was about a half-an-hour to an hour before Sarah and Lily awoke. Landris caught some quick shut eye, and Kalin resumed his sleep. Julian went outside for some crisp, fresh morning air in the woods, and to relieve himself of some fluids.

"Good morning, everyone!" Julian said brightly when he returned and found everyone awake as he crawled back into the den. No one seemed enthused.

"Good morning, Julian," Sarah spoke softly with a smile after an awkward silence.

Lily rubbed her eyes and found her sketchbook. She helped herself to a bottle of water and a plate of steaming hot cakes with syrup. Kalin chose a plate of eggs and some fruit. Landris decided to start his day with another burger, and for Sarah, some fruit and juice. Landris had hoped for coffee but found himself out of luck. Apparently, Lily found coffee to be 'icky.' While everyone munched in contentment on their meals, Julian asked if it'd be alright to help himself to seconds, to which, of course, Lily consented, and had himself a plate of eggs, sausages, and hot cakes as well. They ate mostly in silence with only the sound of eating and an occasional request to pass around drinks or to try a sample of someone else's food.

"You guys seem like you didn't sleep very well," Julian said hoping to break the awkwardness in the air.

Landris responded with a look that made Julian shrug.

Sarah responded with a slight chuckle.

Lily ate her breakfast in silence.

Kalin, sitting closely to Lily, seemed as if he didn't even hear Julian's words.

After breakfast everyone cleaned up, brushed their teeth, and started the campfire they had allowed to burn out.

Sarah still had the task assigned to her by Director Jones that she had to complete. "Lily," Sarah called out to the girl.

The girl turned her head and looked at Sarah with nervous and yet excited eyes.

After what she had witnessed yesterday in the girl's mind, Sarah's task had become difficult and terrifying. The extended silence by Sarah after calling out to Lily caught everyone else's attention, and they stared at the two as the air thickened.

The slight glee in Lily's eyes slowly faded away as the Sarah's search for words lengthened.

In Sarah's mind, the image of the Lily's beaming smiles last night and the image of the Lily's desperate apologies in tears both played at the same time.

"Sarah?" Julian could feel Sarah's uneasiness.

"Why don't we" — Sarah's heart searched for courage — "use my 'gift' to search for your parents?" She couldn't find it in her duty to Director Jones. She couldn't find it at the chance of solving the mysteries of the Witch. But she found it in her hope of helping her friend.

Lily stared at Sarah for a moment before replying, "Okay."

Sarah was thankful of her trust.

Kalin's instincts urged him to protest. Nothing good will come out of this, it said. She'll be hurt, it said. But he settled his urge by reminding himself that this was her prerogative; this was what she wanted, and he knew deep inside that there needed to be some sort of resolution to her past for Lily to find her peace and heal. He walked over to his friend and gently placed his hand over her small shoulder. She looked up at him and gently took his hand from his shoulder into her hand.

"We should get started. The Director will want an update," Landris reminded Sarah as he spat out toothpaste foam from his mouth.

Sarah nodded. After the previous night, reluctance had buried itself into her heart. Partly out of her feelings for Lily. Partly out of her instincts that she was about to open Pandora's Box.

"Lily..." After all morning routines were done, the five sat in the den preparing for Sarah's ritual. Lily and Sarah sat across from one another as the three young men watched. "I have the 'gift' to look into people's minds—their memories. All I have to do is lay my hand on you. Just relax, everything will be alright. You won't feel a thing," Sarah said with a smile to Lily who couldn't even look Sarah in the eyes.

Sarah knew in her heart that she was telling herself to relax, trying to convince herself that the nightmares were just nightmares. She realized she'd have to face reality today, and not just as a bystander, but as the person who lived through what she was about to see. She was going to be Lily, the protagonist. Nothing would be the same. The experience would become part of her.

"Try to think of the earliest memory you have of your parents. I'll guide us from there." Sarah slowly moved her hand towards Lily's head. Sarah remembered the memories of her past summers. The times when she was still an ordinary girl. She used to go cliff diving near the lake at her parent's cabin; you don't think. You just jump.

"You ready?" Sarah asked. She stopped thinking. She placed her hand on Lily's head.

Chapter 22
...BETTER LEFT LOST

Sarah saw the world through little Lily's eyes—the key difference between seeing a dream and a memory. She was sitting in an ice cream parlor sipping on a strawberry milkshake. Lily was staring out the window watching the people pass by. Sarah could see the reflection of Lily who seemed to be maybe four to five years old. Lily wondered at what kind of stories all these people had outside. What were their lives like?

"Daddy?" Lily spoke. "Where are all these people going?"

"Somewhere," the father empathetically spoke.

Turn your head, Lily. Sarah begged in her mind, but Lily kept her eyes on the pedestrians. Through Lily's ears, Sarah could hear the father flipping through pages of what was likely a newspaper. They sat there for a little while as Lily sipped on her strawberry milkshake—which Sarah admittedly enjoyed as well—and watched people pass by.

"We have to go," the father suddenly spoke with urgency. He folded his papers and tossed it on the table as he stood. Lily looked at her father. He was a man who didn't seem to have any standout qualities about him except for his military-styled haircut and sizable stature. He wasn't particularly tall but muscular, and his face wasn't particularly memorable or distinguished.

Lily wanted to finish her milkshake but obediently listened to her father without hesitation. The father grabbed his small daughter's hand harshly and hastily went out the door. They stood outside on the busy sidewalk that Lily had been staring at from the other side of the glass pane.

"Daddy? We should have picked something up for mommy," Lily spoke softly at her father. Sarah was surprised how articulate Lily was as a small child given how limited she seemed now.

"Shut it." The father looked down at Lily with such fierce eyes that it felt more like a threat than a warning. Sarah felt Lily's heart skip a beat and her body tense.

They stood there as people walked past them. The father squeezed Lily's hand tight, and the sweat from his clammy hands drenched Lily's. The father and daughter simply stood in place as more people passed by. Lily peeked up at her father whose agitated face made Lily quickly turn her head away. She didn't want to make her father scold her again.

More people passed by, and the father tapped his foot loudly with impatience. Lily tried to count all the different colors of the cars passing by. One of the cars, a black car—shinier and bigger than the one Lily's dad had—even parked in front of them. Lily stared at the car in awe as she saw a distorted reflection of herself from its gleaming door.

"Kiddo," the father knelt down and spoke gently, his behavior in stark contrast to before. "You stay put right here for a moment, alright? Don't go anywhere. I'm going to get that something for your mom."

Lily broke into a wide smile at her father's change of heart and nodded, but Sarah sensed a hint of nervousness within Lily and her heart slowly sinking into an abyss. An instinctive feeling, but without much thought behind it to justify it.

The father patted Lily on the head and went back into the ice cream parlor. Lily stood there, much like before, but without her father. There were not many people passing now. They must have all gone home. There were not many cars passing now. They must have all gone home too. Lily also wished she could go home soon.

The gleaming car's door opened.

A big, unpleasantly plump man with rough facial hair stepped out of the car. Although it was nearly evening on a cloudy day, he was wearing sunglasses with his big head stuffed into a newspaper boy hat. The man reminded Lily of a bear. When the bear looked down at her, she saw her reflection in his sunglasses looking up at him. She looked scared. He picked her up gently and caressed her into a hug like a father would do for a daughter, but pressed his hand on the back of Lily's head so her mouth was buried into his mushy shoulders. His salty sweat drenched Lily's nose. For a moment, Lily was frozen in fear and bewilderment. The older mind of Sarah wanted to scream at Lily to run and wriggled in disgust, but before anyone could see Lily's fight for her life, he was already back in the car with her.

"Drive. I got her," said the bear-man. He threw Lily onto the car floor and began to duct tape her mouth. The car floor began to rumble as it moved away from the sidewalk. Lily struggled and tried to fight the bear-man. She tried to slap with her little hands and tried to kick with her little feet, and as a response, the bear-man slapped Lily across her face with his paw. In the small, confined space, the bear-man wasn't able to put much strength behind it, but it was enough to numb the small child's entire body. Lily's mind went black and lost all traces of thought and fear. Sarah felt Lily's whole body go limp for a moment before her body began violently pulsating as she began to cry, and the fear surged back into her mind.

"If you don't behave, you'll get another one," the bear-man growled.

"Hey! Be gentle with her! If she's damaged, then all this will be more trouble than it's worth!" the driver shrilled at the bear-man. It was the pitch-y and growling voice of an older woman which reminded Lily of an old cat in her neighborhood.

"You just shut up and drive, woman!" the bear-man snarled back at the old-cat lady as he turned Lily around and duct taped her wrists together. Then he taped up her ankles and legs. And, for good measure, the bear-man taped around her arms and body. He dug into his pocket and pulled out a blindfold to finish packaging up Lily.

"Turn her around so she don't suffocate. If she's dead than all this was…"

"SHUT! UP! I GOT THIS, ALRIGHT?!" The bear-man's roar sent shocks through Lily's body.

"Don't you yell at me! You stupid son of a—!" The old-cat scowled back until she saw a, "—cop!"

The bear-man huddled on top of Lily and kept quiet. The car was filled with only the sound of Lily's sniffles and cries for her dad through the tape.

As the bear-man turned Lily around, Sarah caught a glimpse of the driver's red-frizzled hair.

"Now," the bear-man gently spoke. "If you be quiet and behave, I won't have to hurt you anymore, okay?"

Lily tears kept drizzling down. Beneath the tape, she was calling for her mommy and daddy.

"If you don't behave, I'll hit you again. You don't want that, right?"

Lily didn't want that, but she couldn't stop crying. The bear-man slapped her across the face again. Sarah couldn't tell whether or not it was harder than before, but it wasn't any softer. She cursed at the man with words she rarely used.

The bear-man put a blindfold over Lily's eyes, and the world turned dark. Lily sniffled quietly as the bear-man taped her around her body some more when the car bumped and the bear-man crash landed onto Lily's chest. It knocked the air out of Lily, and Sarah felt Lily's mind black out for another moment again. She was too tired at this point to cry harder.

"You call this driving?!" the bear-man roared again to the old-cat woman.

"I swear to God and to my dead parents, if you yell at me like I'm a dog one more time, I'll murder you in your sleep!" the old-cat hissed back.

"I'd like to see you try, Shelly," the bear-man grumbled as he put a blanket over Lily's body.

'Shelly.' Sarah made a mental note.

"YOU STUPID MORON! I SAID DON'T USE NAMES!" the woman yelled at the top of her lungs.

"SHE'S A KID. WHAT DOES SHE KNOW, AND WHAT'S SHE GONNA DO?!" The bear-man carried his weight and was a bit louder.

"Make sure she can breathe!"

"What do you think I am? An idiot? I kept her face up!" The bear-man climbed up to sit back into the seat and put on his seatbelt.

Lily sobbed until her eyes swelled, and her throat began to ache. Her body slowly grew numb as the tape soldered her body together. Sarah felt Lily's suffering, and even for her, it was unbearable. But the idea that a small child was going through it made her anguish pale in comparison to her anger. The reality that she was simply experiencing the deeds of the past and the frustration of her inability to do anything about what had already been done infuriated her. It was more than a little tempting to stop this memory search—to waste not a second more on her crusade to put these two horrible people on spikes. But Sarah knew the best thing she could do for Lily was to stay with these memories and see how much more they could reveal of the Witch's clandestine past.

The darkness under the blankets distorted her sense of time. Fatigued, Lily fell asleep for a few moments during the ride until a bump woke her up. The bear-man and the old-cat remained mostly silent during the car ride. Perhaps they were too tired to speak to one another, or, they simply didn't want to start another battle of spitfires.

Lily began to rub her head against the car floor. She was, to put it mildly, very uncomfortable but by now accepted the fact that she wasn't going to be able to get her limbs free. At least Lily felt she had a chance with the blindfold since she could still turn her head. She continued to brush her head against the car until the blindfold revealed her eyes.

The struggle chafed her shoulder and neck, but Lily could now peek over with her left eye. She saw the bear-man resting his head against the door and sleeping. Outside she saw the clear blue sky with fluffy clouds. Serene, majestic, and indifferent.

A sign passed by with the number 101. Sarah took note of it.

Lily didn't seem to be able to identify the smell, but the air was filled with manure that Sarah recalled from driving past pastures of farmlands.

The car drove for more or less another hour until it slowed down. After a brief drive on bumpy, non-paved, road the car came to a complete stop. The small jolt of the car settling awakened the bear-man who looked around in a daze, mildly surprised to realize they had already arrived.

"You fat idiot!" The old-cat scowled at the bear-man. The bear-man was too sleepy, still slipping in and out of dreamland, to understand why he was being yelled at. She snapped her fingers at him as if she was waking up a slumbering dog to punish it for the mess it made on the carpet.

"Look!" She pointed at Lily's revealed eye.

The old-cat, Shelly, had stuffed her curly ginger hair under her cap, but it still spilled out of the sides and the back like flowing lava. She wore considerably large sized sunglasses to shield her identity. Despite her geriatric sounding voice, she seemed to be a woman who had just move past her youth.

"Ah, son of a—" The bear-man grabbed the blanket and threw it over Lily's face again with such force that it yanked away from Lily's feet in the process. "Didn't I tell you to behave?!" Bear-man slammed his hand down where Lily's forehead was hidden underneath the blanket.

Lily began to cry again.

"Careful, you ass!" With the ginger woman's protest, the expected blow from the bear-man didn't come. "She might be sent off today!"

"Today? That man?"

"Yeah, he's eager to see her." Lily felt an unexpectedly gentle pat on her head through the blanket.

The bear-man chuckled. "I guess we can get that new TV and even another car pretty soon." The bear-man gently patted the lump where Lily's head was after Shelly was done in appreciation. "Should we move her under the barn?" the bear-man asked.

Under the barn.

"No, unless you got your lazy sorry self to fix the kinks I told you to fix. We're not risking it."

"We already have a couple under there."

"Yeah, well for this one, I don't want to risk it. If we don't move her out by tonight, we'll put her there. Until then, let's just keep her here. She seems fine. Just make sure she can breathe."

"Alright." The bear-man gingerly tugged the blanket around Lily's head. "You cause trouble or even make a peep, I'll smack around your face until your tiny little lips rip right off, kiddo."

The smell of fresh air filled the car with the scent of pasture as the bear-man and Shelly opened their doors and left the vehicle. Lily imagined herself being back at the parlor again sipping on her strawberry milkshake. Watching the people outside and wondering where they were headed. She wondered if any of them saw her and wondered where she was headed that day.

Lily wanted her papa.

Chapter 23
RUBY

Shrouded in the darkness, seconds, minutes, and hours all seemed to collude into a mesh. The time passing by was felt by the skin as the air cooled during nightfall. Lily cried, fell asleep, and dreamt multiple times during the muddled time frame. For Sarah, it was unbearable. The restraints around the wrists and legs, the smelly blanket they were stuffed under, and the darkness—the relentless darkness. She cheated herself from the experience by 'fast forwarding' a bit through the memories.

The 'fast forwarding' process was always a bit difficult to describe in words for Sarah. It was a bit like gliding through the images of the memories, warping the time and seeing the memories within the proximities of the current memory, and Sarah simply skipped or glided around as she pleased.

"Damn it! Today's a good day!" The bear-man's triumphant roar and slamming of the car door as he entered awoke Lily. He heard a yelp. In his excitement, he stepped on Lily by accident and whispered he was 'sorry.'

"Hey, check this out," the bear-man spoke to who Lily and Sarah assumed to be the old-cat, Shelly.

Ch-Chak.

Lily didn't recognized the sound, but Sarah's heart skipped a beat as she immediately realized the bear-man had a gun.

"It feels so good when I do that." The bear-man's voice oozed with self-satisfaction.

"Wipe that stupid smile off your face," Shelly groaned as she entered the driver's seat again and clocked her seatbelt on.

"We should stop by one of those 24-hour places to pick up that TV," the bear-man said jollily.

"Don't count the money we don't have in our hands yet," Shelly scolded.

"You should really keep your mouth shut sometimes, Shelly."

"I have a gun, Ed."

Ed.

"So do I, sweetheart."

"Is the girl asleep?"

Ed, the bear-man, peeled the blanket off of Lily's face. Lily's eyes glistened with moisture as she cringed, her eyes finding even the night's light too bright.

"Nope," Ed answered as he reached into his pocket and pulled out a bottle. He was already aware of what Shelly would demand.

"Put her to sleep, it's going to be a long drive. He's a careful little pervert, but that's good for us too." Shelly flicked her lighter a few times to ignite it. She inhaled the cigarette pursed between her lips deeply after burning off its tip.

"Already on it." Ed grabbed Lily's nose. Fatigued, hungry and decimated, Lily's resistance was composed of fidgeting her fingers and weakly waving her head. Lily gasped for air like a goldfish thrown out of its bowl. Ed shoved the bottle into Lily's mouth, and grape flavored syrup poured down her throat. Lily couldn't help herself from gulping down the medicine.

"I spiked it just in case. She shou… out …til…" Ed's words began to trail off as Lily descended into a deep slumber. The engine turned and the car rocked her to sleep as it rumbled down the highway.

***

Sounds of vast water shattering against its current softly awoke Lily. It was a more pleasant way to be taken out of her slumber than before. The world was still dark and her eyes still shut, but the gentler ambiance soothed her. The air was different. It wasn't the rough scent of a worn out car but a softer scent of a musty room. Right away, she noticed that her limbs felt free, and she was lying on the soft cushions, presumably a bed.

Sarah's mind was twisting in repulse. She was in agony. The pieces were coming together.

"Hey there! I see that you're awake," a tender male voice spoke to Lily. It was far too compassionate to be her father's. Lily had hoped that perhaps the whole thing was a bad dream, and this man would take her to back to her parents.

"Those, crude, crude people. I'm not even sure what they gave you. Though, from your breath, it seems like cough syrup."

Lily opened her eyes. There was no blindfold.

Above her was a round ceiling light that lit the room, and her head was lying on a pillow. She wasn't in a car anymore. It *was* a dream. She looked at the man who was sitting beside her.

Dr. Cowan. Doctor Bradley Cowan. Sarah didn't need to see more but she had to.

He was a man Lily had never seen before, but he had a very comforting smile. His hair was a dirty blond that was barely beginning to

170

gray, and he had warm brown eyes that were slightly magnified by his glasses. He was a well-kempt man and had a runner's physique.

"You're alright now." The doctor smiled and gently touched Lily's face. Lily began to cry.

Lily said, "I want to see my mommy and daddy."

"I'm your daddy, sweetheart," said the man to Lily's surprise.

"You're not my daddy!"

"I'm your new daddy. I'll take care of you and never treat you wrong like your old family did. I'm your new daddy, Ruby, my jewel."

"My name's not Ruby." Lily shook her head with tears still drizzling down her face.

"Yes it is, Ruby. That's your new name now from your new daddy. For your new family."

"No!" Lily reached for her pillow and threw it at the man. She felt cold steel rattling around her ankle. The pillow throw had no effect, and the doctor merely smiled at his Ruby.

Lily looked at her foot to find an iron chain wrapped around her leg and tied to a metal loop skewered to the concrete floor. The room was more of a concrete box than a room, its only decoration being the bed itself and an old rug covering the concrete floor. The chain seemed just long enough for her to walk off the bed to the toilet that was in the corner. There were no windows. The only sign of the outside world was the gentle sound of the tide that she could still hear from the outside.

"I'll let your misbehavior slide today since this is just your first day, Ruby. But you'll have to learn to behave. I'll not let you be a mischievous young lady." The man patted her on the head. Lily smacked the man's hand away from her.

"I guess I was wrong. Maybe it'll be a good time to give you the taste of the discipline you'll receive for such behavior," the doctor stood and headed for the door. Pure darkness was on the other side of the door, and he appeared to seep into it. Lily stumbled and hurried towards the door, but the chain tied around her ankles made her barely out of reach.

"In a minute, you'll even miss having that," the man said as he walked in with bundle of chains in his hands. He tossed the chains on the bed and stood over Lily. She fled to the corner of the room.

"Can I go home? Please, can I go home?" Lily begged.

Watching the child sob brought a satisfied smile to the man's face. She was so small and so helpless. He wanted to protect her and nurture her. Give guidance to the innocent soul.

"You *are* home, Ruby," the man said kindly as he grabbed Lily's arm and dragged her towards him. "...and you're my little jewel.

Think of me as your father and your best friend. The sooner we can get along, the sooner we can find some peace and harmony in our lives together." The man gave Lily a confiding smile. He hoped that she'd like him soon.

Lily kicked and struggled but the doctor proved to be too strong for her. It didn't take much for the doctor to chain each of Lily's wrists and her remaining ankle to the bed, leaving her stretched out like a piece of meat. He reached into his pocket and pulled out a blindfold.

"Since this is your first night and your first punishment, I'll be gentle. In the future, I'll be less magnanimous. Got it, my dear Ruby?" The man put the blindfold over Lily's eyes and kissed her on her forehead.

"Good night, my jewel!" Lily heard the flicking of the switch and the electricity fizzling away from the light above her.

She imagined in the darkness her dad and her mom. Sarah figured little Lily's imagination was probably more rosy and romanticized than how they actually were, but for that short time Lily imagined her parents, there was a small peace in her frayed heart.

Chapter 24
THE LIFE WITH DR. COWAN

Lily quickly learned that for her to be fed, unchained, and relatively unharmed, she had to listen to the doctor. The doctor didn't visit her every day, but when he did, he was almost always calm and gentle with her. He'd read her stories and talk to her about his days even though she was sure that he knew she didn't understand. Sometimes he even brought a computer so they could watch movies. The meals they had were usually fruits and vegetables, and he'd make her brush her teeth afterwards by the sink and the toilet in the room. For showers, the doctor made her wear a blindfold as he led her out the room and up a long case of stairs. At the top of the stairs, Lily would hear the door open and the air would change to warm and pleasant. She enjoyed the shower days because she didn't have to be in the room anymore, and though she couldn't see, the smell of a fresh room and of scented soaps and shampoos made the trips worth it.

Doctor Cowen had a seed. He wanted to grow the seed into a tree big and fine enough to carve into a doll of his liking. Or at least something enough for him to not feel degraded having. After a while, he even let her keep some of the children's books he read to her. Sometimes he'd bring new clothes for Lily to try on, and he'd watch her as she tried on the new clothes. Lily liked dresses.

Some visits, especially the visits when the doctor would be away for a while, the doctor left Lily chained and blindfolded. Darkness quickly became a friend to Lily who learned to not be afraid of it. Even if it wasn't for the blindfold, when the doctor turned off the light, there were only the darkness, a blanket of the sound from the swashing waters, and the occasional thud from the walls.

The nothingness became an open canvass for Lily to create anything and everything. She'd often dream of the ocean she heard every day and visualize what she saw in the books and the TV. What was a once mere imagination became tinder to realized mirages. The darkness disappeared and she could see what she wanted to see, and sometimes she could feel what she saw. The shy kisses of the ocean breeze as the water clashes on her legs, the brush of shoulders as she walked through the busy streets of foreign lands where she would wonder where all the people were headed, and the comfort of her mother's warmth as she buried herself into her chest. Lily wasn't sure how many hugs she received from her mama and papa or if the fading faces of her parents were to be even trusted. But she knew the doctor's hugs and words of his love for her felt empty and bizarre.

Days went by with the familiar routine for years.

On one particular day, the doctor showed up with a new dress and cake for Lily. He said it was her—Ruby's—birthday. Lily wasn't sure what day it was, and in fact, she couldn't even remember what her actual birthday was. But she was happy to see the festive food and the bright mood of the doctor. They had never celebrated her birthday before. He sang a happy birthday song for her and as a treat, he brought his laptop to watch a movie with her. However, when the movie finished the doctor didn't leave as he usually did. The doctor said that he'd spend the night.

"I think it's time," said the doctor with eager eyes and a lustful smile.

He didn't chain Lily to the bed. Instead, the doctor simply lied beside her and placed her head on his arm. He watched her with such intensity that it made Lily feel uncomfortable. He was inspecting and admiring her. His hand gently reached for Lily and…

***

"So how long does this usually take her?" Kalin asked as he watched Sarah and Lily drifting away into a trance.

"Usually seconds. Never more than minutes," Landris replied. He was always secretly fascinated by Sarah's 'gift' and observed carefully anytime he had the chance to witness it.

"When she's done, she can—" Julian was cut short by Sarah.

"GET OFF! GET OFF OF ME!" Sarah screamed as she flung away from Lily. Lily eyes were opened wide with surprise from Sarah's distress. She was frozen between wanting to comfort Sarah and the fear that she was the one who caused Sarah's distress.

Sarah looked around like a panicking animal and realized she was back in their little hut. Her breathing was rapid and irregular and her hands shook as they clenched the dirt beneath her hand until they squeezed through.

"Are you alright, Sarah?" Julian approached Sarah carefully.

"DON'T!" Sarah raised her hand between her and the encroaching Julian. She took a deep breath. "Sorry. Just… just leave me be."

Kalin wrapped his arm around Lily, and, her mind slowly settling, Sarah looked at Lily. The girl seemed as startled as she was and filled with concern. Sarah quickly crawled towards Lily and pulled her away from Kalin, wrapping her into her chest.

"I'm sorry, Lily," Sarah spoke as a small tear rolled down her cheek. "I'm so sorry." Sarah knew her words didn't mean much. What she witnessed for moments were years that were ingrained into this girl's life forever.

"I'm sorry, too!" Lily wasn't sure why she was sorry, but she felt like she was sorry.

"No, Lily." Sarah's voice was firm. "You have nothing to be sorry about. It's not your fault." Sarah pulled away from Lily a little bit too meet her eye to eye. "We'll find your parents," Sarah declared. "We will definitely find your parents."

Lily smiled and Sarah smiled back to her. Sarah had a very different reason and feelings for looking for Lily's parents.

SHE WHO CAST THE FIRST STONE

It was a day like any other. Ruby was lying on her bed in the darkness and wondered whether or not the doctor would come today. She hoped that he wouldn't. The sound of thuds from the walls were orchestrating with the clashes of the tides.

Lights off.

Dr. Cowen flicked the switch at the top of his long stairs out of the basement. It was time for a break from the project that had been taking him all hours of the previous night until morning. He needed coffee. He really needed coffee. And maybe some toast. He braced himself in the darkness before he opened the door. He knew what was about to come. When he opened the door, the bright light of the morning blinded him. He shielded his eyes with his filthy black hands and felt as if his clothes and body were dirtier than they seemed in the sunlight than they were in the dim basement.

"Get back here! Jade!"
Ruby heard Dr. Cowen screaming outside the door. Then a female scream and a thud. Startled, Ruby got up from her bed. She was a good girl last time Dr. Cowan came around; only her left leg was chained and she wasn't even blindfolded.
The door handle jiggled.
The jingle of keys.

Instant coffee was a marvelous invention just like the electric kettle. As he watched the coffee powder melt into his hot water, Dr. Cowan allowed himself to relax. He instantly regretted it. His body felt heavy, and his mind felt cloudy. His head was aching from last night. He searched with his fingers, combing through his hair to find the aching area. His fingertips felt over the crusted blood. It didn't hurt very much anymore, but he still had a mind-numbing headache that didn't go well with his fatigue. He was ready to collapse on his bed. But he wasn't done yet. There was still too much to do, and he needed some fresh air.

"So there really was another. You're too damn quiet, you know that?" An unfamiliar girl entered the room and turned on the light. She was dressed only in an oversized t-shirt that went down to her knees.

Ruby fled to the corner of her room. It felt bizarre for her to see someone other than the doctor after all these years.

"You must be the Ruby that he talks about. My name is Jade. That's my actual name. God, you're so young. Come on, we have to get out of here!" Jade ran to Ruby and started to search through the group of keys she pilfered to find the right one for Ruby's freedom.

"Don't be scared; I'm not here to hurt you. I'm here to save you and me," Jade assured the frightened child. Her hands trembled as she went through key after key. She didn't seem that much older than Ruby.

"Ruby? Ugh, you must hate being called that. What's your name?" Jade asked. She was met with silence. "Can't you talk? God, what has he done to you?"

Ruby didn't speak much to the doctor, and hadn't spoken to a single person other than the doctor since she arrived in the basement. She couldn't find her voice to talk to Jade.

Jade found the right key.

The lock clicked and released itself from the chain. The joy was overwhelmingly evident on Jade's face.

"Come on!" Jade screamed as she grabbed onto Ruby's wrist and pulled her towards the door.

"JADE!" the doctor screamed from the dark abyss.

The fresh ocean breeze was always rejuvenating for the doctor. He sipped on his coffee and watched the endless blue of the sound.

"Hey, neighbor! Do you know what that..." Mr. Barkley from the house next door waved. He was on his patio enjoying his morning cigarette when he turned to greet the doctor, but his greeting trailed off in confusion at sight of the doctor's state. "What happened to you?" Mr. Barkley remarked, staring at Doctor Cowan's blackened white shirt, hands, and smudged face. His hair was a mess, and he hadn't even shaved yet in the morning.

"Late night," Doctor said as he sipped on his coffee. "Decided to clean out my basement."

Mr. Barkley chuckled as he finished his cigarette. He tossed it in the water and waved the doctor goodbye.

"Is that Brad?" Dr. Cowan heard Mrs. Barkley from the other side of the patio doors. "Hi, Brad! Good morning! Boy, you're a mess!" Mrs. Barkley poked her head out and waved at Dr. Cowan.

"Good morning, Leslie!" Dr. Cowan waved back. Mrs. Barkley gave him a wide smile and closed the patio doors. The doctor finished his coffee. He was really pushing his luck with time. Just as he was about to turn back and walk into his home, the doctor saw something he had never seen before. A blemish to his majestic, but familiar, view of the soundfront—a thin pillar of light that pierced the skies over the horizon.

Jade and Ruby ran down the dark and narrow corridor. It wasn't very long until they were blocked by a dead end.

"Jade! You're being a very bad girl!" Dr. Cowan yelled as he struggled to stand up. He felt his head where Jade had struck him. Blood. The doctor let out an incoherent scream as he made his way out of Jade's room.

"Don't worry." Jade held Ruby's hand tightly. "It'll be okay. It'll be okay."

Jade went with her gut and pushed on the dead end. It was heavy but it moved and revealed the actual basement of Dr. Cowan's house.

The doctor decided there was no time for him to wonder about the odd light. He walked back into his home, but he didn't get very far into the house.

The doorbell rang.

The doctor froze. Could it be? He lifted his heavy legs and turned back to the door as slowly and quietly as possible.

The doorbell rang again.

Dr. Cowan carefully approached the peephole on the door.

His heart stopped. He recalled his days as a student aspiring to be a doctor when he had suffered from multiple episodes of sleep paralysis. The sensation he was feeling was uncomfortably similar to that feeling. His whole body was frozen and his eye glued to the peephole of his door. He had to forcefully will his mouth to open and his lungs to suck in air to prevent suffocation. His arm flung out from the shoulder, and his hand slammed onto the door. He didn't mean to do that. The hand was now also stuck.

The girl ringing the doorbell looked startled. But she rang the doorbell again.

Ding-dong.

Dr. Cowan's mouth was gaping and dry, and no words made their way out of his throat.

The damn doorbell rang again.

Briefly, Dr. Cowan wondered if the doorbell had always been that obnoxious. It was the standard two-tone chime of a one high and one low note of electronically reproduced sound. He should really change it.

Ding-dong.

It really was *obnoxious*.

"WHO," the first word came out much louder than he wanted. The doctor cleared his throat. "Who is it?"

"Run! Ruby!" Jade pushed the wall and began to run through the base-ment. Ruby followed after her, but her steps were slow and clumsy. Jade looked back. The doctor was running after them now. Jade turned around and grabbed Ruby by her wrist, pulled her towards the stairs.

"Get help!" Jade screamed as she launched herself at the doctor's legs, causing them to tumble to the ground.

Ruby frantically climbed the stairs, not even realizing the tears drizzling down her face. Her heart was beating much too fast, and the air was too pain-ful to breathe. About halfway up the stairs, she stumbled and climbed the rest of the way on her hands and knees. She heard another incoherent scream by the Doctor and a yelp from Jade intertwined with the loud and disgusting thuds of the Doctor smashing Jade's head onto the ground.

Ruby was too frightened to look back. It was a moment she'd be ashamed of until her last breath. She had to escape and get help.

The girl seemed uncertain how to answer. His little Ruby was mak-ing that familiar slightly distorted face of despair from confusion.

Ding-dong. She decided to simply ring the doorbell again.

Bradley. BradleyBradleyBradley. The doctor tried to piece together his shattered nerves. *Your first mistake was responding to that door bell. If the cops are here, there's not much you can do at this point. Should I run? Run where? Face the music; the cat and mouse game would be more nerve-wreck-ing. Claim that she's crazy or that it was self-defense or something.*

The doctor's trembling hand reached for the door knob. He slowly opened the door and poked his head outside. She really was there. She looked tired and uneasy to see him. As he looked around, he only saw his empty front yard and driveway. If the cops were around, there really wouldn't be a point of them hiding at this point.

So she was alone?

As soon as the thought sprinted across his head, Dr. Cowan grabbed Ruby by her arm and pulled her in. Door shut. Locks locked. The doctor's hand swept hard against Ruby's cheek.

"You ungrateful girl!" the doctor snarled. "You ungrateful, selfish, bad! BAD! Girl!" His hand swept even harder against Ruby's cheek again.

The doctor then pulled Ruby into his chest and gave her a tight hug. He squeezed until Ruby coughed for air.

"But thank you for coming home. You'll be good from here on, right? I'll forgive you if you say you'll be good from here on. Can you say that for me, Ruby? That you'll be good?" The doctor pulled away to look at Ruby in the eye.

Her eyes were different than he remembered. There was a hint of determination he had never seen in her eyes before.

Ruby came out of the basement and ran for the closest door. The stomp of the doctor chasing after her made her frantic.

"Ruby! Stop!" the doctor screamed as he chased after Ruby. The door she opened was the bedroom, but she saw another door that seemed to lead outside.

"What," the doctor carefully began. "What did you do out there? Where did you go? How did you..." He noticed a black, metal-like, armband on Ruby's wrist. "Did you meet someone?"

The doctor ran after Ruby to his bedroom, but slowed his pace once he realized Ruby ran out to the patio. It was a dead end. Ruby confronted the ocean for the first time, and the water violently clashed below her. The doctor walked menacingly towards her with blood running down his face and in his eyes.

"Be a good girl, Ruby," the doctor demanded.

Ruby shook her head. She let out a short scream in defiance. The scream frightened the doctor enough to hasten his pace again to grab Ruby. Seeing the doctor running towards her, Ruby climbed the patio's fence and jumped into the ocean that kept her company all those years.

Ruby followed the doctor's eyes to her wrist.

"Yes," she softly replied.

"An-and? Who was she? He?"

"I don't really know." Ruby looked the doctor in the eyes. He looked relieved at her answer.

"Well, what's important now is that you're home. The world out there is frightening. This is where you belong. Let's take you to your room." The doctor tried to pull Ruby along by her arm, but she resisted. In fact, the more he tugged, the heavier she seemed to get. It felt as if he was pulling on a boulder.

"I'm here for her. And I will be going away with her," Ruby spoke as sternly as her soft voice could be.

"Her?" The doctor's glare changed. He didn't look at her like his lost puppy came home, but rather as an enemy. A threat. The eyes were full of contempt and vex. Merciless and cold. Though he still held her hand, he retracted away from her and towered over her with his back straight.

"Where is she?" Ruby didn't want to look away from the man,

though his sudden change sent chills down her body and made her heart race. Her head began to cloud and numb. But her eyes were steadfast and she continued to face him.

"You mean *Jade*?" the doctor spoke coldly, but his lips stretched into a small smile. His body frozen, only his lips moved. "The terrible, terrible girl that turned you against me?"

The air between the doctor and his once-daughter grew tense. There was a certain joy he felt staring into Ruby's nervous eyes. In them, he also saw the happy days he spent with her and the days that could continue after this mess had been cleaned up.

"She paid the price for what you've done, Ruby. You should ask her to forgive you sometime," the doctor finished.

"I want to see her. I want to go away with her." To Ruby's dismay, her words trembled.

"Oh. OH! You're going? With her? Of course! That's why you came back! But where to, Ruby? This is home! You're going to be a bad girl and leave daddy again?"

The doctor's palm struck across Ruby's cheeks again.

"You haven't learned a damned thing, have you?"

Blood rushed through her white cheeks, and her head turned from the impact. But it didn't faze her. It had been a long time since he could reach into her and make her feel something. She faced the doctor again and looked him in the eyes. The doctor twitched. The courage did not derive from desensitization to the pain and the humiliation. She could be numb, she could disassociate herself, and she could escape with the desensitization. She had already given up on herself long ago before she even realized she gave up on herself. She had gotten used to—was groomed—for the life that she had with him. But Jade was the knife that tore through the veil of her misguided contentment. Jade was her courage.

The doctor stared down at the insolent Ruby. His hands wanted strike her again. And again. And again. Until the girl was bleeding from her lips and looking up at him with pleading, begging eyes and asking for forgiveness. After that, all would be well. Their lives will go back to normal again. But he had a better idea.

"You want to see her? That's what you want?" the doctor snarled.

Ruby nodded.

"Come then." The doctor briskly walked away from Ruby. Ruby was engulfed by the doctor's shadow as he led the way. His back was cold and sinister. He sauntered either as if he dreaded what he was about to do or was relishing in the seconds leading up to it.

The hallway was sprinkled with a distinct aroma that tickled Ruby's nose and senses. As they approached closer to the door, the smell became more cloying and Ruby's hand rose up to cover her nose.

The doctor's hand turned the knob and opened the door, and a monsoon of stench flooded out, making Ruby gasp for air. The doctor looked back and smiled at Ruby's suffering in amusement.

"Not going to stop now, are you? We are almost there to her." The doctor's hand reached out to Ruby's head, but she swatted it away and went down the stairs. It was dark, much like the night before.

"Jade?" Ruby weakly cried out. Each step, she seeped deeper into the dark. And as she went deeper into the dark, the more potent the stench became. It was hard to believe that the stench could grow more and more foul…

"Jade?"

…and thicker. Each time she called out to Jade, she felt as if she could bite down and chew on the rotten air inside her mouth.

When her feet touched the familiar concrete, she knew she had reached the bottom. The descent down the stairs felt like an eternity compared to the previous night's ascent up. She looked up at the doctor who still had the same smile on his face. The light had engulfed him and left only a silhouette of a man.

"Jade?" She searched in the darkness until the tip of her foot struck a hard, rubber-like stump. As the thin surface layer of the stump crumbled on her toe, Ruby felt a chill down her spine.

Lights on.

The doctor's feet echoed with each step. The light turned Ruby's worst fears into reality.

"It was quite rash of me, really. I admit it. You two put me in a panic," he spoke into the air as he gradually descended the stairs

A peculiar feeling.

Although Ruby didn't know for certain what she was looking at, but at the same time she *knew exactly* what she was looking at. The stench that only lingered around her nose now felt as if it was inside of her. She felt as if her friend was inside of her.

"Of course, my better instincts were screaming that there were better ways to take care of the problem, but sometimes an urge just prevails through any sort of common sense or logic." He stopped his descent for a moment and relished in watching Ruby struggle to accept what she was looking at.

"But, why?" Ruby whispered.

"Fear…" The doctor didn't seem to hear her. "…rage, joy, and love. Those fundamental emotions of what makes humans, human. It's amazing how these emotions can revert all the progress a man and his species has made to civilize themselves."

Ruby turned her head back to the doctor. His words were air, a buzz, a screech.

"I was quite frightened, Ruby. You almost ruined my life." The doctor finally reached the basement. "I was distraught how quickly my two bundles of joy could become my biggest source of anguish. You two were all that I had."

The doctor slithered over to Ruby.

"I was enraged. Perhaps I just wanted to see her burn. Punish her for causing me such pain. Make her feel what she had made *me* feel. And perhaps, I hoped that you'd come back and see what your betrayal had done. Punish you for thinking of leaving me. Make you feel what she had to endure because of you."

Stop talking.

Ruby's hollow eyes delighted the doctor. She seemed frightened and in despair. Hopeless and gutted, and riddled with guilt. She would never dare think of being so audacious again.

"But as soon as I saw you, I was overjoyed and forgot all the anger. And now, my little Ruby..." The doctor placed his hand on Ruby's bony shoulder. "My love for you is going against all of my common sense to forgive you and give you another chance at our life together."

Stop. Talking.

The doctor finally made eye contact with Ruby again. His lips stretched into a smile.

"What do you say?" The doctor offered his dove and olive branch.

The ground beneath the doctor began to quiver. Startled, the doctor stood and looked around to discover the entire house was shaking.

"Get down!" the doctor cried, bringing Ruby to the cold hard ground with her face right next to Jade's as the doctor lay on top of her.

"Off." Ruby commanded.

The doctor did not hear her.

"Get. OFF!" Ruby shouted.

The doctor ignored her.

The frustration and anger came out of Ruby in a sob and a wail. The house and all that was in it began to violently shake until the Doctor finally realized it couldn't be a simple earthquake.

Outside were Dr. Cowan's concerned neighbors who were watching their beloved local doctor's home turning paranormal. First that light and now this. Some responded by calling for the authorities, while others responded by recording the event, but they all gasped when the entire house evaporated into dust that swirled around like a small hurricane.

And within the dusty hurricane, they saw a young girl they had never seen before and the doctor floating, flailing and screaming.

Later, Dr. Cowan's long-time neighbor Mrs. Barkley, described watching the doctor as if she was watching a man drown in the air. His pleading and cries were swept away in a storm of dust that was once his home. And they were hopelessly lost to the Witch.

When all the dust had settled, the Witch stood in an empty space that was once a home filled with the life of a Bradley Cowan. All of his light and all of his shadows were gone without a trace. Around her was a crowd recording and giving birth to the one who would forever be known as the Witch. The Gifted who threw the first stone against the mankind.

Chapter 25
THE MANHUNT - ONE

"Wait!" Sarah stopped Landris for making the call to Director Jones. Her voice was not only authoritative enough to stop Landris, but it also left him silent without any snarky remarks or comebacks.

"You." Sarah pointed at Kalin with such ferocious eyes that it startled him. "I need to talk to you." Lily squeezed Sarah's arm and looked between her and Kalin in confusion.

"It'll be alright, Lily," Kalin said.

"Yes, it'll be alright." Sarah gently brushed her hand through Lily's hair.

"Sarah? Everything okay?" Julian whispered into Sarah's ear.

"I don't know yet," Sarah whispered with her rage-filled eyes glued on Kalin. She grabbed Kalin by his wrist and dragged him outside. They walked away from the hut, heading into the woods. When Sarah felt the distance gave them enough privacy, she let go of Kalin's wrist and crossed her arms. She looked at him with a look of contempt but said nothing.

"Did you know?!" Sarah finally spoke. Heartbeat fast with anger, she tried to remember that Kalin didn't deserve to be on the receiving end of all of what she was feeling right now. Not yet, at least.

"Calm down! I don't know much of her past! She never talked about it, and she didn't seem like she wanted to. I could only piece things together from little clues, and from what little I figured, it didn't feel like something I should dig out of her." Kalin never expected this side of Sarah.

"Calm down?! You...!" Sarah stopped her sentence as if she was halting an eruption. She snatched up Kalin's hand. Instantaneously, all that Sarah saw with her eyes inside Lily's mind was transferred to Kalin. In a fit of rage, Kalin let out of scream and smashed his fist against the nearest tree. Aided by the streams, his fist went right through the trunk, and the other end exploded with splinters.

The noise of Kalin's rage echoed throughout the woods and didn't go missed by the three waiting in the hut. Lily immediately got to her feet and headed for the exit, but Landris grabbed her wrist. Perhaps it was how quickly and forcefully Landris grabbed her, but Lily's body reacted to the haunting memories engraved into her body and tore her hand away from Landris with a yelp. She looked at him as if she had seen her worst nightmares looming right in front of her.

"Sorry, sorry," Landris said gently and raised his hands in the air in submission. "…Everything will be okay. They're alright. I promise you, they're alright. Just trust them."

There was gentleness in Landris's eyes that Lily had never seen before. He pleaded with concern, and she reluctantly sat back down and grabbed her folding papers. Something to distract her mind from everything else.

"You had NO IDEA. *NO IDEA* of what that girl had to go through, and you dragged her around the world?! FOR WHAT?!" Sarah erupted.

"I DIDN'T KNOW!" Kalin ripped his hand out of the tree trunk. His hand was torn and bleeding, but the streams immediately ignited from his hand and began to heal it.

"Both of us…." Kalin's voice was soft and beaten. "…didn't have a place to stay. No home and nowhere to go. We were both being chased for our own reasons. I guess both of us knew we had a past we wanted to run away from, but we never dug it out of each other. We didn't need to or want to. When we were with each other… we didn't care about each other's pasts."

Kalin felt guilty and selfish, and his shame prohibited him from looking Sarah in the eye. "What mattered was the here and now, and taking care of one another. We both wanted to just get away and see the world, enjoy our lives living in the moment. Never sit still long enough for the past to catch up. Seeing how big the world was, how many different lives there were, it made us feel small and, strangely enough, that made us feel better.

But the problem was"—Kalin smiled with a mixture of endearment and embarrassment—"anytime she saw someone in need, she couldn't help herself. She always said…" Kalin stopped himself.

"Anyway… After seeing all the good that we were doing, I thought that maybe this is what we were supposed to do. It felt right, you know? And I thought it would help clear her name. But the world had a way of twisting things and ignoring all that we've done. They just wanted to see us for what they wanted us to be."

Kalin paused for a moment and inspected his healed hand. It was as good new. "I don't get it," Kalin continued. "How did turning us into their nightmares help them sleep better?"

"She needs help," Sarah said. "She needs a chance to heal. Don't get in her way from getting better."

"I was always planning to find her—us—a sort of a safe haven. Find us a way to make our lives better. Looking for her parents was part of that! But now… after that…"

"Are you guys…" Sarah wondered if she should finish her sentence. "Are you two in… because you know that you can't be, right? That's not fair for her. That's not right."

"No! Of course not! She's my best friend! She's more like a sister than anything!" Kalin quickly rejected Sarah's implications.

"Good," Sarah said. "At least, you can't be right now. After all this is over, as soon as we find the chance—we need to get her help."

"Yeah," Kalin answered weakly. "Are you sure this Director Jones can be the help that she needs?"

"Yes," Sarah said adamantly. "I truly believe that."

Kalin nodded. He rested his hand on the damaged tree as if he was telling it he was sorry.

"I want to make them feel what she felt," Kalin said. "Her parents."

"Yeah. Me too," Sarah answered. "I don't know about even looking for them, or if it's even worth it. But I feel like Lily deserves at least that."

"Let's head back. Let's get this done," Kalin began heading toward the hut.

"I'm sorry," Sarah spoke as Kalin walked past her. He stopped in his tracks. "I probably shouldn't have even shown you that. It's just…" Sarah began to shiver and her voice began to shake. "What I've shown you are just images. I chose to do that. When I see it… I experience everything Lily experienced, and it's just…" The strength from Sarah's leg gave out and she fell to her knees. Her head was dizzy. Kalin walked over to her and helped her stand, and then he took her into his arms and held her shaking body.

***

"I think the easiest way would be if Lily could open that portal for us to where Ms. Jones is?" Julian suggested as he munched on an apple from Lily's book.

"If I can see the place and if it's not too far." Lily munched on a cookie from her book. She was folding more of the tiny cranes that Sarah taught her. Kalin took the cookie from her hand.

"You've had enough," Kalin told Lily who was shocked by her cookie theft. Kalin tossed the rest of the cookie into his mouth. It was the last cookie, and he hadn't even had one yet.

"What a party-pooper," Sarah remarked and put her arms around the now sad Lily who had been denied indulging her sweet tooth. "You're getting good at folding these," Sarah complimented as she picked up and looked at Lily's latest crane. It was a blue one.

"For a tiny girl, she can pack down cookies. Was that like her 6th?

7th?" Landris grabbed Lily's book and flipped through the pages for a snack himself.

"How far is too far?" Julian wanted to get back on topic.

"I'm sure we don't have to worry about sending you guys over. We have gone across the ocean to other countries before." Kalin's answer battled Julian and he stared, wide-eyed. He felt envious and inadequate as someone with a similar 'gift.'

Makes sense. Landris thought, thinking of how Kalin and Lily popped up all over the world. Landris pointed at a bag of spicy potato chips in the book and handed it to Lily.

"It's harder, though, when it's far." Lily took the book from Landris. "This is Kalin's favorite. And it's the last one." Lily gave a sly smirk to Kalin as she popped the bag out of the page. Cookie vengeance crossed off the to-do list.

Landris made certain to maintain eye contact with Kalin as he thoroughly enjoyed the first chip.

"Did you ever try to…" Julian's question was cut short by the expected phone call.

"Yo," Landris answered the phone as he popped another chip into his mouth.

"'Yo'? You've gone and lost your little mind, baby brother." Director Jones replied.

"You have to call us on a video call." Landris ended the call.

The phone rang immediately again, but this time with an option to answer the call with a video feed. When Landris answered the call, his phone screen lit up with face of Ms. Jones and her office in the background. He could also see Yuri sitting on the sofa in the background sipping on what he assumed to be either coffee or booze.

"So why was it so imperative that I contact with video…" Nancy paused for a moment and studied the background of Landris's video feed. "Where are you guys staying?"

Landris glimpsed behind him. "What does it look like? It's shelter formed with trees and tree roots."

"Right." Nancy saw Lily huddled with Sarah next to Landris. "Is that *her*?"

"Yep. The famous Witch. Making paper cranes."

Nancy studied the Witch. She was not impressed. The child reminded her of a beaten dog or perhaps a stray cat? A stray-beaten-kitten.

"Right, well," Ms. Jones continued. "We figured out how to get you guys home."

"Right, well." Landris waved the Witch and Sarah over. "We don't need any fancy pick up now. Our friend, Lily"—Landris pointed at the Lily—"will take care of that for us." Landris handed the phone to

Lily.

"Oh, really?" Ms. Jones smiled brightly. "You are quite the talented young lady, aren't you? It's good to finally see you, Lily!"

Lily looked away from Ms. Jones and her cheeks blossomed red.

"Could you point the phone somewhere else?" Lily asked.

"I'm sorry?" As Ms. Jones was about to ask for clarification, she felt Yuri standing behind her.

"Hello, there!" Yuri squeezed into the video screen. "You must be the Witch! I'm Yuri! You're even younger than I thought! And quite the pretty little thing, aren't ya!" Yuri laughed heartily.

"Don't mind him," Landris whispered to Kalin who seemed concerned.

But Lily was frozen stiff and merely stared at the video call.

"You're frightening the poor girl, Mr. Ivanov!" Ms. Jones pushed Yuri out of the frame. "Now, what exactly did you want me to do?"

"She needs you to point the camera somewhere in the office where there's an open area," Kalin spoke out of the frame. Lily shifted the phone so it included Kalin who was standing behind her.

"Hello, young man. You're different than I imagined. Your hair really is very red," Ms. Jones noted as she flipped the phone toward the area where Mr. Ivanov was sitting at the beginning of the call. "Move the sofa out of the way, will you, Mr. Ivanov?"

Mr. Ivanov obliged and moved the coffee table with the sofa to clear the area.

"Will that be enough?" Ms. Jones asked.

Lily nodded and handed the phone to Kalin. He held the phone in front of her so that she can see the office, and she took a few steps back. The three students who stood behind her stepped back with her.

The Witch raised her index finger and closed one of her eyes, gently biting her lower lip as if she was aiming a gun. Each second felt like minutes as Mr. Ivanov and Director Jones waited in anticipation, though they weren't exactly sure for what.

When Lily felt ready, the tip of her index finger began to glow a luminescent light. She crouched down and led her finger to the ground. From there, she led her finger up and over her head and down again until it formed an arch that resembled a door.

"Look," Though he was not in the frame, they could hear Mr. Ivanov's voice. He pointed out to Director Jones the same arch that was vaguely visible—like a shattered glass panel—in their office.

With the door formed, Lily began to makes lines across from one end to the other over and over and from side to side, top to bottom, and at times, even over the other lines until the inside of the door seemed like shattered pieces of glass held together.

Mr. Ivanov and Director Jones watched as the pieces formed

themselves in their office as Lily drew them.

Lily stood in front of her door and rested her whole palm on the cracked pieces of the plane.

"Don't embarrass yourself, Lily," Kalin teased.

Lily turned her head and gave Kalin a look. Her entire palm glowed like her fingertip before as it rested on the cracked pieces. After she breathed in some air through her nose, Lily pushed. The fissures throughout the door began to erupt with light. As the pieces fractured, they resisted, trying to stay put. But Lily grunted and pushed harder.

Director Jones and Mr. Ivanov watched the pieces bulge as Lily pushed. The dimension was fighting back hard as it could against the Witch's might.

"Should we help her?" Julian asked.

"To us, it's like trying to push air," Kalin answered.

Lily pushed harder and harder. The task was definitely more difficult than the time when she rescued Kalin and her three new friends. After another loud grunt, the pieces of the dimension scattered. Much like before, they dangled in the air as if still attached to their former position by an invisible cord. The Witch, however, lost her balance and fell flat on to the ground—half of her body still in the woods and the other half in Ms. Jones' office across the nation.

"My God, will you look at that," Director Jones remarked, observing the pieces of dimension floating around. Yuri hovered his fingers around one of the pieces contemplating whether or not he should touch it.

"Want me to help you up?" Kalin asked in a mockingly jovial tone at Lily's fall.

"No, thank you!" Lily cried as she quickly picked herself up, dusting off her one-piece dress. She quickly retreated into the woods side of the portal. Yuri and Nancy, far too impressed by the feat, were at a loss for words.

"I wonder if I can learn to that," Julian murmured.

"In your dreams," Landris replied.

Sarah picked up her belongings and headed toward the portal. Before she went beyond, she handed Lily a crane she had folded.

"Keep practicing! I'll check to see how much you've improved next time we meet." Sarah gave Lily a gentle hug. "Thank you for everything. We'll find your parents. We'll *definitely* find your parents."

Lily returned the hug. She liked being in Sarah's embrace and didn't really want to let her go. Kalin could go. Sarah could stay. Actually, they should both stay. Julian and Landris could go. She just really liked Sarah's hugs.

Julian scrounged around the area and checked to see if he had all of his belongings. As he began to walk towards Ms. Jones' office, he noticed Landris's feet were planted next to Kalin.

"Aren't you coming, Landris?" Julian asked.

"Really?" Landris stared at Julian as if he was looking at the dumbest person in the world. His eyes were full of disappointment and pity for Julian.

First, Julian was flushed with anger. Then he realized why Landris had to stay. He walked over to the office without another word.

"Stay out of trouble!" Director Jones yelled across the portal. "That means you, Landris!"

Sarah and Julian waved goodbye at the three remaining in the woods. Lily was the only one to return the wave. Soon after the good-byes, all of the shattered pieces from the doorway returned to place, and the fissures made by Lily disappeared as if they were never there.

"Some trick that is," Mr. Ivanov remarked.

"Welcome home…" Before Director Jones could properly welcome back her two students, Sarah walked briskly to stand in front of her. "Sarah?"

Sarah's eyes were ignited in ways Ms. Jones had never seen before.

"Ms. Jones, we have to—no, we *need* to find Lily's parents." Sarah approached Ms. Jones' forehead with her hand, but stopped a hair before it made contact until Ms. Jones gave her a nod. When the palm of Sarah's hand touched Ms. Jones forehead, Ms. Jones witnessed all of Lily's past that Sarah had witnessed.

Chapter 26
MANHUNT - TWO

Nancy stepped back. Her eyes widened and her tongue tied, she distanced herself from Sarah's hand. The Director looked around her office. Yuri's curious eyes grew worried when he saw Nancy's startled look. Julian seemed to be waiting on Nancy's response. Sarah seemed as if she expected this. How long was she gone for? Nancy always asked herself this after Sarah showed her the visions. She knew it was probably only seconds that had passed, but it always took her a moment to believe that. The director composed herself and let out a small cough to clear her throat.

"That's quite the turmoil she had to endure," Nancy spoke softly. She walked over to the coffee table that had been pushed away to prepare for Lily's portal and poured herself a cup of tea.

"Show me child." Yuri stomped over to Sarah. "Show me," he demanded.

Sarah was startled for a second, but Nancy gave her the nod.

"I need Mr. Ivanov to know all the details regarding this case if we are going to find the Wit—Lily's parents," Nancy told Sarah.

Sarah placed her hand on Yuri's forehead as she had with Ms. Jones, and after few seconds Yuri's eyes widened and he took a few steps back as Nancy had just moments ago. A misstep caused Yuri to lose his footing, and Julian ported next to the old man to prevent him from falling.

"I forget how tiring seeing your movies can be, child." Yuri chuckled as he patted Julian on the back to let him know that it would be alright to let him stand alone.

"Even seeing the condensed version, it still feels days, weeks, have gone by," Nancy commented as she took a sip of her tea.

After standing tall and taking deep breath, Yuri pulled out a cigar from his pocket and placed it in his lips. Though normally this would bring upon quite the scolding from Nancy, she gave him silent consent for this instance.

"I'm glad I don't have a daughter. I'll never have a daughter." Mr. Ivanov clicked on the lighter and ignited the tip of the cigar. He took a couple of puffs from the cigar and let loose a grand white smoke. "If God could see what we did to the world He gave us, He'd burn us all and spit on the ashes for good measure," Mr. Ivanov spoke as the white smoke poured out of his mouth. "Then again, we are His creations after all." Mr. Ivanov nearly choked on his smoke as he chuckled.

"Is there anything else you can tell us regarding how to find her parents?" Ms. Jones asked.

Sarah shook her head. "No. We probably have a clearer vision of her earlier memories than she does. I tried speaking to her a little bit about it, but her memories seemed to be dominated by her time spent with the doctor. Lily's times with her parents seem like they are mostly faded, and it appeared to disturb her quite a bit when I delved further into the topic, so I decided to leave it alone."

"Probably the wise thing to do considering what happened to her with the doctor." Ms. Jones finished her tea and set the cup down on the table. The idea of bringing the Witch under her wing—under her direction—seemed more difficult than before. But the reward for the effort seemed to glitter more than ever. No time to waste, she had to act fast. "Thank you for all the hard work, both of you. Now go get some rest," Ms. Jones gave them a smile to take with them.

"Ms. Jones," Sarah wanted to add on something. To emphasize the urgency of finding Lily's parents. But at this point, Sarah realized she was being petulant and digressed. "Please let me know if you need me for anything. I'll do everything that I can to find her parents."

As the thick doors to Ms. Jones' office closed behind them, Sarah felt a certain sense of relief that she could trust Ms. Jones to be able to do what would be a near impossible hunt for most others.

"Many naive people in the world..." Yuri spoke as soon as the door closed and left him and Nancy in their own private world. "... believe there is no such thing as *evil*." Yuri chuckled through the smoke fuming out of his mouth. "They think it's childish to think of the world in such black and white terms. They don't realize they're the ones too afraid to admit that the evil in the world is real. Bad guys do exist." Yuri grinned and gave Nancy a playful look. "I'm glad we are at least bad guys with class." Yuri laughed at his own not-exactly-funny remark.

"We have names, a highway sign, knowledge of their probable occupation, some physical characteristics, and I'm guessing we can assume they were somewhere within the area of where the doctor lived," Nancy began her investigation.

"You think tracking the traffickers will help you find the parents, Nancy?"

"Well," Nancy reached for tea biscuit. "It's a starting point. And I'd like the chance to meet them myself."

"Oh?" Yuri smiled in amusement. "I'm not sure if I should feel sorry for them or congratulatory that the great Nancy Jones decided to meet them herself."

Nancy headed for the sofa and the table that had been moved out of place. When she came to stand beside one of them, she looked at Yuri. The old man took the hint and hurried over to help her set the room as it originally was before Sarah and Julian had returned with the Witch's help.

"If they're still alive and in business, they probably haven't gone unnoticed by the actual scary folks whose territory they're stepping in on," Yuri grunted as he set down the final piece of furniture back into place. "I'll tap into my contacts with those people, some people in the bureaus, and probably will have something for you by tomorrow afternoon? Maybe the morning?"

"I bet you can do it by tonight, Mr. Ivanov." Nancy smiled.

Mr. Ivanov returned the smile and swiftly left the room. Left alone, Nancy sat in her chair and buried herself in her thoughts. The vision of the Witch's past played in her mind and she felt disappointed how messy things had gotten.

✻✻✻

"I'm sure Director Jones will find them. Don't worry so much, Sarah," Julian consoled Sarah as they walked through the dorm halls.

"I think I'm going to get cleaned up and be ready just in case the Director needs me." Sarah looked forward to a shower, and some momentary rest from her thoughts and the memories.

As they approached their rooms, the door to Howard's opened and Kiara stepped out. She had a small paper in her hand and her eyes seemed swollen.

"Kiara!" Julian and Sarah both happily called out their friend's name.

Kiara's head quickly turned and she stared at the two like a deer staring at headlights. She'd never thought until that moment that she would feel anything other than happiness to see her friends.

"Julian! Sarah! You guys are back!" Kiara roused up a smile as she shoved the paper into her pocket.

"It's only been a few days, but it feels like it's been ages!" Sarah approached Kiara for a hug.

"Oh my!" Kiara gently stepped away from Sarah. "Have you guys been rolling in the dirt? You're filthy!" She didn't want to take any chances making contact with Sarah.

"Oh, I'm sorry!" Sarah examined her own body. "It was a bit a wild journey."

"Did you guys…?" Kiara carefully began, fully knowing what the answer will be. "Did you guys meet the Witch?" She hoped that by some chance the future had been averted.

"Yes we did!" Julian cheerfully replied for his friend.

"You may find it hard to believe, but she's a joy!" Sarah added on.

"Yes, I do find that hard to believe." Kiara found it hard to maintain her smile.

"Well, this filthy girl is going to take a shower, but we all should have dinner afterwards!" Sarah combed her hair with her fingers to judge its condition.

"I'll go take a shower too and then let Nada and Howard know. I'm sure they're very curious about our little adventure," Julian eagerly volunteered.

"And maybe next time we have dinner, it'll be with Lily." Sarah seemed to really enjoy that idea. "I miss her already, Julian."

"Lily?" Kiara squeezed the question out of her tightening throat.

"Oh, that's the Witch's name," Sarah clarified. "I'm sure you'll love her as well when she comes," Sarah assured Kiara. "Well, I really should get going if I'm going to fit in a shower and a nap by dinner time. I'll see you two later."

"I'm going to head off, too. See you later, Kiara." Julian waved good bye.

The two friends went their separate ways, leaving Kiara where she still stood. She reached into her pocket and pulled the paper out again. On the paper was a list of ingredients Howard asked her help to procure—ingredients needed to give Kiara the means to stop the Witch.

Chapter 27
THE BAD & THE UGLY

It was long drive home, both a pro and a con of living on a farm miles away from the city. Every time she looked up at the stars, she felt like a young girl again lying down on the fields of her family's farm and dreaming of the future. She caught a glimpse of herself in the rear-view mirror. Her eyes were embedded into bags of skin and her face molded by callouses from work and time. She was barely the girl she was twenty years ago. Even her emerald eyes seemed only dimly green, dull and faded. The stars and its memories were as depressing as they were nostalgic, but to her, the pain was worth the mending it gave her.

She was careful not to get too mesmerized by the night sky as she drove down the empty highway. The night sky was perverted by that Light these days, anyway. The road shrouded in darkness only revealed itself as far as the headlights could reach and hid everything else. It was scarcely littered with a few rare stragglers and those on a long journey. If she was to get in an accident on this highway, it could be hours before any help would arrive. But that was another benefit to living so far out; it was secluded. It wasn't messy with people. Her beat-up truck riddled with dirt and mud was the only thing roaring down this empty stretch of concrete.

At night, the surroundings seemed like they were on a loop like an old time cartoon. She drove like that for hours out of the city until she saw the familiar stretch of green and pulled off the highway to an off-road dirt path that led through the fields and to her farmhouse and barn. She could already feel the comfort of her couch perfectly positioned in front of the fireplace and the television. She can taste the soup and the sandwich she picked up from the city warmed up in the microwave and then slushing down her throat. She'd watch the news for a while before attending to the cattle in the barn.

As she passed the fields and her sweet home came into view, her dreams for the evening shattered. The lights were on. Someone was in her home. From the smoke out of the chimney, they were making themselves cozy with her fireplace and probably—they'll burn in hell if they are—lounging in her couch too. Could it be that some of *them* got out of the barn?

She parked her car next to her black SUV and stared at the house for a little while. Where were their cars? Trying to find any hints or clues to who could be inside, she took out her sandwich from the brown paper bag next to her and took a big bite out of it. As she munched away the bread, the meat, the cheese, and the veggies in her mouth, she opened up the soup container and took a small sip, never taking her eyes off the house even for a moment. After she swallowed enough of her dinner, she reached for the shotgun behind her on the gun rack in her truck. It was a typical pump shotgun that she had with her since she was in her teens. The gun was always loaded. She opened up the glove compartment for the box of shells and stuffed her pocket with a handful.

Before doing something that could be unnecessarily reckless, she pulled out her phone and dialed a number by memory. No answer. If it was those people who were in the house unannounced, she was as good as dead anyway.

Shutting the door quietly behind her, she ran towards her front door like those soldiers in the movie where they stormed the beach. She pressed her back against the wall next to the door like the movie star did in so many action movies. Her hands, a bit stiff from the nerves, grabbed the door knob. She slowly turned it enough that it was clear the door was unlocked.

Breach.

The ginger-haired middle age commando slammed the door open and yelled, "WHO'S HERE?!" at the top of her lungs. She could see her fireplace lit and her television turned on. And worst of all, she could see a tiny blond head sticking above the back of her couch. Someone had dared to sit on her couch.

"I was starting to think maybe you weren't coming home tonight," a soft woman's voice responded to her ambusher.

Her hands holding the shotgun stopped trembling. The perpetrator was just a woman. From the voice of her, it was just some petite, young city girl who was probably a lawyer or something like that.

"You are trespassing on private property, girl. I'm calling the cops." Shelly's voice was calmer and had more confidence. The perpetrator scoffed and stood.

"Don't you move, you little whore!" Shelly warned.

The perpetrator turned around. She had a mocking smirk on her face, and she was definitely a girl from the city from the way she was dressed and how she pampered herself. Her pretty face made her mocking smirk and her look of disdain even more despicable.

"I don't think *that's* a good idea," the blond whore said tauntingly.

"Who are you? I suggest answerin' unless you want your face full of lead."

"Then again..." The woman ignored her question and began to

march towards her. She was unarmed with only a tablet in her hand.

"I SAID DON'T MOVE!" Shelly tightened her grip on the gun and adjusted her aim to compensate for how much taller the woman was than her, but the certainty the woman had in the few steps it took to be right in front of her made her trigger finger freeze in its place.

"Maybe you hadn't called the cops in the first place for a reason."

"What?" The woman was close enough that the tip of her gun was already touching her forehead.

"Maybe you didn't shoot just now because you think I'm a cop." Even with the barrel of a shotgun on her head, she was looking down at her.

"You little…" Before Shelly could finish her sentence with a curse, the blond woman slapped her across the face with such ferocity that Shelly felt her breath escape her lungs as she collapsed to the floor. But the slap did knock enough sense out of her that she decided it was time for her to put the blondie down. As she pointed her gun at the woman from the ground, she saw several barrels of military rifles surrounding her. There were men dressed in military gear, Kevlar, earpieces, sidearms, and the rest of the works surrounding her.

Shelly slowly lowered her gun as she studied her surroundings like a scared dog.

"They've been here the whole time." The blond woman fully lowered Shelly's gun for her as she knelt down so she was at the same eye level. The two women shared a brief moment of silence as they stared at one another. Shelly stared at her with the stunned eyes full of fear while Nancy stared right back with that smirk and eyes full of dominance.

Before Shelly could ask her anything, she felt Nancy's backhand striking across her nose. It was deliberate. The blow was painful and made a mess, and as Shelly yelped in pain and dropped her gun to cover her nose with both of her hands, blood guzzled through between her fingers.

"This," Shelly shouted, although it was muffled by her hands covering her nose and also partially covering her mouth. "THIS IS PO-LICE BRUTALITY!" Her eyes were watering as she glared at Nancy. In her mind, she was pinning Nancy to the ground and smacking her with a hammer. The fact that she couldn't do just that infuriated her and could only threaten her. "I'll sue! I'LL SUE THE WHOLE LOT OF YA!"

"Who said we were the police?" The tormentor was amused at her victim's desperate struggle.

"WHAT IS THIS, THEN?! WHO ARE YOU PEOPLE?!" Shelly's voice was muddled by her own gushing blood.

"For me, this is just another day of overtime at work. For you,

Shelly Robins, I suppose this is your sentencing. As for who I am, I am your judge and jury."

Shelly stared at Nancy with a blank look on her face. Did she not pay up the proper amount this month? Did they want more? Or did they just want to take over the operation?

"Your name is Shelly Rosaline Robins. Age forty-six, born on the eleventh of July," Nancy began to read from her tablet. "Your parents were Adam Gabriel Jackson and Sarah Daniel Jackson, her maiden name being Washburn. Both locals of this town and had been in the farming business since they were old enough to pick up a gardening hoe."

"You went to Everwood High School," she continued. "Got yourself a respectable GPA, went to the local state school, and you were earning yourself a degree in sociology until you dropped out after two years in. After that, you took jobs here and there at local grocery stores and what not until you married your late husband and ironically became a farmer's wife after your long struggle to escape that fate." Nancy finally looked back up at Shelly again.

"You have a decent credit score. You have a daughter named Dorothy Sarah Robins, age eight, who is currently being raised by your sister, Deborah, in the city. I heard you visited her today."

Shelly's expression with a mix between baffled, violated, and a dash of vengeance.

"Does she know, Shelly? Because we found them."

"Found what?!" It was more of a snarl than actual speech. Shelly bluffed even though she knew her judge was aware of her crimes.

"How you pay the bills. How you pay your daughter's bills," Nancy searched for the right words for the moment. "Your... assets under the trapdoor in the barn. Quite a little daycare you got there."

"You little stuck up Goldilocks whore." The can of worms had been cracked open, and Shelly felt unleashed. She would show this woman who she was messing with. The people was messing with. "You get these stupid goons over here with their guns, and you think you can scare me?" It was Shelly's turn to be amused and return the smirk Nancy had given her. "DO YOU KNOW WHO YOU ARE DEALING WITH?!"

Shelly's scream was like a lioness finally let loose, and she roared at them with all of her fury. She would put them in their place. But a lion roars not to fight, but to avoid them—to scare away the enemies with loud noises. And that's all it was, and deep inside, Shelly already knew it. Her words were just loud noises. "MY PEOPLE WILL MAKE YOU THEIR BLOND PET FOR WHAT YOU ARE DOING RIGHT NOW." But she roared anyway out of fear and anger.

She looked into the eyes of another lioness that for not one second stopped looking down at her. Though Shelly was uncertain when in the beginning, she realized now that she had been looking upward this whole time as if she was facing a giant. She spat a mixture of spit and blood from her nose at Nancy's face. It was a futile attack, but it was her last struggle.

As soon as the conglomerate of saliva and blood landed on her snow white face, Nancy slapped the other woman across the nose again and bent it the other way. The whipped cat screamed in pain as the blood started to gush out with renewed vigor. Nancy reached into her coat pocket and pulled out her handkerchief to wipe off her face.

"Trash," Nancy said. It was the first real emotion Shelly was able to draw out of Nancy—a very small victory for Shelly. "Call your scary people."

With Nancy's permission, Shelly quickly snatched out her phone from her pocket. Again, something in the back of her mind was telling her to just get a hold of herself. *She's just letting you to call for back up. She KNOWS your backup.* But she ignored reason. "Y'all gonna get it now. Y'all can kill me, but I'll see you in Hell in pieces."

She dialed the numbers with her hand crusted and sticky from her blood. It made a mess of bloody fingerprints and smudges all over the phone. After she finished punching the numbers, she held the phone up to her ear as she glared at Nancy. She tried her best to stare her down with blood all over her nose and mouth and the left nostril still drizzling more blood. She sucked it in to clear the airway as she waited for someone to pick up. She tried to enjoy the little smudge she managed to leave on Nancy's pretty little face. But it was only a brief enjoyment until the distress began to set in again and no one answered on the other line. Much like earlier, when she tried before she entered the house.

Shelly watched Nancy as she pulled out her own phone and dialed a number. Someone seemed to answer her call almost immediately. Nancy graciously offered her phone to Shelly.

The ginger farmer carefully approached the phone to her ear.

"Hello?" Shelly's sheepish voice broke the silence.

A familiar raspy voice answered back, "You're on your own." The answer was quick and tart, and the call disconnected as soon as the sentence finished.

From the crumbling look on Shelly's face, Nancy figured the call went exactly as she thought it would. "You see, Shelly, we are the scary people that your scary people are afraid of." Nancy took the phone from Shelly's hand and closed in on her. "So why aren't you begging yet?"

"What... what do you want? Money? You can have it all. You want in? We'll do eighty-twenty, your favor. That's giving you fifteen more than the other guys. You can take a few of them right now for the boys here and yourself, on the house... please. Just please. Let me walk out of here and don't mix my daughter up in this. She doesn't know anything."

Nancy stood and towered over the defeated woman begging for mercy. A disgusting bug she wanted to torment, but at the same time, simply stomp on right away.

"In a way, we are both villains in this world. But I'm the devil, and you're just gutter trash." Nancy tapped on her tablet and faced the screen toward Shelly. "I could have done this an easier way, but I didn't want to involve my friend. So cooperate, and we may spare your family.

This man." Nancy's tablet screen showed a picture of the late Dr. Cowan. "You sold a girl to this man sometime around six to eight years ago. I'm looking for her parents."

"That's the doctor that was killed by the Witch. Yeah, I remember them," Shelly answered.

"So you watch the news, Shelly. That's great. Answer the question: where and who did you get her from?"

"You the government or something? Why should I tell you? What's in it for me?"

"I take long and painful death off the table and I take your sister and your daughter off the table." Nancy watched as Shelly's face turn into a face of disgust. "As I told you, Shelly, I'm no saint. I'm a villain."

"...she was a halfy and young—*real* young," Shelly reluctantly relented. "They're *crème de la crop* and go for great rates. He paid about eighty grand for her."

"You're testing my patience, Shelly. I need something useful here."

"I don't know his real name, but I can tell you where we met and probably the town he's from. I may also have a photo I took of him just in case in my hidden safe. That's all I have." Shelly looked at Nancy with pleading eyes.

"Good. You'll lead a couple of my men here to those pictures." Nancy gave Shelly a smile, and the smile gave Shelly hope.

"What's going to happen now?" Shelly asked.

"After we leave, we'll call the police to check up on that barn," Nancy said.

"You're going to have me arrested?" Shelly thought it was better than death.

Nancy tilted her head. "No, Shelly," Nancy chuckled. "You thought you were going to get off that easily?"

The last bits of hope were starting fade away from Shelly's eyes.

"I will be sending you to my private prison. You'll spend your time there until I see fit. Expect no less than a couple of decades, though." Nancy waved over a few of her men who picked Shelly up to her feet. Shelly couldn't find the energy to stand on her own, and the men held her standing.

"While you search for those photos, Mrs. Robin, I recommend you pick out a book. I'll allow you to bring just one. Choose one that you don't mind reading for a while." Nancy smiled at Shelly once again. It was a smile that was as despicable as it was lovely.

Chapter 28
BACK IN THE WOODS

"So…" Landris sat next to Kalin and Lily by the campfire. Lily hummed an abomination of a tune as she folded more paper cranes that only Kalin could began to decipher from knowing Lily's musical history. He threw branches into the fire as he continued their conversation. "You guys went around the world in hopes of clearing the Witch's name?"

"No," Kalin said. "…well, that was my idea of it, anyway. Ms. Tone-deaf here—"

"Hmm?!" Lily turned her attention from her crane to Kalin, giving him a glare before turning her attention back to the task at hand.

"—Ms. Rhythmically-challenged here," he amended. "…wanted to see the world. I guess I did too. But the helping others part—at least, for her—is an impulse. She can't help herself."

"That's dumb," Landris answered immediately. "You guys think it's noble and all that, but none of it really matters; that's just naïve. At the end of the day, people will choose to be selfish if it means making their lives a little easier. It's every man for himself. Protect yourselves; no one else will do it for you. Those people who you helped will not help you in your own time of need. I mean, come on! You guys are walking proof of this."

Kalin said nothing as he grabbed a stick and poked at the fire.

"Because we can," Lily said.

"What?" Landris turned to look at Lily. She was still folding her paper cranes.

"We help because we can," Lily said as she finished up her paper crane. "It's just that."

"Alright, so let's just accept that you're a child and you don't know better, but you"—Landris pointed at Kalin—"aren't you suppose to protect her? You can't let her be what she is and still have her head in the clouds at the same time."

Kalin remained silent. Somewhere deep inside, he felt Landris was right.

"The world isn't simple, and it isn't nice, and as long as people are around, it'll never be simple or nice. We kill each other for money. We kill each other for fun. And we don't think twice about throwing words around like honor and justice as we kill, rape, and cheat one another. We have laws to be polite, but it's only there for people who care for it to be there. That's the kind of the world we live in."

"I don't think anyone is born bad" Lily spoke calmly. "But life is confusing and tough. Somewhere along the line, we just forget or lose our way on what it means to be good. But those who are good can't give up or forget being good even during the worst times because then there'll be nothing good left. They will remind others what they've forgotten. To keep it alive." Finished with another crane, Lily picked up the next small folding paper before continuing, "I might not really understand much, but I think sometimes people complicate things. It can be simple. Maybe the world would be less complicated if we help one another. We just have to do our parts to be good no matter what others are doing."

Lily looked up and smiled at Landris. "At least, that's what I like to believe." She turned her attention back to the paper and began humming her strange tune.

Baffled, Landris looked at Kalin for an explanation.

The sound of a ringtone suddenly coming to life startled everyone in the hut.

"Hello?" Landris answered the call.

"Yes, Landris. It's me," Nancy said. "We're ready for you guys."

"You... found them?" Even though she was his sister, Nancy still regularly managed to surprise Landris. "Already?"

"Shocked, little brother?" Nancy playfully answered.

"No, not really. Anyway, so what now?"

"Turn on your video."

Landris tapped on his phone and saw Nancy on the screen. Behind her was their private jet in its hangar.

"This is all that's needed for you guys to come on over, correct?" Nancy asked.

Landris turned to look at the Witch and her friend. They had already packed their things. Lily gave a wave of the finger and a clap. The roots that formed the hut began to slither away back to where they belonged.

"Are you ready?" Kalin asked Lily. With an already a nervous heart, Lily nodded. She walked over to Landris who presented her with the screen of the hangar, and she raised her finger in the air where it glowed with a brilliant light.

Chapter 29
AN ANSWER FOR THE END

"Almost done," Howard spoke with his eyes fixated on the schematics for the cylinder of the gun displayed on his computer. He had taken his gloves off, and within his naked hands were the knickknacks he had Kiara collect such as paper clips, nails, and any other metallic objects she was able to scavenge from around the facility. As Howard clasped his hands tightly, Kiara heard a metallic scream through Howard's fingers as the objects were crushed and twisted. Accompanying the sounds was a brilliant light and some sparks. Various sized chunks of metal from small to very, very small slipped out through the cracks of his hands. Howard let out little grunts here and there, as well as an occasional 'ow' of pain, while remaining fixated on the schematics.

"Done." Howard held up a shining cylinder as he looked through each of its six slots to make certain they were up to his standards. Although to Kiara, his desk seemed cluttered and disorganized with various parts lying freely about, Howard reached for them without ever needing to look back at where his hand was going in order to assemble the gun. Before Kiara could utter a word, Howard's hands began to move again. They reached through the seemingly cluttered and disorganized desk and grabbed the exact pieces needed to assemble the gun. Howard's hands danced across the table as they swerved through the chaotic mess for a piece and snapped back from the madness to assemble his new magnificent creation.

"Now, really done." Howard held up the shining hand cannon. He turned his head towards Kiara with glee and pride, and he fully expected her to be floored with amazement.

"That's outstanding, Howard. You really are the Inventor!" Although she meant every word, Kiara felt like she had been somewhat forced to say those words from Howard's gaze.

"Thanks. I've really gotten better the second time around." Howard set the gun back down on the table. He looked at his hands, and they were scarred with cuts and burns with new additions from his latest creation. It was an unpleasant sight. Sensing Kiara's eyes behind him, Howard shyly wiped off the droplets of blood on the gun with a handkerchief he kept in his pocket and cleaned his hand before hiding them into his brown gloves.

"Second time around?" Kiara asked, though not entirely surprised by the revelation.

"Yeah," Howard reluctantly confessed. "I always thought guns were cool and stuff, y'know? From, like, an engineering perspective? But more than that, I wanted to see if I could do it. After all the training here and what not, and being surrounded by guns, one day I just went for it."

"What happened?" Kiara could connect the dots that punitive actions must have taken, seeing as how she wasn't simply offered his first creation.

"Apparently someone found out and told Director Jones. It was garbage compared to this, but she was still impressed. Though, she did warn me pretty sternly about making any sort of weapon again."

After one last inspection, the gun was finished. "Here." Howard placed the glistening revolver into Kiara's hand.

As soon as the heavy steel landed on Kiara's virgin hands, the reality of her task crashed upon her. Her hand sank from its weight and her heart dropped. For a moment, she simply stared at the weapon.

"It's a semi-auto revolver," Howard's voice broke through Kiara's trance. "I modified and enhanced it from the schematics of an existing model. I made it small enough so you can hide it, and it's simple to use, accurate, and powerful enough to put a hole in a grown man. You're not going to have much practice shooting it, so I thought this would be the best." Howard took the gun back from Kiara.

"Press down on this small latch here with your thumb"—Howard demonstrated on the gun—"and the cylinder will flip down to the side like that. A bullet for each hole goes in here, and you just click the cylinder back in. This little switch here is the safety, and once you've flipped it, you're ready for the day of reckoning for the Witch. You don't even need to cock the gun. If you look at the top of the barrel, you'll see the front sight." Howard pointed at a little piece of metal protruding from the top of the muzzle at its tip. It was shaped and sharpened to point forward. "I tried to make it easier for you to point and shoot. Think of the point of the front sight as a point of an arrow. Just point that to where you want to shoot." When he was done with his demonstration, he placed the weapon back into Kiara's hands.

"Right, the bullets." Howard opened his desk drawer and handed her four bullets. "I don't feel too comfortable dealing with gunpowder in general, so I had to channel my inner kleptomaniac to score these. You won't be fully loaded, but the way I see it, if you miss your first shot, you won't get another anyway. Wait 'til you're close enough to her, or maybe even until she's asleep before you roll the dice."

In one of Kiara's hands was the gun and in the other, the ammo it needed to fulfill its purpose. As her mind slowly came to grasp the tangible reality of her decision, she took a moment to marvel at the fact that this piece of equipment which seemed so magnificent to her eyes was made from simple paper clips, nails, and other knickknacks of materials they collected from around the facility. An odd time to marvel at a thing like that while trying to grasp her task of killing someone.

"Howard, why didn't you make the gun so it looked like one of the ones carried by the security here?" Kiara asked as she noticed a distinctive "Lexi" engraved on the side of the barrel.

"Because I didn't think they'd be good enough," Howard answered.

"But I'm sure Director Jones will..."

"She'd of found out anyways. Besides, I'd be more than proud to know that it was my work that helped you with this, and that it was my work that killed the Witch and saved the world." Howard gave a shy smile.

Kiara put the gun and the bullets into a bag she had brought with her to Howard's room.

"It's a bit silly asking now, but are you sure about this? I mean, absolutely sure?" Howard, who could easily tell how nervous Kiara was, asked.

No words. Kiara simply nodded.

Howard tried to think of some wisdom to pass on to his dear friend.

"Don't miss."

Chapter 30
TWIDDLING THUMBS

The sky was ash gray and anxious to wash itself pure with the rain. Not sunny and not rainy, but simply cloudy—Kalin found the weather matched how he was feeling perfectly. It would have been great if there had been some sunshine today, but it wouldn't feel honest. But he digressed, and his thoughts were consumed solely again by Lily. This was her day. She seemed entirely more nervous than excited and had not slept nor ate well during the short plane ride and then the long car ride.

"What're they doing just sittin' in their cars?"

The father spoke to himself as he sipped on his stale morning coffee. He peered through the openings between the window blinds and watched the large vehicle he assumed was the guests he was expecting. Though Nancy tried to rent a vehicle that would be inconspicuous, she had underestimated the depravity of the neighborhood. He walked back to his couch, sat, and took another sip from his coffee. He relinquished himself to the fact that once that girl walked through those doors, his world would never be the same. Much like the day she was born.

Lily's parents lived in a town that had long forgotten better days, and it was filled with people who had long forgotten better lives. It was somewhere that was nowhere. A dead end. A kind of place where a gray sky fit better than the blue kind. The roads were filled with cars long worn out of their prime, garbage scattered about to feed the rats and stray cats, and people who searched for their better days hunched inside their coats with their eyes onto the ground. Her parents' house itself was probably once a home-sweet-home for a young newlywed couple decades ago. It probably saw a few families grow and wither until it itself began to wither away as well. Now a mere hag of a house, the paint had lost its shine and was chipped off in more places than it still remained. The grass lawn was spotted with death, brown and barren, and the front porch was littered with never completed chores worth a thousand weekends. But the dirty floor mat said 'Welcome.'

"Lily? Sweetheart? Still not ready yet?" Ms. Jones called out to Lily who was having a harder time dealing with the meeting than anticipated.

Nancy had sent Yuri out to meet with the parents the night before they arrived. It only made sense to minimize as much risk as she could in order to not create a sequel to Dr. Cowan.

"I didn't explain to him very well who we were, but he understood very well what we could do to him if he didn't behave," Yuri explained over the phone.

"What of the mother?" Nancy asked.

"She's… uhh… how do I say… should be just kept out of the meeting? Not a good sight, that woman. Lost her soul. I told him to put her somewhere out of sight and say that she's out of town on business or something. Or better yet, that she's long gone." Yuri chuckled.

"I see. Alright, thank you, Yuri. I'll see you back at the Facility." Though she still had her reservations regarding the meeting, Nancy ended the call and dialed for Landris.

"Lily?" Ms. Jones called out to Lily once more who seemed to have failed to hear her the first time. Lily was humming to herself. Another of those mysterious tunes that probably only Kalin had any chance of deciphering. She'd stop soon and recite…

"Hello, my name is Lily, and I am your daughter. I've looked for you to let you know that I am okay," Lily quietly recanted this to herself every once in a while. Nancy thought it might have started since the airport, but Kalin, who sat next to her on the plane, caught her mumbling to herself while they were in the air. She'd hum, take a deep breath, and then recite her monologue. The incantation became more and more frequent as they got closer and closer to the parents' house, and he heard many variations to the chant as Lily tweaked the words until it felt perfect for her. And the perfect chant always ended with, "I am okay!"

"I don't think you need to worry too much, sweetheart." Ms. Jones turned her body to face Lily. Her face was riddled with concern and nervousness, her breathing was awkward, and Nancy could swear Lily's whole body was shaking. She was back to humming. "This should be one of the happiest days of your life, Lily. You won't have to impress them. They'll just be happy to see you. They've been waiting for this day as much as you have." Nancy smiled and grabbed on to Lily's hand. Ms. Jones' hands were warm and gave comfort to Lily. Maybe her mother's hands will feel like that. Could they hug? Could she hug her mom? Hug her dad? How would that feel? Would it be the same as hugging Kalin?

Lily gave a very quick hug to Kalin leaving him and Ms. Jones bewildered. The hug, no offense to Kalin, with her mom would probably feel a lot better. A lot warmer. She sort of wished Sarah could have come so that she could practice hugging her mother with Sarah.

"Right, Kalin?" Ms. Jones looked at Kalin for support after a moment.

Did she really believe everything was going to be alright? Kalin was still adamant about his reservations for the meeting. To him, it felt certain that something was going to go wrong. He already felt angry for what was to come. But ultimately, he felt angry because he wasn't sure. This could be the best day of Lily's life. This *should be* the best day of Lily's life. She deserves a happy family waiting for her and for her parents to not be some deadbeats who let their daughter be sold off as a slave. Perhaps he didn't know better because he was young and the things he saw in Sarah's visions were misleading. Or perhaps Ms. Jones knew better than him. Or perhaps she made certain that this meeting would go well. Kalin would rather let Lily have a play of a happy ending than the reality that ends with a metal pipe to the head. "I'm with you no matter what," Kalin finally answered.

An acceptable answer, though he could have been more positive, Nancy thought. But the boy was smart and above all seemed to have an honest heart. Noted. He gave the best answer that he could manage to say without having to lie.

"Can I go by myself?" Lily asked. She had asked before.

"No." After denying Lily's request in unison, Ms. Jones and Kalin shared a moment of locked eyes. The motivation for the denial was clear to one while a bit convoluted to the other.

"Why not?" Lily protested.

"Because," Landris said, poking his head out from the seat behind Lily and Kalin. "You're hopelessly odd, and this meeting is going to be painfully awkward as is. They'll be there to make things go smoothly."

"Lan—" Before Nancy could scold Landris, Lily spoke up.

"You're being mean, Landris," Lily told the boy.

She's done it now. Nancy waited for Landris to snap at Lily with a comment that would make his last seem gentle and kind.

After looking dumbfounded for a moment, Landris spoke. "Sorry. It'll be alright. Just don't let it get to you too much."

Lily nodded.

Nancy stared at Landris, but before she could decipher Landris's intentions she heard Lily cry, "Papa!"

They all looked out the window. A tall and endomorphic man stood outside the front door of his house with a mug in his hand and a stressed and confused look on his face. He studied the car and found himself in the predicament of whether or not to approach it closer. Lily made the decision for him. His daughter jumped out of the car and stared at her father, her legs frozen and the chant she practiced lost somewhere in her throat. It never even made it close to her lips. Her father, although he didn't recognize her face, knew right away that he was looking at his long lost daughter. Parent and child stood and stared in silence, drowning in mixed emotions.

Chapter 31
MEET THE PARENTS

"You sure this is a good idea?" Landris asked as he followed behind Nancy and her bodyguard. They trailed behind Lily and Kalin who were taking their first steps into the home in silence after the father gestured them in without words.

"I took all the precautions I could, given her demands and given our circumstances. It'll also be a good test to see how volatile she may be." Nancy hastened her pace towards the house which in turn hastened her companions. "But if anything does go wrong..." Nancy turned her head and gave Landris a soft smile. "That's why I have you with me, right, little brother?"

Landris remained silent. He didn't need her to remind him or ask him to do the things he thought to be his natural duties. He was well aware and fully committed, and Nancy herself knew of her brother's conviction for her—his whole family—without needing to hearing the answer from him.

"I'm curious though," Nancy continued. "What's the actual reason behind your concern for this meeting?"

The father held the door open for Nancy and her followers. As the last of them made it into the home, the door closed behind them.

$$***$$

The house had a distinctive aroma that none of its visitors could really properly identify. It wasn't pungent or putrid, but neither was it pale or pleasant. It was a scent that was a mixture of home and outdoors; it was the scent of a place where a person lived, but didn't really cultivate. The house was small, filled with the basic necessities to present itself as a place where people found shelter: a couch, a TV, a few cabinets, a few pictures, and a few surviving plants. But surrounding those few necessities were boxes filled with a collection of newspapers and various magazines, and there were piles of empty liquor bottles and beer cans of different brands piled around the TV like decoration. They tried to clean the place up, and to them it was clean. But clean was relative, and the house couldn't shake off the obvious facade.

"You can keep your shoes on," the father said as he led the group to the living room. Nancy didn't plan on taking her shoes off whether she had permission or not.

Closest to the father was his daughter. She stole quick glimpses of him from time to time but mostly kept her eyes either forward or downward. Her heart pounded, and she worried that she might puke. This was much more difficult than she had imagined. Then again, at this point, she wasn't sure what she really imagined this would be like. Maybe everything was going as well as it could be. Maybe this was what it was supposed to be like. Maybe this was home.

"Sit anywhere you like," the father said as he turned off the TV and sat down on the cushioned chair—his humble throne. With the chair occupied, there was a couch adjacent to it. The father turned his seat from facing the TV to face the couch.

Lily looked at Kalin, and he pointed at the far end of the sofa that was closest to the where the father was sitting. Kalin looked at Nancy who nodded at him to take the middle seat next to Lily. Nancy then looked to Landris who replied, "I'll stand with you."

The father sat in his seat and studied everyone in the room except Lily who he only glanced at once in a while. Lily stared at her feet. *Hello, my name is Lily and I am your daughter. I've looked for you to let you know that I am okay!* Her chant repeated in her head with the image of her filled with confidence and equipped with a bright smile as she said it to her father. And her father would smile as he heard those words and would tell her how happy he was that his daughter was home. Lily began to hum quietly without realizing it; it calmed her nerves. The father raised an eyebrow and looked at his daughter as if she was mad.

"This is my first but this has to be the gloomiest long-lost-daughter and father reunion ever," Kalin broke the silence that was probably a lot shorter than it actually seemed.

The father looked for a moment at Kalin as if Kalin had called his mother a dirty word. He then glanced quickly at Nancy that was only noticed by her and her brother.

"You're right. You're right!" The father smiled. "I'm just, uhhh. This was all so sudden and I just… I just don't know how to feel right now."

"Happy?" Kalin smiled back at the father. "Happiness is a good place to start."

"Of course. Happiness." There was a hint of bitterness in the father's inflection with the word 'happiness.' He didn't appreciate Kalin's assertiveness.

"So, are you like her boyfriend or something?" the father asked.

"Just a friend, and I think you're taking an interest in the wrong person," Kalin answered.

The father chuckled. The cheeky, redheaded kid was right. Embarrassed for being called out for his cowardice, the father finally looked at his daughter, and to his surprise she was staring right back at him. His daughter had grown up, but he could still see the image of the last time he saw her. Sort of.

"Hello, my name is Li…"

There were moments in her life when Lily felt she could only hear the sound of her heartbeats. She'd count them as they were always moments that she wished would pass soon. But counting the beats wasn't her way of running from those moments, it was her way to stay in them. Her way of *fighting* to stay in them. *One. Two. Three.* Don't run. *Four. Five. Six.* If she let the heartbeats take over, she'd be left with only regrets when silence returned. *Seven. Eight. Nine.* Last time she let them take over, she lost her parents. *Ten. Eleven. Twelve.* She abandoned Jade. *Thirteen. Fourteen. Fifteen.* And then, she murdered a man. *Sixteen, Seventeen, Eighteen.* And this time, she might fail to have her parents see her. The man before her, her father, the man who looked the same as she remembered him. He might not see that she is his daughter.

"Screw this. I don't even care!" Her father didn't hear his daughter mumble and interrupted her. "I know people like you, alright? I know no matter what happens, I'm not getting out of this. At least I can be straight with myself and straight with the girl."

Lily forgot her incantations.

"Hey, Melody. Yeah, I remember your name," the father continued his tirade. "What do you want, huh? Why'd you come back? Revenge? Money? What is it? What did you think you can accomplish by coming back? 'Cause I got nothing. I had nothing for you then, and I got nothing for you now. So, if you want to kill me or something go ahead. Free me from myself."

A pang. It reminded Lily that she was alive. A reminder she rarely felt through the numbness. There were times when she wondered if she smiled because she wanted to smile or felt like she had to smile. Times when she wondered if she spoke the words she spoke because she believed the words or because she liked how they sounded. She needed a reminder once in a while to remember what was important to her. What was real to her. But this sort of reminder—pain—was something she had thought that was long lost to her. The tear drizzling down the side of her face wasn't planned, nor was it a reaction but a screaming echo from something deep within her that had been awakened from its slumber. All that was, all that is, and all that she had hoped would be colluded into an unrecognizable and indecipherable mess. For once, she didn't feel numb but lost in a jumble of feelings.

"Ah, damn it," the father said, seeing his daughter's tears. "I didn't want to do that to you, alright? But It's not... It's not like I wanted you either?" The father scratched his head. "God that came out wrong. Alright, look kid. I'm sorry. Alright? I'm sorry. You... ah geez." He let out a deep sigh and looked up at the ceiling before facing his daughter again. "Alright. Stop. Stop crying, that's not going to help anybody. We did what we did 'cause we had to. What's done is done. Life's not fair, and it's too long. Too long for you to be dwelling on this."

Kalin fists couldn't be clenched any tighter.

The father continued, oblivious to the tensions rising in the room, "Think that we, as parents, gave you the most valuable lesson in your life early: that the world—more like the people... yeah, the people in the world are cruel. They're merciless. They will take a bite at you at the first chance, chew you up, and won't even have the decency to crap you out if it means they'll get even a half-a-step ahead. We weren't good parents, but because of that you got an edge over most other kids in the world. Carry that lesson with you, and go live your life. Go with this boy. Make babies and make a family of your own, alright?"

Without a sound, Kalin leaped from his seat and grabbed the father. Before the father could react, he was already thrown onto the ground.

"Landris!" Nancy looked at her little brother who did not budge.

"He sort of deserves it," Landris said empathetically. Nancy looked at the father and thought perhaps she should let Kalin have a couple more blows.

Lily was frozen, staring at the empty seat where her father was. The world had no sound to her, and only the jumbled gibberish of her heart filled her ears.

Before Kalin could strike down on the father, the father punched him on the nose, and Kalin's nose began to bleed. He was happy how little it hurt. Kalin struck back at the father. No stream—just his own strength. His knuckles burned and were already starting to redden with blood.

"Stop!" Lily cried out to Kalin. She scurried over and covered her father's face with her body.

"Move out of the way, Lily!" Kalin shouted. "This man isn't your father!"

"This man IS my father!" Lily shouted back at Kalin. She looked at him with soaked and swollen eyes, and gave him a look of contempt that Kalin had rarely seen from her.

"Please, don't hurt my papa," Lily sobbed. Kalin was baffled and lowered his hands in defeat. All the energy he had drained out of his body. The room was silent.

A creak from the stairs.

"Baby?" A squeamish voice of a woman cried out from the stairs. Each step creaked as she slowly descended. They could hear her humming a tune of sort.

"Oh god," the father groaned. "Yuki! Stay up there!"

Yuki did not listen.

Chapter 32
MEANING OF FAMILY

Leading out of the small living room was an arch. Yuki stood in that arch and observed the group with blank eyes. Shorter and lankier than an average woman, her long black hair loosely ran down her shoulders. It was oily and unkempt. She was dressed in an oversized shirt that probably belonged to her husband and dirty sweatpants. She was pale. Perhaps even more pale than Lily. Her eyes were sunken and darkened with bags, and her lips were cracked and dried, and there were signs of dried drool by her lips.

"Baby, you didn't tell me you had friends over," Yuki said. Her words were slow and slurred. She sounded groggy.

"Hello, everyone." Yuki waved with her bony arms and scrawny hand. Nancy and Landris noticed scarred spots on her arm. After waving, she began to hum gently under her breath as she walked over to her husband.

"Mama?" Lily picked herself up from her father and faced her mother. Her words froze Yuki in her tracks. Their eyes met, and tears began to drizzle down Lily's cheeks again.

"Mama!" Lily's voice cracked and rolled as it drowned in tears. She was having a hard time catching her breath, and her sniffles began to sound like hiccups. She cried like she never cried before.

"Mama!" Lily wailed as she ran over to her mom and wrapped herself around her and buried her face into her womb.

"Lily…" Kalin picked himself up and thought of pulling his friend away from another potential heartbreak, but he decided let her be.

"Oh god," Yuki finally spoke after having stood there like a post as her daughter sobbed into her shirt crying for her 'mama.'

"Oh god, oh god, oh god, oh god." Yuki pulled her daughter away who looked at her as she sobbed.

"PAT!" Yuki cried. "PAT! I'm seeing her again! But… but she's different! I've never seen her like this before. PAT! PAT! I can feel her PAT! Oh god, oh god, oh god, oh god, PAT! Please, PAT!" Yuki began to sob and pushed her daughter away and ran by her husband who had picked himself up and sat on the floor watching the whole fiasco.

"LOOK!" Yuki bellowed as she pointed at Lily. "It's her!"

"Yeah, it's her, Yuki. Get a grip and shut up, will ya," Patrick said as he wiped the blood off his face with his hand.

"NO!" Yuki screamed. "She's dead! Pat! She's dead! She's supposed to be dead!" Yuki crawled to Lily and embraced her.

"You're supposed to be dead," Yuki whispered into her daughter's ear as she cried with her. "You're supposed to be dead."

"I'm here, mama. I'm here, mama," Lily told her mother.

"No, angel, you're not. You're not here. If you're here that'd mean terrible things. Horrible things. You're not here. You're in a better place. Because if you were here... I shouldn't have..." Yuki words were becoming harder and harder to make out. "... I should have been better... I should have looked harder... I... I shouldn't have... been a..."

"No, mama. It's me. Mel..." remembering her name and being able to say it again bore heavy weight on Lily's lips. "...Melody. I'm here!" Lily said.

"No! Angel, don't do this to me. You're not here anymore. And I'm sorry, I'm sorry, I'm sorry, I'm sorry, I'm sorry, I'm sorry. You don't have to forgive me but I'm sorry, I'm sorry, I'm sorry. Oh god, why do you feel so real?" Yuki hugged her daughter even tighter.

"But, mama, I *am* real!" Lily was frustrated of being a ghost.

"You *can't* be. You CAN'T be!" Yuki stood up and ran out of the room and up the stairs.

"She died a long ago," the father said. "That ain't a person you're seeing."

Nancy blamed herself for her ill-preparedness. This could have gone better. It could have been much smoother. Why did she decide to give Lily an even remotely honest meeting? In the corners of her mind Nancy knew the truth. She knew exactly why she took the risk. It wasn't for her, it was for Lily.

The mother walked back down, cradling a colorful mass of folded papers. She dumped that on the ground in front of Lily. They were paper cranes.

"I prayed, I hoped, and I even wished that you were at a better place," the mother said. "So you can't be here."

"You've got to be kidding me." Landris's mutter wasn't really under his breath. By the look of Kalin's face, he shared Landris's sentiment.

Lily picked up one of the cranes and observed it. She unfolded the crane until it was a creased paper. The daughter felt the creases made by her mother with her thumb. She followed the creases, and folded the paper back into a crane as her mother had before.

After a moment of silence, Lily spoke.

"Hello. My name is Lily," Lily spoke with strength. She sat the paper crane down with the rest of them. "I am your daughter. I am okay." Lily looked at her parents. "And I will be okay," Lily continued. "I will make it okay. With or without you. No matter what. That's all I came here for." Finished with her speech, Lily headed for the door. Kalin, Nancy, and Landris slowly followed after her.

"WAIT!" As Lily took her first step outside, Yuki called out to her. She ran over to Lily and embraced her into her arms. "Just a little more," Yuki said. "Just let me dream a little more." The mother whispered into her daughters ears. A whisper so soft that no one else could hear. After she was done, she finally let her daughter be free.

***

"What are you going to do with them?" Landris asked his sister as their plane took off.

"Nothing," Nancy answered to Landris's surprise. "They're harmless. Besides, I think it's more fitting that they live in their own self-imposed purgatory than anything done by me."

"Is that all there is to it?" Landris questioned his sister. She brushed it off without an answer as she flipped through her tablet.

Lily had pulled out some more folding papers and laid them out on the table. She stared at the papers, deep in thought. Kalin felt uncomfortable sitting in the silence. His friend hadn't spoken a single word since they left the house. He wished he was better with words; it bothered him tremendously that at this moment, he didn't know what to say.

"Do you want me to call you 'Melody'?" Kalin finally broke the silence.

Lily looked at her friend with wide, confounded eyes.

Then she smiled. "No, I am Lily," Lily answered. "I'm not Ruby. Not Melody. Not anymore. I want to be Lily. I want to be remembered as Lily."

"Alright." Kalin cleared his throat. It was weird. He could always talk to her about anything. He never had to think or worry, even when he teased her. But at this moment, it felt like the night he first ran into her all over again.

"Kalin," Lily softly called out to her friend. "Why was I born?"

Kalin felt his heart squeeze and his body numb when he heard the question. She had asked it with a bittersweet smile. The feeling that it felt as if it was a fair question coming from her made him feel like a traitor to himself and to Lily.

"Lily," Kalin finally managed to open his mouth. "We don't have to be bound to our pasts. Our future—our lives—can be whatever we want them to be. After this journey is over, we can go somewhere where we never thought to go and do something we never thought do. Wherever we decide to go and whatever we decide to do—or we don't even have to go anywhere or do anything, but whatever we do, it'll be by our choice, and that'll be our lives. We'll make new pasts with our future. And..." Kalin was struggling to find the right words again and felt his face redden. It didn't help that Lily was staring at him as if she was studying his soul. "...And I guess... whether you like or not, I'll be with you. Whatever you decide. Because that's what being family is."

Kalin watched Lily's eyes widen, and it made him feel even more vulnerable and embarrassed.

"What?" He asked.

The girl gently placed her hand over Kalin's. "Good," Lily said with a smile. Kalin turned his head away from her. He had to.

Lily looked at her left wrist with the black band dangling from it. The last step of her journey before she was done. Feeling pressed for time, Lily began folding more papers. She wanted to be ready for the journey's end. Her wish had to be ready in time.

"What are you wishing for, anyways, Lily?" Kalin asked, finally being able to face Lily again.

"It's a secret!" Lily said as she finished up another one.

The plane began to move. Soon, they would be up in the air heading towards the end. And Kalin hoped, a new beginning.

Chapter 33
WAR PREPARATIONS

Director Hamilton's Office.

The director sat alone at his desk as he mulled over his part in all that would happen in the next couple of days. It was the right call to make. He didn't lie to himself, at least when he was alone with his conscience. His decisions were selfish, but the selfishness didn't rob them from their righteousness. Needing a break from his own thoughts, director Hamilton turned on the television.

"I'm not saying our government is doing everything right. Let's take a look at what they're calling the Light," Mr. Brian O'Connor of The Point spoke to his audience. *"It was revealed last year that the governments around the world knew exactly where the Light was, but somehow failed to notify us, the people, of their findings. It was not too far off from our own coast when we the media—the eyes and voice of the people—tried to report on the Light and were stopped by military vessels on threats of death before we were able to approach any meaningful distance. We did, however, see this."*

A picture came up on the screen. It was an aircraft carrier far off in the distance. Behind it was a thicker than usual visual of the Light.

"Now!" Mr. O'Connor clasped his hands and gave a meaningful, if not slightly playful, look into the camera. *"What could they be hiding from us that it would require one of the most powerful machinery in our military—in the world—to have its presence there? Our fellow reporters from around the globe have told us that any nation that can afford to have their military present at the Light has done so. Their reasoning being that the Light is an event that triumphs any normal circumstances of jurisdiction, sovereignty, law, and et cetera. However—"*

A phone call interrupted the Director. It was one of his personal phones that only a select few were provided the number for. He turned off the TV with his remote.

"This is Director Hamilton," he answered the call.

Morris sat in his car parked outside the McKinley's Headquarters. Within the hour, he was to be leading a team of the McKinley's men to raid the secret facility of the Silver Aegis assisted by the group of wild Gifted who called themselves the Wolf Pack. He had phoned the director with the desperate hope that he might stop the madness.

"This is agent Graham," Morris said. "It's urgent, sir."

"What is it, Graham?" Director Hamilton replied.

"I think it'd be as good a time as any for us to step in and stop this war between McKinley and Jones, sir."

"No, Daniel, we will not be doing that," Director chuckled a bit in disbelief.

"Sir? Am I missing something here?"

"Daniel..." the Director paused for a moment and contemplated whether or not to share with his agent the next set of information. "For Nancy Jones' secret facility to be off the grid in this day and age is impossible without the cooperation from the government."

"You mean..."

"Yes. We were fully aware of the facility that Ms. Jones had started in order to deal with the Gifted. Though, obviously, all this is still classified information."

"Then..." Morris began connecting the dots. "...was it us who supplied McKinley with the location?"

"Of course," the director replied.

"But, why?" Morris masked his contempt as much as he could.

"'Why'? *Why* shouldn't be your concern, agent Graham. It is the decision made by your superiors, and it is the decision that you will carry out."

"Sir, people may die from this. If Nancy Jones does have a facility filled with the Gifted the chances are high that they'll be children."

"McKinley and Jones were becoming too big and too unpredictable. They were taking advantage of this situation to build an empire of their own. Who knows what they would have done if they succeeded. McKinley took care of itself, and now it's Jones who needs a check. Let McKinley do our dirty work if they so desire. Let them tear each other apart. We'll step in afterwards to make sure they and anyone else thinking of taking advantage of current circumstances will not dare to do so. It's about balancing order, agent Graham. Throw in Ms. Wolf and her gang of thugs, and we've got ourselves an unexpected bonus. If a few of those other 'freaks' are taken care of in the process, then good riddance; that's fewer anomalies to keep us up at night. We are not living in a world of dreams and ideologies anymore, Daniel. Whether people realize it or not, or whether they want to admit it or not, we are in a time of chaos. A time where the world as we knew it is about to be ripped out of our hands and reduce our society to anarchy. So if you will, agent Graham, just do your job."

The call ended.

Morris stared at his phone in the silence of his car. He was uncertain whether or not to trust his superior's decision and what it meant to doubt his superior. Before too long, a car pulled up next to him. The music and banter was loud enough to leak out of their car, and it seemed like they were here more for a school field trip than for a military operation. It was Emily Wolf and her crew of three others. Two of the three were brunettes, one a girl who seemed to be in a passionate discussion with Emily while the other was a boy who seemed timid even from a glance as he stared down at his phone with his ears covered by his headphones. The third member was a black man who clearly seemed to be the oldest of the four, though was still young compared to Morris. His face had strong, bony features and looked stoic. Perhaps he seemed even more mature surrounded by his rowdy bunch of friends.

Morris exited his car coincidentally at the same time as Emily, and they looked at one another. Morris saw his reflection in Emily's aviator glasses. She gave him a smile and a wave hello.

The leader of the McKinley's crew and the leader of the Wolf Pack's crew went around the car and gave each other a handshake.

"Ms. Wolf, I presume," Morris said. "You and your friends are younger than I thought. I am—"

"Mr. James Morris. You have quite the prestigious reputation. So much that I wonder if any of it was fabricated," Emily said with a friendly smile. The rest of her party gathered behind her with suitcases and backpacks as if they were on vacation.

"Coming from you, Ms. Wolf, it's an honor," Morris replied while a small part of him worried about Emily's last statement.

"Let me introduce you to the crew." Emily motioned and gave a drum roll sound as she looked behind her and pointed at the brunette girl first.

"Introducing—she's the spunky punk with an attitude but..." Emily turned around and faced James. "... carries a heart of gold. It's Norah Howl!"

"Shut up, Emily," said Norah. "'Hey, I'm Norah."

"Next! He's scrawny! He's puny! He's hasn't hit his growth spurt yet! And he's so shy he's scared of his own shadows! Don't make him mad because he'll cry!" Emily imitated a drum roll again and pointed at the wavy-haired brunette boy standing next to the girl. He was the same height as the girl he was standing next to, and the boy looked as if he was the youngest.

"I hate you," the boy said to Emily.

"No, you don't. It's the boy genius and the other half of the wonder twin! Noah Howl!"

"Last but not least!" Emily's drum roll began again. "He's the rock, he's the oak, he's the big brother of the pack!" Emily looked behind her and pointed at the tall, structured man who caught Morris's intrigue earlier. "Leon Lukeba!"

Leon slowly walked up to Morris and offered him a handshake, and James obliged. Leon's hand was coarse and had a firm grip.

"You guys really are young," Morris said with a smile that was hinted with disbelief. "So what are their 'gifts'?"

"That'll remain a secret as agreed on the contract!" Emily said as she walked over to her crew and grabbed one of the backpacks. "But don't worry. All of us have enough experience to not be shy around you boys and girls. Especially with the Gifted. It's sort of our thing."

Emily motioned to her crew and Morris to begin walking over to the main building.

"It's a mad world to have young people like you be part of something like this. Then again, I guess the world has always been a little crazy," Morris said as he walked next to Emily. "What are you getting out of this, Ms. Wolf?"

Emily glanced at Morris for a second. It was a silly and pointless question.

"My cut of the madness, I suppose," Emily answered.

END OF PART TWO

PART THREE

LILIES IN THE FLOWER SHOP

The street was as quiet as Kalin remembered during night. Even with the street lamps, the neighborhood was mostly shrouded in darkness. Ruby liked it this way. She found comfort in seclusion. The occasional bark from a dog off far and the occasional car driving by were the only signs of life. Holding her hand, Kalin guided her through the streets as she held in her other hand the flowers they had bought earlier on the way. *Lilies,* Kalin called them as he gave a name to the prettiest flowers Ruby had ever seen. He said they were for someone very special to him. Ruby constantly marveled at the white and sizable flowers and would have been lost if it wasn't for Kalin guiding her.

"We're here," Kalin said. "It's been a while." He smiled, but his voice was melancholy.

Ruby looked away from the lilies and at the building. There were giant wavy letters that simply spelled, "FLOWERS" above the entrance. The doors to the entrance were secured with cold, metal chains that were intertwined between the handles and hitched with a heavy lock. Kalin quickly tore away a bright red paper that had been thoroughly taped to the center of the entrance before he dug into his backpack and found a bundle of keys. After looking around to see if they were in the clear, Kalin opened both the lock and then the door, and they headed inside.

It wasn't much warmer than the outside and the building also smelled funny, but the smell was vaguely familiar to Ruby. There were empty shelves and counters stained with of what used to be there, and the floor was peppered with dead leaves.

"This used to be my family's flower shop," Kalin told Ruby. Ruby looked up at Kalin with curious eyes.

"Where?" Ruby asked.

"You mean, where's my family?" Kalin was getting better at understanding Ruby's broken speech. Ruby nodded.

"I only had my mom and my dad," Kalin said. "They're both gone now." His voice quivered ever so slightly. Kalin wondered why. He had accepted their departure for a while now, but something about saying it out loud shook him. Across the building, he saw the register he used to man after he came home from school. As soon as he opened the doors, he'd see his mom who'd greet him with a smile.

She'd always tell Kalin he didn't need to help out if he was busy, but Kalin always tried to at least put in a couple of hours as soon as he got home. It gave his mom time to take a break or attend to some of the flowers.

Ruby replied with silence. She held his hand and looked around the desolate lot.

"I know to you it probably looks lifeless and empty," Kalin said. "But we used to live here. It was our home."

Ruby nodded.

Kalin usually didn't talk much, but with his new silent friend, he found himself talking quite a lot more than he was used to.

"Come on." Kalin tugged on her hand and led them to the door behind the counter. It opened to reveal a stairway that led upstairs. Ruby hesitated for a moment as the dark stairs brought unwanted flashbacks of her past back to mind, but she shook it off quickly before Kalin grew worried.

"We shouldn't turn any lights on. Actually, I don't think we can even turn them on. I wonder if there's any water..." Kalin led them to the kitchen and turned on the faucet. After a short spurt of water, the faucet made a noise of death and gave no more.

"Well." Kalin looked at Ruby who didn't seem concerned at all and was mostly curious about her surroundings. "I think the bed is still there and we can use the bottled water to brush our teeth. I still have the apples left from the store."

Ruby stared at him without words or emotion.

"Right." Kalin began walking towards his old room. He then stopped. "Oh, we still have a donut we picked up as well."

He turned and saw Ruby's eyes glisten with life.

"But it's for me," Kalin said. Ruby's eyes quickly died and her emotionless face somehow radiated disappointment and sorrow.

"I'm..." Kalin quickly felt the sting of guilt for his teasing. "...kidding. It's all yours."

They headed into the room. All of Kalin's belongings were nearly just as he had left them. Surprisingly, Kalin could tell the subtle disturbances in the room that he suspected were done by the police in an attempt to search for his whereabouts. His room had never been clean, but to Kalin it was organized in his own way.

"Wait here. Make yourself comfortable." Kalin let go of Ruby's hand. Ruby felt startled at how deprived she felt as her hand was freed from his. Though she didn't show it in any way, Kalin felt something off with his friend. "...I'll be back soon. I'm going to find something to put the flowers in."

She nodded, and with a little assurance from her, Kalin grabbed the flowers and left the room.

Ruby sat on the bed and looked around the room with fascination. There were posters and books, television and toys, and many things she didn't recognize. She wanted to touch and play with them all, but in fear of being scolded, she resisted the temptation.

"I used some of the bottled water for the lilies, but I think we still have enough for the night." Kalin had returned with the flowers in a clear glass vase filled with a little water. He set the vase on his desk which was coated with a thick layer of dust.

Kalin grabbed his bag and found the apples he had mentioned earlier.

"First apples, then you can have your donut," Kalin said as he also reached for his knife. He cut one of the fruit into four slices and handed them all to Ruby who began to munch on them right away.

"Where's your Papa?" Ruby asked as she finished her first slice.

"He got sick and died," Kalin answered as he cut his own apple.

"Where's your Mama?" Ruby asked as she took a bite of her second slice.

She got killed to protect YOU and people like YOU. Kalin nearly erupted with those words. He stopped cutting the apples. Shame for having such a thought engrossed Kalin. *It wasn't her fault,* Kalin reminded himself. If it was anyone's fault, he felt as if it was his own. Him...

...She got killed to protect me. The final realization made Kalin lose his appetite. He finished cutting the apples and handed them to Ruby. She looked confused and worried but still accepted them—albeit carefully like a squirrel taking a cracker from a stranger.

"She died protecting what she believed was right," Kalin said.

"Why?" Ruby asked. "Why die?"

"Why die?"

"Why die for what she believes in?"

"Because sometimes," Kalin started off the sentence confidently but quickly realized what a tremendous question was asked of him. "... because life... I..."

Ruby stared at Kalin with the eager eyes of an enthusiastic student.

"I don't know," Kalin finally said with a defeated smile. "Maybe it's silly to die for something you believe in. Sometimes it makes me mad when I think about it because what does it matter what you believe in and what you fought for when you're dead, right? But I guess maybe it's because even though we only live once—no, maybe it's *because* we only live once that there are times when we can't be afraid to be strong. Strong enough to risk losing everything we have and everything we want so we can protect something that's even bigger than us. Something that'll have meaning for people other than just us. Something that'll protect their lives."

Kalin thought of his mom and realized he was living in the echoes of her actions in more ways than he imagined.

"I… I talk too much with you, I think," Kalin felt puzzlingly embarrassed.

"Was your mama killed?" Ruby asked.

Kalin was surprised by the question but found no fault in it. He simply nodded.

"You only live once. Life is important." Ruby thought of the doctor. He had had a life as well. So had Jade.

"Yeah, very important. Might as well make it the best it can be and maybe help others do the same if we have the chance to."

"Killing is always bad then?" Ruby asked.

"Yeah, always. Killing is always bad," Kalin answered quickly. His reply was snappier than he intended. He quickly remembered the news of the Dr. Cowan, but unlike before he had met Ruby, Kalin's feelings regarding the case were unclear and confused.

"Well, I guess, um… maybe sometimes…" Kalin tried to redact his statement, though he was uncertain why. As far as he knew, she did murder the doctor but after getting to know the Witch, he felt like she couldn't have done what they said she's done. But then again, how well could he know her in such a short amount of time?

"Why are you with me?" Ruby asked. "I'm not a good girl. I'm horrible."

"I…" Kalin searched again the right words. "Well, to be honest I'm not sure why I'm helping you. But it feels like the right thing to do, as if I'm taking care of unfinished business." Kalin realized as he answered that perhaps he was trying to see if his mother's sacrifice was worth something through Ruby.

"And I know… that you're the Witch. And maybe you killed the doctor like everyone says." Kalin grabbed a slice of apple from Ruby. "But… I don't know. I don't think you're a horrible person. Everyone has their stories, I suppose. How can we judge a person from what others say they've done without knowing the real story behind it. I guess that's something I've learned while I was living out there on the street."

Kalin took a bite of the apple and looked up at Ruby. She was staring off into space with tears drizzling down the side of her face.

"Ruby?!" Kalin dropped the slice and stood. He sat next to Ruby uncertain of what he had done or should do next.

"I didn't want to be there. I don't know why I was there," Ruby spoke quietly with tears still flowing from her eyes. "I didn't want to do all those things. I don't know why I had to do all those things." Ruby's voice was still quiet.

The silent ambiance was broken by a car driving down the empty street, and Kalin leaned in closer to hear Ruby's words better.

"I didn't want to go there, I didn't want this." Ruby looked at her left wrist with the black band. "I don't know why... I don't know why...." Ruby's voice had begun to quiver. "I didn't want her to die, I didn't want to kill him, I didn't want to be the Witch, I don't want to be the Witch, why do I have to be... why am I..." Ruby stopped speaking. Her sniffles filled the room.

Kalin looked out the window. Although he couldn't see much from where he was sitting, the faint glow of the Light was still visible. If he let his mind slip back into the past, Kalin could still hear the gunshots. He wouldn't dare walk up to the window to stand where he stood that night.

"I don't know," Kalin said. "I don't know the answers to any of those. But let's figure it out together, and maybe I'll find what I'm looking for too."

Ruby shook her head.

"No, you'll be hurt," she said. "I'm not good."

"I'll do what I want to do," Kalin replied. "And I promise I'll be more help to you than not. If anything goes wrong, I won't blame you either."

Ruby shook her head again, and buried her face into a pillow. Her head felt fuzzy and ached, and her eyelids felt heavy. Her sniffles still filled the room.

Kalin grabbed the extra pillow next to Ruby and cleared some space on the floor for him to sleep on. They laid in silence both entranced in their thoughts.

"Good night," Kalin finally spoke. He figured Ruby had already fallen asleep. What was he doing, Kalin wondered. What was it that he was even looking for? There was an emptiness that asked for answers that Kalin could not give. He was a soulless body wandering in search for nothing.

Without knowing the word itself, Ruby wondered what her destiny was. Why God, the gods, life, fate, or whatever it was that determined her life had determined it to be the way it was and where it was determined to take her next. She wondered if she had truly escaped or if there was ever any escape at all.

The very thoughts that kept the two awake gradually led them to deep into their slumber.

Chapter 34
FACILITY ZERO

In the small reception area outside of Director Jones' office, Sarah and Julian sat on the couch waiting to reunite with their new friend. There were some magazines to read and a TV to watch. Julian folded a plane with the page he ripped out from one of the magazines.

"I can't sleep some nights." Julian said as he looked down and folded an airplane from the paper. "I feel like there's a storm coming, and I won't be able to do anything about it."

Sarah listened quietly to her friend.

"I was..." Julian paused for a moment, too embarrassed to continue. "...afraid...when I first saw Kalin up on that rooftop. I'm not like Landris. I can't do what I should do, what I want to do... or even know what to do in situations like that."

"You brought him to us, Julian. Don't take that away from yourself," Sarah told her friend.

"Yeah, but it feels like I was just lucky, you know? When I think back, I don't know how I did that. When the time comes for me to step up again... I don't know. I actually wish that time never comes. Especially when I think what if... what if... I had to protect my friends? You?" As Julian muttered the last few words, he wished that they had never left his lips.

The plane was done.

"I'm sorry," Julian said. "I... I should be stronger, I know."

"None of us are invincible, y'know? Not even Landris." Sarah smiled at her childhood friend. "You don't have to be stronger for me. You don't have to be Landris. I just want my dear Julie to be Julie."

"I thought we agreed you'd never call me that again," Julian complained.

"No one's around, Julie," Sarah playfully remarked. "And don't forget I'm here for you. I'll protect you."

The words felt bittersweet to Julian.

"Because I know you'll do the same for me, too," Sarah continued. "You always have. When I'm scared or uncertain about being here—being a Gifted—I'm glad you are here with me. I'm glad you're my friend. My *best friend*." Sarah nudged Julian who was still staring at the ground. "Isn't being there for one another what being best friends is all about? Bestie?"

"Yeah." Julian finally smiled. Despite his deeper feelings, he was thankful that someone like Sarah was his best friend.

A helicopter roared from afar.

"It must be them!" Sarah said.

On most occasions when Nancy arrived at Facility Zero by helicopter, it only turned a few of the students' heads; they were used to the noise. This time, however, word of the less than ordinary guest arriving with Director Jones had spread among the students and the staff, and the students had gathered outside at the sound of the helicopter coming their way. They chatted amongst themselves in excitement and, for many, in fear.

One particular girl, her body frozen staring at the sky, was petrified in fear. Her body felt heavy, and her lunch teased on clawing its way back out. Kiara looked to the sky and saw the helicopter. The lunch managed to make its way out.

The aircraft landed on the helipad at the top of the main office building.

"Welcome to Facility Zero!" A tall, heavy man yelled over the roaring helicopter with his arms wide open. He was an old man, but he had the energy of a youth. His long gray hair had been combed neatly back, and his face was shaped with age and rough with stubble. He wore a suit, but his top buttons were unbuttoned and it lacked a tie. With a youthful air, Mr. Ivanov seemed younger than his actual age. There was a hint of trendy cologne hanging around him.

The roar from the helicopter died down.

"I am Yuri!" The man walked over to Kalin and offered a handshake. His hand was rough and large, and his grip was impressively strong. "You must be the weird redheaded friend of the Witch! I wish I still had a young man's stupid bravery!" Yuri chuckled and then quickly turned his attention to Lily below who was a bit frightened. The air around Yuri became gentler as he crouched down to meet Lily at her level.

"And you must be Lily! The Witch!" Yuri gleefully picked up the tiny girl. "You're so light, little girl! Have you not been eating?" Yuri asked the bewildered girl. She noticed something flying over her head, and Lily looked up at a bird-like figure hovering in the sky.

"For heaven's sake, Yuri! Put her down!" Before Kalin could say anything, Nancy stepped in.

"Nancy! This child is adorable! She may look even more beautiful than you when she grows up!" Yuri laughed and gently set Lily back down. "There you are, little miss!" he said as he patted the still confused Lily on the head.

"You alright?" Kalin asked.

"That's not a bird," Lily said.

"What?" Kalin looked up and saw the shadowy eclipse of the bird as it flew below the sun. Blinded by the sun, Kalin quickly looked away.

"Landris! My Boy! Good job on your trip! I hear there's a birthday present waiting for you!" Yuri patted Landris on the back. There was enough force that if it had been Julian, it may have knocked the wind out of him. Landris groaned and hastened his pace for the door.

"Everyone, please follow Landris!" Yuri said. He waited until Nancy walked past him to walk along with the group.

Yuri leaned over so his head was close to Nancy and whispered, "Obviously, I didn't let Hamilton and his people know about you coming here today with the Witch. He's been calling, and he's getting antsy. If you're really planning to take her *there*, you might as well let 'em know sooner rather than later." Yuri pointed at Lily. "…that tiny girl is still too much of a giant to keep secret. We may be able to use her to make things a bit more favorable for us."

"I'm hoping we have at least a day or two before we have to figure out how to coordinate everything." Nancy kept a smile on her face and didn't look at Yuri as she whispered back to him. "Hamilton is at least smart enough not to be overly brave. He knows better than to do anything rash."

"You hope," Yuri said.

"What about the other details I asked you to look into?" Nancy asked as they reached the doors.

"The redheaded boy is a bit of mystery. There are leads that he could be a runaway from a town not too far from where that doctor lived, but we are not sure yet. No one will see the farmer woman for a little while. And as for the parents…" Yuri held the door open for Nancy. "…untouched as you've requested. You sure about that?"

"They're harmless," Nancy replied.

"Even if they were to disappear, no one would miss 'em," Yuri reminded Nancy.

"She might."

Yuri stopped in his tracks.

"Really?" Yuri walked hurriedly to catch up with Nancy and began to whisper again. "Is the child gone in the head or what?"

"She's something. Not sure what, yet."

"Very interesting." Yuri scratched his beard. "Slightly surprising. Overall, another fine demonstration of sensationalism in media, and their taking advantage of people's fears… it's like…"

"Enough, Yuri. I have neither the time nor the energy for your political commentary."

"You used to at least pretend to listen to my mindless ramblings," Yuri complained as he boarded the elevator. Nancy ignored him.

The group rode on the elevator in near silence while Yuri hummed with the elevator music as he snapped along.

At the ding that signified its arrival, Sarah and Julian turned their heads towards the elevator.

"I thought it'd be nice for you to see your friends again," Nancy told Lily as they got off the elevator.

"Lily!" Sarah cried out soon as she saw her friend. She ran up the girl and gave her a hug.

A crude concoction of emotion brewed inside Lily from the happiness of seeing her friend to the residual feelings from her recent events.

Sarah pulled away to see Lily's face, and Lily tried to smile. Seeing a forced smile, Sarah hugged her again. It was out of part concern, part love, and also part apology for her hand in leading Lily to her parents.

"Hey, Lily!" Julian threw a paper airplane her way. It caught Lily by a surprise and poked her in the head. Some smiled, a brother and sister cringed, and for Yuri, the incident sparked a certain curiosity. A crack in the castle wall.

"Oops," Julian said as he walked over and picked up his airplane. "Sorry about that."

Lily pinched Julian's cheek. It was an act that left Julian confused but before he could really think about it or ask, the door to the Director's office opened and they were all ushered inside.

Chapter 35
DESERT HIGHWAY

Amid the infinite stretch of barren desert and canyons, mankind carved out a lonely artifact. The usually undisturbed highway was a long connection between the barrens and human civilizations. It was only traveled by those who didn't have any other choice to reach their destinations and by those who wanted to see the beauty of the forgotten lands. A herd of vehicles headed towards the only significant landmark made by man that was unknown to the rest of the world: Facility Zero.

"It's real funny," Henderson said as he drove. He looked at Morris sitting in the passenger seat next to him. "My kid's complaining that I won't be there for her recital, and my wife is telling me about the latest gossip with her girls. It's like… if we weren't part of any this, we wouldn't even know how much the world has changed. The 'Gifted,' the 'Witch,' the 'Light,' and what not. It's like war, man. People know about it, but if you aren't there, it ain't real, y'know? The only thing that's real is what's in your own bubble. Sometimes I think maybe we're just causin' trouble by makin' all this into trouble. Maybe we should just let it all be. Be part of some other bubble."

Henderson sipped on his jug of soda that they had picked up while they were still in the city. The car smelled of the greasy burgers and fries that everyone took part in. A soft buzzing of music echoed behind them from their VIP passenger. Morris stared at the small portable camera that was the size of his thumb.

Nancy and the Witch have arrived at the facility. Everything is on schedule, a female voice from HQ patched through Morris' earpiece.

Henderson peeked behind him at their guest. Emily's ears were buried beneath large headphones as she rested her chin on her hand and stared out the window. The girl seemed a bit too relaxed for someone about to head into a potential battlefield. The Wolf Pack's leader was separated from her crew. The leader with Henderson and Morris, the twins in the car behind them, and the oldest looking one of them all, Leon, was in the car up ahead of them. To Morris's surprise, they obliged the McKinley group's request for separation without much fuss.

"You gonna go through with it?" Henderson softly asked Morris. Morris turned his attention from the camera to Henderson.

"Yeah," Morris answered after a long pause. "It's an insurance of sort."

"For what?" Henderson asked.

"When things go too far," Morris said. "When I get to a point where I need to choose between being able to call myself a decent man or a decent soldier."

"I got you, Morris," Henderson said. He raised his fist, and Morris bumped his fist into his.

Morris looked behind him to check on their star guest. He couldn't tell if her eyes were open or closed behind the aviator sunglasses. "You doing okay back there?" Morris asked in a raised voice hoping to beat the music blaring through the headphones. He felt a little silly asking given how relaxed Emily seemed to be.

As expected, Emily did not hear him. His voice was lost to the music. Faran, sitting next to Emily, watched Morris helplessly trying to get the attention of the girl. With his eyes fixed on Morris, Faran yanked off Emily's headphones.

"—the hell's your problem?!" Emily violently spun her head towards Faran who ignored Emily's rage.

Faran simply pointed at Morris. "Man asked you a question," Faran said as he kept his eyes on the uneasy Morris.

Even with her aviators hiding her eyes, it was easy to tell Emily was aggravated. "WHAT?" Emily asked Morris.

"Go ahead, team leader," Faran said.

Morris's concern for how the girl was doing seemed moot at this point, but he couldn't exactly say nothing anymore. He figured if he did, all the trouble would have been for naught. "Are you doing alright?"

Emily gave Morris a look that highly suggested she was reevaluating his level of intelligence. "Yes, I'm fine. Thank you," Emily replied with each word carrying a begrudging oomph. "Are there any more fries left?"

Morris shook his head.

"Water?"

Morris grabbed a bottle of water from the plastic bag by his feet and gently tossed it to Emily.

"Thanks," Emily replied as she quickly tore open the bottle top and chugged down the water.

"You sure your ragtag crew can handle what they've been told to do?" Faran asked with a slight hint of condescension that made Emily wonder if she was being overly sensitive.

"Yep," Emily replied. She wiped the residue of water off her lips and crumpled the empty bottle. Morris gestured for the plastic, and Emily tossed it over. He tossed it back into the bag that it came from.

"Scope out the secret base and help you kick some Gifted butt."

"I guess they better do a good job given how much you're being paid and how we have their boss hostage," Morris said.

"Don't worry. They'll do their job whether I'm dead or alive," Emily replied with an easy smile. "They're the best of the best."

Faran rolled his eyes.

"It's a shame what the world has come to that children are hired to kill people. The Gifted are nothing more than a bane to mankind. A cancer. An error by mother nature," Faran said.

"Yes, *we* may be a bane to mankind. A cancer. An error by mother nature—but it's not because we're 'Gifted,'" Emily corrected.

Faran raised his eyebrow and finally turned his head toward Emily. She was putting on her headphones again as she looked out the window.

"Can I smoke?" Emily asked.

"No," Morris expectedly answered. "You're too young."

"You are aware—" Emily tried to retort.

"Yes, I am aware of the irony, Ms. Wolf. Our car, our rules," Morris cut Emily off.

Emily shrugged and studied the canyons of the barrens as she planned for tomorrow after all that would happen today was past.

✳✳✳

In the car ahead of them, Leon shared the ride with a group of the McKinley's men. Much like his boss, Leon stared out the window.

"So, I hear you're going to help us scope out the place," Cooper asked as he drove.

Leon didn't answer. He'd been silent during their long ride.

"The man doesn't want to talk to us," Carlos said.

"We're trying real hard to be friendly here, man," Cooper said.

"Leave the man be. If he don't want to talk, he don't need to talk," Carlos said, trying to calm Cooper down.

"I don't like being ignored," Cooper said menacingly. "Especially not by some no-good guns-for-hire. How do you feel about working for a little girl, by the way?"

Leon didn't turn away from the window when he finally spoke, "I picked up my first gun when I was six. I remember thinking how heavy it was. Cold, too. It was exciting for me to be like the bigger boys—like an adult. Killed my first man about three hours after that. The second about five minutes after. The gun just became a gun after that. I remember the first few people that died by my hands and the last one, but everyone else in between is a haze. I learned quickly that life is cheap. People think it's so much more than it actually is, but taking away a life filled my belly easier than trying to save one. When the Light came, it meant nothing to us. Those with the 'gift' that couldn't protect themselves died. Those with the 'gift' that survived learned to make profit with it. The world didn't change. People adapt; the only thing different is that the bottom just has more things to play with."

"You going somewhere with this story?" Cooper asked.

"The day Emily came to the bottom of the world was the day of reckoning for most of us. She was the angel of retribution and mercy. She was the one who ended up changing everything and saving everyone. You underestimate a child who did more than God did for a place forgotten by Him and the rest of the world. That child is destined for greater things than any of us are meant for." Leon reached down into his bag by his feet and pulled out a sizable and exotic pipe. He began to pack it in with tobacco.

"Sounds like you've really fallen for her," Carlos said.

"Maybe Nancy Jones don't have the Witch. Maybe Ms. Wolf is the Witch," Cooper said.

"I do not believe in the Witch. I do not think of her. I do believe in Emily." Leon lit his pipe and took a deep breath from it. He let out an unnaturally large amount of smoke.

"At least open up the window if you're gonna smoke," Carlos said. He pressed the button to scroll down the window by Leon's side.

The smoke was sucked out the window. From the car behind, Emily watched the smoke shape into a bird before flying away.

***

In the car behind Emily's, the Howl twins were fast asleep. Norah's head rested on Noah's shoulder and Noah's hands were barely holding onto his portable video game console.

"What are we doing with a bunch of kids, man? We could die here today, and we're supposed to count on them to make our chances better?" Daniels asked Thomas as he drove.

"What makes you think it'll be violent? Maybe it'll be all chill-like," Thomas said.

"There's, like, eighty to a hundred of us coming. This is going to be a war. If Mr. McKinley wanted peace, we could have just stayed out of all this. Let the government boys handle it," Daniels scoffed. He grabbed his bottle of soda and took a big gulp before continuing. "Nancy Jones has probably got kids there, man. It's never rubbed me the right way to shoot a kid."

Thomas reached for his own soda only to be disappointed at how little of it was left.

"Man, haven't you seen that show *The Point*?" Thomas began. "You can't think of them like kids. They're *walkin' bombs*. If you saw them with guns, would you hesitate?"

"I guess not."

"Exactly. You knew when you signed up for this gig, we weren't just going to be providing 'security' for some rich folks. We were trained to kill and that's the skill we have to put the food on the table. Difference between killing these freaks—"

"*If* we have to kill them."

"Yeah, whatever, *if* we have to kill them, the difference between these *Gifted* and some of them *freaks* living in huts and caves coming at us with guns is that we'll be doing the world a favor. Shoot, we'll be doing the world a favor by killing either of them, but with the *Gifted* it's like we're fixing God's mistakes, you know?"

"If there's a God, you think he'd make mistakes?"

"I don't know. But people do. And we'll be the ones to fix it. Mind if I drink this?" Thomas grabbed Daniels' soda. After a little thought, Daniels gave him the nod.

"I don't know, man. You're thinking about this too much," Thomas continued after hydrating his dried throat. "We just do our job and get paid. Sure, it'll be best for everyone if no one died, but I guess I wouldn't mind the action or having shot one of them *Gifted*. Seriously, those things are trouble. There's only a little left," Thomas said as he shook the bottle as if that demonstrated his point. "Mind if I just finish it?"

"Go for it," Daniels gave him permission.

"Look," Thomas said as he placed the empty bottle into the holder. He pointed at the car leading the herd as it turned off the road and onto the bumpy dessert.

"Guess we're gonna get started soon," Daniels said as he turned the car to follow the pack leader and the line of cars behind followed after him.

Choppers are waiting on your go, Morris.

The radio feed buzzed into all of the McKinley unit's earpieces.

Chapter 36
NANCY'S TEA PARTY

"Yuri, would you mind grabbing us some tea and some sweets?" Nancy asked as she walked over to her desk. Yuri nodded and opened the cabinet in the office and prepared some cookies on a plate before he turned on the electric kettle. As Nancy walked over to her desk, she saw the giant black case in front of it—Landris's birthday present. But for now, it was not to be spoken of.

The group sat on the couches set up around the coffee table.

"Hey kiddo," Yuri tossed a cookie at Lily. The flying baked good caught Lily by surprise and she fumbled around with it in the air until finally being able to grab hold of it.

"Thank you," Lily answered. She was happy with herself that she caught the cookie. Yuri gave her a smile as he sat the tray of cookies and tea on the table. "These are the cookies I said we should get before!" Lily told Kalin as her eyes glowed at the sight of the baked good.

Nancy took the single chair at the head of the table.

"How is it?" Nancy asked Lily.

"They're delicious!" Lily answered with a smile while munching on the cookie. "I told you these would be good!" Lily said with a hint of glee and moxie that Kalin had missed since their trip to her parents.

"They better be for how much they cost." Kalin took the remainder of the cookie from Lily's hand and popped it into his mouth. Lily gasped and gave him a spiteful look before grabbing another one.

"We got plenty more where that came from," Yuri chuckled as he watched the Witch. "Rest of you, dig in!"

Julian and Sarah grabbed a cookie for themselves while Landris chose to simply sip on the tea.

Nancy grabbed a cookie as well and took a small nibble, then a small sip of the tea.

"So Lily…" Nancy set her tea down and lowered her cookie to the plate. "The Light. Why do you want to go there?"

The room quickly became solemn. The tea and cookies quickly realized their place as mere distractions.

"As you are probably aware," Nancy began, leaned back into her chair. "It's a place of immense controversy, mystery and security."

"Ground zero for the 'magic' phenomenon." Yuri took a big gulp of his tea. "You and the Light are the center of this whole thing. I guess it only makes sense that you want to go there."

Lily remained silent.

Nancy continued, "Military and other government officials from all over the world have placed a sanction around the whole area. Any country that can place military presence there has done so. There's not a single news organization that has been allowed or has been able to get close enough to even see the source of the Light, and even the best pictures we have are of the barricade made of military ships from all over the world deterring one another from doing any decent investigation."

"No one can even explain why, yet we can see the damn Light everywhere and anywhere," Yuri interjected again. "Funny enough that you were also all over the world." Yuri chuckled at something funny in what he said that no one else seemed to get or appreciate.

"Anyway," Nancy continued. "It's already near impossible for anyone to go to the Light. And considering you're a bit of a star yourself—"

"Some countries even think you are a spy or a secret project for a new weapon commissioned by some government." Yuri chugged the rest of his tea in one go.

"...at the most, the world thinks of you as dangerous. At the very least, they have a lot of questions," Nancy continued as if she hadn't been interrupted, watching as Lily's face became gloomier and gloomier. "That's not to say it can't be done." This time, her words brought hope back to Lily's face. "But it'll be difficult, and will take a lot of deliberations, precautions, and luck. So then, I hope you can understand why we may have some questions for you."

Lily nodded, and Nancy watched Yuri pour himself another cup of tea as she debated what her first question should be.

"The Light can be seen because it wants the world to know that it's there," Lily spoke. "It can be seen so that the person who must go there can find it."

Lily raised her arm with the black bracelet.

"This. This is what it wants."

That?

Was Lily playing Nancy for a fool? Making a mockery of her? Or was this girl out of her mind? Nancy cringed for a second before she reminded herself to maintain composure.

"What is it?" Julian asked. "What's at the Light that it wants... *that?*"

"Yes, what is that exactly?" Nancy asked calmly. Yuri stood, stretched his back and leaned forward to closely inspect the band in question. Sarah and Landris felt as if they were seeing the bracelet anew.

"I..." Lily sorted through her thoughts and memory. "I'm not sure what it's called. I'm not sure what it exactly does. I don't know if I ever knew, but I know that it's very important for me to get this to the Light. It was a promise that my friend wanted me to keep."

"What friend?" Sarah asked.

Lily's face looked desperate. "From another world that began to disappear as soon as I returned. A friend who I know was important to me, but I can't remember his face now. It's as if it was all a dream." Lily looked at her black band. "This is the only reason that I know that it wasn't."

"You said from another world?" Landris gave Lily a funny look.

"I fell in the water. I couldn't breathe and everything was dark, and then I fell asleep. When I woke up, I wasn't here anymore," Lily recollected the fragments of her past. "That's all I really remember. The next thing I remember is waking up on the shores by the same water I fell into and seeing the Light."

"Child," Yuri said, licking his dry lips a bit. "If the world wasn't the way it was... I would have thought you've done either too much of the funny stuff or you hit your head real hard somewhere."

"So let me get this straight..." Nancy massaged the bridge of her nose with her thumb and index finger. "You're telling me that your goal is to go to the world's most heavily guarded and hostile place to deliver an accessory from who-knows-where?"

Lily shrugged.

"If I may be frank, Lily, this is a bit out there," Nancy confessed. "I helped you with your first task because it at least made sense and it was feasible. But this... this just seems lunatic."

The room was silent again.

"I understand this may seem crazy. If you cannot help us, Director Jones, I..." Kalin stopped himself and placed his hand over Lily's hand. "...*We* will make the journey ourselves."

Lily didn't show what she felt by Kalin's words on the outside. Nancy studied Lily while weighing her options. She sipped on her tea as she recalled the dream that was once described to her by the Oracle-Who-Sees-Forward, but whatever awaited them at the Light had something powerful enough to be worth the risks.

"...And then I—" Lily looked at Kalin. "...We will come back and keep our promise to you. For helping us find mama and papa."

"You don't know why you're doing this, you don't who you are doing this for, but you are doing it to keep a promise?" Nancy said.

"Yes," Lily said. No one responded, silent with disbelief thick in the air. Lily spoke again, "It was a promise."

"Let me see that thing," Nancy said after a moment, reaching out to Lily with an open palm. Though slightly hesitant, Lily relinquished the artifact into Nancy's waiting hand. As soon as the cold black steel-like band touched her skin, Nancy felt a jolt of energy travel down her body. The feeling was more instinctive than anything else. Her eyes widened and her hand pulled the band closer for inspection. It was matte black inside and out, and as thin as it was, Nancy could tell just by touching it that it was a formidably durable piece of metal. Or whatever it may be made of. Nancy was briefly startled when Yuri reaching for the band from behind her. He placed his fingers on it and looked at Nancy for approval. She answered back in silence by letting the band go.

"It's so simple that it's almost boring." Yuri studied the black band for a bit until he was bored of it and spun it around his finger. "I think it's too big for your tiny wrists, little one?" Yuri looked at Lily with a sparkle of amusement in his eyes and then gestured to Lily to lean over the table.

Lily obliged and Yuri placed the band on top of her head. "Maybe it's meant to be a tiny crown!" Yuri laughed heartily while Nancy groaned in embarrassment.

"So what exactly is there at the Light, Lily? Any ideas?" Nancy asked.

"All I remember is something very important for this world," Lily answered carefully.

"You are dead set on going?" Yuri asked.

"Yes," Lily answered.

"And you." Nancy pointed at Kalin. "Mr. Witch's Friend, you're not going to stop her from this foolishness?"

He wanted to. Maybe when they were alone, he would talk to her about it. But now, when they were in front of the others, he would stand by her. Kalin felt as if it was his duty to stand by her. "I don't think I could stop her even if I wanted to," Kalin answered.

Yuri, a man of many laughs and chuckles today, gave another performance with clapping added. "I wish I was that young and stupid again!" Yuri exclaimed as he looked over at Nancy to see how she had responded. "Boss, I don't think we can convince them otherwise."

"I don't think so either. So therein lies the problem." Nancy considered the gamble again. Did the rewards outweigh the risks? Deep inside, Nancy knew she had already made the decision a while ago.

"We will need some time to talk about this, Lily. Perhaps we might even ask Sarah to help you remember your time in this other world you spoke of. But for now why don't you all get some rest while Mr. Ivanov and I discuss these matters." Nancy smiled at Lily. "I'll do everything that I can to help you."

Lily smiled back.

"Thank you, Director Jones. Really, thank you," Lily said.

"You can thank me when I actually have some good answers for you." Nancy stood. "Now, children, shoo! Shoo! Sarah, Julian and Landris can show you guys around the facility. We'll call for you when we need you." Nancy froze for a moment as if she had just remembered something. "Oh, wait. Except you, Landris. You stay. I've got something for you."

Landris shrugged.

"We'll introduce you to our friends," Julian said.

"I think you'll really like what we have here," Sarah said.

Everyone except Landris watched the children head for the door. Lily grabbed another cookie for the road. After getting a nod from Kalin and then a nod from Director Jones, Lily grabbed a couple more.

"Wait!" Yuri stopped the group. He picked up the plate of cookies and began to walk towards them.

"Witch's friend," Yuri called out to Kalin. "You have to let the girl live a li—"

Stumbling over his own feet, Yuri fell to the ground with a loud clash, the plate shattering.

"Clumsy me!" Yuri said with a guffaw while on the floor.

"Yuri!" Nancy cried.

"What?" Yuri looked at Nancy and saw the worry in her face. Blood dripped from his hand to the carpet below.

"Mr. Ivanov! Are you alright?!" Sarah ran over to the old man and the rest of the group quickly followed.

"Yeah, yeah, it's nothing," Yuri dismissed as he sat up and quickly pulled out the few shards of plate embedded in his hand. "Sorry about the carpet, Nancy."

"Kalin! You can heal him, can't you?!" Julian cried.

"Yeah, yeah." Still a bit dumbfounded, Kalin quickly composed himself.

"Can you do such a thing?" Yuri asked with eager eyes as placed the last shard he could see in his hand onto one of the bigger broken pieces of the plate. "Please help me, boy. I am making such a mess on Nancy's precious carpet."

"Yes, I'm terribly sorry, Kalin, but please help Mr. Ivanov," Nancy pleaded.

Kalin quickly hovered his hand over Yuri's bloodied hand. Even sitting, Kalin seemed smaller than he actually was next to Yuri. Even their hands demonstrated Yuri's sheer colossal stature.

Streams began to vapor out from Kalin's hand and then engulfed Yuri's hand. The two hands looked as if they were lit on fire with the streams.

Lily gathered all the pieces of the plate and looked at Nancy for guidance as they hovered in the air. Nancy pointed at the coffee table and all the pieces, big and minuscule, neatly piled themselves on top of the table.

"Sorry, it's usually faster if it's for myself," Kalin said.

"Is that right?" Yuri made a mental note in his mind, and something within Kalin told him that he had made a mistake revealing more information than was necessary to this man.

The bleeding stopped, and the blood that was once there incinerated into the stream. In less than a minute, the wound had closed itself. Once his work was done, Kalin moved his hand away.

Yuri looked down at his hand, and wiggled his fingers. No pain whatsoever. "Fantastic!" Yuri clapped in joy. "Look how clean it is! Thank you very much! What a fantastic 'gift' you have!"

Kalin gave a forced smile.

"You can go now!" Yuri said with big smile. "Off you go!"

"I'm so sorry about that, Kalin," Nancy said. "But thank you."

With an air of confusion regarding what just occurred, the group left the Director's office and closed the door behind them.

Chapter 37
THE WITCH KILLER

Emily let out a playful whistle.

"That's a pretty sweet secret base," Emily remarked as she pulled her eyes away from her binoculars.

The sun was beginning to set in the rugged terrain of the canyon desert. The McKinley's armada had halted their march still far away, barely within eyesight of Facility Zero. They tried to hide as much of their armada behind the rugged canyon terrain.

"I assume they have some sort of satellite surveillance if they were able to build a place like that out here," Emily remarked to Morris who was also looking at the facility with his own binoculars. "But I guess them not seeming to notice us here must mean either you guys have really good tech support or you have the approval from friends in high places for this mission."

"I think the Witch can be killed," Yuri said as he studied his hand. It didn't even leave a scar. "It just has to be a surprise. Mangle her enough in one blow that she doesn't see coming. Keep her relaxed. Have her trust her surroundings. And then… BANG!" Yuri chuckled to himself. "A big gun should do it. A hole big enough that her little friend can't heal her fast enough to save the girl. Maybe even with a twist of a big knife."

"Is that what all that was about?" Landris looked at Yuri with slight disgust—a look that Yuri just smiled off.

"I figured," Nancy said with a sigh. "It's good to know that there's a chance the Witch can fall if we need her to, but she's more useful to us alive than dead. For now, anyway. By the way, Yuri, you owe me a new tea set. Not to mention I expect the carpet to be free of any bodily fluids by tomorrow."

"Fine, fine. It'll be done." Yuri didn't seem to be bothered much by Nancy's requests.

"Are you planning on taking her *there*?" Landris asked his sister.

"You don't know your sister very well!" Yuri guffawed. "I'm sure that's been determined since the beginning when we acquired the little girl."

"It doesn't change the fact that we still have variables to consider—none of which were answered by the Witch. I didn't expect her to be so clueless," Nancy said.

"The child is frighteningly, illogically human," Yuri chuckled.

"Illogically human?" Landris asked.

"Promises. Keeping promises. The entire idea and the practice is such a human thing to do. It's entirely unnatural, and yet so natural. It's what keeps the world sane and together. A simple trust." Yuri seemed like he was rambling more to himself than anyone else.

"Illogically decent, maybe. But, human?" Nancy corrected Yuri. "I think this makes her more inhuman than anything."

"That's the point!" Yuri laughed. No one understood.

"So, why are we going? What's the point, Nancy?" Landris asked.

"My, my, Landris. You're only born once; you have to think big. If we aren't there, someone else will be. You can't be afraid of being a pioneer." Nancy paused for a moment. "Whatever made the world this way, the answer lies at the Light. My gut tells me so."

"We should have asked the Witch—Lily—if the Light did have anything to do with all this. I mean, I guess it seems logical, but—" Landris got cut off by Nancy.

"I'm pretty sure her answer would have been, 'I don't know.'"

Landris couldn't disagree.

"Anyway, Landris. Time for your birthday surprise!" Nancy carried out the black case which had been by her desk over to the coffee table. With a little grunt, she placed it on top of the table.

"What is it?" Landris asked as he unlatched the locks on the case and opened it up. Inside the dark metal casing was a set of two identical swords that were long enough to make sense of the case's great length. The scabbards glistened black down to the hilt where there was a line of silver. Right above the line was the simple design of a silver aegis.

Landris unsheathed one of the blades so he could see it for himself. The blade was ebony without any shine. Although the sword was long enough to be a two-handed weapon, it was balanced perfectly in weight to feel comfortable carrying it one-handed. He marveled at the blade and its dark metal that refused to shine under the light.

"I figured having a weapon like this suited your 'gift' very well. The boys at the lab called it XNC1-1. The material for the blade was entirely invented by our R&D for a different project and is currently considered indestructible which means you'll never have to sharpen it and it'll just cut about anything as long as you have the strength for it."

"XNC1-1, huh?" Landris touched the business end of the blade with his finger. With only a slight press, the blade cut through his skin. He suckled on his bleeding wound.

"And since swords are the symbolic weapon for a hero, I thought it may suit the role you'll have to take on in the future. If it works out

well enough, I thought I'd make it a standard issue for the more quali-
fied students, but currently those are the only two in existence and
quite costly to make. They actually had a nickname for it other than
the official name, XNC1-1."

Landris looked at Nancy waiting to hear the answer.

"They called it the 'Witch Killer.'"

"Really?" Landris remarked with a grin. "They didn't think that
was a really dumb name?"

"They're convinced that in the hands of someone like you, it
would even be capable of bringing her down. It's the best weapon our
technology can offer to the hero to take down the villain."

Done marveling at the blade, Landris sheathed it back into its dark
scabbard. He ran his thumb over the silver aegis icon on the scabbard
and then locked the blades back in their case. "Thanks, Nancy. This is
a nice gift," Landris said as he locked up the case.

"Happy birthday, boy," Yuri said. "You're growing into a fine
man."

Landris scoffed and headed for the doors. He paused mid step,
wanting to say something but forgetting what it was he wanted to say.

Nancy walked over to her large window which oversaw the facility as well as the crowd of students that had gathered outside the
building, but her attention was on the Light beyond the horizon. For
once, the Light didn't annoy her. "The Witch is ours, and the Witch
can be killed." Nancy turned her head to Yuri and smiled. "Just a little
more, Yuri. Just a little more."

Yuri smiled and helped himself to another tea.

Chapter 38
EYES OF THE BEHOLDER

"Leon..." Morris ignored Emily. "Have you found the generators yet?" The stoic member of the Wolf Pack inhaled from his pipe again and let out another smoke. The smoke formed into a bird and took flight. "Not yet," Leon answered.

"Let me know as soon as you do. As soon as the sun is down, we'll make our move." Morris looked to Henderson. "What's the word on the second wave?"

"They'll be here in an hour. So, by sundown," Henderson answered as he munched on a small bag of chips.

"That'll make it about twenty something in cars as well as a few choppers. We'll be more than a hundred strong storming that place." Morris looked through the binoculars again.

Noah's eyes widened at the number. His sister, Norah, still sat in the car in an attempt to dodge the sun, but kept the door open for air.

"Should be enough," Carlos said.

"I guess that'll depend on the Gifted they have and the Gifted we have," Henderson answered.

Landris was greeted by little paper objects being thrown at him as he left Nancy's office.

"Frog!!" Julian and Lily cried out as they threw paper frogs at Landris when he exited.

"Right," Landris spoke to himself.

"We thought we'd wait until you were done," Sarah said.

"Happy birthday," Kalin said.

"Thanks." Landris didn't seem comfortable with the congratulation.

"Frog!" Lily picked up the frog and threw it at Landris again. She obviously wasn't entirely satisfied with Landris's earlier reaction.

Landris caught the paper frog midair and crumpled it in his hand. After seeing Lily's silent, but notable reaction, Landris gestured to Julian for his frog.

"Frog," Landris said as he tossed the frog back at Lily.

She caught the frog and smiled. Landris didn't mind playing along if it meant putting a smile on Lily's face since her meeting with her parents.

"What are you guys going to do?" Landris asked.

"We thought that maybe we'd show these two around the facility. If we have enough time, possibly grab dinner together at the cafeteria as well," Julian said.

"Well," Landris said. "I don't want to do any of that. What if I just borrow the ketchup-head, and you guys do you own thing and we'll meet up whenever?"

Kalin raised an eyebrow.

"Yeah, that's right. I want to bond with the Witch's best friend. You okay with that?" Landris asked Kalin.

Kalin shrugged. "Sure," he said, curious of Landris's intentions. "You okay going with Sarah and Julian?" Kalin asked Lily.

Lily nodded.

"We'll take good care of her, Kalin, don't you worry," Sarah said as she grabbed Lily's hand.

"You sure, Lily?" Kalin asked Lily again.

"I'm gonna have fun with Sarah! You have fun with Landris," Lily said with a smile. "But join us soon! You too, Landris!"

"Alright then." Landris walked towards the elevators. He pressed one button for going up and the other for going down. "You and I are going to the roof."

***

"It'd be best if we could wait until a bit deeper into the night," Emily said to Morris.

"I know," Morris said. "But Mr. McKinley's worried that Nancy may move the Witch if we wait too long."

"Figures." Emily instinctively placed a cigarette between her lips. It was her 'thinking-buddy.' But sensing a glare from Noah, Emily glanced behind her to confirm that her senses were true. She reluctantly spat the cigarette back out.

"Leon works best outside the action. Somewhere where he can oversee the events," Emily told Morris.

"Alright." Morris looked at his men. "We're going to start setting up for the operation. Henderson, you are our best sharpshooter here. I want you to take a few of the men and try to find some vantage points. Leon, you may join them if you wish. No cars. Get to your positions on foot. The rest of us will wait for the second wave, and at night, we'll storm them from all sides."

Leon looked at Emily who gave him a nod. He walked back to the car he had arrived in and grabbed his belongings.

Kalin and Landris walked onto the rooftop baked from the heat of the sun. The helicopter they arrived in was resting at the helipad.

"Whew, can't say I missed this much," Landris said as he walked over to the edge of the building where there was a small fence. "Look." Landris pointed below them.

Kalin walked over to find a large group of students scattered around about the courtyard all facing towards the building they were on.

"They're all excited for your little friend," Landris said.

"Damn it," Kalin said as he turned to head for the door.

"Stop," Landris grabbed Kalin with his free hand. "You need to stop babying her. All that's going to do is make her weak."

Kalin hesitated for a moment and studied Landris as he processed his suggestion.

"They're not bad people," Landris added. "They might be curious and maybe even afraid, but none of them are bad people. As Gifted they all share the feeling of being hunted and hated for being different."

"You seem different," Kalin said.

"This is my home. This is my family," Landris said.

Kalin nodded and walked next to Landris near the edge. He couldn't see Lily, Sarah or Julian yet. They must have been taking their time leaving the building.

"I thought about what you said. About protecting her," Kalin said after a bit of silence.

"Yeah? And?"

"I... I don't know. I don't know what that means anymore."

"..."

"I obviously want what's best for her, but I don't know if I know what that is. I don't know if what I've been doing has been good for her, and, whether it has or hasn't been, I don't know if I can do what's good for her in the future. I don't... I don't know if I can protect her—guard her—from what she has to face. What she had faced. For God's sake, I'm just turning seventeen this year, and I don't even know what's right for myself, let alone having to have someone else's life in my hands."

"You chose this," Landris said.

"What?"

"From what you've told me, you chose to stay with the Witch. It's sort of unfair for you to get so weak now, isn't it?"

"That's..."

"And from what it sounds like, she's not only dependent on you, but you're dependent on her. Look, man. We make choices in life without ever knowing for sure where it's gonna go. But when we make our choices, we have to be ready to deal with whatever consequences it may bring. If not, you're just playing with yourself."

"What if my choices are the wrong choices? What if I should have never chosen... No, never mind..."

"Yeah, you hold that tongue. I'll give you that you really do seem to have her best interests at heart. Whatever you do, you'll do what you think is best for her. That means a lot. More than the mistakes you'll make along the way."

"Thanks, Landris."

"Don't thank me. Just stop being such a whiny brat about it. Man up."

"Right."

"Guard what's important to you. No one else will do it for you."

"Right."

Kalin and Landris noticed as the crowd below them slowly and carefully began huddling closer near the door of the building. Sarah, Julian, and Lily walked out the door a second later.

***

"We're ready for the air support. Have them be here in an hour." Morris *hung up the phone.*

Just then, Emily's phone gave a jingle. A text message. "Leon says he found the generators," Emily told Morris.

Morris nodded. He put his hand in his pocket to make sure the camera was still there.

Faran walked up next to Morris.

"I don't like this," Faran whispered to Morris. "I want to keep them all where I can see them."

"Whether you like it or not, we have to work with them. Make the best of it with what we've got. They have a base full of soldiers and, and far as we're concerned, possibly trained Gifted over there." Morris gave a slightly defeated look to Faran. "I don't like it either, but what other options do we have at this point?"

The elevator door opened to the first floor of the office building.

"Yeah, so Julian used to wait for me by the baseball field every day after school," Sarah told Lily.

"Really?" Lily's eyes glowed as she looked at Julian. "Do you love Sarah?"

"What?!" Julian's face reddened and he spoke louder than he had intended. "No!"

"No?" Lily looked a bit puzzled.

"No?" Sarah looked a bit disappointed.

"I mean, but, I do *love you* but I don't *love you*… you know?" Julian stuttered.

"Oh, I see." Sarah smiled as she pushed open the door to exit the building.

"I think…" Lily had to stop and swallow her words. Outside, she was greeted by what seemed like a hundred eyes staring at her. She wanted to hide behind Sarah but managed to stand tall—though her feet still felt rooted to the ground.

"Hey, everyone," Sarah announced. "This is Lily!"

The crowd stared blankly for a moment and then looked at one another.

Sarah looked down at Lily and saw the fear and dejection on her face. She grabbed the Witch by the hands and led her to others.

"Shannon!" Sarah smiled and walked over to the petite, orange-brown haired girl near her who tried to mask her surprise and awkwardness as Sarah approached her with the Witch herself.

"Hiiiiii…" Shannon said trying to sound as excited as she could be.

"Lily, was it?" Shannon offered her hand to Lily, and Lily carefully reached out and grabbed Shannon's hand. Shannon tried to smile.

Lily couldn't.

"Look! Magic!" Shannon snapped both of her fingers, and from behind her, wave after wave of butterflies flew out.

Dazzled, Lily watched them as they took to the sky before Shannon snapped her fingers again, and they all disappeared into sparkles of glitter.

"I just tried to show off in front of the Witch," Shannon said, her face clearly showing her discomfort. "I'm sorry. I was just trying to make the awkward situation better." Shannon put her head down in shame as she heard a few chuckles around her. It wasn't like her to act and feel so odd.

"You're fine, Shannon! Jean! Jamie!" Sarah called out to the twin girls who had been standing next to Shannon. "Come say hello!"

They waved and shook their heads at the same time.

"Hi," a deep voice startled Sarah from behind. A skinny but muscular, tall boy with swaying dark brown hair and bony facial features stood next to a sand-toned girl about half his height and twice the length of hair as his.

"Gus! Maria!" Sarah greeted the two. She was thankful for them and glad that Lily's first acquaintances would be friendly.

"My name is Gus." Gus offered his hand to Lily who carefully offered hers.

"My name is Maria," Maria said with an accent that Lily found very charming.

"Tara! Dominique!" Sarah called out to the two who were watching them from afar. Without Landris, the two always seemed the most reclusive as if they thought everyone else had fleas. Tara, who took advantage of the desert sun to properly tan, looked at Sarah with her big, squirrel-like eyes as if Sarah had offended her and spoke quietly to Dominique. Rubbing his dark buzz cut head, Dominique nodded and began to walk away with Tara.

"Don't worry, Lily," Julian said. "They're jerks to everyone."

Sarah wasn't too surprised by their reaction.

A small girl who was observing the Witch from afar began to walk toward her. Marched towards her. She carried books that seemed even bigger carried by her, and she had a child's eyes but it was intense and focused like that of an adult's. "Hello," She spoke strongly and stood tall in front of Lily. The girl was shorter and looked even younger than Lily.

"Nada!" Sarah smiled with joy. "Lily, this is Nada! She's the youngest of all of us here but probably the smartest of all of us as well."

Lily and Nada locked eyes in silence. Sarah had gone unnoticed, tuned out. Nada looked at her intensely while Lily felt awkward and uncertain at the sense of animosity from her. "I don't blame you," Nada finally said. "I really don't."

Lily and Sarah sensed something wrong but couldn't interrupt Nada. She spoke softly in her still very childlike voice but sternly and without fear.

"I'm from a small village far away where people are still ruled by superstitions and beliefs," Nada continued. "When the tales of the 'Witch' and the Light appeared, most people believed the end was near. They spoke of it daily and how we should prepare for the end. To cleanse ourselves to prevent from becoming a 'cursed'—a 'devil's soldier'—like the Witch. I was young when I discovered my 'gift,' and I did not know what I was doing when I showed it to my friends. I thought I could trust them."

Tears began to fall from Nada's eyes. But her eyes did not lose any of its strength. "My mother and I were dragged out of our homes that night. Me for being cursed, and her for giving birth to a cursed one. My father was beaten to death in front of us as he tried to stop the neighbors. My mother... they threw rocks at her as she pleaded with them to let at least me go until her voice just stopped. If it wasn't for *her*, I would have died as well. If it wasn't for her, I would have been lost."

Nada wiped her tears with the palm of her hand. "I don't blame you. It's not your fault," Nada said. "But did you... did you really kill that doctor?"

There was silence for a moment as everyone turned their attention to Lily.

"Yes," Lily answered.

"Why? Was it worth it?" Nada was disappointed that her voice shook.

"I don't know," Lily said. "I don't know. I'm sorry."

Nada shook her head and walked away.

Sarah and Julian shared a look. Julian walked with Nada to console her while Sarah began to walk Lily towards the dormitory as she whispered apologies and defenses for Nada's usual self that wasn't shown.

Howard stood in the middle of the stairs looking at the entrance of the dorms debating whether or not to take a look at the Witch or retreat up into the hallway that led back to his room.

The padded doors opened.

Howard saw a glimpse of Sarah and the raven hair of Lily before he quickly turned around and went into his dorm.

Sarah looked up at the sound of a door closing. She felt bitter, but said nothing of it. "Come on," Sarah said as she led Lily through the living room area of the dormitory.

Lily paid no attention to the grand piano, the fireplace, the giant television with its collection of movies at it side, and the other details that she'd normally be fascinated and infinitely entertained by.

As Sarah made it up the stairs, she saw one of the doors swing open.

Kiara.

Sarah stopped herself from calling out to her too brightly. She felt the need to be cautious. "Hi, Kiara," Sarah said with a small smile and a soft wave as she held tightly to Lily's hand.

Kiara paid no attention to Sarah. Her eyes were glued to the pale girl who came up to about shoulder length next to her friend. Was her heart still beating? She had to say something back to Sarah, but Kiara's lips were frozen.

They were closer now.

They were right in front of her.

"Hi," Kiara finally squeezed out the word. And then she was able to manage a smile.

"This is Kiara," Sarah told Lily. "She's one of my closest friends here."

Hearing that she was Sarah's close friend, Lily tried to smile for Kiara and offered her hand for a handshake.

Kiara carefully grabbed Lily's hand. Was her hand shaking? Was it clammy? The Witch's hand was soft, but the visions of her dreams that were whispering to her were now screaming. Kiara tried her best not throw up again.

The Witch let go of her hand.

"I'm going to show her my room," Sarah said. "Let's all have dinner later."

"Okay," Kiara tried to smile again.

Her friend led the Witch to her room.

Kiara stared at her hand that shook the Witch's hand. She swiftly walked back into her room.

Hearing Kiara's door close, Howard made his way over to her room. "You should really lock the door when you're dealing with that," Howard said as he saw Kiara with the shining gun in her hand. Her hands and legs were shaking.

"I don't know if I can do this," Kiara said.

"Then you shouldn't," Howard said.

"I have to." Kiara looked at Howard with determined eyes. "It's not for me. It's for everyone else."

Chapter 39
THE TWO ORACLES

Julian knocked on Sarah's door. He heard a gentle song playing from the room. As Sarah quietly opened the door, Julian caught a face of concern that Sarah quickly hid behind a smile.

"I had a chat with Nada. She wanted me to tell you that she was sorry. She's in the library reading. I think, maybe sometime later, we can reintroduce the two of them," Julian spoke softly to Sarah. Over her shoulder, Julian could see Lily sitting on Sarah's bed folding more paper cranes. "Is she okay?" Julian asked.

"She hasn't spoken much since we came to my room. We've just been folding papers," Sarah said.

The McKinley's men waited patiently and bided their time. Most waited in the cars taking in what they thought could be their last moments of rest and peace. The more restless of the bunch kept themselves occupied with whatever the dessert had to offer them. Emily and Morris stood next to one another and watched Facility Zero light up in the desert evening.

Sarah opened the door a little wider and allowed Julian to come into the room. Lily seemed too focused on her paper folding to notice him enter.

"Hey, Lily." Julian sat next to Lily. "Folding more of those cranes?"

Lily kept folding with her hands and turned her face to see Julian. Without words, Lily grabbed Julian's cheek and pulled on it a bit before letting go. Julian was as confused as the first time he experienced Lily's cheek pinch.

Emily pulled out a cigarette from her beat-up cigarette box. The cigarette was worn, but she hoped that it wasn't stale. She placed it between her lips and lit it up with her finger.

Not stale. A small victory.

"It'll kill you," Morris said as he walked up next to Emily.

Emily chuckled as she pulled the cigarette out from her lips. "Yeah, I'm sure that's what I should worry about killing me today." Emily placed the 'cancer stick,' as her boyfriend called it, back between her lips, "We all choose our own poison, I guess."

Emily let out a puff of white smoke from her pink lips.

"But it is a disgusting habit, so I'm doing a one-a-week—one-a-month?—whatever sort of thing. It's none of your business though, right? Can't you just see me as a co-worker?"

"Wait!" Kiara called out to Sarah before she could close the door.

"Kiara?" Sarah was surprised and happy to see her friend again. Kiara peeked behind Sarah to look at Julian and Lily.

"Why don't use your magic to fold those papers?" Julian asked.

Lily didn't answer right away. She quietly finished her crane.

"Can I talk to you for a sec?" Kiara asked Sarah.

"I want to make them with my own hands," Lily answered Julian.

"Sure," Sarah answered as she quietly shut the door behind her.

Morris didn't answer right away. "It's weird for me too, feeling all paternal. But you all are so young. I mean, what'd you all want to do before all this?" Morris asked.

"What do you mean?" Emily asked back.

"Before the Light—before all this. I'm sure being a leader of mercenary group wasn't something you planned on for growing up."

Emily turned her head and gave Morris a confounded look. "What, are we bonding now?" Emily choked on her own smoke as she chuckled.

Kiara and Sarah stepped out a few paces away from the door. Kiara rested her arms on the railing as she looked at the empty lounge below them.

"Look, Kiara," Sarah spoke first. "I know you don't feel too comfortable about Lily, but just try to get to know her. She's not what they say she is."

"You mean the Witch?" Kiara said.

"Yeah," Sarah replied.

"What if…" Kiara composed her voice from trembling. She didn't look at Sarah; it'd be too hard. "What if I told you that I had a dream about her?"

"It's just…" Morris wasn't really sure himself why he asked such a question. "Forget it."

"I don't know. I always wanted to do something with my guitar. Be the front-man and the lead guitarist. Greedy, yeah, but I loved it and was pretty good at both." Emily smiled with a certain sense of pride. "If I may toot my own horn." Emily took another inhale of the cigarette. "My not-a-teenage-dream-but-an-actual-plan was to go to college. Maybe go to law school. That seemed interesting. But shit happens and we make do."

Morris tried to hide his smile that he knew would offend Emily.

"What was that?" Emily didn't miss it. "Was that a you're-just-a-kid-after-all-smile right there?"

"Yeah, yeah it was," Morris said. "That'd been better than this."

Emily grumbled.

Morris' earpiece patched in.

Sarah walked up next to Kiara and rested her arms on the railing. "What was it? Sarah asked.

"What if I told you she'll do terrible things? What if I told you that because of her, a lot of people will die?" Kiara finally faced Sarah. She watched as Sarah's eyes widened and stopped blinking for a moment.

"You saw all this?" It was now Sarah who looked away from Kiara and looked below at the lounge.

"I did. It was horrifying," Kiara told Sarah. "She's just a disguised lamb, Sarah. That girl, *Lily,* will be the end of us all."

Sarah thought to herself in silence. After few moments a small smile bloomed on her face. "I always envied your 'gift,' Kiara," Sarah said.

"What?"

"Your 'gift.' To see forward instead of having to see backwards." Sarah faced Kiara who looked dumbfounded. "There are things I've seen that I wish I had never seen—especially like what happened to that girl in my room right now. Because, you see, my 'gift'… it doesn't allow me to do anything about what I see. What I feel. What I… they… experienced. I'm just a bystander. All I can do is witness what's already been done and accept that none of it can be changed."

"Sarah…"

"But your 'gift,' Kiara," Sarah continued. "At least if we know what's ahead, we can do something about it."

"Sarah, I've never been able to change anything I've seen. Ever." Kiara's words robbed some of the confidence and fragile hope from Sarah's face. It was only for a brief moment that Kiara almost missed it.

"But at least we have a chance. A hope." Sarah placed her hand on Kiara's. "I didn't see what you saw, but I believe you. But you have to believe me when I say that Lily isn't someone to harm anyone. And just in case, I'll be there. I'll help her anyway I can to walk the right path. Give her a chance."

"It won't matter, Sarah." Kiara gently removed her hand from Sarah's.

"We have to at least try. I have to at least try if that's what it means to protect her. She's gone through enough. What else can we do, Kiara?" Sarah began walking towards to her room. With her hand on the door handle she turned her head to Kiara once again. "Thank you," Sarah said. "For your concern. Let's have dinner later. All of us. I want you to meet her."

Kiara remained silent.

Sarah's door swung open unexpectedly, and Sarah stumbled backwards as Julian stepped out.

"Sorry!" Julian said. "It's Director Jones! She says she's ready for us."

Lily, with her backpack strapped on her back, was hidden behind Julian.

"Let's go!" Sarah said as she hurried into her room and gathered her personals. As she walked out, she patted Lily on the back. "We'll have dinner afterwards!"

The three briskly walked past the Oracle-Who-Sees-Forwards.

"See you later, Kiara!" Julian said as he walked past her.

Sarah gently touched Kiara's shoulder as she walked past her.

Lily and Kiara's eyes met briefly as the Witch walked past the Oracle.

Kiara watched the three leave the building standing exactly where she had stood when she was speaking with Sarah. The childlike eyes of the Witch was disturbing and foul.

"We have to at least try," Kiara said to herself. She brushed her hand against her back and felt the hard steel of the gun. Slowly, she headed for the exit herself, gathering courage with each step.

"We're moving out in twenty minutes," Morris said. "Better go get your team ready."

"Yeah," Emily put out her cigarette with her tongue and placed it in her inner pocket of her jacket to save it for later.

"You know," Morris said as they both turned towards the cars. "I hope the world goes back to the way it was so that you can pursue those other dreams and goals of yours."

Emily gave Morris a look as if he had said something silly. "Goes back to the way it was? But I've already adapted."

Chapter 40
CALM BEFORE THE STORM

Large falcons of smoke dispersed into a flock of sparrows, and the flock landed on top of the building that housed the generator powering facility zero. They were silent, and, in the evening's shade, they were ignored. The sparrows dispersed into a swarm of mice and breezed into every crevice of the building without any of the Silver Aegis agents knowing any better.

"I'm ready," Leon said on top of one of the smaller canyons outside of Facility Zero. In front of him were a couple of men of the McKinley Security taking aim with their rifles.

Yuri put the phone down from his ear onto his lap. He sat alone with Nancy who was sitting across the coffee table from him looking at her tablet.

"Still not picking up?" Nancy asked.

"Nope," Yuri said. "It's almost as if he's dodging our calls."

"Something's up," Nancy said. "It's not like Hamilton to be so quiet. Especially with news like, 'I have the Witch.' I would have expected him to be sulking in his office, sipping on his whiskey, and running the gerbil in his head trying to figure out how to turn the tide, but not this silence."

"So what does it mean?" Yuri asked.

"It means he's already done something and doesn't want us to affect it in any way until it's done." Nancy didn't look up from her tablet. "Or just licking his wounds. He's not an audacious man. Whatever the case, it shouldn't affect our plans very much."

"Just go to the port?" Yuri brushed his beard with his hand.

"It'd have been ideal if we had a way to simply bypass the military barricade, but since that's impossible, it'd be best for us to just put Hamilton on the spot—while making it seem like we're still playing ball, of course." Nancy looked up. "Why fight if there's a way to keep everyone happy, right?"

"Or at least pretend to. Not sure if Hamilton will remain docile if he knew you were planning to take sole ownership of whatever it is at the Light. Especially if he knew of that girl's dream," Yuri chuckled.

"Ignorance is a blissful thing." Nancy smiled.

A momentary silence.

"Nancy," Yuri said. "I have to ask again. Did you really think it was such a good idea to take that girl to see her…'parents'?"

"The way I thought of it," Nancy murmured, her focus back onto her tablet. "If it worked out, great. She'll feel indebted to me. And if it didn't work out, there were three likely scenarios. One, Landris kills her, and then great, the Witch is dead by our hands. Two, Landris doesn't kill her and we're all dead. There isn't much we can do when we're dead. Three, nothing really happens other than the Witch feeling as if she has nowhere else to turn to other than to us."

Yuri quietly brushed and scratched his beard.

A knock on the door interrupted the two's conversation.

"You've got eyes from above for the whole facility, team leader," Henderson, on a different hill, whispered into his earpiece as he watched Facility Zero carry on with their nightly routines through the scope of his rifle.

"Choppers are coming in soon. Everyone else good to go?" Morris asked from the driver seat watching the buildings glow brighter as the night grew darker.

"We got the whole place surrounded and just waiting on your go, team leader," Faran said in one of the vehicles at the other side of the Facility Zero. He was moved under suggestion by Morris to spread around the Gifted they had on hand and to prevent any more frictions between him and Emily.

Morris scrounged up from his pocket the small camera. He secured it to one of the many outer pockets of his tactical vest.

Yuri opened the door for Sarah, Julian, and Lily.

"Where's the friend and Landris?" Yuri asked as he ushered them in.

"Kalin and Landris went off by themselves," Julian answered as he guided Lily around the giant.

"I see." Yuri looked over at Nancy who was still sitting by the coffee table. "Should I call them over as well? Maybe over the intercom?"

"No need. This will be simple and quick." Nancy stood up and smiled. "Come on in, everyone."

The group sat around the coffee table again much like they had earlier that day. Except now, instead of Kalin, Sarah sat next to Lily.

"We'll find him right after this," Sarah told Lily who seemed a bit uneasy without her constant companion.

"Yes, Lily. I'll get straight to the point. I just called you up here to let you know that we'll be taking you to the Light." Nancy watched as Lily's face lit up brightly.

"Look how happy she looks!" Yuri pointed at Lily who blushed at his remark.

"But there is one thing, Lily. One thing we must do first," Nancy said.

Kiara walked through the empty halls of the director's office building and pressed the button to summon the elevator. She brushed her hand against her back, near the hip to feel for the hard steel. Her hand gently jiggled the gun to make sure that it secure. But even moving the gun that slightly worried her that it might go off.

A bell dinged to notify that the elevator had arrived.

As she walked into the confined space of the lift, Kiara could smell the familiar scent of her friends.

"You good?" Morris turned his head to Emily sitting behind him. She had her ears buried under the headphones again but still managed to give him a single thumbs-up. Sitting next to her was one of the McKinley's men she had barely met... was it Simpsons? Sampson? And sitting between them was a shadow of a man waiting patiently for his turn.

"...so that's why I dyed my hair red." Kalin rested his back on the railing and casually swung one of Landris's ebony swords. He didn't say it, but it was obvious that Kalin seemed to appreciate the sword quite a bit. The other ebony sword rested in its opened case.

"Basically, so that she can find you easier?" Landris said as he sat next to Kalin.

"Yeah, and I guess I grew to like it a bit," Kalin admitted.

Landris heard the door to the rooftop open and watched as a couple of the staff brought suitcases to load into the helicopter.

"I guess Nancy made up her mind," Landris said.

"We're going to the Light?" Kalin asked

"Guess so." Landris stood as he heard the sound of helicopters echoing from afar.

"You guys expecting more visitors?" Kalin asked as he stood and looked at the general direction Landris was looking at.

"No. I don't think so anyway," Landris answered.

They can probably hear the choppers now. We should get moving, Morris, Henderson's voice patched through Morris' earpiece.*

"Copy. Kill the lights on my go. Make sure you get both the main and the backup generators," Morris gave his orders to Leon.

"We'd like to ask you to allow Sarah to see into your past again," Nancy told Lily. "To find out more about this... other world you visited... and perhaps learn more about what's at the Light."

"Sounds like the perfect idea to me," Yuri remarked.

"Sure. Maybe then we can also find out why you were asked to do this Lily," Sarah turned to Lily who seemed uncertain but not in disdain of the idea.

"Okay," Lily quietly replied after a short pause.

"5." Morris started his car. "Keep our own lights off."

"Alright, should we just start this then?" Sarah glanced at Director Jones then back to Lily.

Another knock on the door interrupted them.

Yuri walked over to the door and slightly cracked it open. He turned his head back to Nancy.

"4."

Leon focused on his smoky beasts. They seeped into the generators and waited on their master before they finished their purpose.

"It's the One-That-Sees-Forward," Yuri told Nancy.

Nancy stood and saw through the crack under Yuri's arm a nervous Kiara.

"Her name is Kiara, Mr. Ivanov," Nancy gently chastised.

"3."

Noah took deep breaths through his nose. His heart was pounding. He wondered if he'd ever get used to these sorts of things. His sister, Norah, gently massaged one of his shoulders.

Nancy stood and walked over to the door. Even though it already seemed as if she was trying to hide, Nancy could see that Kiara looked even more tense than usual as she got closer.

"2."

Emily flicked her finger and ignited it on and off as if she was playing with a lighter.

From the other side of Facility Zero, Faran gripped tightly onto his steering wheel. His mind focused like a zealot.

"What's the matter, Kiara?" Nancy brushed Yuri aside and tried to step outside her office, but Kiara darted through the gap. Without words or hesitation, she reached for her gun, Lexi. Her thumb automatically flicked off the safety as she her arm swung forward to pointed the gun at the girl in a black dress next to Sarah. The practice she had paid off. The Witch was exposed enough for even Kiara to feel confident in her shot.

Yuri leaped after the oracle.

"1."

Blackout.

Lexi's barrel lit the room for a flash second as its loud roar filled the room.

Chapter 41
BATTLE ROYALE - ONE

Darkness fell on the facility and the engines and the rotors of encroaching intruders grew alarmingly louder.

"What was that?" Kalin and Landris spun their heads away from the dark horizon to the floor below them. The gunfire was deafening and Kalin's mind was immediately filled with only thoughts of Lily.

The clamor of the staff and the piddle-paddle of their scurrying footsteps filled the Facility.

"Something's—" Before Landris could finish his sentence, he was interrupted by loud crashes that were followed by a barrage of shouts, screams, and gunfire.

McKinley's vehicles crashed through the fences and gates all around the Facility. The security members of the Silver Aegis immediately fired upon the vehicles, but the bullets couldn't penetrate them.

A couple of years ago, only a day or so after the Light had appeared, Landris was a young teen. He was a teen with a timid heart hidden behind a persona. His mother was standing in front of his fallen body and screaming at his father.

The thunderous sound of alarms screamed throughout the facility.

"Those must operate on an independent power source," Morris said as he waited in the car with the rest of the members for a break in the hail of bullets.

"Go!" Landris pointed at the sword held by Kalin. "Do what you have to do to protect her." He grabbed the sword's twin from the case and leaped off the rooftop.

One of his eyes would be swollen shut and blue by the morning. His mouth was filled with the metallic taste of blood as the leak dripping from his nose mixed with the leak from his lips. He watched as his father slapped his mother. He hit her hard and then even harder. When his mother fell on the ground, his father's foot buried itself into her stomach. But Landris couldn't pick himself up. He was a slave to the fear ingrained into his being of his father.

Kalin wasn't certain what he would do with the sword, but he took it with him anyway. He leapt down to the building closest to the dormitory.

The noise from the helicopters were now loud enough to match the sirens of the alarms.

He looked up at his father, a man who he'd look exactly like in a couple of decades. Even though he was already as tall as his father, to Landris, his father was a colossus.

A distinctive orchestra of gunfire meeting with return fire joined the fray.

The colossus breathed heavily with his large chest caving in and out. Landris couldn't remember anymore why his father was so enraged that day. His father choked the vase with the flowers he had gotten for his wife.

Carlos was in one of the few cars that trailed behind the herd. He blazed through the warzone and headed straight towards where the Witch was supposed to be—the office. A young man appeared before him.

The flowers slipped out as the father raised the vase over his head. The vase came down in a moment, but to Landris it moved gradually and fluidly in his eyes as if his father had constricted time for his son to capture every single moment before it shattered on his mother's head. His mother let out an animal-like squeal—a yelp—that only lasted a split second. It was a noise that would forever echo in Landris's mind. The water from the vase and the blood from his mother pooled beneath the mother's still body.

Carlos cursed and made a quick decision to simply run over the young man, but moments before the collision, Landris disappeared from his sight. In the split second before the young man disappeared, Carlos noticed something odd about the boy. He'd come to realize later that he had witnessed a young man become something more than what once defined as human.

This was the last time Landris cried. When Landris came to, he felt the warm tears drizzling down the side of his face as his eyes were staring outdoors through a new gaping hole in their villa. In the dark woods outdoors, he heard every droplet of the heavy rain splashing on the leaves and grass. From below he heard the last breath of his father dissipating into the air. Landris looked at his arms with its veins glowing white. He looked behind him and saw his mother's lifeless body drowning in pool of red. Yuri and Nancy arrived minutes later. The cocktail of emotions on Nancy's face as she stared into Landris's eyes was another memory of the night that'd never fade.

With his eyes glowing white along with all of the veins in his body, Landris effortlessly tossed the car into the air as it crashed into him. The car spun high in the air and halted some of the gunfire and screams as people watched, awed at the spectacle.

The sound of an unexpected wreckage turned Landris's head. The car had struck one of the helicopters in the air approaching the office building. The helicopter, entangled with the car, fell straight on top of the office building. Before he could decide what he wanted to do, the decision was made for Landris. Squads of the McKinley's men surrounded Landris with the laser sights of their guns decorating him. In this familiar situation, Landris recognized a familiar face.

"Freeze!" Morris screamed at Landris. The team leader wondered why he didn't simply squeeze on the trigger.

A moment of hesitation. A moment of cowardice. A moment too late to protect when it mattered most.

"Never again," Landris muttered to himself as he drew his black blade.

Chapter 42
BATTLE ROYALE - TWO

...There are still sorceries that are a mystery to the world, including the phenomenon of individuals with sorceries that were not taught but seemingly were born with. One of the rarest of such sorcery is the power to have the sight into the future. The guild has recorded these rare gifts, once every few generations to a varying degree of potency. However, this gift of foresight has caused quite a stir and controversy among the academics regarding just what it could mean in terms of preventing another catastrophe like the Great Calamity and the Witch. Some of the visions from these seers have prevented possible tragedies while also many of their visions were seemingly immune to interference. This has led many scholars to believe that the future is either malleable or perhaps the seers are prone to false visions and cannot be relied upon.

My counselor, Arch-Recorder Liam, however, shared with me his belief that to me seemed simpler, more elegant, and perhaps more troubling. Counselor Liam believes that there may be grand schemes that are determined by a force greater than man that makes certain events, no matter how relevant or irrelevant it may seem to us, definite. And only the irrelevant pawns, be that a person or events, outside of those schemes are the ones that are allowed to change....

The silence seemed thicker after the earsplitting gunfire. As the last of its echoes faded in their ears and minds, the silence became riddled with the chaos outside and a girl's sob.

"Everyone alright?" Yuri grunted as he picked himself up while keeping Kiara under his foot. He had ripped the gun out of the girl's hands.

Julian and Nancy all lit up their phone and tablet to use as a makeshift flashlight.

"Lily?!" Sarah had huddled over Lily. She quickly pulled out her own phone and shined its light on her small friend. Lily's eyes were wide, and it took her a moment for her eye to shift towards Sarah. There was a sizable bullet hole on the sofa next to her head. Sarah pulled Lily into her arms again.

"No!" Kiara cried as she tried to drag herself away and towards the Witch by scraping away at the floor with her fingertips. "She has to die!"

"You've gone mad, child!" Yuri grabbed Kiara by the back of her shirt and dragged her away to a corner. In the darkness, he took off his suit jacket and belt and quickly tied Kiara's arms and legs with them.

Julian was still speechless and motionless. It was induced by shock but remained due to shame. Ashamed that he hadn't budged—that he was still sitting across from Sarah. Embarrassing memories of all of his shame in the past rushed to fill his mind. For a moment his eyes met with Sarah's and he quickly turned away as the light from his phone shut off. He pressed a button again to light it up.

"Are you alright?" Julian asked squeamishly.

"What is the meaning of this, Kiara?!" Nancy's shout drowned out Julian's whisper. She stomped over to Kiara.

"You've all lost your minds, Director Jones! You're making a deal with the devil! She and you will be the end of us all! It's too late! It's all too late! Nothing can be changed! Sarah! Nothing can be changed!" Kiara screams were muddled with tears.

Mr. Ivanov, unidentified vehicles are approaching. Fast.

Yuri pulled out a walkie-talkie from his pants pocket.

"If they don't stop, fire at will," Yuri spoke into the walkie-talkie.

After several loud noises presumably of things crashing into other things, an orchestra of gunfire raged outside.

"Looks like it's that boy's work. I don't recognize the gun." Yuri inspected and tinkered with the gun he took from Kiara before handing it over to Nancy. "You might need this. Stay here I'll go check what's going on."

Nancy took the gun and used her tablet light to study it for a second. It only took her a brief moment to learn of its features and check its ammo. The name 'Lexi' engraved was the final nail in the coffin that Howard was its creator. The boy always had cheesy sensibilities.

Yuri closed the door behind him.

The tremendous sound of helicopters muted out most of the noise outside.

"Why?" Lily whispered only loud enough for herself to hear.

The sound of glass shattering screamed from beyond the doors of the office.

Men were shouting orders.

And then gunfire.

"It's too late," Kiara, her tears dried up, said apathetically. "I'm already dead, and so are the rest of you."

The deafening shatter from much closer this time stunned everyone as the McKinley's men rappelled down and broke in through the window of Nancy's office.

The shouted orders obscured one another.

The group remained uncertain like deer caught in headlights. Julian's heart pounded fast and hard enough for him to feel embarrassed. He felt powerless and imagined again how Landris would have been in his shoes.

Sarah stood and placed herself between the invaders and Lily.

"Why?" Lily whispered to herself again.

"RAISE YOUR HANDS!" the men shouted at Sarah with their guns pointed at her. Sarah still considered her options as she'd rather have them point the barrels at her than at Lily.

"Oh god," Kiara whimpered from the ground. "I think it's now."

An explosive crash from above turned everyone's attention to roof. The helicopter spiraled out of control after being hit by a car thrown into the air. The vehicles caressed one another and crashed onto the top of the building. For a moment, there was only relative silence compared to the explosive noise of moments before. The invaders quickly recovered and pointed their weapons at the group again.

With a thunderous crack, the entire roof of the office caved in on top of everyone, and a slab of concrete raced down towards Kiara's face.

Just like in her dream.

Chapter 43
THE HERO

Morris fired one shot by Landris's feet. "Live ammo for you, kid. Get your face on the ground. Let's not spill any more blood than we need," Morris warned Landris.

Landris looked around at the dozen or so men surrounding him. His 'gift' was now kicking into his brain as well, processing everything faster and better. They all seemed so small.

"Let's just shoot, Morris! He's already killed our own!" Thomas yelled.

My sight is on the freak's head, Henderson patched through Morris headset. On a hill, far enough away to oversee the entire Facility, Henderson watched Landris through his scope, not realizing that his target could see him better than he could on his rifle.

Landris kicked up the first piece of rock the size of his fist he saw on the ground and caught it his hand.

"I said GET DOWN!" Morris screamed at Landris.

Landris, paying no attention to Morris, turned his head towards Henderson. To his glowing eyes, the darkness of the night or the distance did not matter.

It's like he's looking at…

As the rock left Landris's hand there was a loud crack in the air that overcame the surrounding commotions. Immediately, Morris and his men fired on Landris.

As the guns blazed, a wet explosion in his earpiece told Morris of Henderson's fate.

Landris eyes allowed him to see any slight titillations of the world, his mind granted him to ability to process it all, and his body granted him the strength and agility to react. As the barrage of bullets came towards him, it was clear to Landris where they came from and where they were headed. He calculated all the different responses he could make, and all Landris had to do was choose which outcome he wanted.

There were no improvisations or uncertainty in Landris's movements. Some of the bullets were cut by his blade and some were dodged as he quickly closed in the distance between him and the McKinley's men. He moved faster than their eyes could follow with his dance, and the blade soon found itself flowing through many of

McKinley's men's limbs and bodies until Landris was in front of Morris himself. Landris grabbed Thomas next to Morris and threw him over his shoulder. The man screamed and flailed his limbs as he flew over the facility.

Without words, Morris reached for his sidearm and fired directly at Landris forehead.

Landris did not move.

Morris watched in terror as the bullet flattened on Landris forehead, not even leaving a scratch. Landris smiled and kicked Morris in response.

Morris' body skipped over the ground like a stone over water. He looked up into the dark sky as the pain rang from all over his body and the nausea made his stomach turn.

The lights came back on.

Chapter 44
THE OTHERS

Dominique was finishing up a few more reps in the swimming pool when the light went out. He and Tara had had a particularly heated argument, and Dominique wanted an outlet to let out his frustration. After hearing the commotion and the explosive pops of gunfire, Dominique thought it'd be best for him to stay put.

A loud crash echoed from outside.

He submerged himself back into the dark water. Water was where Dominique felt most comfortable. It wasn't long until the McKinley's men swarmed into the pool area. He poked his head out of the water and gently kicked his legs to stay afloat.

"Put your hands in the air," they screamed.

Dominique was amused how much this was like the movies. It was cliché. Given the current circumstances, they must have realized how silly their requests were.

His thick black hair was buzzed to a pitch black fuzz. Though not very tall, his almost religious attendance to the gym showed on his sculpted body. Wearing nothing but swimming trunks, Dominique wondered where they thought he'd be hiding his weapon.

"Come out of the pool!"

Now they were making more sensible demands. From the sound of their feet, Dominique guessed there were probably five to six of them.

One of the McKinley's men reached the limits of his patience and pulled out the tranquilizer pistol assigned to them for this mission. He took aim and fired.

Before even hearing the gunfire, Dominique raised the water around him and formed a dome. The dart was stuck in the spiraling water that surrounded him.

The lights came back on, and the intruders looked around in surprise.

There were six intruders. As they came to, they were startled by the sight of a sphere of water spiraling in front of them. The top half of the sphere absorbed into its bottom half and revealed a cocky young man with a slanted smile and the dart in his hand.

Dominique studied the tranquilizer dart a bit before tossing it away.

"Why are the lights back on?" one of the men spoke into his ear-piece. "Team leader? Team leader? You there?"

Without warning, the water formed a pair of serpent-like limbs and whipped two of the intruders and then launched them into the walls. The four left raised their guns, but before they could pull the triggers, the water formed four tentacle-like limbs and ensnared the four men. The tips of the limbs formed into balls of water and trapped the intruders inside. Dominique walked on top of the water and sat by the poolside. He kept his feet in the water and watched the four men dangling in the air as they slowly drowned.

Too easy, Dominique thought. He wondered if even Landris could have handled the situation better.

Tara. He had forgotten about her for a moment. Too much time already wasted, he had to end this quicker.

Before Dominique could command the water to rid him of the intruders, a pair of hands reached out from the shadows and pulled him in. The aquatic limbs lost their solidity and fell back into the pool with the intruders.

***

Across the rec center where the pool was located was the library connected by a catwalk. The twins, Jean and Jamie, hid behind the non-fiction section of the small but adequate library. As the doors quietly opened and the march of footsteps echoed through the quiet library, the sisters latched onto one another.

Jean and Jamie looked at one another and nodded. There was another in the building, and they had to reach her before they left. Jean put her finger by her nose and let out a quiet shush. To test if it had worked, Jean snapped her fingers. The snapping made no noise. She grabbed onto Jamie's hand and Jamie snapped her fingers. Jamie's snapping was as silent as her sister's. Jean nodded at her sister once more, and Jamie nodded back, took a big gasp of air and closed her eyes.

The twins disappeared from sight.

Jean guided her sister along through the dark library. The last they saw of Nada was of her reading as she usually did at the tables in the center of the room. She had been between stacks of books with her head buried in the one she was currently reading. The intruders were already gathered around the center where only the piles of books remained on top of a table. One of them started to make hand gestures at the other men. Jamie tugged on her sister and they quickly found shelter behind one of the other book shelves. Jean looked over the corner of the shelves to look for Nada as Jamie silently gasped for air. Once ready, Jamie squeezed Jean's hand to let her know that she was ready to go again.

Invisible and silent, the sisters brazenly ran by just a hair away from the intruders. They checked quickly, bookshelf after bookshelf, until they finally found Nada in the corner of the room behind a bookshelf at the history section.

Jamie silently panted for air and startled Nada when the twins appeared in front of her. Nada quickly covered her mouth as she let out a gasp while Jean reached her hand out to Nada.

As Nada reached for Jean's hands, a dart pierced Jean's neck.

Her sister's scream shattered the silence, and another dart found its way to Jamie's neck, followed by a couple more that landed on her chest. The two sisters crumpled to the floor as they lost consciousness.

"Stay away!" Nada screamed as she was reminded of the nightmares from her past as the men encroached upon her.

"This one's real young," one of the intruder said as if he felt a bit of guilt that he was about to shoot her.

"Just do it," one of the other men behind spoke with authority.

A sudden figure appeared behind Nada that stunned all the men.

"Do you guys see that? Cooper?" a man beside the authority figure asked.

"Yeah," Cooper, the one who spoke with authority, replied.

A woman, mangled and torn, limped from behind Nada and towards the men. Her ethereal legs went through Nada and the woman's eyes didn't blink as it stared at the men with fury and menace.

The man who was to shoot Nada shot at the ethereal woman instead, and the dart landed on her chest. It pierced her not as if it was piercing skin, but as if it was trying to pierce through thick smog.

Don't cry, child.

The woman spoke in a tongue that some of the men recognized, but none could understand. Her raspy voice struggled to be coherent as it made its way through her mangled vocal chords.

Don't be afraid.

Her words, however, were as clear to Nada as they were when they were first spoken to her.

Don't cry, child. Don't be afraid.

Nada collapsed onto the ground and buried her head into her knees.

The men holstered their tranquilizers and raised their guns at the woman.

"Stop!" Cooper yelled. "You might shoot the kid! Lead that thing out to the middle of the room."

"Do we really care at this point?" one of the man argued.

"Cooper," the one furthest back spoke with a shaking voice. "There's more of them."

Through the walls, the fallen gathered to answer the call of the child. The freshly fallen of the Silver Aegis and McKinley, the fallen that had been long forgotten, and even the beasts and insect long dead and gone. The intruders huddled in the middle of the library and fired their guns at the ethereal as they quickly realized their ill fate. The fallen grabbed onto the McKinley's men as the beast and the insects began gnawing on their limbs. Some desperately fired their guns without caring who or what their bullets were hitting in the process.

Nada kept her head buried as the men screamed in terror and agony. She heard their flesh being torn and wept for her part in it. Sensing something amiss, Nada raised her head to see the sleeping twins devoured into the shadows and disappear.

A hand appeared behind her. It didn't touch her, but was offering itself for Nada to take. Nada's hesitation ended quickly when she turned and saw the first of the ethereal to appear as if it was staring at her. She took the mysterious hand and followed it into the shadows.

When the lights came back on in the library, it was silent and void of life. The floors and the furniture were painted red and decorated with the limbs and pieces of the newly fallen.

Chapter 45
THOSE WHO STAY, THOSE WHO RUN

Shannon and Tara were both returning to their rooms when the lights went out. Out in the open when the havoc was unleashed, the two girls ran into the nearest alley when their route became littered with armed men. They rested their backs on the walls as Tara gradually slid onto to her bottom as she tried to calm her breath. Shannon conjured the illusions of walls on both ends of the alley way.

"We'll be alright, Tara," Shannon tried to sound as confident as she could be as she rested her hand on Tara's shoulder. Tara pushed Shannon's shaking hand off of her.

"Don't touch me. I... I..." Tara snapped as she tried to control her breath. "God, I should have stayed with Dominique."

The explosive crash of a car hitting a helicopter startled both of them. Tara screamed and Shannon lost concentration of her 'gift' for a moment, causing the walls to disappear.

"What're you doing!" Tara screamed.

"Shut up!" Shannon screamed back. One of Silver Aegis men caught a glimpse of the two of them and ran towards them.

"Help!" Tara yelled at the man.

"Are you guys alright?" he asked. Before he could hear an answer, a bullet pierced through his head.

Tara screamed once again as the man's body dropped to the ground. Shannon stumbled backwards trying to bring the walls back up, but she couldn't shake the dead body in front of her out of her mind.

"Shannon!" Tara shouted.

With a wave of her hand, Shannon raised the walls again.

"Tara, help me. Tara, HELP ME!" Shannon's face wasn't trying to mask her fear anymore. Tara nodded hesitantly and ran up to Shannon. She placed her hand on Shannon's shoulder and channeled her 'gift.'

"I swear he was talkin' to someone here," the two heard one of the intruders say.

"Maybe it's the redheaded kid that got Donny's group."

"This wall…" The intruder knocked on the wall erected by Shannon. "It seems out of place."

Shannon noticed Tara's breathing getting heavier and quicker.

"Just keep concentrating, Tara. I—we—can't afford you to lose it now," Shannon whispered to Tara.

"Come on, it's getting crazy out here. We need to join up with Donny," the other intruder hurried the one knocking on the wall.

"Yeah, but I'm sure Donny won't mind if we got the kid who manhandled his men that we're replacin'?" The intruder took a step back from the wall and fired his rifle at it.

Tara let out a yelp at the roar of gunfire. For a moment, the walls lost solidity, and the bullets whizzed past Shannon and Tara.

"I'll be damned," the other intruder began to believe his friend.

"We have to run." Tara clenched Shannon's shoulder and snarled, "We HAVE to RUN!"

"Neat trick," the intruder said. He pressed on the wall only to find that the wall was solid again.

"Get a grip, Tara!" Shannon snarled back. Tara lost concentration again, and the intruder's hand still placed against the wall went straight through. The two men exchanged looks and raised their guns.

"Damn it!" By the time Shannon turned around, Tara was already fleeing.

The walls disappeared.

"Raise those hands in the air and don't even blink," the intruder said as he approached Shannon with his partner.

"There's one running!" the other intruder alerted.

Shannon waved her hands and swarms of hornets appeared and stormed the two intruders.

The other intruder's screams were drowned out by the noise of the hornets. He swung his rifle around the swat off the hornets.

"Calm down, you idiot!" The intruder grabbed his friend by the collar and yelled in his ears. "This is an illusion! It's not real!"

The two walked through the swarm and caught a glimpse of two girls running away. They fired warning shots at their feet, and Shannon, startled by the noise, tripped. Tara didn't—couldn't—look behind her and kept running.

As Tara turned around the corner, a hand from the shadows grabbed her ankle and pulled her into the darkness.

Shannon rolled onto her back and waved her hands as she screamed. Illusions of all kinds of beasts from the air, land, and sea filled the alleyway and turned it into a circus and aquarium. Each one was less concentrated than the other, and the two the McKinley's men approached Shannon fearless of the beasts.

"Neat trick," the intruder said as he stood over Shannon.

"You don't have to get up," the other one said as he pulled out the small tranquilizer pistol.

"Don't worry. It's a tranquilizer, sweetheart. It'll all be over when you wake up."

Before the other intruder could squeeze the trigger, a hard blow to the head dropped him to the ground. The intruder looked behind him and saw bluish streams streaking from the attacker's arms as his black sword sliced down his gun.

The lights came back on to reveal the attacker's dark crimson hair. One of his hands held the scabbard that struck down his first victim while his other hand held the ebony blade that sliced the rifle in two.

"Leave," Kalin said with the tip of his blade pointed at the intruder.

"And what're you going to do if I don't?" the intruder asked as he tossed aside the half of the rifle that was left.

He didn't have more time to waste. Kalin stabbed the blade through the intruder's foot, and the intruder screamed in pain. Shannon's eyes widened and her breath caught in her throat.

"You can either limp away now, or I can make you crawl away on your hands later." Kalin wiggled the blade a little bit in the intruder's foot. He screamed in pain once again as he described Kalin with flavorful but harsh words.

When Kalin pulled the blade out, he and the intruder stared each other down briefly until the intruder finally relented and limped away.

Kalin offered his hand to Shannon. Feeling lightheaded, Shannon shook off the blank stare on her face and took a deep breath. Shannon's hand cautiously approached Kalin's.

"Thanks. You must be the Witch's… friend… right?" Shannon asked as she gently grabbed onto Kalin's hand.

Kalin nodded as he helped her up. "Do you know where she is?" Kalin tried to shake off the blood from the blade before sheathing it.

"I think… I think I saw her go to the office building," Shannon told Kalin.

"Damn it!" Kalin slammed his fist into the wall. "Are you going to be okay on your own?"

"Are you going to the office?"

"Yeah."

"Didn't you see what just happened there?"

"That's why I have to go."

"I'll be okay on my own," Shannon answered.

"I suggest you find a better hiding place." Kalin turned away from Shannon and towards the courtyard again.

"Hey!" Shannon tried to call out to the Witch's friend as he sprinted away with the streams jetting off from his body. He seemed to be as quick as Landris. "Thanks, and be careful…"

Shannon took a deep breath and debated whether to hide in this alley or find a better place as the Witch's friend suggested. As Shannon turned to head towards where Tara had run off to, a hand from the shadows of the wall reached out and covered her mouth from screaming. Its other hand around her waist, the shadow pulled her into the darkness.

Chapter 46
THE STORM

On top of the hill from afar, Leon smoked his pipe as he watched the small war unfold in Facility Zero. He was reminiscing about the spectacle of the car that was flung into the helicopter when his phone vibrated in his pocket.

It was a text message from Emily.

'Do it.'

Leon stood and took a deep inhale through his large pipe, unleashing a tsunami of smoke upon exhaling. The smoke split into two large clouds and formed into the shapes of men. They silently approached the two the McKinley's men looking over Facility Zero through the scope of their rifles. The smoke men's cloudy hands went over the mouths of the McKinley's men and they struggled violently, trying to gasp for air until finally passing out.

The smoke men dragged the bodies of the McKinley soldiers to Leon, and he checked for their pulses. They were still alive. The smoke men took a portion of themselves and formed cuffs for the wrist and ankles of the unconscious men, then place a puff of smoke over their mouths to keep them silent.

Leon stood over the edge of the hill and watched over Facility Zero shrouded in darkness and lighting up in sparks from the flash of gunfire. Over the horizon he could clearly see the Light surrounded by the stars. Simply for a dramatic effect to amuse himself, Leon snapped his fingers and light returned to the facility.

The guns of the Silver Aegis were now on equal footing as the guns of the McKinley's.

Chapter 47
A PURPOSE TO LIFE

Kiara was surprised to find that she could still open her eyes. In front of her was a slab of concrete that would have turned her head into a mush of red goo. Slowly, it rose further and further away from her head. She turned to the only person who could be responsible for such an anomaly.

Lights returned. The few bulbs and light stands that remained functional lit the collapsing room.

"I was supposed to die right here," Kiara told the Witch who was standing with her arms stretched out by her chest. The Witch returned a confused and slightly resentful look. The hint of the latter emotion from Lily surprised Sarah as she caught a glimpse of it.

Above Lily's head were giant pieces of concrete, and the shambles of a wrecked helicopter wanting to follow their natural course and collapse.

The three intruders slowly picked themselves up and quickly removed their night vision goggles. As their eyes came to, they marveled at the sight above them.

"I SAW MY DEAD BODY! I WAS SUPPOSED TO DIE!" Kiara screamed at Lily.

The noise jolted the intruders enough to remind them of their jobs, and they raised their guns.

"Shut it, Kiara," Sarah's voice carried enough menace to frighten Kiara. The anger in her face was something Kiara thought she'd never see in Sarah. The Witch had stolen Sarah from her.

"I guess we are in your debt," one of the intruders spoke. "But we still have a job to do, and that's to bring you all in. Especially you, *Witch.*"

"I'm not sure who hired you, but it certainly wasn't for your smarts." Nancy pointed towards the crumbling ceiling. "I wonder how hard it'd be for her to simply let your side fall."

The intruders remained silent just for a moment.

"You're right," the intruder who spoke before replied. "That's why if even a crumb of that falls down, we'll just shoot everyone in this room. I guess then we'll find out just how talented the Witch is."

Lily turned her head towards the intruders. The sound of war screamed from outside. Emotions that she had forgotten within her were stirring. Perhaps they were there all along, brewing until the proper boiling point came. She stared at the intruders with disgust, vex, and anger. It was a look they always imagined the Witch would have.

"Why? Why do all this?" Lily asked, this time not to herself but to them.

The intruders seemed dumbfounded by her question.

"Because you're the Witch, of course. And if you come with us quietly, no one has to get hurt," one of the other intruders answered.

"SHOOT HER! END IT NOW!" Kiara yelled. "MS. JONES! SHOOT HER! THERE'S A CHANCE! WE CAN CHANGE THE FUTURE!"

Nancy rebuked Kiara with simply a glare.

Julian took deep breath and swallowed the saliva that pooled in his mouth. Without any additional movement, he dispersed into countless particles of light.

The intruders turned their attention to the empty seat but didn't realize that the boy had appeared behind them with a sound barely audible in the room.

Julian quickly grabbed the intruders on his left and right with his hands and rested his chin on the shoulder of the one in the center. He closed his eyes and prayed for the best.

"JULIAN!" Sarah called out to her friend.

By the time the last bit of Sarah's voice registered in his ear, Julian already knew that his teleportation had failed. He couldn't tell how high, but they were high enough to see Facility Zero glittering in the far distance.

"Oh, god! I didn't mean to!" Julian's voice was impossible to hear with the wind gushing at their face. He saw the men screaming something at him. Julian reached out to them with his hand, but before his hand could reach them, one of the men pointed his gun at Julian.

Julian screamed as he dispersed into light just in nick of time while the bullets passed through the air where he used to be.

"NOOOOOO!" Particles gathered and Julian's scream carried through back into the office space as he fell near the floor.

"Julian?" Sarah rushed over to her shivering friend. She could feel the cold air still around him as her hand went closer to him. Julian swatted her hand away and covered his mouth from vomiting. He looked up and met eyes with Lily who looked at him worriedly, still holding up the debris in the air. He had been gone for merely a few seconds, and in those mere few seconds, he had become a killer.

"I didn't mean to," Julian told Sarah.

Sarah looked at Julian, puzzled until she connected the dots. She wrapped her arms around him.

"It's okay," Sarah told Julian.

Julian whispered into her ear and Sarah told him the same answer again.

"I'm sorry, but we have to go," Lily told the group. "This is getting heavy, and there's something I have to do."

"Come on!" Nancy grabbed Kiara by the collar of her shirt and pulled her up to her feet while she dragged her towards the doors.

As Nancy opened the door, the space was blocked by gargantuan Yuri. He seemed startled as she was to be seeing one another. His white shirt was splattered with red, and in his hand was a smoking gun. When Yuri moved out of Nancy's way, the disarrayed corpses of the McKinley's men were revealed behind him.

"You alright?" Yuri asked.

"Yeah. You?" Nancy returned as Yuri took Kiara from Nancy and swung her over his shoulder.

Nancy nodded and hinted at him with a glance to check the office.

Julian and Sarah passed by Yuri as he headed into the office. Lily walked toward Yuri, and above her, Yuri saw the power of the Witch. His eyes widened with amazement like a child as he guffawed. He moved out of the way for Lily to pass by. Once out of the room, Lily let the debris fall into the office as gently as she could.

"Let me down, Mr. Ivanov," Kiara asked Yuri. Yuri looked at Nancy for permission. She nodded in response.

"Sure." Yuri set Kiara down and took his coat and belt off of her legs.

"I need to find Kalin," Lily said as she walked away from the group.

"Absolutely not!" Nancy grabbed Lily's arm. "You're staying with us. It's far too dangerous for you to be out there."

"Let her go, Nancy," Yuri said as he fixed on his belt and wrinkled jacket. "She can take care of herself. Just make sure you come back in one piece, little miss."

Nancy marched toward Yuri. "What makes you think this is your call, Yuri?" Nancy snarled.

Yuri pointed out the window with his thumb. The guns, the screams, and the occasional explosions. "Once that's over, it'll be your call again, Director Jones," Yuri replied. "But for now, my words may as well be words from God. Your safety is my priority.

Go," Yuri told Lily.

"Wait!" As she headed towards the window, Kiara's voice grabbed the Witch's attention and stopped her in her place. The Witch turned her head to the oracle.

"I think you're done talking for today, child," Yuri warned.

"You saved my life," Kiara spoke almost yearningly. "That means my dreams—the future—can be changed."

Lily seemed apathetic.

"So why not kill yourself?" Kiara pleaded. "End your life for all of us. That'll stop the coming calamity. One life for the entire world. What more purpose could a person's life have?"

The other oracle strode over to Kiara and slapped her across the face.

"What's the matter with you?" Sarah's face was contorted with sorrow and anger at her friend.

"If you had seen what I've seen, I wonder if you would still put your trust in the Witch so much." Feeling betrayed and alone, Kiara stared back at Sarah with resentful eyes.

Lily hopped out the window. Perhaps if she climbed the sky, she would be able to see Kalin's telltale red hair.

"Not everything you see is true or definite, Kiara. If anything, what happened in that room should be a testament to that." Sarah's gaze matched that of Kiara's.

"And if you're wrong?" Kiara turned her head away from her friend and sat with the dead bodies. She felt indifferent to the blood and their deaths. For her, it was fitting for what was to come.

"Anyway, whoever wants to come can come with us. I'm taking the Director to our helicopter," Yuri said as he pillaged another gun off one of the dead bodies on the ground.

"The helicopter?" Nancy asked.

"From what I saw out there, that's our best chance. Especially with one of theirs down like that." Yuri placed the gun in one of his pockets and began walking towards the elevators.

Sarah, Julian, and Nancy followed after him.

"Kiara…" Sarah looked back at her friend. "Come on. Time to go."

Kiara shook her head feeling as if there was nothing left for her.

Sarah walked over to her friend and pulled on her arm, but Kiara tore her arm away from Sarah's hand.

"Go," Kiara said.

"If she doesn't want to come, leave her! We don't have the time or luck to deal with someone who'll slow us down!" Yuri yelled from the other side of the hallway.

"Whatever happens, I'll make sure to see it through," Sarah told Kiara. She didn't respond and just stared at the ground with her head hanging.

Sarah ran after the group to catch up to them.

…I won't deny that the inevitable question that arises from this notion seems unanswerable. In this grand scheme, who's who and what's what? When I asked this of my mentor, his answer was simple but unsatisfying:

'whose prints remain are who, and what's been done is what. To seek for more clarity is a desperate and futile attempt to satisfy our need for at least an illusion of control in the scheme that's beyond our reach.' I asked him where that left us with the question we began with. He answered, 'Back at the beginning where's there's everything, but no one wants to see anything. That the answer never mattered, but only that we all played our parts right...'

Chapter 48
JUST A DOG

Team leader, get the lights off again!

We lost contact with a few of the squads. Need some instructions here.

Foxtrot needs back up! What the hell are those freaks we hired doing? Has anyone seen them?

Morris!

I saw a couple of them trying to help those guys in the car.

Anyone checking on the backup call with Cooper's group? They went cold.

Is our Team Leader dead too?

Don't know about you guys, but I'm shooting first. Screw this taking them alive business.

Yep. Soon as I saw that car fly, my mind was made.

Keep the Witch alive if you see her. Boss will be pissed. She's worth more alive to us than not.

No one's seen her yet, right?

First one to find her, finders keepers.

His head was shaking, and the noises from the earpiece didn't help with the already ongoing chaos. Morris lifted his head from the ground and watched the glowing-eyed monster walking towards him with blood still dripping from his black sword.

"Need…" It was harder to talk than he thought it'd be. He coughed and cleared his throat. Each cough was accompanied by a searing pain from all over his body. "Back up. Courtyard. Need backup."

"The rooftop was one thing, but you thought you could come to my home and threaten my family?!" Landris yelled at Morris as he sauntered over. As if he had changed his mind about his approach, Landris tore through the sound barrier and appeared in front of Morris. The noise jolted Morris awake.

"But you're all just dogs following orders, right?" Landris raised his sword above his head.

Morris laughed. Coughing and laughing didn't have much difference on how much pain it caused him. "And what are you?" Morris asked. "What do you think you are with that sword? Some kind of a hero? A knight in shining armor? The guardian of the freaks?"

With his sword raised, Landris watched Morris laugh, cough, and moan in pain.

"You think you're doing anyone a favor right now? This is what's wrong with the world now. Even stupid kids who didn't even have time to grow a brain yet can go on murderous rampages. You and I are no different. We chose not to have choices. All that power, and you're just as much a dog as I am. At least I know what I am. But you…" Morris chuckled and then groaned from the pain. "…You thought you were something else. Something bigger. Just kill me kid. Just kill me. End this stupid puppet show."

Morris raised his hand and pointed his finger at Landris's face. "But do me a favor and think real hard sometime what you could be doing with yourself. There's no such thing as a hero, but you sure as hell can learn to be something damn close." Morris shut his eyes and chuckled a little more.

Landris's stomach twisted as he looked at the man stare at him not as a dying man, but as someone older and wiser who was passing on his knowledge to a lost boy. Without a sound, Landris swung his sword down.

Landris's enhanced eyes caught a glint of something as it buried itself into the dirt next to Morris.

Before his sword could make contact, the hard ground by Morris formed into the shape of a large fist and launched Landris into air. Landris cut through the air until he crashed into the wall of the rec center.

A glint of light again.

The walls of the rec center formed into a shape that resembled a face and clenched Landris in its teeth. Streams, similar to ones he saw Kalin use, poured out through its cracks and crevices.

"That guy's a psycho!" Norah ran up next to Morris. "Are you alright?"

Landris punched the concrete-face-thing and it shattered from his might. The dust from the blow clouded his view, but he could feel the face-thing clench down even harder. When the dust cleared, it revealed the shattered pieces that still remained tied together by the stream. It gathered more pieces to recover itself.

Slowly, Morris struggled to pick himself up. Norah didn't help and kept her focus on the psycho with both of her hands directed at the wall-face. "Sorry," Norah told Morris. "This takes a lot of concentration, and that nutjob isn't making it easy. Where's that idiot brother of mine?"

Chapter 49
GLOVES OFF

Emily found a safe spot behind one of the cars from the gunfire. She pulled out her phone and pressed her number two speed dial.

"Da?" Olivia's somnolent voice quickly answered the call. Unlike her voice, however, Emily could hear Olivia's fingers playing a choppy concerto on the keyboard of her computer.

"You got eyes on here yet?" Emily asked as she peeked around the cars to see if there were any Silver Aegis security members she had to worry about.

"Nyet, sorry." There was the rare hint of urgency and remorse in Olivia's usually lethargic voice.

"Stay here." Gus sat Maria down in the corner of his room. His room was four doors down from Howard's in the opposite direction of Sarah's. Their only source of light was from Gus' small handheld flashlight. When the gunfire ensued, the unofficial couple became trapped in the room.

"Where're you going?" Maria grabbed Gus's arm as he walked away from her. "The rules are that when the alarms go off, we find cover and stay put."

"I think we might have been the only ones in the dorms when all this started. I have to see what's going on. See if anyone needs help." Gus tore out a few pieces of paper on his desk and crumpled them up roughly into balls the size of a small rock. He shoved them into his pocket and grabbed some pens as well. Director Jones made sure there were not many belongings in any of the students' rooms that could be conveniently used as a weapon. Though restrictive, the Gifted understood why. The only one who regularly went around the rule was Howard.

"It's alright, kiddo. Just..." Emily was interrupted by a McKinley's soldier screaming in pain as he fell near Emily, The night vision goggles had been knocked off, and his eyes met with hers. For a brief moment, his eyes desperately pleaded without words. As Emily quickly approached him, she saw the muscles around his eyes relax as if he had found peace at the last moment, and she watched his eyes quickly turn to glass.

"Emily? Emily!" Olivia was showing more emotion today than she usually did.

Emily checked the man's pulse with her fingers on his neck just to make sure.

"Oh my god! Emily!"

"Sorry," Emily said as she left the body and returned back to her original position. "Just make sure you keep us all connected."

"Okay." Olivia was a bit mad for the panic Emily caused, but the relief that she was alright overcame the anger.

"Were ya worried?" Emily mischievously asked.

Olivia grumbled in her mother tongue.

Emily poked her head out and assessed her position once again. "There's one more thing I want you to do for me," Emily said as she readied herself for a run.

"Well, then I'm going with you!" Maria's accent became more prominent when she was flustered.

"No, Maria," Gus rejected.

"Excuse me? Augustus Bakker! You do not tell me what to do and what not do. I'm not letting you go out there by yourself!" Maria's eyes were lit with fire. This always meant that Gus had to be gentle and choosy with his response.

"I'll be real quick," Gus spoke calmly. "The doors are locked and I just want to check out the nearest dorms to see if anyone needs help getting in."

"And?!"

"And even though your 'gift' is powerful, I don't know if it'll help us right now. We'll need to move around and cover a lot of ground quickly. You'll be safer in this room, and I'll be safer and quicker by myself." Gus hoped that his words got through her.

"I haven't found Faran yet. I don't think he's been using his 'gift.' I want to find him before he does something, so tell everyone to be on the lookout," Emily said and hung up her phone. She ignited her hands in flames and dashed out into the warzone.

A loud explosion halted their argument.

"Stay here," Gus told Maria. Maria reluctantly sat back in the corner as Gus handed her the flashlight.

After blowing out the locked doors to the dormitories with charges, Daniels led his team down the dark hallway. They stepped over the bodies of the Silver Aegis sentries as they stepped inside when the sound of something whizzing through the air followed by a loud crack on the ground surprised the team.

The McKinley's men all pointed their weapons towards the general direction they felt the object originated from. They found a rather tall boy hiding behind the railings above.

"We can see you kid!" Daniels shouted. "Just come quietly and there will be no trouble. We're here on government orders! Silver Aegis isn't what you think it is!"

"Daniels..." One of the men tapped on his shoulder.

Daniels looked back and the man handled him a crumpled up paper.

"What's this?" Daniels asked as he crumpled the paper in his hand. "It's just paper."

The man chuckled and pointed at the small crater in the ground.

"You never know what these freaks can do," he said.

"Leave us alone!" Gus yelled.

"We can't do that kid!" Daniels yelled back. "Our orders are to take you guys with us. You'll be safe with us!"

"We were safe here! We were safe without you shooting at us!" Gus reached into his pocket for another paper ball.

"You're right!" Daniels yelled. "You kids are caught in a nasty crossfire! But the choices you have right now are either come with us quietly, or we force you to come with us. And we don't have orders to bring all of you with us—just whoever we can! So think real hard before throwing another one of those, kid!"

Gus's hand trembled in his pocket. What was he fighting for? What's the difference if they were with these guys or Silver Aegis?

He shook his head.

If it was just him, he'd take the gamble. But he couldn't risk it for Maria. Who was to say these guys would treat them well as Silver Aegis if well at all? Gus pulled his hand out of his pocket and clenched another paper ball. He took a deep breath.

"Gus!"

Gus heard a familiar voice in the darkness. The footsteps from below were slowly making their way towards the stairway.

A loud crash outside distracted the McKinley's men for a moment.

"Come here!"

Howard. His door was slightly cracked open. Gus quickly crawled, then ran towards Howard's room. He heard loud popping noises echo behind him, felt something whizz by his face and heard it pierce the wall between the doors. He leaped into Howard's room as more darts whizzed by.

"Damn it," Daniels angrily muttered to himself. The McKinley's men made their way up the stairs and spread themselves out in front of the door of Howard's room.

Howard had fortified his door with a wooden door bar. He flipped a switch and a generator began to whir. The room was soon brightly lit. Gus stood surprised by the state of the room. It was torn apart as if vultures had a feeding frenzy and took chomps out of anything and everything. At the other end of the room, surrounded by scraps, was a gleaming suit of knight's armor.

The McKinley's men pounded on the door, startling the two of them.

"Quick!" Howard hastily paced over to the armor and began inspecting it one last time. "The size should be alright. I just used whatever I could to finish the job, but it should be fine."

"Come out!" Daniels yelled. "We're already irritated, kid! Don't go and piss us off now!"

"Just charge it up like you would with paper and what not," Howard said as he strapped on the armor on Gus. "You might have to give it more juice than usual because obviously metal isn't paper. I wish we had the chance to test it, but…"

"It's alright. Thanks Howard." Gus put on the helmet himself. "You might have saved us all."

A forced, bittersweet smile stretched across Howard's face.

The poundings evolved into tremendous slams as one of Daniel's squad members began using a portable ram. The wooden bar between Gus, Howard and the intruders let out a loud crack.

Abruptly, the lights returned to the entire dormitory. The McKinley's men glanced at one another hoping for an explanation.

"Keep at it!" Daniels yelled at the man as he tore off his goggles. "Foxtrot needs back up! What the hell are those freaks we hired doing? Has anyone seen them?" Daniels yelled into his earpiece.

"I think that door needed to be replaced anyway," Howard told Gus.

"Howard…" Gus tried to refine his voice to hide his nervousness. He tossed the key he had taken out of his pocket before. "Maria is in my room. Can you watch over her while I… while I'm out there?"

Howard grabbed a bunch of scraps and, with a few sparks and a crackle, turned it into a small, unrefined dagger.

The slams relentlessly continued. The wooden bar verged on tearing in two.

"Leave her to me." Howard took the key and patted Gus' armored back.

With Howard's assurance, Gus focused his energy into his metal shell. When he needed to exhaust as much energy as he did to an object, Gus found flexing all of his muscles as much as he could to help. He guessed, perhaps, that the sensation of physical exertion helped his mind trigger the ability to exert his 'gift.'

"Wait," Daniels told his team as his instincts told him better.

A war cry and loud clanking stomps pierced through the doors. "MOVE!"

As Daniels yelled at his team, Gus exploded through the door like a runaway train. He was faster and stronger than he had ever felt and the power was awkward to control. As it was the layer above his skin that held all the strength, Gus had to maintain the thin awareness of what his body wanted to do and the devastation that the his outer shell was capable of.

The armored Gifted struck Daniels and ran through the railing before falling to the ground. Daniels flew across the air and slammed into the wall above the entrance. A small backup group that had arrived scurried to catch Daniels as he fell.

With the couple of men left in the corridor outside his room fallen and incapacitated, Howard bolted out towards Gus' room.

"Holy crap!" Gus fought through the slight motion sickness as he picked himself back up, his armor clanking as he did. The armor was heavy, but nothing he couldn't manage. He felt none of the impact, and when he inspected the armor, it seemed as pristine as it was just moments ago. Like the paper balls, there were no real indication of the charge he gave the armor. Unlike usual, however, from crevices of his armor where it was most thin or where the armor was non-existent, yellowish streams of flames, or thick smoke, gently poured out.

"Don't move!" one of the new group of men yelled with his gun pointed at Gus with the rest of his men.

There were five of them. Eight total with the three picking themselves up outside Howard's room. A part of Gus didn't want to fight the men. He didn't want to hurt anyone. There was also a part of him that wanted to see what he was capable of. Could he be someone like Landris and protect everyone? His conflicting feelings aside, there was no part of him that was scared anymore.

"Leave!" Gus told the men. His voice sounded hollow and echoed through the helmet. "No one else has to get hurt!"

"Too late for that kid. You and your friends are coming with us, and we wouldn't mind bringing you specifically with us in a body bag," one of the new intruders answered.

Gus didn't reply or move. For the McKinley's men, the decision was already made when they saw Daniels fall from the sky. It didn't take long for the men to fire their weapons.

The barrage of gunfire was loud, but the noise of the bullets hitting the armor was ear shattering. Gus consoled himself with the thought that at least he didn't feel any of the bullets. He stood as the flattened bullets piled up by his feet.

Each of the McKinley's men quickly reloaded their guns as soon as the last bullet dropped. The gun smoke didn't need to clear for them to realize how futile their attempt was.

"Barry and I will keep him busy here," the man who seemed like the leader of the group said. "The rest of you head over to that room the blond kid ran off to."

As the squad began to split up, they heard a clank of a footstep. The armored boy began to move.

"Leave," Gus spoke.

"Go! Go!" the man yelled at his squad members as he and Barry opened fired again. The bullets began to ricochet all over the living area of the dormitory as Gus ran after the men heading towards the stairs. Gus grabbed one of the men and threw him across the room, and then he grabbed the other and threw him at the leftovers of the Daniel's group on the second floor. The last one fell to the ground and screamed as he emptied his gun at Gus. Gus picked him up and tossed him at the man and Barry.

Gus walked back to the center of the room. He was starting to feel the weight of the armor. As the man and Barry tried to pick themselves up, they were offered a hand.

"You guys take the injured and get out of here," Faran said as he helped Barry up. "I'll take over from here."

Gus could feel himself wearing out. He felt as if he had ran a marathon and then stayed awake for a couple of days. He stood tall hoping to not show any signs of weakness.

McKinley's men helped one another to slowly clear out of the dormitory.

Only one man remained standing in front of Gus. He had a square body, a square jaw, and a face as if he could have been someone who might have never laughed once in his life. The man stared right at Gus and walked up to him slowly with his gun hanging from its strap on his shoulder.

"Leave," Gus breathed heavily. "Unless you want to end up like those guys."

"Another victim of the 'gift,'" Faran muttered quietly to himself as he rolled up the sleeves of his shirt. There was always a sense of hesitance and disgust before he did what he had to do. To overcome those feelings, he thought of the world before—an imperfect world, but a world where there was still sense to the madness and wickedness. A world where the boy in front of him would have been better off.

"I'm serious!" Gus pushed himself to keep standing. The armor was heavy and only getting heavier, and the high pitched ringing in his ears from out of the blue didn't help Gus's nausea.

The explosion that followed the ringing was deafening and magnificent. Gus flew into the air and smashed into the side of the corridor before flopping down back to the hard ground.

The lights flickered until the dormitory was engulfed in darkness once more.

Another high pitched ringing.

A smaller explosion from his side tossed Gus sideways.

Gus was at his limit. His helmet was humid from sweat, and his body trembled. He couldn't lift the weight of the armor.

Another high pitch ringing.

From the opposite side of before, a small explosion tossed Gus nearly back to his first landing spot.

Faran walked toward Gus who lied helplessly on the ground coughing and barely conscious. Gus felt his strength slip out from the armor, and it returned to being just a shaped hunk of metal.

"That was for my comrades. And now…" Faran pulled off Gus's helm. "… I pray you be given a better life someday for having had to live this one."

A high pitched ringing.

"Faran!"

The high pitched ringing stopped.

A voice familiar to Faran distracted him from delivering the killing blow as his attention shifted. He didn't need to turn to see who the voice belonged to. "Ms. Wolf!" Faran said as he stood and dusted off his pants.

"I don't think killing a helpless kid is part of your job!" Emily stood by the door-less doorway dimly lit by the orange glow from the fiery remnants of Faran's wrath. She reached into her coat pocket and put on her shades.

"This is none of your business. Don't you have your own job to do Ms. Wolf?" Faran turned around and faced the Wolf Pack's leader.

"I think you and I both know this is doing my job." Emily remembered to relax her shoulders. She had to always remind herself to relax her shoulders.

At the sound of armored fingers scraping on the ground, Faran turned his head and watched Gus desperately fighting from seeping into the shadow.

Before Faran could act, Gus was already gone. He turned his attention to Emily once again.

"And what exactly would be the meaning of this?" Faran asked.

"I'm sure you already know the answer," Emily replied.

"This is Faran. Situation in the building C is under control," Faran spoke into his ear piece. He smiled at Emily. "I don't want the men having to lie and make up excuses about whatever happened to dear Ms. Emily Wolf."

"We don't have to do this, you know." Emily fixed her shades on her nose bridge with her finger. "You can do your thing. We can do our own thing."

"It seems that your 'thing' and our 'thing' seem to be the same *thing."*

"No, that's where you'd be wrong," Emily said. "Your *thing* is to survive this war you all started. Our *thing* is to make sure innocent kids aren't caught in the crossfire."

Faran smiled bittersweetly.

"Just to be clear, I don't enjoy this." Faran thought about reaching for his gun, but as he watched Emily's hands ignite into ball of flames, he thought it'd be more amusing to beat her at her own game.

"I don't buy it." Emily was surprised to see that her response seemed to irk Faran the wrong way.

A high pitch noise rang in Emily's ear.

Chapter 50
WOLVES

The explosions from below didn't frighten Maria or Howard any-more. However, it did worry them for their friend. The light went out again and the two sat in the darkness with only their flashlights as a source of light.

"It'll be alright, Maria. Gus can handle himself," Howard spoke as he grabbed for any metallic object he could find and presented them to Maria for permission. He had already barred the doors to Maria's room as he had before and now was working towards turning his dagger into more of a spear. Had he still been in his room, Howard figured he probably could have slapped together some sort of a fire-arm, but he made do with his circumstances.

Maria switched between pointing the flashlight at the door and at Howard as she swiveled her body back and forth every once in a while. She hoped that the only person who'd come through that door next would be Gus.

The door.

Howard.

The door.

Howard.

The door.

"Maria! Run!" Howard screamed as half of his body sunk into the ground. He tried to stab at the shadows but was devoured by it before he had the chance.

Maria shined her light at where Howard should be but wasn't. She didn't need a specific target for her 'gift' to take effect, and its range was enough to at least cover the room. Without hesitation, Maria un-leashed her 'gift' in hopes that whatever was in the room would feel the way she felt—but worse. Much worse.

For a moment there was nothing but Maria and the muffled chaos outside.

Suddenly, a man pulled himself halfway out of the shadows. He breathed heavily and muttered in a language Maria didn't recognize. She shined her light on him.

"Who are you?" Maria asked with her fear and surprise masked behind a stern look.

The man pulled his whole body out from the shadows and struggled to stand. He was skinny and somewhat short for a man, and dressed in a white dress shirt with a skinny black tie, all encased in a formfitting black dress vest, and black dress pants. Maria flashed him with the light. He had long, styled black hair, and a face defined by the shadows cast by his cheekbones. Though he seemed young, the shadow man seemed older than the students at Facility Zero.

"What. Have. You. Done?" the man asked with an even thicker accent than Maria. His accent reminded her of Jean and Jamie, though it was slightly different. He pressed onto the wall with one of his hands to push his quivering body up. His eyes occasionally opened wide as if he had a sudden great realization, or as if there was a moment where the discomfort of what he was feeling suddenly spiked into pain.

"You're feeling fear. Perhaps the worst feeling of fear you've ever felt," Maria told him matter-of-factly. "I have the power to make people feel certain emotions to any degree that I want. So tell me what you've done with Howard, or it might get much worse for you."

The shadow man's mind fought against the unnaturally imposed emotions. His hand on the wall slid down as his legs collapsed. Memories associated with the feeling began to replay in his mind like a strobe light.

The man chuckled.

"You're. Weak." He took a deep breath and tilted his head up to stare Maria in the eyes. His string-like lips was stretched diagonally to resemble a smile. "You think. This fear? My country. What I've done. What I've seen. My life. This. This Nothing."

"I'm sure I can top it," Maria replied. She concentrated a little harder.

The man began to breathe a little faster and raggedly. His lips remained stretched upward.

"You're friend. Not. The only one. I have all. All your friends," the man said with some strain. "I don't know. What will. Happen. If I lose. Control. Maybe. They die. If you. Had the strength. To do worse. You would. From start. No? Now. You know. What do you do?""

Maria stared at the man for a moment without words. She was careful not to show a single sign of the chaos reigning in her mind. "Why are you doing this to us?" Maria asked.

The man sighed in relief as Maria's powers waned. He took a moment to compose himself and muttered something to himself in his native tongue. From the sharp tone of it, Maria imagined he was cursing at her or something like it. The man stood in front of Maria fixing his tie before giving his vest a few quick swipes down to dust it off. It was already clean to Maria's eyes, but it seemed to make him feel better.

"Not enemy," the man said as he offered her his hand. "Not friend. Just rescue."

*****

Faran stared in disbelief.

"Wow, that's still loud as hell." Emily massaged the ear ringing from the explosion. It was still louder than she had anticipated. She coughed a little bit to clear her through from the dust. "You can still go, Faran. Apparently there's not much you can do. I'm sure you and I would be much better off if we didn't have this little showdown. And trust me, Faran, I dug into your past a bit, and I really wouldn't mind having the chance to kick your ass. So why not take my offer while you still have my generosity?"

Emily pulled out her cigarette that she had saved from earlier. As she lit it, she heard the familiar and obsolete high pitched ringing again.

This time the explosion happened further away than Emily wanted-ed. It claimed the piano as its victim. Emily took a deep inhale of the cigarette and exhaled a cloud of smoke. She looked at her addiction and thought to herself that she really needed to quit. But it was so, so hard to give up.

His 'gift' had never missed before, and its magnitude never differed from the scale that he intended. At least, not since when he first discovered his 'gift.'

"Go, Faran," Emily said as she worked on her small and dwindling cigarette.

With a frustrated cry, Faran raised his hand in the air. In an instant, a javelin of flame ignited in his hand. Without hesitation, Faran chucked the flaming spear at Emily.

Surprise disrupted the near rhythmic timing of Emily's smoky exhale. Choking a bit on the smoke, Emily lightly coughed as she stomped her foot on the ground, and a slab of the earth erected in front of her. As the javelin hit the earthen shield, it exploded into magnificent burst of flame.

Faran threw another javelin without hesitation.

"What do you have against the Gifted anyway?!" Emily yelled once the roar of the explosion receded. She had to cough a little more to clear her throat. "Do you just enjoy being an ironic villain?!"

"I'm the villain?! Does any of this seem natural to you?!" Faran yelled back. "Do you think any of this is okay?! For a man to be able to do these things?! We're abnormalities! Abominations! We don't belong in this world! The only thing the Gifted will bring to this chaotic world is more blood!"

Faran hurled another flaming javelin at Emily.

"I've killed men!"

Another javelin struck Emily's earthen shield. It shook and rained crumbs on Emily's head. The cigarette was almost done. She played around with the fire in her hands and tried to mold it into shape. A shadowy figure of a man appeared in front of her.

"I've killed women!"

This javelin was considerably weaker—he was running out juice. The shadow man waved at her, and Emily nodded back. She watched as the shadow man disappeared out of the room.

"I've killed children!" Faran breathed heavily. "And I'll kill myself when it's my time! But someone has to clean up this mess! And I'll be dying knowing I've done my part! That I've done what I could to cleanse myself for my part in this! I may be a villain, but I'm a necessary evil! And someday when the better days come, people will appreciate people like me who were needed for the greater good."

Faran breathed heavily as he raised his hand for another javelin but couldn't gather the flames. He reached for his rifle and unloaded at the slab until it was empty. There was silence as the smoke cleared.

Before Faran could reload his gun, Emily darted out from behind the slab and threw at Faran a smaller flaming javelin of her own. Faran leapt out of the way as the javelin burst in brilliant flame.

"Thanks for teaching me a new trick," Emily said as she walked towards Faran. She spat out her depleted cigarette and picked up a piece of debris the size of her fist from the ground.

"I'm pretty sure..." Emily spoke as she observed the debris.

Faran quickly reloaded the gun and pointed it at Emily, and the debris in Emily's hand scattered into countless particles of light. Faran didn't notice his gun change until it hadn't fired. In Emily's hand where the debris once was, a part of Faran's gun now rested in her palm. He studied the rock embedded in the body of his gun and tossed it away.

"I'm pretty sure this is self-defense now. I'm pretty sure people will agree I gave you a fair chance to walk away." Emily tossed the metal chunk of his gun that had switched places over her shoulder.

As Faran reached for his sidearm, Emily clasped her hands together. The moisture around Faran gathered and frosted over him. He was left encased in ice from head down.

"What are you?! What is your 'gift'?!" Faran finally showed slight fear in his eyes. He couldn't see Emily's eyes to get insight into her mind. The shades only showed glistening reflections of the flames scattered around them.

Emily pointed at her head. "I told you before that this is my 'gift,'"

Emily said. "I'm a bit quicker at picking up things than others. Including these 'gifts.'" Emily smiled. "My idiot boyfriend and I have a bet to see who can learn more of these. I hate to admit it, but even though I have the unfair advantage of having him teach me whatever he knows, he seems to be winning."

Faran struggled to free himself.

"Yeah, anyway, the point is you and the world are going on about this 'gift' and the Light the wrong way. It's not what can we do to stop this. It should be, 'what can we learn to do with these.' Because I'm sure as time goes by, more and more people will start picking these things up." Emily kept her distance from Faran.

"Those who choose to take part in the madness…" Faran spat at Emily. It landed nowhere near her. "…should burn for their own madness."

"Not going to change your mind?"

"Never."

"I know." Emily moved one of her hands across her chest. A zephyr, traveling the direction Emily's hand went, began to circle around Faran.

A high pitched ringing.

Emily ignored the ringing and moved her hand again once more the same direction. The zephyr turned into an uncomfortably strong wind.

"Thanks for at least making this easier." There was no smile on Emily's face.

Carefully placed explosions freed Faran from his icy prison. He quickly reached for his sidearm.

"See ya," Emily gently told Faran.

What followed Emily's farewell halted the small war in the desert.

Chapter 51
COLLISIONS

With a roar, Landris finally freed himself from the clench of the concrete-head-thing's teeth. The concrete-head couldn't retain its shape any longer. As Landris fell to the ground, above him the piles of sand and lumps of concrete rained down on him.

Morris scavenged off a rifle from one of his fallen men. He quickly checked the gun for its ammo and rummaged through the body's pockets for any extra. Norah walked up next to him.

"Don't think that'll help much," Norah said with her eyes locked on where Landris had fallen.

"Got to do something, right?" Morris readied his gun. "You alright?"

Norah didn't answer. She knew Morris asked because she was visibly tired and probably shaken at this point. A glint of emerald light appeared in Norah's hand, and another glint of emerald light flew over from where the concrete-head thing had been and landed on the palm of her other hand. With a wave of her hands, the two lights pierced the ground around her.

The ground around them violently rumbled and cracked. With tremendous noise, the large chunks of the earth formed into a pair of what resembled humanoid beings that were as tall as two story buildings. It had a large obtuse torso and hefty limbs. Within the cracks between the pieces of rocks held together was a gentle stream of energy that fluttered off into the air.

"That's more assuring," Morris said as he stared, awed at the towering beings.

Norah wasn't so confident. She commanded the two golems to go after the enemy.

Landris took a moment to catch his breath. That *thing* took more energy than he had wanted to fight off and destroy, and the earth shaking stomps coming his way suggested there were more like it. He wasn't sure how much longer he could last in this state.

An explosive boom echoed throughout the facility as Landris bolted toward the golems. Using the momentum and all the strength his leg could give, Landris flung his body onto one of the golems. The golem exploded into a firework of rubble. As soon as he landed, the second golem threw a punch at Landris with all of its force. Its fist met with Landris's fist, and the golem's arm erupted and shattered into pieces.

"Noah!!" Norah screamed.

Landris grabbed one of the falling stones and threw it at Morris. The moment he saw Landris looking his way, Morris subconsciously raised his gun to shield himself, and the stone struck and buried itself into the gun instead of him. The impact knocked Morris off his feet. His fear had saved him.

Before the golems could gather themselves, Landris bolted towards Norah. Another boom echoed throughout the facility.

Julian?

The countless particles of light gathering in front of the cowering Norah stopped Landris in his tracks, but the boy that appeared before him was much shorter and looked even younger than Julian.

His eyes were fierce and unafraid, and his arms were stretched out in front of him. "Sorry, Norah. Things were getting messy back there," Noah said. "I also had to let Emily know about that guy she was looking for."

"What could have been more important than your dear sister?!" Norah snapped at Noah.

Landris wound up his arm and threw a punch at the boy. He didn't flinch. The punch struck an invisible wall between Landris and Noah's hands. The tremendous blow echoed and stirred the ground around them.

The protector of the Silver Aegis had finally been halted as he retracted away from Noah and grunted in pain. Landris realized he was getting weaker and weaker. He had to act quickly.

Noah's legs shook. The acute stress from blocking the blow shocked his system and nearly made him vomit. "What is this guy, Norah?" Noah asked as he tried to compose himself.

"A monster. A psycho. A freak. All of the above," Norah answered. "But I'm he's sure nothing the Howl twins can't handle."

Noah wasn't so confident. He knew Norah wasn't either. The siblings, however, knew neither one of them would ever let the other come to harm if they could help it.

"He's coming again get ready to run," Noah warned his sister.

With a roar Landris tried his might against the barrier again. Noah disappeared into countless particles along with the barrier and Landris punched through nothing but air. Norah sprinted away towards Morris who was a few feet away from them.

Landris's eyes briefly tracked the instantaneous movement of the particles of light heading behind him. As Landris turned around, the world as he had seen with his gifted eyes reverted back to normal. It always took a moment to readjust. It felt dizzying, as if he was nearly blind when he reverted back. For a moment, he couldn't trust his eyes that he saw three of the boy.

The eyes of the monster reverting from glowing white to a human's natural color didn't go missed by Noah. Even without full realization of the 'why,' a wave of confidence rushed through him.

Landris struck at the first Noah only to watch it disperse into streams that quickly dissipated into the air. The second Noah produced the same result. Before Landris could reach the third Noah, the boy clasped his hands. The air around Landris became frigid, and in an instant trapped him in dense ice from the neck down.

He was tired. It felt like he could fall asleep at any moment. His heart pounded, and breathing became difficult while he was infused in ice. Landris realized he had ran out of time, and it was much sooner than he had anticipated. He watched as the golems stomped over in his direction. One of the golems crumbled down into pieces during the journey as Norah grew weary herself.

***

Moments before, from afar, Kalin watched the battle unfold and debated whether to help Landris or to see if Lily was safe. Before he could make the decision, he was surrounded by the McKinley's men.

"Kalin!"

The voice of a young girl turned all of their attention to the sky.

"It's the Witch!" one of the men yelled in excitement. The McKinley's guns turned their attention from the redhead to the Witch in the sky. Without even lifting a finger, the Witch crumpled their guns like paper. They all reached for their tranquilizer pistols only to witness the same thing happen again.

Lily lifted all of the men into the air until they were as high up in the sky as she was. Some of them yelled and cursed at her while some of them were silent with fear. A few of them pleaded with her for their lives. The Witch stared into the eyes of those few and studied the emotions on their faces.

"Lily?" Kalin's voice reached Lily. They both saw and felt something from one another that they had never seen or felt before. Lily gently placed all the men down back onto the ground.

"Run," Kalin told the men.

The men listened.

Lily began climbing down the sky. When she neared Kalin, Lily decided to skip the last few steps and leapt into Kalin instead. Kalin embraced her into his arms and was glad that he didn't lose his footing.

323

"You alright?" Kalin asked as he pulled away from Lily slightly.

Lily shook her head and buried it in his chest again.

"What happened?" Kalin asked.

Lily remained silent.

"Where are Sarah and Julian?"

Lily pointed back at the rooftop of the office building.

"They are with Ms. Jones and the Mr. Yuri. They said they're going to the helicopter. I came here to get you."

A loud boom echoed through the facility as Landris bolted towards the golems.

"Lily…" Kalin pulled away from his friend more completely. "Listen to me carefully, okay? I'm going to go help Landris, but I want you to go meet up with Sarah and them. Landris and I will catch up with you."

Lily shook her head.

"Don't go anywhere," Lily's words surprised Kalin.

"He needs me, Lily," Kalin said. Lily remained silent for a moment.

"I'll go with you," Lily pleaded.

"No, Lily. They're here for you." As he saw the change in Lily's eyes, Kalin felt as if he had made a mistake saying those words. "And it seems like they've got other Gifted with them. I don't want to risk losing you."

Lily was left without words again. She nodded her head, and Kalin nodded back to her.

"Go! Hurry! I'll see you soon, alright?" Kalin said as he turned his back on her. He looked back at her once more, and she looked small and hollow. He wished that he hadn't looked back.

Lily watched Kalin as he jetted off to Landris.

***

"Listen we're not here to hurt you guys," Noah told Landris still encased in ice. "I know it seems really hard to believe right now, but you have to trust me, okay?

Morris picked himself up from the ground. He couldn't remember the last time he was thrown onto his back that much. The gun was broken. Even if it hadn't been, it wouldn't be any less useless as he learned that day. He—no, *they*—were outclassed. If there was such a thing as natural selection, they were certainly not going to be around for long. For a moment, he caught a glimpse of the Light over the horizon and cursed at it. Then he caught a glimpse of a familiar redhead coming at them in lightning speed. "Kid! Watch out!" Morris yelled at

Noah.

By the time the words reached Noah's ears, Kalin's fist had reached Noah's face. Noah's small body did a full rotation before he hit the ground.

"Noah!" Norah linked her anger to the lone golem.

The golem swung at Kalin and he leapt on top of its arm.

"Hey! Free me first! Tomato-head!" Landris yelled.

Kalin hung onto the golem with great toil as the golem vigorously swung around its arm to free itself from the pest. When he saw the chance, Kalin scurried up to its lump of a head. The streams that permeated from the golem felt familiar to Kalin.

"That's the Witch's friend!" Noah said as he picked himself up and spat out blood.

"You okay?!" Norah asked her brother.

Noah placed his hand on the ground and the earth encased his arm into a crude gauntlet and formed a shield. He ignited his other hand with fire.

Kalin placed his hand on top of the golems head. His gut feeling told him that he could manipulate—communicate—with the streams that flowed within the beast. Before he could give it a serious attempt, Norah gave the golem an idea inspired by her brother. It placed its lump of an arm near the ground where it collected the earth to form a hand. The golem grabbed the pest on its head and threw him across the courtyard.

Seeing the tomato-head failing to be his rescue, Landris concentrated as much of his energy as he could.

Noah teleported to where Kalin landed.

"Listen." Noah dissipated the fire from his hand. "It's us. The Wolf..."

Kalin swept Noah's legs and darted for the golem again. On the ground and looking up at the sky, Noah let out a grunt of frustration before teleporting back to the battleground.

"Go for the girl!" Landris yelled as he saw Kalin hop across the golem's arm and onto its head again.

Noah appeared in front of Norah with his earthen shield and hand ignited with flames once again.

Kalin sat on the head of the golem much like before. If his theory proved correct, Kalin thought, he could end this fight with harming less of the people involved. He placed his hand on top of the golem's head and let loose his streams. He felt his streams intertwine with the streams within the golem. They didn't get along. The streams within the golem were trying to rip the foreign streams away from its source and absorb it.

The golem struggled to keep its shape and struggled to move its hand towards Kalin, inching closer and closer with much effort.

"What is he doing?" Norah asked.

"I think I know what's happening, but I don't think I can believe it," Noah answered.

"What are YOU doing? A little help, maybe?" Norah gave her brother a confounded look.

"Just… just give it a second," Noah said as he keenly observed Kalin.

For a brief moment all of his veins glowed white again, Landris used all his might and shattered out of his prison.

Noah shielded himself and Norah from the chunks of ice flying off. He felt irritated that he had to turn his attention away from Kalin to Landris, but was relieved as he watched Landris fall to his knees.

"Do something, Kalin," Landris muttered between his heavy breathing as he tried to pick himself up.

"Seriously?!" Norah prodded Noah.

Noah gave an uneasy smile and a shrug to Norah. He wanted to see if his hypothesis was correct.

Kalin amplified the amount of streams flowing into the golem and overloaded it with a burst of his own energy. The crevices of the golem erupted and exploded with streams. As the golem lost structure and crumbled to the ground in pieces, Kalin leapt off before he could be buried under the rocks.

"That was amazing," Noah exclaimed. "He controls the energy itself."

"I'm glad you got to learn something, genius, but now what?" Norah complained. "Hermes and Gaea are both too tired, and now, so am I." The glinting emerald lights were absorbed into Norah's hands.

"They don't look to be in too good shape either," Noah said observing Kalin who was helping Landris stand. "I bet they're ready to—"

By this time, nearly everyone at Facility Zero were used to loud noises of gunfire, explosions, shouts, and screams, but the sheer roar of Emily's deed shocked them all, and its power terrorized them.

"Your girl's crazy," Norah said as she hid behind the slab of earth erected by Noah.

"Damn it, Emily," Noah muttered under his breath.

Shielding himself from the heat and the wind with his arm, Morris couldn't help but laugh at the lunacy of it all.

Chapter 52
THE WOLF & THE WITCH

Yuri hurriedly led Nancy, Julian, and Sarah through the hall leading to the rooftop.

"Yuri! Wait!" Nancy tried to grab on to Yuri's arm, but Yuri quickly moved it out of her hands' reach. They were right at the door. The chaos and the scenery felt all too familiar for Julian and Sarah.

"Let me check first," Yuri told the group. He carefully went out the door and found the gaping hole on the rooftop where the helicopter had crashed into. Other than the rubble and smoke, there was just a single man of the McKinley's struggling to survive. Their own helicopter on the helipad seemed intact. The McKinley's man reached his hand out to Yuri and tried to form words that came out more as a jumbled groan. Before returning to the group, Yuri ended the man's struggle.

After a single shot of gunfire, Yuri opened the door and simply waved the group to follow.

"Yuri!" Nancy's voice was close to a yell as she followed after Yuri's swift pace. She was finally able to grab Yuri's arm and yanked him back hard enough for him to turn around. "I'm not leaving without my brother!" Nancy demanded.

"Your brother will be fine." To Nancy's surprise, Yuri appeared almost mad as he spoke to Nancy. "If anything happens to you, however, he will not be fine. I will not be fine. None of us will be fine. You understand?"

"No, I don't understand." Nancy's eyes were cold and stern. "I'm not leaving him behind. Not again."

"I will pick you up and carry you like luggage if I have to, child." Yuri's eyes were just as stern.

Before Nancy could respond, a deafening roar of howling winds silenced them all.

Yuri leapt forward and pushed the group to the ground. They watched in disbelief as the dormitory fiercely tore apart and sucked into the flaming tornado. The intense heat wave from the violent wind made the air unbearable to breathe, and the brilliant flames blinded their eyes from staring into it. Julian and Sarah held each other's sweat drenched hands tighter and tighter as the seconds went by.

The tornado, with all of its fire and fury, dissipated like magic. As if it was all a momentary nightmare, the night returned and silence ensued. The group looked at one another to confirm what they witnessed was indeed real.

"Everyone okay?" Yuri asked. He wondered if they could hear him when he could barely hear himself.

Nancy nodded as Yuri helped her up. He then helped the kids stand, and Yuri guided the disoriented group to the helicopter. As the kids boarded, Nancy and Yuri remained outside. Nancy was adamant about staying.

The idea of what exactly he was trying to protect Nancy from struck Yuri, and he paused for a moment, smiled, and shook his head. From his coat pocket, Yuri pulled out one of his cheap cigars. "When did we let it slip?" Yuri chuckled as he lit his cigar with a match he got from a rundown motel. "The world we once knew. Our world."

Nancy shrugged her shoulders. It was one of those silly questions Yuri liked to ask.

"We're on the verge of becoming the relics of the past, Nancy. Relics from the world that once was, and I think I'm too old for that kind of change." Yuri let out a sigh with smoke.

"The world's no different than it was before the Light," Nancy said. "It has always demanded the people to adapt if they wanted to survive."

Yuri tasted his cigar once more before he tossed it. He then grabbed his flask from one of his other pockets and took a swig. Only a droplet ran down his throat. Yuri chuckled as he tossed the empty flask over his shoulder. "Come on," Yuri said as he headed toward the corpse of the lone McKinley's man on the roof. "Let's get you a nice gun and go see about that brother of yours."

✳✳✳

The leader of the Wolf Pack stood alone surrounded by nothing but the burnt debris and ashes of where Facility Zero's dormitory used to be. "Damn, I'm all sweaty now," Emily complained on the phone.

Lily walked into the charred lot. She could still feel the heat emanating all around her.

"Yeah, I know that's my own fault. We're almost done here," Emily continued on the phone. "I'm sure my little stunt also took the fight out of the lot of them. Tell Gabriel to standby somewhere close though. What? What's going on with the twins?"

Emily heard the gentle footsteps and turned around, and for a moment lost her train of thought.

"Hey now," Emily spoke into the phone. "The *V.I.P.'s* right in front of me. Call you back later." She hung up and dropped the phone into her coat pocket. "Hi," Emily said playfully as if she was talking to a child.

Lily ignored her and walked past Emily. She stood where Faran once was.

"Someone died here," Lily said, staring at the spot where barely any ashes remained. "You killed him."

Emily scratched her head.

"Yeah," Emily admitted with slight repentance in her voice. "Someone did die there. And yeah, I killed him."

Lily turned around and faced Emily. She didn't speak, but Emily felt that the Witch was demanding an explanation.

Emily didn't understand why, but she obliged the Witch. "I don't enjoy killing anyone," Emily said as she folded away her shades. "But he was a bad man. Killed many people, and probably would have killed more. He was trying to kill me, matter of fact."

Emily wasn't sure if the Witch had lost interest in either the conversation or her, or if she had just drifted away somewhere as the Witch's eyes rolled down from her to the ground and became like glass.

"You're the Witch, right?" Emily began to walk closer to Lily. "I mean, I'm sure you had a good reason yourself when you killed that doctor, right?"

Lily looked up. She looked almost offended.

Emily stood right in front of the Witch. She had about a head over the Witch in height, though they both could probably use a sandwich or two.

"Or would I be correct to guess that was more of an accident?" Emily raised an eyebrow.

Lily didn't answer.

"Whatever your story is, it's nice to be able to finally meet you in person. I'm Emily." Emily offered her hand.

For whatever reasons that Lily couldn't quite grasp, Emily rubbed her the wrong way. She didn't accept the handshake. "Why?" Lily asked Emily the question she had asked so many times that day. "What's all this for?"

Emily raised her other eyebrow. It was a small talent of hers. She scratched her head as she contemplated the Witch's question. "It wasn't for you if that's what you're wondering. At least, not for us anyway," Emil answered. "Y'know... I was never really into the Witch's hype, but I have to say this meeting is a bit disappointing."

Lily's eyebrows furrowed, and her lips tightened.

"A lot of people, especially the Gifted either look up to you like their messiah or think of you as the devil." Emily looked down on Lily only because she was taller than her. "But it seems like you don't even know what you are—like a lost child. You don't fit your role."

It was quick, but seemed nonthreatening. Emily let Lily feebly slap her across the face. The blood in the Witch's eyes suggested that she gave it all she had, though it didn't feel like much to Emily. She was more intrigued by the odd black bracelet on the wrist of the Witch's hand that had slapped her.

"You don't know me." Lily's voice was quiet, but solid—gentle, but wrathful. "I didn't choose this. I didn't choose to be the Witch."

"Glad you at least have some fight in you." Emily eyes never left the Witch's. "You're going to need it, because it's not going to get any easier."

Emily poked and buried her finger into Lily's sternum. It hurt, but Lily didn't show it.

"No one chooses what they're given in life. We just choose what we do with them." Emily's tone grew stronger with the pressure of her finger on Lily. "Whether you like it or not, you're the Witch. A lot of people look up to you, and lot of people want to see you dead. What you do has a lot of effect on everyone. You'll either have to learn to deal with that, or roll over and die while cryin' and askin' pointless questions like 'why.' It is what it is."

Lily felt for the first time what it was like to be scolded like a child from someone other than Kalin. It was embarrassing, and she felt strangely frustrated towards Emily.

Emily took her finger off of Lily.

"No one should have that much baggage, and if I could take it from you, I would. You already seem like you're ready to break. Don't." There was a sudden gentleness in Emily's eyes that startled Lily. "Because it's too damned unfair for you that your one life has to be ruined by something you didn't choose. While you're alive, make the best of it. Make it worth it. It's your life, your story; fight for it."

"Sorry, I can be a bit preachy sometimes." Emily looked away from Lily for a moment and scratched her head again. "Anyway, even if strangers who're affected by you don't matter, you still have that guy who probably cares about you a lot, right? Be alright for him if you can't be alright for yourself."

Emily's eyes widened for a moment as she seemed to recall something important. "Oh yeah, that guy! We should probably go find him." Emily began walking away from Lily. "I owe him and I guess you an explanation and some kind of apology."

Lily was confused by what had just happened. She stood still, puzzled, as she stared after her while she walked away. Emily had a confident and wide stride as she whistled away.

Emily stopped and looked back. "Come on. Let's go find your boyfriend." Emily waved Lily over.

In the darkness Emily couldn't see Lily's pale face blush. As she began walking away again, Lily trailed behind her from afar with her little steps.

Chapter 53
THE BLURRED LINE

The uproar halted at Facility Zero. The Silver Aegis and the McKinley soldiers stared as they made way for the leader of the Wolf Pack and the Witch as they walked towards their companions.

Many were tempted to take a shot at the Witch and the leader of the Wolf Pack, but the smoldering ashes of Emily's fury was still burned into their minds. Instead, a soldier took advantage of the temporary peace to take the life of his non-Gifted enemy instead. With a single shot and another dead body the war resumed.

Safe from the bullets, Emily and Lily walked a sacred path amidst the chaos.

"Was that your girlfriend?" Landris asked Kalin referring to the storm of fire.

"Never," Kalin answered.

Morris asked a similar question of Norah and Noah to which Noah answered similarly, "No, I'm pretty certain that was the work of that leader of ours."

"Emily?" Morris exclaimed in disbelief.

"Landris!"

Kalin and Landris turned their heads at the familiar voice. Nancy was running towards them with a rifle in her hand with Yuri, Sarah, and Julian close behind her.

"Nancy!" Landris yelled back. "Stay back!"

Nancy didn't listen. Soon, the twins and Morris were face to face with Nancy Jones of the Silver Aegis, Yuri, Sarah, Julian, Landris, and the Witch's friend.

"What now?" Norah asked Noah. "It just got messier."

"I think it'll be fine since it's almost time for us to leave anyway," Noah answered Norah.

"What part of 'stay back' did you not understand, Nancy?" Landris asked.

"Shut it, baby brother," Nancy replied. She raised her rifle and aimed it down at Morris.

Morris could tell from her form that Nancy at least seemed to be proficient at handling the weapon. It was also obvious that it had been one of their guns.

"You weren't able to beat them?" Julian asked in disbelief as he noticed Landris's worn out state.

"You're welcome to do better, Julian Badass Caldwell." Landris dusted off his clothes.

"The two over there are Gifted. Pretty frightening ones at that." Kalin didn't take his eyes off of his enemies.

"Well, at least we outnumber them." Yuri handed Sarah his sidearm and aimed his rifle that he had looted off of one of the dead bodies. "Point and shoot. Have you ever used one before?" Yuri asked Sarah with his sights on Noah.

Sarah held the gun as if someone had dropped a parcel in her hands, but it didn't take her long to study and recognize the bits and pieces of information she had learned in the past. "Yes," Sarah answered Yuri after a short moment as she pointed the gun in the general direction of the twins and Morris.

A small wall of fire sprinted across the no man's land between the two warring parties. As they all turned to look in the direction of the fire's origin, they all watched as Emily and the Witch walked towards them.

Before, Morris felt nothing more than a bit of surprise to hear of Emily's deed, but as he watched Emily and the Witch coming their way, Morris felt a pang in his stomach. He—they—everyone—knew the Gifted were capable of havoc, but the Witch was always the only one thought to have the power for catastrophe. Emily had singlehandedly changed that for all who had witnessed her otherworldly tornado. How many more like them were out there? Were even the twins next to him capable of something like that?

"Don't y'all think both sides have had enough?" Emily cried as she waved her hand and dissipated the flames.

"Lily!" Kalin ran after his friend. He stood in front of Emily and hesitated, uncertain as to whether or not she was an enemy.

"Go ahead." Emily moved out of the way for Kalin. He didn't waste time running to his friend.

"You're Emily Wolf, aren't you?" Kalin had never met or even seen a picture of the girl, but his gut feeling told him the fake blond with the smug smile was her.

"Bingo, bingo, little dingo," Emily said as he walked past Kalin, giving him a playful slap on his behind.

Lily didn't appreciate it.

As the leader of the Wolf Pack made her way to her crew, she paused for a moment as the realization of who the boy was sunk in. She let out a small sigh and scratched her head.

Morris, it's a mess out here. What the hell's going on? One of the men patched through Morris's earpiece. *We're losing contact with more and more people every second here.*

334

"Are you okay?" Kalin asked Lily.

Lily nodded.

"You got the Witch?" Morris asked Emily who walked past him to the twins.

"Not sure yet, James." Emily inspected the twins quickly with her eyes for any damage. "You good?" She asked Noah. He nodded and Emily pulled him in close and get him a peck on his cheek.

"How about you?" Emily turned to Norah with her arm still around Noah.

"Yeah." Norah gave Emily a fierce glare. "Are you the one who did the fire show?"

Emily gave a slightly reluctant nod.

"Emily Wolf," Nancy murmured just loud enough for Yuri and Landris standing next to her to overhear. "It all makes sense now."

"Mr. Morris! I think it's time for you call for a cease fire!" Emily firmly suggested loud enough to be heard over the commotion.

"What are you talking about?" Morris was afraid to hear the answer, but in the back of his mind, he was already beginning to connect the dots about what Emily was about to tell him.

"I mean, there's no point of this war for the McKinley's anymore," Emily continued. "We have all the Gifted except for the ones right in front of us," the leader of the Wolf Pack said indicating Lily, Kalin, and the Silver Aegis group.

Yuri chuckled at the revelation. "So that's the little wolf girl?" Yuri asked Nancy.

She nodded stoically.

"I like her."

Morris! another man screamed his name through the earpiece. Morris chuckled as he massaged his nose bridge.

"Somehow... somehow that's just perfect, Emily," Morris remarked.

The outcry of gunfire echoed all around them.

Morris weighed his options. Either stop now or lose more lives. If the Gifted were already gone, their mission was already over.

"Just so you know, Mr. Morris," Nancy spoke sternly. "If you wish to continue this war, we're prepared for that as well. Our own reinforcements should arrive soon."

"And if I were to tell you that we're here with government support?" Morris replied just as sternly.

"Then you'll learn tonight two things. First, that perhaps you aren't the only one. Second, how little that means compared to what people of importance will do to stay important."

Morris contemplated Nancy's words for a bit. "This is Captain Morris," Morris spoke into his earpiece. "Cease fire. I repeat, cease fire immediately. Take the wounded and carry them to the vehicles while you wait for further instruction. This operation is over." Morris's decision was more or less based on being sick of the lives lost to the games of the few.

Morris looked at Yuri with demanding eyes who simply repaid the look with a smile.

The gunfire didn't cease.

"Thought I'd let my men get a few more shots in," Yuri chuckled as he pulled out his walkie-talkie. "This is Yuri. Hold your fire. Let the intruders go for now. Their leader and we are in negotiation," Yuri spoke into his walkie-talkie and placed it back into his pocket before he could hear the complaints from his men.

"This is Morris again. Ceasefire is still in place. Get yourselves to the vehicles," Morris reassured his men.

"What about those guys, then?" Landris pointed at the twins and their leader.

"It's an odd sensation, Ms. Wolf. A paradoxical mix of being very surprised and yet not very surprised to see you here." Nancy lowered her gun. "Do you think we'll let you leave?"

"You'll never be able to find my friend with rest of your Gifted. They're already long gone," Emily spoke with confidence. "So unless you want to have one hell of a pointless bloody brawl, I think it's in your best interest to let us go. Especially, since you might not lose anything out of this because of us."

"This might be the most costly phone call I ever took." Nancy smiled. "Was a small war part of your little scheme as well?"

"Things just happened that way." Emily smiled back.

"I get it now," Kalin spoke with slight distaste. He held Lily's hand.

"Heya!" Emily waved. "I kind of sort of owe you some sort of apology, I think."

"You definitely do," Norah said.

"Yeah." Emily looked down to the ground and cleared her throat. She needed a cigarette. Like a seasoned machine, her hand reached into her pocket for the carton, spanked it, and her lip whipped out the stick from its home. Before she could light it, Noah yanked it out of her mouth. Her face showed her frustration, but she didn't complain and simply let out a sinking sigh.

"What phone call, Nancy?" Yuri kept his gun raised.

"She's the one who sold us the tip to find the Wi... Lily and Kalin," Nancy answered. "Saying it was 'too hot' of a case for them to touch."

"You believed her?" Yuri flashed a smile at Nancy that oozed with I-will-tease-you-for-years-for-this.

"Given our circumstances, I didn't see the reason not to take the chance. The money she asked for was cheap enough to pay but high enough to take seriously. The girl's clever," Nancy answered Yuri.

"Dreams are a dangerous thing," Yuri chuckled. He wondered if anyone got his joke.

"Hey." Emily approached the redhead and his small friend. "I'm… all this… look…" She cleared he throat. "I'm sorry, and if it means anything, the rest of the pack was really against this idea. This is my selfish crime.

Ever since that Julian kid's video and Nada's disappearance, we knew someone was collecting the Gifted kids. I just had to find out for what," Emily told Kalin.

"You used us both," Kalin said with profound disgust. "You used everyone. I reached out to you for help!"

Emily accepted Kalin's reproach in silence and a bittersweet smile.

"Reach out to her?" Julian asked.

"An email. It's not too hard to find out how to contact us. It's just that we only contact back when it's a case we feel necessary for us to step in. Usually for Gifted in trouble and, I suppose, for the infamous Witch and her friend. We figured it was really you when you mentioned that you were a certain runaway," Noah answered. Though the boy spoke confidently, his voice was quiet.

"I'd have gone myself," Emily continued. "But I didn't know the circumstances. I knew most likely that the great Nancy Jones wouldn't be harming the Gifted; it didn't seem like her style. But I didn't know if I could spring everyone—let alone myself—out without being able to see what's going on. I wouldn't have done it if I wasn't certain you two wouldn't be harmed, and the way I saw it, it was the two of you for who knows how many other Gifted."

"Your idea of rescue was waging a war against us?" Sarah interjected.

"I have no idea how the McKinley's got a whiff on this. It wasn't supposed to be like this. Though I have guesses." Emily glanced at Nancy who remained silent. "I figured if the McKinley's got involved, it'd get messy, and I thought maybe it'd be good to stick with them to get some more answers and maybe even get a better control of the situation. Especially since I figured the government was involved somehow."

"Aren't you a fine specimen for a decent human being," Landris remarked.

"Ironic coming from you, isn't it?" Norah said. "How easily one forgets himself."

Landris didn't have a response.

"Look." Emily sounded sincere. "I'm not trying to give you two a bunch of excuses. I'm just giving you guys an explanation. You two deserve at least that. I'm sorry. I really am."

Emily offered her hand. Kalin didn't oblige her.

"And what do you plan to do with the kids?" Nancy asked calmly.

"Nothing really," Emily said as she retracted her hand with a small sigh. "We'll let them know what happened and of their circumstances. We'll inform them the risks of being part of a private military company given what they are, and offer them alternatives. For example, being part of a group that actually cares about them and can help them learn better what they can do. But if they want to leave, we won't only let them go, but we'll help them go wherever it is they want to go with an open invitation to reach us if they ever need to."

"We're just supposed to believe you?" Sarah asked with a bit of venom in her voice.

"Yep," Emily simply answered. "I just didn't want these kids to be victims of a war they didn't start. I also welcome the rest of you to come with us. Nancy Jones isn't a person who will care for you out of the goodness of her heart, and as long as you're a part of a private military company, you're nothing more than pawns and soldiers at the end of the day."

Helicopters roared from afar.

Morris I think we're all loaded up. That's probably the Silver Aegis reinforcements we're hearing.

"Director Jones isn't like that. We'll take our chances with her," Sarah snapped.

"I don't think you sound that great either," Julian followed right after Sarah.

One of the McKinley's vans drove up right by Emily and the twins. Leon walked out from the driver's seat, and two men-of-smoke placed two unconscious McKinley agents by Morris' feet. "They'll be fine. Maybe have a headache," Leon told Morris.

"Well." Emily dug into her pocket and pulled out some business cards. "Guess that's my cue to leave then. Just in case you change your minds."

Emily walked up to each of the Gifted and handed them her card. It was a simple white business card with "the Wolf Pack" in bold letters, below that was a long series of digits, and finally below the digits was an email address.

Julian and Sarah took the card more out of confusion than out of consideration.

"Are you getting the help you need from her?" Emily asked as she handed Kalin her card. "I know it's was a bit messy, but our offer to help the two of you still stands."

Kalin snatched the card out of Emily's hands. He looked down at

Lily and looked back up at Emily again.

"We'll stay with Ms. Jones," Lily answered. "She helped us to get this far. Not you, Emily."

Emily nodded. It was expected and a risk she understood. She gave Lily a gentle smile, and tried to hand her a card. Lily shook her head.

Landris looked at Emily with disgust and walked away from her.

As Emily went up to Yuri and Nancy to hand them a card, Nancy leaned in to Emily's ear.

"It's a thin line, Emily," Nancy whispered. "A thin line between you and I."

Emily pulled back from her with a crinkled face. She walked away from the group and headed towards the van. Before she hopped into the passenger's side, Emily looked at Morris one last time.

"I highly recommend you also find a new boss." Emily seemed like she had more to say but closed the car door.

With that, the Wolf Pack disappeared into the night desert. Soon, several helicopters flooded the Facility Zero's airspace as the Silver Aegis agents rappelled down from them.

Emily's words reminded Morris of the camera in his pocket. He pulled it out to see that it had been damaged—perhaps even broken. He wondered how much he could recover out of it.

"And what'll you do now?" Yuri asked Morris.

"Let him go," Nancy said.

"What?!" Landris was furious.

"We're neither the military, nor the police. If the government was involved as Mr. Morris said, this is especially something we have to be more sensitive in handling. We don't have the authority to hold these men, nor will they let us hold them without more people being killed. Some diplomacy seems to be the only sensible solution to this," Nancy spoke calmly in contrast to her brother.

"Everyone be ready to move out," Morris spoke into his earpiece.

"But please, do let Mr. McKinley know, Mr. Morris, that there wasn't much more he could have done than this to ensure an early retirement," Nancy told Morris.

Morris nodded. He turned and headed towards the nearest the McKinley vehicle.

"Take care of things here, Yuri. If something happens to me, take care of my brother and mother," Nancy said. "We're going to go and force Hamilton's hand."

"To the Light?" Yuri asked.

Nancy nodded.

"If anything happens to you, I'll take care of them like my own family," Yuri replied. "I'll catch up as soon as I'm done with the clean up here."

"Come," Nancy told Kalin and Lily as she walked past them. "It is time for us to leave. Landris!"

"What about us?" Sarah asked.

"You guys are staying here. Yuri will watch over you," Nancy said.

"Director Jones, we want to be there for Lily!" Sarah complained.

"Absolutely out of the question." Nancy had more than a few reasons at this point to keep Sarah and Julian out of the equation.

"Ms. Jones..." Lily tugged on Nancy's sleeve. "Can Sarah and Julian come with us?"

"What?" Nancy was frankly annoyed at this point.

"I..." Lily seemed nervous, sensing Nancy's frustration. "I don't feel safe leaving them here. I'd feel better if they came with us."

Nancy glanced at Yuri who simply shrugged.

"Alright." Nancy was defeated. "Just Sarah, though."

"Director Jones," Julian said. "If Sarah's going, I'm going. I don't think you'll be able to stop me either."

Nancy was surprised by the newfound boldness in Julian. And she knew from this day on, that boldness would get in her way. "Fine," Nancy said. "Come on, we don't have much time."

Lily opened her bag and checked if she had her important belongings. The cranes were in there safely. The rest of the group had already begun walking towards the building with only Kalin waiting by her side. As Lily closed her bag and looked up, she happened to see something in particular that she lifted into the air and pulled her way.

Landris felt a tap behind him as they entered the office. Lily was holding his black sword.

"Isn't this yours?" Lily asked with smile. "I saw it out there! It's heavy!"

"Thanks," Landris said as he relieved Lily from the blade. "The sheath should be up on the roof." Landris looked at Kalin pointedly.

"I..." Kalin stumbled on his words. He surveyed the area quickly. "I think that rock thing knocked the sword off of me."

Landris looked as if he was angered for a second, then simply smiled. "It's alright, marinara-head," Landris said. "I'm sure Yuri will pick it up."

The group headed for the roof to begin their long journey to the Light.

***

It was a quiet ride back to base in the McKinley's vehicles. Morris pulled a cell phone out from his inner pocket and dialed a number.

"Graham, what happened out there?!" Mr. Hamilton himself answered the call right away. He had been waiting for a while to hear back from Morris.

"Mission failure, sir. I have a feeling you can expect a call from Jones soon," Morris said.

"What?!"

Morris heard a glass shatter from the other end of the phone.

"What happened exactly?!" Mr. Hamilton demanded.

"Your games," Morris said. "You, Jones, and Wolf. All of it happened at the cost of our lives."

"Are you forgetting who you're talking to, you twerp?" Morris could imagine Hamilton's face red with anger.

"What's wrong with the world hasn't changed much, Hamilton," Morris said uncaring of his former superior. There was a certain, profound realization of how little these titles people gave one another mattered.

"You've gone and lost your mind, Graham," Mr. Hamilton said.

"It's people like you and me." Morris rolled downed the window. "I quit." Morris disassembled the phone and took the battery out. He then threw all the pieces out into the desert.

"What'd you do that for? We ain't getting paid for this; you have to save on the little things," Daniels said. "Then again, you did just quit."

"You alight?" Morris asked.

"I'll live," Daniels answered. "Though I'm not sure where we're going."

"We're going to pick up Henderson's body," Morris answered.

"No, I mean, after this," Daniels said. "Where we going after all this. What's tomorrow for us?"

Morris didn't have an answer for Daniels. He wasn't even sure if he wanted to know what tomorrow was yet. For him and many others, today was, more-or-less, enough.

Chapter 54
THE FINAL TASK

Landris woke up with a searing headache. The bed creaked as he lifted up his body. For a moment, he didn't know where he was. The salty air, the fake impressionist painting of the ocean and lighthouses hanging from the dully painted cream walls, the cheap TV, and the outdated phone and lamp by his bedside table all worked together to help him remember that last night wasn't a dream, and he was in a cheap motel by the ocean.

Into the wee hours of the morning, they left Facility Zero and transferred from one vehicle to another until they arrived at the harbor motel where all of them shared a single room and passed out together.

For a moment, Landris thought he was in the room by himself.

"You're finally awake." Nancy was sitting by the small coffee table as she tapped away on her tablet. On the table was a muffin and the bargain mug that came as part of the room steaming with whatever was inside of it.

"How long… what time is it?" Landris asked in a tired voice. His muscles were sore, and sharp pain shot through up his body as he tried to move it.

"It's late afternoon. You're the last one to be up. You must have pushed yourself a bit too far last night." Nancy sipped from the white mug. He guessed she was sipping on whatever tea they had had.

"Where's everyone else?"

"Out," Nancy said without looking up. "I told them they could go look around town until Hamilton gets here—which is supposed to be soon, so I'm assuming they'll be back in a little while. Thought they could use a small break after a day like yesterday before they have to deal with Hamilton."

"You thought it was a good idea for Lily and Kalin to head out?"

"Hamilton already knows we're here with them, and they managed to elude capture by themselves for a couple of years, so I'm sure a few hours would be fine."

Nancy watched her brother get out of the bed stretching his muscles in the vain hope of relieving some pain. When she saw him looking her way, Nancy pointed at the large muffin. "That's for you. Grabbed it this morning while they were doing the continental breakfast."

Landris collapsed on the chair across the table from Nancy. He took a big bite out of the muffin and stared out the window. The sky was already darker shades of blue. The seagulls, the ocean, and the boats all worked together to form a picturesque image of a budget vacation at the harbor.

"I thought the Light would seem…. bigger from here," Landris said as he looked at the Light behind the ocean horizon. He finished the muffin quicker than he anticipated.

"That's what I thought when I first came here a year or so ago as well." Nancy looked away from her tablet for a moment and stared at the Light with her brother.

"I need new clothes," Landris said, looking at his dirty and ragged attire that he fell asleep in. "Didn't you say you brought some yesterday?"

"Check the closet." Nancy sipped a little more of her tea. "I hung them already."

Landris walked over to the closet and opened its doors. "Seriously?" Landris asked in disbelief as he looked towards his sister with resentment.

Nancy didn't return any sort of reply and went back to tapping away on her tablet.

***

"Maybe we should have worn those things that Director Jones brought," Julian complained as he and Sarah sat in a café on the corner of the block by the docks. They drank barista-made lattes while sharing a small coffee cake.

"You can't be serious." Sarah giggled a bit in disbelief.

"We're so dirty, though. I think people are staring at us." Julian looked around a bit.

"Oh poo! Who cares, Julie," Sarah said as she tore off a piece of the coffee cake with her fork.

"Quiet, Starchild," Julian growled.

Sarah gasped. "We agreed we'd never speak of this!" Sarah lifted her fork and pointed it menacingly at Julian.

"I still remember when we first met," Julian chuckled. "I was like, five? I was playing in the yard when your family moved in. Your dad had that ponytail still at that time, and you were wearing that tie-dye shirt."

"Yes, I was an adorable child," Sarah added.

"When your dad told my dad that his name was John Starchild—"

"You said, 'what a dumb name!' and that made me realize that my neighbor and I would be enemies," Sarah interrupted.

"Aren't you glad your dad changed your last name to Starr?"

"Like I said, that's apparently what the family name used to be 'til he had his phase during high school or college or something." Sarah waved her fork in the air, uncertain whether or not to take another chunk of the cake.

Julian took a sip from his latte. He hadn't liked it at first, but he learned to like it after drinking it so much with Sarah.

Sarah chuckled. "We used to play together a lot when we were little, man," Sarah said as she cut a chunk off the cake. "I remember when we dug holes in your yard to build trenches, and your parents were furious with us."

"Yeah…" Julian smiled as he drowned in fond memories. "I was… really happy that you and I got stay friends even in school."

"Of course. Did you even ever worry about that?"

"I mean, yeah. You were, you know… that girl in school that everyone liked and stuff. I was just… Julian Caldwell, that kid who was friends with Sarah Starr."

"To me, you were my best friend." Sarah smiled as she played around with the cake with her fork. "I remember you used to wait for me by the baseball field every day so we could walk home together. And I *know*, Julian, that some days you used to just wait even when I had stuff to do after school even though you could have just gone home."

Julian blushed and quickly took a sip of his latte.

"So thank you for that, and I'm really sorry about those idiots… that…" Sarah stopped herself.

"It's fine." Julian nodded, remembering the events first hand that most people saw through a video on the Internet.

"…Connor used to be really jealous of you sometimes."

"Really? Why?"

Sarah shrugged.

"I guess if it wasn't for that video, though, none of this would have happened as well." Julian took a chunk of the cake. "Ms. Jones did find me through that."

Julian paused for a moment. "I always wondered, though, Sarah. How did Ms. Jones discover you? I never said anything to her."

Sarah didn't answer but simply smiled. "Aren't you glad that I came with you, though?" Sarah asked with a smile.

"Definitely, I'm just…" Julian was interrupted by the ringing of Sarah's phone.

"I bet its Ms. Jones," Sarah said as she scrambled to get the phone out of her bag. "I'm guessing this means our little break is over."

Although he never heard the answer, Julian knew that Sarah had, in one shape or form, volunteered to come to Silver Aegis with him. It was the only explanation that ever made sense. He promised himself that he would make sure no harm would ever come to her because of him.

***

Lily and Kalin sat at the edge of a dock and watched the tide and the seagulls. Kalin pulled out a single jelly-filled donut powdered with sugar and handed it to Lily. Lily took the donut and immediately took a big bite. Jelly gushed out from the donut and left trails around her lips, and Kalin readily wiped away the strawberry goo off before handing her a napkin.

They hadn't had a serious talk since the night before. Just the usual banter and comments about the new city they were visiting. There seemed to be an unspoken agreement to keep the topic of what happened yesterday, what was to come tomorrow, and what will come the days after a taboo for a little while.

"I'm selfish," Lily said with her eyes set on the ocean and the Light. She took another bite of the donut—a bit more carefully this time so that it wouldn't make such a mess. "I think I'm a bad person."

"What makes you say that?" Kalin took a bite of his maple bar.

"What if Kiara was right?"

"Kiara?" Kalin asked as he took another big bite from his bar. He was hungrier than he thought.

"She was Sarah's friend. She said she can see the future."

"That's neat. I'd have asked her so many questions."

"She said in the future, terrible things happen, and it'll be my fault." Lily saw that Kalin finished his maple bar and was grabbing another donut—a chocolate donut with custard filling. Lily slapped her friend's hand. "That's Landris's donut!"

"Well, I think she's ridiculous." Kalin set the donut back in the bag.

"She said that maybe if I died, it wouldn't happen."

Kalin stared at Lily with a blank expression as the words left her mouth so nonchalantly. "Screw her," Kalin finally said.

"What if she's right?" Lily looked at Kalin. She had a soft smile on her face, and it puzzled Kalin.

"She's not," Kalin answered immediately. "And screw her."

Lily shook her head and stared at the ocean again. "It's really pretty. I really like the ocean," Lily commented. The noise and the smell brought back memories she wished she'd forget, but the view made it all worth it.

"We can just go somewhere," Kalin said. "We don't have to do this. We can just go wherever, and it can be like none of this ever happened."

"We'd know," Lily smiled.

"Hey, we don't have to know anything. If we wanted, that Light doesn't even have to be there." Kalin's voice was more emotionally charged than he had intended.

"You're acting funny," Lily chuckled, and for a moment, neither of them spoke.

She was right. But she had a way with making him act and feel funny.

Lily let out a sigh.

"Maybe we can go to that bakery again? The one with the cakes with thin leaves of chocolate?" Lily placed her hand over Kalin's.

"Sure, why not? Maybe we'll learn to bake from them and open up our own shop."

"Yeah? Maybe make jelly donuts, too?" Lily asked enthusiastically.

"We'll make the best donuts, cakes, cookies—whatever you want. We'll be fat and happy," Kalin smiled at his silly dream.

"Whatever I want," Lily spoke quietly together.

"When this is over…" Lily grabbed Kalin's hand tightly. "Let's do all that together and more."

"Sounds good." Kalin intertwined his fingers between Lily's and held her hand.

"And then—and then, let's find a home!" Lily's excitement brought some comfort to Kalin after how she had been the last couple of days.

"A home?"

"Yeah! A home for us!" Lily seemed as if she could already see their dream home in front of her eyes.

"Sounds good," Kalin answered her with a content smile.

"I know." Lily smiled right back.

Lily suddenly unstrapped her backpack and rustled through it. "Look!" Lily handed Kalin her large paper crane with countless smaller and more colorful paper cranes embedded within it by her talents.

"How many are there?" Kalin said as he admired the crane.

"One thousand," Lily said with a proud smile.

Kalin looked at her with wide eyes. "Congratulations! That's great, Lily!" Kalin said as he wrapped his arm around Lily's shoulders and pulled her in. "What was your wish?"

"I'm not telling yet," Lily said. "I'll tell you when it comes true."

"Why?" Kalin asked.

"Because it might not come true if I tell you," Lily said as she rested her head on his shoulder.

Kalin's pocket began to vibrate. He pulled out Julian's phone that was loaned to him. When he answered the phone, Sarah informed Kalin that it was time; Mr. Hamilton had arrived to meet them all.

Chapter 55
TO THE LIGHT

Director Hamilton, or Mr. Hamilton as he'd be introduced by Nancy, arrived at the motel with two other men. The men were dressed in casual attire, though they walked with a menace that warned people around them they might not have been as casual as they seemed.

Mr. Hamilton took a moment to compose himself. There had been many times before he even arrived at the motel that he needed time to regain composure. As the moment passed, Mr. Hamilton knocked on the door.

"Director Hamilton," Nancy said as she opened the door.

"Nancy! It's good to see you." Mr. Hamilton put on a smile.

One of the men stood outside the door of the motel room while the other entered the room with Mr. Hamilton.

"I imagine it's more of a surprise than good!" Nancy said as she guided the men through the small motel room.

"Well, it was a bit sudden that you decided to bring the Witch and demanded to take you all to the Light." Mr. Hamilton tried to maintain his poker face. "But I suppose I can appreciate the urgency."

"Is that what we're talking about, Bill?" Nancy smiled as she sat on the edge of one of the two beds.

"I don't know what else we could be talking about, Nancy." Mr. Hamilton friendly expression changed to that of startled and disturbed.

"Look, Bill, I forgive you. If not because I'm generous, then because we still have work to do together. You've tried to assert yourself, and you've failed. Now you know without a doubt where you and I stand. But understand that my patience is finite, and our cooperation is more out of convenience than necessity. All I need is someone with the title of your position, Bill," Nancy spoke with such poise and confidence that Hamilton felt that he had already lost.

"I…" before Mr. Hamilton could respond, the door nearest to the exit opened and Landris walked out in his new clothes.

It was a custom designed the Silver Aegis formal uniform meant for the Gifted at Facility Zero. With emphasized collars, fitting design, and everything else that made the wearer look crisp like a cut out. The basic design of the uniform took great inspiration from a military formal except with a silver palette. Around his waist was his sword attached with a leather sword strap.

"Hello." Landris offered a handshake to Mr. Hamilton.

"Yes, Landris, was it? We've met before." Mr. Hamilton received a quick handshake before Landris walked away buttoning the buttons of his suit jacket.

"That's the new uniform I'm thinking of giving to all the students at Facility Zero." Nancy stood next to her brother and quickly glanced over to check if he was dressed properly.

"I see. Mentioning those students, where are the others? Where's the Witch?" Mr. Hamilton asked.

"Wait a moment, Bill." Nancy brushed off the dust from the shoulders of her brother. "I believe you were about to apologize."

"What?" Mr. Hamilton watched as Nancy's head turned from her brother's suit to him. Her green eyes stared into his soul.

"You were about to apologize for your indiscretion," Nancy said. "Apologize."

The man who came into the room with his boss looked at him uneasily as he wondered what to do.

"I'm sorry," Mr. Hamilton squeamishly said. "I'm sorry, Nancy."

"The kids should be returning soon," Nancy replied with a smile.

"You… you let them out?" Mr. Hamilton was startled.

"They're not animals to be caged, Bill."

As soon as the words left Nancy's mouth, there was a gentle knock on the door. Mr. Hamilton looked at Nancy who gestured to him to open the door.

"It's… it's the Witch… I think, sir," The man standing outside told him as he let the gang of Gifted in.

"Kids, this is Mr. Hamilton. He'll be taking us to the Light," Nancy introduced Mr. Hamilton.

"Hello, I'm Sarah." Sarah shook Mr. Hamilton's hand, careful not to invade his privacy as she did it.

"Hello, I'm Julian." Julian was next.

Kalin shook his hand without a word.

"You must be the infamous redheaded friend of the Witch," Mr. Hamilton said as he shook Kalin's hand.

"Yeah," Kalin answered as he matched the strength of Mr. Hamilton's grip.

"Nice grip you got there, kiddo. Guess you have to be strong to protect someone like her."

Mr. Hamilton let go of Kalin's hand and turned his attention to the only one he really cared to meet. "You, miss, I'm guessing is the Witch," Mr. Hamilton said as he offered his hand, "You're much smaller, younger, and prettier than I imagined."

"Her name's Lily," Kalin told Hamilton.

"And what a lovely name that is," Hamilton said as Lily gently grabbed his hand and they shared a soft handshake. Lily felt uncomfortable with this man.

"Thank you," Lily spoke softly.

"Oh? For what?" Hamilton asked.

"For taking us to the Light." Lily grabbed Kalin's hand and guided him to the bed Nancy was sitting on and sat themselves next to her.

She tried to give Nancy a donut to which she declined at first but relented at her wordless insistence. She then gave the custard filled chocolate donut to Landris. He ruffled her hair as his way of saying thank you and finished the pastry in a few quick bites.

"Well…" Mr. Hamilton cleared his throat. "To introduce myself, I'm Bill Hamilton, and I'm the Director of the… well, I guess it'd save time to just say that I'm in charge of the security for our country." Mr. Hamilton sounded very proud.

"Then did you know about what happened yesterday?" Lily asked innocently. "It was terrible."

The entire room stared at Mr. Hamilton for an answer.

Nancy gave a light chortle. "Why don't we move on to the topic of the Light," Nancy suggested.

"Yes." Mr. Hamilton cleared his throat once again. "If you guys weren't aware, we'll be taking the helicopter to the carrier."

"A carrier? Wow," Julian remarked.

"It shows other countries that we're not messing around." Mr. Hamilton smiled.

"But before we go" — Mr. Hamilton paused for a moment to see how delicately he wanted to word his next question — "What exactly are we planning on doing at the Light?"

Lily lifted her arm with the black band, but before she could open her mouth, Ms. Jones interrupted her. "Let us discuss all this when we're actually at the carrier first, shall we?" Nancy said.

Mr. Hamilton thought through the suggestion for a moment before he agreed to it. They packed lightly and only took a small delay to allow Julian and Sarah to change into their new uniforms at Ms. Jones' insistence. To her dismay — but to Kalin's relief — Nancy did not have a set for Kalin and Lily.

The sun was already setting as they embarked on a long flight on the helicopter to the carrier over the dark blue ocean.

Chapter 56
THE NIGHT BEFORE THE END

As the helicopter neared the carrier, the group saw the infamous international barricade they had only heard about and seen on the news. Though most of the other members of the barricade seemed small compared to the carrier boasted by Hamilton, the warships from the other nations still seemed impressive and fierce.

It was deep into the night, and the Light at the center of the barricade seemed brighter than ever. The wide-eyed Gifted children didn't have time to admire the incredible sight of the jets and the routine of running a carrier being performed by the military personnel when the helicopter finally landed. Instead, they were quickly ushered into the captain's quarters where the captain gave a quick salute to Mr. Hamilton and left the room. As hastily as they were escorted to the room, they were seated just as quickly.

"Now, let's talk." Mr. Hamilton had a newfound confidence from having the home advantage, and opted to start the conversation as soon as everyone found a seat on the couch and the chairs around the small table.

"To approach the Light right now requires approval by those present at the barricade. Technically, it should be approved by all the nations in the union, but this is more of a gentleman's agreement anyway—especially for countries in our position. Regardless at this point, the rules are even more lenient because no one can figure out a single damned thing about that Light." Mr. Hamilton paused for a moment to look around the room as if to study their faces for answers. "The Light itself comes from the tip of a giant crystal spire. Only the tip of it is right now is above the ocean surface, and the Light itself seems... harmless. We still don't know how and why it's there. And I don't understand how it is... the way it is. You'll understand when you see it for yourself. The crystal itself, as far as we know, seems to be *indestructible*. We can't even chip the damn thing. But the damnedest thing about it is that it seems to stretch all the way down to the bottom of the ocean. There's what seems to be a structure of some sort at the bottom, but everything beyond that is a mystery. Obviously, the bottom of the ocean isn't the easiest or the cheapest thing to explore. And, that's all we know. By 'all,' I mean that is the entire accumulative knowledge we have of that Light in this world. I had hoped that the Witch would have more answers for us. What do you know that I don't that you insist on going there?"

All the heads in the room naturally turned to Lily.

"Lily believes," Nancy spoke before anyone else could. "Taking that black band around her wrist will trigger an event with the Light."

"What kind of an event?" Mr. Hamilton immediately asked.

Lily searched for her place to speak.

"We don't know. She doesn't know," Nancy immediately replied.

"So we're just supposed to take her word for it? How do we know whatever event that she triggers doesn't bring the world's end or some other tragedy?" Hamilton glanced at Lily, "No offense."

"I doubt it," Landris said.

"Lily's not someone who'd do that," Sarah also defended the Witch.

"Bill, what we are going through is probably the event that will be noted in history as the event that changed the world forever. At the heart of it all is that Light and our Lily here. We have a chance to make it our nation who took the reins during this time," Nancy said. "I think the gamble's worth it, and knowing this girl, I don't think it'll even be that much of a gamble."

Mr. Hamilton pondered for a moment. "Could I see that black band of yours?" Mr. Hamilton asked Lily.

Lily nodded. She walked over and placed the band in his hand and stood by as he inspected it.

Mr. Hamilton saw nothing really special with the band, but he was surprised how cold to the touch it was and how durable it felt regardless of how thin it was. He held it up with his finger and thumb and rotated it one way, then the other, and even studied the inner ring of the black band.

"I don't understand what's so special about this," Mr. Hamilton said.

Nancy thought she would have been offended had he noticed something when she hadn't.

"Where did you get this?" Mr. Hamilton asked.

Lily opened her mouth to speak, but before a word could come out, Ms. Jones interrupted her again.

"She doesn't remember that either," Nancy said.

Lily closed her mouth.

"That's just perfect, isn't it?" Mr. Hamilton chuckled as he handed the black band back to Lily. "How am I going to convince anyone to make this happen?"

"I'm sure you'll find a way, but I'd advise you not to let the other nations know that we have Lily with us." Nancy leaned back into her chair.

"Of course." Mr. Hamilton let out a deep sigh. "I'll need a day or two to make this happen. We need to do it quietly, but we need to do it right. We'll have exactly one shot at this."

"The sooner, the better," Nancy said.

"So what now, then?" Landris asked.

"It's late." Mr. Hamilton looked at his watch to confirm. "I've asked them to prepare a sleeping quarter for all of you. It'll be cramped, but you'll all get a taste of what it's like to be a crew member on a carrier. I will also ask them to prepare you all some supper."

The childlike excitement in Julian's eyes made Sarah smile.

"Well then, shall we?" Mr. Hamilton stood and gestured towards the door.

As the group headed for the doors, Sarah reached out to Nancy.

"Director Jones!" Sarah called out as she grabbed Nancy's hand.

"Yes, Sarah?" Nancy turned to see Sarah's eyes turn glazed for a moment, and her face wash over with an ominous expression. Feeling an instinctive sense of violation, the director tore her hand away from the oracle.

"What…" Nancy composed herself. "What is it, Sarah?"

"Can we go outside?" Lily asked Mr. Hamilton as they walked past Nancy and Sarah.

"Sure." Mr. Hamilton turned to the captain who was waiting at the other side of the door. "Can we get someone to escort miss… ummm…"

"Ms. Jones, I…" Sarah stumbled on finding her words.

"Lily," the Witch reminded Mr. Hamilton of her name.

"Right, yes. Lily." Mr. Hamilton awkwardly smiled. The captain nodded and began to ask into his walkie-talkie for an escort.

"I thought we should try to find out what happened in Lily's past. In that other world." Sarah finally found her words.

"Yes, of course. I thought the same," Nancy replied. It wasn't a question of if she had read her memories, but of what she had read.

"Should we do it now?" Sarah asked, hoping that she had her usual face.

"You two coming?" Mr. Hamilton asked the two stragglers. The captain began walking out Lily and Kalin.

"Why don't you and Julian go grab something to eat first?" Nancy suggested. "Landris and I will check the sleeping quarters first, and we can all do it before bed tonight when we have some privacy. It seems Lily wants to go explore a bit anyway."

"Sure, of course." Sarah smiled and walked past Nancy to stand next to Julian.

"Everything okay?" Julian asked with a worried look.

"Yeah, everything's fine," Sarah answered with a smile, though she knew that Julian wouldn't believe her.

"Nancy?" Landris asked as his sister stood by him.

"It's nothing," Nancy told Landris.

"Well then." Mr. Hamilton closed the door behind him. "Let us head to the sleeping quarters first, and then for those who want to eat, I'll take you to the mess hall afterwards."

The four followed Mr. Hamilton in an uncomfortable silence as the oracle and her director contemplated their next move.

Chapter 57
BLACK HALO

Mr. Hamilton's description of the sleeping quarters being cramped was an understatement. They had room to stand and get around the bunks, but the size of the room was as efficient as it could be. The beds were against the wall and had three stacked one on top of the other with a little gap for a person to squeeze into each one of them. They reminded the group more of drawers than of beds. After seeing the room, Sarah and Julian followed Mr. Hamilton to the mess hall while Landris and Nancy decided to 'relax' for a bit in the sleeping quarters. On top of one of the bunks was Lily's bag that Nancy took from her on her behalf.

Landris sat on the cold, hard floor and rested his back on the metal frames of the bed. He unsheathed his ebony blade retrieved by Lily and admired it once again. "I can't believe you convinced Hamilton to let me keep this on board," Landris remarked.

"Ignorance is bliss," Nancy said as she sat next to him and opened up her handbag. "He doesn't know what you or that blade are capable of."

"So what's bothering you?" Landris asked as he flipped his blade around and studied it again.

"I'm thinking that…" Nancy caught a glimpse of the shining revolver in her bag. She looked over at Landris to see if anyone else was in the room. The revolver, whose name Nancy figured to be "Lexi" by its engraving on the side, was different than any she had seen before, but the basic functions of it were akin to any other revolver. She opened its cylinder to check the number of bullets again.

Three.

That was either just enough or one short in case of an emergency.

"Where did you get that?" Landris asked. "Guess they didn't check your bag?"

"Landris, I'm thinking that we go to the Light tonight. Just you, me, Lily, and her friend—because I'm guessing we won't be able to get rid of him."

"You mean tonight?"

"Yes. Tonight." Nancy buried the revolver into her bag again.

"What about Hamilton? Sarah and Julian?" Landris stood up and sheathed his sword. Though he was asking questions, Landris was ready to follow his sister.

"Hamilton would probably prefer it this way, and if he's there with us, it may make things more difficult for us to take control. Whatever happens, he'll be the one to take credit while we'll take the blame if there is any. If we're there by ourselves, at least we'll be able to shape the story as we see fit. Sarah and Julian... it'll be better for all of us to go without them." Nancy stood up as well. About a head short next to her little brother.

"Hamilton left a guy by the doors when he left. I'm guessing that guy will be following us around wherever we go," Landris said softly.

***

At the mess hall, a humble dinner of burger and fries was quickly prepared for Julian. Sarah declined to eat anything. As Julian chowed down on his meal and made comments regarding it and their trip, Sarah simply nodded or occasionally smiled in response.

"Julian," Sarah finally spoke as she stared at their table.

"Yeah?" Julian said as he worked on the last few bites of his burger.

"I don't think Director Jones intends good things for Lily."

"What makes you say that?" Julian finished his burger and grabbed a fry.

"I... I accidentally read her memory."

Julian's follow up fry froze before it reached his mouth. "What did you see?"

"Director Jones and Mr. Ivanov were having a conversation. I think this was just after we left them yesterday afternoon." Sarah tried to replay what she had seen in her mind. "They were talking about how it was possible to kill Lily. Landris was there too... I didn't see much because... I just... I just naturally stopped it as quickly as I could since I didn't mean to see into her memories."

"What... what should we do?" Julian set the fry back down back on the plate.

"Let's go find Lily." Sarah finally looked at Julian. "Let's... let's go to the Light ourselves."

Julian nodded and glanced behind over his shoulder at the military man who'd been standing by the exit the entire time they had been in the room.

Outside, the sound of the ocean and the mechanical noises of the carrier clashed. The air was gentle, but cold and ingrained with salt.

"Do you have to stand that close behind us?" Kalin and Lily sat by the edge of the carrier and watched the view that was similar to the view they had enjoyed by the docks, but strangely more grand. A man in military uniform stood right behind them.

"I'm here for your own safety. You two normally wouldn't even be allowed out here," the military man gave an excuse to hide his real duty of keeping an eye on them.

"I'm sure you can watch us just fine from about twenty steps behind us." Kalin and the military man had a little, not entirely hostile stare-down until the man relented and gave Kalin and Lily their space.

They didn't really have secrets to share, nor had anything particularly intimate to talk about. Lily personally didn't mind too much if the man wanted to watch over them. Kalin, however, felt a need for the two of them to have some time of their own.

The Witch and her friend watched the dark ocean and listened to the songs it sang. It didn't take much for them to tune out the sounds made by the man-made machines around them and simply listen to nature. Kalin stared at the Light wondering what would be there while the Witch looked within herself, deep in thought.

"Are you cold?" Kalin asked.

Lily didn't seem to hear him.

Regardless, Kalin took his jacket off and set it over her shoulders.

With her eyes still on the ocean, Lily grabbed the jacket and pulled it closer to get cozy inside of it, and the two returned to their silent pondering. Kalin felt like he knew what his friend was thinking about.

"I've decided!" Lily stood up sprightly.

"Nope," Kalin quickly answered Lily spryness with a dry response.

"I'll go by myself!" Lily pointed at the Light.

"Nope." Kalin's tone remained unchanged.

"But—"

"Nope." Kalin stretched out his arms and let out a yawn.

"You want to come with me?"

"Yep," Kalin said as he stood and dusted off his pants.

"Really?"

"Yep." Kalin finally turned his head from the ocean to Lily.

"Okay." Lily gave a defeated smile.

Kalin smiled and turned his head toward the Light again. Perhaps they could finally put this chapter of their lives to rest and move on. "Just the two of us sounds about right."

"Ready to go now?" Lily asked excitedly as she formed a monocle with her finger and thumb. In the darkness of the night, she could vaguely see the tip of the crystal where the Light was originating from.

Kalin glanced behind him at the military man watching them.

"Yeah. Let's be quick about it, though." Kalin took back his jacket from Lily as she offered it to him.

Lily focused on her finger and it gave a gentle white glow. She kept the image of the crystal in the ocean alive in her mind.

The military man began to carefully take a few steps towards them, sensing something was amiss.

"Lily!" Sarah yelled as she walked down the runway of the carrier with Julian after finally finding her.

"Lily!" Nancy's voice overlapped with Sarah's as she and Landris spotted the Witch at the edge of the carrier's runway.

The oracle and the director found each other at the other sides of the runway both converging at Lily.

"Sir, something's up," the military man spoke into a walkie-talkie.

Lily poked into the air and began drawing the arch with the light trailing off of her finger.

"Sir, the Witch is definitely up to something." The military man began to run towards the Witch and her friend.

"Hey! HEY!" he yelled at them, and Lily, without turning around, froze him in place. She finished her arch and started crisscrossing inside the arch to turn it into a stained glass piece.

What's going on? Hamilton's voice cried out from the man's walkie-talkie.

Lily began to push on the shattered pieces in her arch.

Both Nancy and Sarah started running towards Lily and Kalin with their escorts running after them.

"Hold on Nancy," Landris said as he lifted his sister off of the ground. The veins of his legs began to glow white.

The pieces of the arch shattered through and scattered about at the destination.

Sarah and Julian ran as fast as they could and saw Landris getting ready for a sprint.

"Risk it, Julian!" Sarah cried.

Julian grabbed Sarah's hand and tried to turn off his brain to overcome his nervous heart, but he remembered the screaming men falling to their deaths from the night before.

"Julian!" Sarah grabbed her friend by his shoulders. "Believe in yourself!"

Lily and Kalin stepped through the arch, and their feet landed on top of the dark ocean. The tide went around their feet, and the water beneath them flattened to provide a platform.

The sheer speed let loose by Landris knocked the wind out of Nancy, and Landris restrained himself from going any faster in fear of hurting his sister.

Julian found courage in Sarah's words, and they safely appeared at the other side of the gateway made by Lily.

"Lily!" Sarah yelled. Lily turned her head in surprise and quickly made sure that they wouldn't fall into the ocean.

As the shattered pieces began to return to their proper places, Landris darted through the gateway. Before he either crashed into the rest of them or fell into the ocean, Lily's powers caught him, and Landris and Nancy were gently set on top of the ocean.

Nancy and Sarah exchanged looks.

"We wanted to do this by ourselves." Lily's voice almost sounded apologetic.

"Well, we can't let you do that," Sarah said. "We're your friends, remember?"

"Yes, this was quite reckless of you," Nancy also complained as she shivered from the cold.

"So this is the Light, huh?" Landris slowly picked himself up wondering how stable his footing on the ocean water was.

The group all turned to see the brilliant Light right in front of them that they had all only ever seen far past the horizon. The Light was not much thicker than as they had seen it from a distance, and it began from the tip of a large, nigh translucent crystal.

The black band quietly awakened and began to gently swivel around Lily's wrist. Lily took a few steps and stood in front of the crystal. Five thin lines of light appeared on the band and segmented it into six pieces.

"Lily…" Kalin worryingly reached out.

Before Kalin could reach her, Lily placed her hand on the surface of the crystal's tip, and the black band ripped apart into its six segments. Surprised, Lily pulled away from the crystal, but the black band pieces continued to rapidly rotate around her wrist until the segments slithered up her arm and found their place above her head. They gently rotated above Lily's head, detached from one another but still resembling the shape they originally were.

"It's… it's like a halo," Sarah said.

Lily turned around and saw Kalin looking at her with worried eyes. She felt different, though she was unsure exactly in what way.

"Ka—"

Before Lily could speak, the ocean around them erupted.

Chapter 58
TEMPLE OF THE UNKNOWN

"Where the hell did they go?!" Mr. Hamilton yelled at the crew as he walked out onto the runway of the carrier where the Witch, her friend, and rest of the Silver Aegis were last seen.

The violent outburst of the ocean as it erupted into mountains of water around the Light gave him his answer. The loud explosion alerted all the other nations surrounding the Light, and the quiet night ocean was quickly filled with chaos.

Starting from beneath Lily's feet, the water turned into streams, then quickly turned into hard ground until it formed a circular plaza the size of a large stadium.

The ocean around them rose up into the air like monstrous serpents, and the serpents entangled and turned into a violent squall of streams which fed into the crystal and raised it to a pristine crystal spire. With the crystal spire as its center piece, the streams stormed around at its base until it formed into a grand white temple. Only speckles of the streams remained as it formed into the last finishing touches. At the tip of the crystal spire, now tall enough to be seen with naked eye from miles around the ocean, the brilliant Light still pierced the skies.

The ships around them raised their alarms.

Countless little tiles that formed the plaza illuminated its surface brightly enough that the plaza was lit as if it was in daytime.

"Sir, we're getting messages from all the other ships asking if we had something to do with what has just happened," the captain informed Mr. Hamilton.

"Deny everything," Mr. Hamilton said. "If Nancy wants to do this on her own, then she can take the bullets on her own."

"All this seems man-made," Julian said as he looked around the plaza. He noticed the very far edges of the plaza seemed black.

"And yet, it doesn't," Nancy remarked as she studied the temple. "I've never seen anything like this before."

Without words, Lily began heading toward the temple. There was a stairway leading to its great gated entrance. Each step of the stairway was a bit larger and further apart than she had ever seen before in man's structures. Before she could place her foot on its pearly step, Kalin grabbed her hand.

"We're going together, alright?" Kalin said.

"In there," Lily said. "It wants me to go in there."

"Come on." Landris helped Nancy up and headed towards the steps.

Julian and Sarah quickly followed after them.

"Look," Julian told Sarah. Each step they took lit up the pale tile below them as what looked like foreign writing flashed across the surface.

They stood in front of the grand white gate that was as tall as a small building. It was engraved with elaborate patterns that not even Nancy could recognize.

From a distance away, one of the nations could barely make out the vague image of the group at the plaza. It was unacceptable, and they determined that whichever country or whoever that had triggered the event without consent of all the other nations warranted an attack for the sake of their own security in the matter. No one country was to have the Light unfairly or before others. They fired their cannons at the temple, and the sound was deafening as it froze the hearts of many with the realization of the line that had been crossed.

Not long after they heard the explosive boom, the shells struck the temple and shook the entire plaza. The explosion was as brilliant as it was loud, and the heatwave from it baked the group despite the chilly night air.

The militaries of the world watched with bated breath as the smoke cleared to see that no damage had been made on the temple.

Landris, looking to provide cover for his group, focused his strength and ran in front of Lily and Kalin. He pushed on the door with all his might, but even with his immense strength, the gate did not budge.

More cannon fire roared, but this time from multiple sources.

Lily raised her hand in the air and the shells froze in place. A gentle twirl of her hand spun the shells higher up into the sky, and a clench of her hand into a fist collided all the shells into a magnificent ball of fire that lit up the night. The heat from the blast was felt by all the men on the ships as the legend of the Witch solidified in their memories forever.

Nancy desperately hoped that the crack Yuri had seen in the Witch's seemingly unstoppable power was real.

Tranquility returned to the ocean with only the sound of the waves filling the air. Landris moved out of Lily's way as she approached gate. As soon as her small palm rested on its surface, light spread across the gate, and it opened.

"Other nations seem to be sending their teams out there, sir," the captain told Mr. Hamilton.

"Send a team of our own as well," Mr. Hamilton ordered.

Beyond the gate was a large corridor that seemed to lead to yet another gate just as large as the first. The corridor was as white as it was outside and bright as the day.

Lily took the first steps into the temple followed quickly by her redheaded friend. Sarah and Nancy shared uneasy looks with one another until they quickly followed after Lily and Kalin. The gate closed behind them.

... Though the story varies from teller to teller, the trait that always remained the same is that the hero Landris and the Witch Who Brought the World's End both walked into the Light but only the hero with his blood-soaked blade walked out...

Chapter 59
THE WHITE CHAMBER

The group's steps echoed as they walked through the bright white corridor. The structure of the temple featured the craftsmanship and dedication of whoever or whatever had built it. But there were no signs as far as they could tell that it was an earthly culture or civilization which had built the temple.

Nancy placed her hand on the wall, and was surprised how smooth it was to the touch as she appreciated the beauty of the architecture.

Lily stood in front of the second gate. The halo gently rotated above her head while small writings in a foreign language illuminated the surface from time to time.

She placed her hand on the gate, and like before, a light quickly spread out from where her palm had touched it throughout the door. The gate opened, and they could immediately see a grand stairway at the end of the revealed room leading up to another large door that was relatively much smaller than the others.

Lily and Kalin looked at one another. Kalin gave Lily a nod, and Lily nodded back. Together, they stepped into the white chamber.

As Nancy moved to follow them, Sarah grabbed her wrist. "Director Jones," Sarah spoke quietly, but intensely.

Nancy quickly buried away her surprise and stood tall. "Yes, Sarah?" Nancy said.

"What do you want with, Lily, exactly?" Sarah's fierce eyes barely hid her fluttering heart.

"What exactly did you see when you looked into my memories without permission?" Nancy's tone made Sarah feel like a scolded child.

"I..." Sarah stuttered but quickly found her tongue again. "I heard the conversation you had with Mr. Ivanov." Sarah looked over Nancy's shoulder to see Lily and Kalin in the next room looking back at them.

"And?" Nancy sounded agitated.

"And I heard... you discussing with him... about..." Sarah caught a glimpse of Landris who was staring her down like a beast about to take a bite out of her.

Julian placed his hand on Sarah's shoulder and stood by her side.

She found great comfort and confidence from her friend.

"Hurting Lily," Sarah finished with newfound confidence.

"I see." Nancy was glad that Sarah hadn't seen anything too dire. "And I can see how this may have startled you."

"Why, Director Jones?" Sarah asked with the ferocity melting away from her eyes.

"Because that's the reality of things, Sarah," Nancy said. "She is the Witch. You know very well what she's capable of. Now we're in this… in this… *place,* and who knows what this is supposed to be. If the unthinkable is about to happen, we at least have to know there's a hope for us to stop it."

"I…" Sarah couldn't find the words. Was she convinced that easily that what Director Jones saying had any credence? From the pit of her heart, she felt shame.

Nancy and Landris left Sarah to her thoughts and quickly followed after Lily and Kalin who were taking their first steps to the final door.

"Is it alright for us to go further?" Landris quickly asked.

"Too late now to turn back now. Might as well take a chance with whatever's beyond that door," Nancy replied just as quickly before turning her attention to the two further ahead of them. "Wait!" Nancy called out to Lily.

The two turned around.

Before Nancy could speak another word, her steps stopped as she was struck with awe by the chamber she had entered. It was as illuminant and grand as the temple had demonstrated itself to be to them so far, and the chamber was reminiscent of an amphitheater. Above their heads was a dome that made the ceiling feel as high as the sky.

"We'll be right back," Lily smiled and turned for the door again.

"Stop!" Nancy chased after the Witch and her friend with Landris following close behind her.

Lily and Kalin made their way down the stairs to meet the director at its base.

"Lily, I think perhaps I should be the one to walk through that gate," Nancy suggested.

"It's alright, Director Jones," Lily replied with a smile. "I can do it. Thank you very much for helping me to get here. I don't want to burden you further."

"It won't be a burden, Lily," Nancy said. "It's just the responsible thing for me to do." Nancy reached out and grabbed the piece of halo rotating gently above Lily's head. As soon as her fingers touched the piece, the halo stopped rotating.

"It won't budge," Nancy said as she struggled to pull the piece away from Lily's head.

Landris walked up to Lily and gave a try himself to remove the halo from Lily. His fist clenched one of the pieces and tried to yank it away from its place; however, like his sister, Landris also failed.

"And I'm guessing that door won't open for anyone but you," Nancy said.

"It'll be okay, Ms. Jones," Lily assured the worried director.

"We'll go through the gate together, but before that, Sarah!" Nancy called to the oracle who was slowly catching up to the rest of the group with her friend.

As Sarah walked up next to Nancy, she didn't give any verbal reply but simply looked at her.

"If it's alright with Lily, will you read into her past regarding the 'otherworld' she spoke of?" Nancy moved to give Sarah room.

Sarah gave Nancy a disgruntled look as she passed her. She looked at Lily who was looking up at her with her curious eyes. "Would it be okay, Lily?" Sarah asked with smile.

Lily nodded with a smile in return. "I'm not sure if it'll work," Lily said.

"We'll give it a try." Sarah placed her hand on top of Lily's head and concentrated. In an instant, Sarah recoiled and tore her hand away from Lily.

"What is it?!" Julian reached out to steady Sarah.

Sarah let out a painful groan. She blinked rapidly before she opened her eyes. "That's never happened before," Sarah quietly spoke. "It was like I was staring into the sun. Just brightness. It felt like my head... like my head was getting crushed."

Lily grabbed Sarah's hand. "I'm sorry," Lily said. "I think... I think *this* might be... it's doing something."

"What's it doing?" Nancy asked.

"She said she feels as if she's connected to the building," Kalin answered.

"Look," Landris said looking at his feet. He lifted his feet off from the paper white floor and then placed it back down. Lights like circuits dispersed quickly and faded away.

Julian tried the same and walked around a bit while looking at his feet. Each step produced the same results.

"Let's open the gate," Nancy said. "Hopefully, it'll have answers rather than more questions."

Each step of the stairway was larger and further apart than what was comfortable for a human, much like before. At the end the of the stairway, there was a short walkway to the door, and in front of the gate which was as elaborate as the gates before, Lily placed her palm on its surface. The gate opened and revealed nothing but bright luminescent light. Only Lily could look directly into it as the others covered their eyes and looked away.

"Kalin," Lily spoke softly.

"Let's go, Lily," Kalin said as he grabbed her hand with one hand and shielded his eyes with the other.

Lily shook her head.

"I have to go alone," Lily said.

"What is this?" Landris complained as he tried to walk into the light. An invisible force pushed him back as if there was a wall of air.

"Lily, no." Kalin pulled her away from the light. "You're not going wherever that is by yourself."

"I don't think I'll be gone for long, Kalin." Lily held Kalin's hand with both of her hands. "I'll be back soon."

"No," Kalin said. "You can't. I won't let you."

"We have to move on from this part of our lives." Lily tried to keep a smile on to hide her scared heart. "We'll both be better after this."

"I…" Kalin's head were filled with the things he wanted to tell Lily and the things he wanted to yell, and all those rushed in at once and choked them from coming out.

"I can't say it's a good idea either, Lily," Nancy said as she remembered Kiara's dream.

"Lily…" Sarah wasn't sure what position she held for Lily. "Do you have to do this?"

Lily nodded.

"Why?" Julian asked.

Lily thought for a moment and chuckled. "I don't know. I know I sound silly, but I think I have to do this," Lily said.

"Is it that thing telling you to?" Landris asked.

"Maybe," Lily replied back. "Maybe I'll understand better why I have to when I'm there."

Lily walked up to Nancy and gave her a hug. A hug that the director wasn't quite sure how to react to. "Thank you for everything," Lily said.

She then gave Landris a hug. "Thank you," Lily said.

"Don't make this weird, idiot," Landris said.

"You're a good guy, Landris," Lily told him as she stared into his eyes and smiled. "Don't forget that."

Sarah was next. Unlike the two before, Sarah embraced Lily back perhaps even tighter than she had embraced her.

"Thank you, Sarah," Lily whispered into Sarah's ear. She felt her cheek moisten with warm tears flowing down from Sarah's eyes.

"Don't thank me, Lily. I don't know where you're going or why you have to go or even what you have to do. I don't even know if I should let you go or not. I don't know… I don't know… if I was any help to you on this hard journey you've been on." Sarah's voice shook more than she would have liked.

Lily pulled away from her and looked at her with a surprised face. "I'm so happy to have met you, Sarah," Lily embraced Sarah again. "You're amazing."

Sarah laughed.

"When you come back—and you will come back—let me teach you new things to fold and get more of those donuts that you like," Sarah told Lily with a smile.

Lily nodded back.

"I'll be there too!" Julian said.

Lily looked at Julian.

"Why do you always look at me like that?" Julian asked.

"I like your face!" Lily answered with a smile. She waved Julian to come closer and gave him a hug followed by pulling on his cheek. "Thank you Julian," Lily said as she continued to pull on Julian's cheek. "Please be there when we go have fun."

"Uh-huh, of course," Julian tried to speak with his cheek stretched out.

"Good!" Lily let go of his cheek.

Only her redheaded friend was left. She walked up to him, and he looked as grumpy as he had when she first met him.

"Are you going to cry?" Lily asked.

"Don't be stupid," Kalin replied back.

"I'm really going to be back soon," Lily told Kalin.

"You better," Kalin said.

Lily reached her hand out to Kalin. He lifted her off of her feet and gave her a hug.

"It's going to be real awkward when you come back after all this," Kalin whispered into her ear.

Lily giggled. "I know," Lily said.

"Come back as soon as you can," Kalin said.

"I will."

"I'll be waiting," Kalin told Lily. He tried to put her down, but she gripped onto his back.

"Not yet," Lily whispered. "Not yet."

"Are you going to be okay?" Kalin asked as he held her tight again.

"Mmhmm, I better be. We have to find our home. You can't do it by yourself."

"That's right, you better be okay."

"Do you trust me, Kalin?" Lily asked.

"What?"

"Do you trust me?"

"Of course."

"I know," Lily smiled like a child as she pulled away from Kalin. "Time to go!"

Kalin set her down, and Lily stood in front of the light once more with the group watching from behind her.

She turned her head one last time and smiled again as she usually did. "I'll be back!" Lily waved her hand.

"Just come back in one piece!" Kalin said

"Go already!" Landris said at the same time.

"We'll be waiting!" Sarah told Lily.

With that, Lily seeped into the light, and, as she disappeared from their sight, the gate closed behind her.

Chapter 60
WITHIN THE LIGHT

The room beyond the door showed no end in sight. When the sound of gate closing behind her made her look back once more, she saw that the door simply stood in place without being attached to any wall. Lily quickly ran to the other side the door only to find the other side to be much like anywhere else in this room—endless. Above her, there was no ceiling. Just white.

Although she thought she had steeled her heart, Lily felt loneliness quickly creeping over her.

Footsteps.

She heard the footsteps before she saw him.

A robed man appeared in front of her and he sauntered over. Even from afar, Lily could see his long, silver hair shimmering with each step. His gaunt and tall stature made his night sky robe seem like drapes fluttering in the wind as he came closer and closer to her.

Frozen by the task at hand and paralyzed with indecisiveness, Lily stood still until the man came to stand right before her. He was taller than any man she had ever seen before, and it made her feel smaller than she had ever felt when standing next to a person. He knelt before her and gave her a soothing smile. The man's eyes, silver with a tint of blue, stared into her hazel eyes. He placed his hand which was as pale as the moon on her shoulders. They were large enough—or perhaps she was small enough—for his palm to cup her shoulder while his fingers wrapped around her back.

"Such a small and young child to carry such a burden. The crown truly knows no mercy." To Lily's ears, the man spoke in a language she had never heard before. If the wind could speak, Lily imagined it would sound similar to that of this man's. But in her mind, Lily understood all that he was saying. "The crown does not belong to this world, nor was this world ready for it; however, the crown works in mysterious ways. The path that you must have taken to be here was, I imagine, an arduous one. It always is." The man stood up. "Do you know why you're here? Has it told you?"

Lily carefully nodded.

"You have the power to do what you wish with the world. If you wish to save it," he spoke peacefully. "You must end it. That is your duty and destiny as the bearer of the crown."

Chapter 61
THE WORLD IN HER HANDS

"At this moment, you're one with this world and the world is one with you," the man said. "It is bound to your will and your choice."

"Who are you?" Lily asked.

"I am the one who bore that crown before you in a different world at a different time. But who I am matters not. Not anymore. What I am now is the one who will be your guide until you reach your decision."

Lily shook her head. "Why me?"

"Whether it is coincidence or fate, it matters not. You're here now and the decision has been given to you," the man answered.

His words reminded Lily of Emily.

"This world," the man began as he swept his arm across the room, and with it, the room became the sky above the ocean. Lily looked below her at the warships firing cannons at the temple again. He waved his hand once more, and they traveled through the world and witnessed all kinds of people and their sins. The man observed the girl as they saw together the most grotesque sufferings of the people and those who relished at their anguish. Many would accuse the girl of lacking heart and empathy from the little emotion she showed on her face. But the man knew better.

"This world is no different than the one I was once a part of," the man waved his hand again, and the room returned to the ocean where the temple was. He then placed his hand over Lily's head. Lily watched as he pulled his away and his gentle face broke into a slight cringe.

"As I suspected you, yourself, are aware of this world's ugliness — of its sins," the man said as he recalled what he witnessed. "You must not make the same mistake as I had. You must be above being a mere man. The only way for you to save this world — to grant it its salvation — is for you to start it over and guide it to a true utopia. You are the only chance that it has. The crown, or the halo as you have deemed it, has granted you the gift and the responsibility to be this world's savior. The power to turn the world into whatever you desire it to be has been granted to you."

Lily looked at the door behind her.

"You can make certain that no one will suffer as you have," the man said. "You can build a new world."

"I'm..." Lily said. "I'm not a witch. I'm not a savior. I'm just a girl. I'm just... Lily. That's what I want to be."

"But you're not anymore and you have to be more than that, child," the man spoke softly. "With the halo, you have to be this world's... god. As its god, you have to be responsible with the power granted to you. For all of this world's people, whether they know it or not, depend on you."

Lily looked at the man with uncertain eyes and looked into herself for the answer.

Chapter 62
LILY'S STORY

Sarah, Julian, and Kalin sat on the walkway outside the last gate and waited for Lily. Outside, the group could hear the rumble of cannons firing on the temple. Although at first the noise worried them, but soon it became apparent that the cannons were futile against the temple walls.

Nancy and Landris walked away from the rest of the group. The brother and sister explored the room and eventually made their way out into the first hallway.

"You have to kill her," Nancy spoke quietly. "Get in close. You can either use my gun or stab her with your sword, but you have to be quick enough that no one — not even her — can stop you. Catch her by surprise. I'll take care of the rest."

Landris looked at his sister. She was sincere.

"Why?" Landris asked.

"*Why?*"

"I…" Landris was always surprised how small his sister could make him feel. All it took for her was to give him a certain look or take on a certain tone. "I just don't understand why that's necessary."

"My goodness!" Nancy looked at her brother in disbelief. "You're really taken with the Witch, aren't you?"

"It's not like that!" Landris protested. He had to remember to lower his voice. "She's… she's a good girl, Nancy. I don't think… I don't think we have to kill her."

The temple rumbled again.

"You hear that? I'm guessing that's not just Hamilton, but everyone surrounding this magic castle. Everyone that saw us walk into this place with the Witch. I'm betting that right outside that gate are pissed off armies ready to kill each other and us. If we go out there with the Witch, we'll be branded as enemies of the world, regardless of what the Witch may actually be like or what the Witch may be doing right now."

"Wasn't this the risk we decided to take when we set off for the Light? Since the day Kiara had that dream?"

"No!" Nancy's face grew red. Landris was probably one of very few people who actually got to see Nancy's true emotions. "The risk we decided to take was that if we were ever in this kind of situation, we would risk trying to kill the Witch. We have a life to live after this day, Landris. We have things we still need to accomplish, and we have people who depend on us. Or did you forget?"

"No," Landris said.

"Then be ready to use that sword for its namesake!"

Landris looked at his sword and then the ground. His lips remained sealed as his sister impatiently waited for his answer.

Morris and Jung suddenly came to his mind.

"No," Landris told Nancy. "I'll protect you and everyone else for whatever happens next, but I won't... I won't hurt her. We'll find another way, Nancy. I'll find another way."

Nancy stared at her brother's back as he walked away from her and headed towards his friends. At the bottom of the stairway, Landris unstrapped his sword and dropped it on the floor.

"No, brother," Nancy said taming back her emotions. "I'm the one who will protect you — as always."

From the crystal spire, a tsunami of stream unleashed in all directions and passed through all within the temple and the temple itself. The tsunami continued as it passed through the warships and on until it went beyond the horizon.

The ones within the temple inspected themselves and each other. The stream seemed harmless. After unleashing the streams, the Light dissipated, and as the Light faded away, the crystal spire dimmed and the temple lost its sheen.

The door reopened. Lily walked out from the light, and the door closed behind her.

"It is done. You'll feel weak for a little while," the man said as Lily's decision was fulfilled.

The black halo above her head became whole once again and landed gently on her head. Lily grabbed the halo and placed it around her wrist.

"Kalin," Lily muttered as she tried to find her balance. Kalin quickly came by her side and helped her stand.

"Your people... I hope they will appreciate what you've done for them. And I hope that you will be happier with your decision than I was with mine. Rest now child, and rest well. There could be no greater duty a mortal could have done."

"I'm here, Lily. I'm here." Kalin carried Lily in his arms.

"Lily!" Julian and Sarah ran gleefully to the Witch's side.

As they walked down the stairway, Landris met them halfway.

"Welcome back," Landris told Lily. Lily smiled brightly.

Near the bottom of the stairway, Nancy waited for them all.

Kalin placed Lily back on her feet. She was weak, but smiled at Nancy as she closed the gap between them and they embraced one another.

"But tread lightly. If even the gods are not free from resentment, what chance does a mere mortal have?" With these last words, the man disappeared much like how he first appeared before Lily. The door opened behind her.

Nancy whispered softly into the Witch's ear as she drew the revolver out of her handbag and pulled the trigger.

The gunfire was more chilling and louder than any other gunfire they had ever heard or ever would hear in their lives.

The white room splattered with red.

Her clothes dirtied with blood, Nancy dropped Lily's body and quickly stood and pointed the gun at her next target.

"LILY!" Kalin screamed.

Another gunshot, and Kalin felt a heavy impact on his shoulder and fell to the ground. The white room was tarnished with even more red.

Nancy pointed the gun at her next target.

Julian saw that the director's gun was now pointing at Sarah. He thought of quickly grabbing Sarah's hand to disappear, but another idea occurred to him, and that other idea seemed cleaner and neater. He had just enough courage for that idea but not enough for the first.

"NANCY! NO!" Landris shouted as he leapt for his sister.

The last bullet.

Before Landris could interrupt Nancy, her finger squeezed the trigger. But the bullet that was meant for Sarah's heart pierced Julian who appeared in front of her. Julian fell to the ground as he coughed up blood.

Landris tore the gun away from Nancy and crushed it in his hand. Before he could do anything, Landris saw his black blade jet across under his arm and pierce Nancy in her abdomen. The impact was strong enough to lift Nancy off balance and onto the ground.

The boy who would be remembered as a hero in the legend stood without words or wits over what had transpired in just seconds. He turned his head to where the sword had flown from, and, as expected, saw the Witch's friend. Their eyes did not meet. The redhead breathed heavily as he bled from one of his arms and stared at the still body of the director. He then quickly ran to the Witch.

"Lily!" Kalin cried as he saw Lily staring at the ceiling in a crimson pool. The black hole in her stomach where the blood spilled from blended with her black dress. He quickly placed his hand over the wound and began pouring in his stream.

"You're hurt, Kalin. You're hurt," Lily said, seeing her bloodied friend.

"I'm okay, Lily. And you're going to be okay, too," he lied to her and to himself.

"Oh god, Julian," Sarah knelt by her best friend. She quickly took off her uniform jacket and pressed it on the wound. Julian's face was already pale. "Stay with me, Julian. Stay with me."

Landris walked over to his sister. Her eyes wide from the pain and disbelief of her oncoming demise, they rolled down from the ceiling to her brother.

"What happened?" Lily asked.

"I don't know, Lily. I don't know." Kalin frantically poured his streams into the wound. The bleeding slowed down, but he could sense that the wound was too grave.

"Did I do something wrong?" Lily asked.

"No, Lily," Kalin said.

"Kalin…" Lily coughed violently and splattered blood on Kalin.

"Don't talk, alright? You're going to be fine. Just don't talk," Kalin pleaded.

"Kalin, why was I… why was I b…" Lily bit her lip from asking the question.

Landris took his uniform jacket off. He wrapped it around the sword and pressed it over his sister's wound. "The wound is too big, Nancy," Landris said. The blade had gone through Nancy when it initially struck her and pushed out as she fell to the ground onto her back, causing the wound to widen. "I don't… I don't know what to do."

As the crew from the warships gathered composure after the tsunami of streams, they fired their cannons once again. The cannons struck the dim temple and the crew cheered as the building exploded under their weapon's might.

Landris huddled over his sister's body to block the debris.

"It's alright, Landris. It was a risk we were willing to take," Nancy said. "Pull this blade out of me. Tell them the blood on the blade is the Witch's. Yuri will help you with the rest."

"What for?" Landris looked at his sister in disbelief. "What was all this for?"

"For you!" Nancy snow-like skin was getting whiter. "For you, Landris! You're… you're still so young. Still so naive. I still see the helpless boy I came home to that night."

"It didn't have to be this way," Landris said. "Nancy, it didn't have to be this way."

"But it is now, Landris. And for us to survive, it had to be this way..." Nancy fought through the pain as she gasped for breath. "Sometimes we have to do what we can't do or don't want to do. It's not fair and it's not easy, but..." Nancy's breath became heavier and more rapid. "...it's the way it is," Nancy told her brother who didn't seem convinced. With each second passing, Nancy felt her consciousness lose its grip.

"It doesn't matter now. Just promise, Landris. Promise you'll take care of mom and yourself. That you'll survive. Don't let all this go to waste. Survive." Nancy couldn't find the words anymore. The world around her was fading away.

"Kalin," Lily called out to her friend. "Kalin," her voice was getting weaker. She tugged on his arm as hard as she could for his attention. "Thank you," Lily couldn't help but smile as Kalin finally turned his attention from her wound to her. "Thank you for everything."

"Don't talk like that, stupid," Kalin said. "It's going to be alright." The blood flowing out from the wound lessened. Kalin felt no comfort, not knowing if the streams were actually working or simply teasing him.

"Kalin, I'm glad I was alive because of you," Lily said, her cold hand touched his face. "I was *happy* to be alive when I was with you."

Kalin struggled to speak. Part of him wanted her to stop talking. Stop reminding him of what was a possibility. The other part of him wanted to not miss the chance to give her a proper farewell. Not to miss the chance to let her know what her life meant for him.

"I just..." Lily's voice began to shake. "...I just wish we could have had more time together." Lily didn't want to cry. She didn't want Kalin to remember her crying. She tried to smile, and thinking of the memories of their adventures gave her some peace to do just that.

"I was alive because I was with you, stupid," Kalin said. He didn't want Lily to see him cry. He didn't want her to think that he gave up. He didn't. Not yet. But his tears were grasping reality better than he was. "So don't leave me, Lily," Kalin pleaded as he grabbed her hand on his face with his. "Please. You don't get to go yet."

Another shell struck the temple. The building cracked and crumbled around them, but the destruction wasn't enough to shake anyone within.

"My wish..." Lily's tears were drying up, and her face lit up with her smile. "My wish was for us to be happy after all this was over. Even though I'm gone, please let my wish come true."

"No. No, Lily. No..." Kalin shook his head. "Don't give up."

"Kalin, find..." Lily's hand only stayed by Kalin's face because he held on to it. "...find a home and..." Lily scrounged the last bit of life she had to maintain her smile. "Smile more."

Julian drifted in and out of consciousness. The voices and the chaos around him sounded like hollow echoes. Above him was Sarah who looked more desperate than he had ever seen her. He could see the temples falling apart around them. Inching his hand towards Sarah felt as if he was moving boulders.

With his fingers touching Sarah's arm, Julian thought of the fond memories of waiting for her at the field by their old school. The anticipation that built up until he finally saw Sarah walking up to the field with her glowing face as she waved hello.

For her, Julian had to once again find courage because soon all would crumble into the ocean. Without a logical reason, he felt certain that he wouldn't let her down.

Sarah and Julian dispersed with countless particles of light.

Landris stood by his sister's still body.

"Nancy..." he muttered his sister's name even though he knew she couldn't hear him anymore. He gently relieved her of the sword piercing her body.

Landris's mourning for his sister was cut short by the gunfire outside as the soldiers of different nations fought to enter the temple. He looked behind him to see only Kalin and Lily remaining.

"Come on!" Landris hurried over to Kalin whose bloodied hand was still pouring stream into Lily's wound.

The Witch's eyes were closed as if she was asleep.

"Kalin!" Landris yelled.

The Witch's friend did not hear him.

"We have to go!" Landris grabbed Kalin's shoulder.

Kalin slowly turned his head to Landris before turning his attention back to Lily.

"Go," Kalin's voice was barely loud enough for Landris to hear over the chaos.

"You'll die!" Landris shouted in frustration.

"Where could we go?" Kalin turned his head towards Landris again. "My home, where I belong, is wherever she is. Go, Landris. Save yourself."

The soldiers were now beginning to fill the first hallway.

"Damn it!" Landris headed towards the hallway with his blade in hand. "I'll hold them back. You just find a chance to escape somehow."

Hopelessness of the situation wasn't lost to Landris. He simply didn't want to accept it. When Landris opened the gate to the hallway the frantic soldiers turned all of everyone's attention toward the boy with the bloodied sword. Before Landris could speak or take any sort of action, a loud explosion turned all of their attention behind him. As the rubble from the temple fell above them, Landris saw Kalin embrace Lily as he gave her their first and last kiss. The crystal spire cracked in two and fell over the temple.

It was the last image of the Witch and her guardian.

BORN AT A GRAVESIDE

Kalin laid the bouquet of lilies by his mother's headstone.

"I still don't know where to go or what to do, mom," Kalin said. "But I think… I should help this girl. I think, maybe, that's what you'd have wanted me to do. Would it be alright?"

Ruby looked at Kalin and then looked at the headstone. Was his mother going to speak back to him?

Kalin didn't say much and just sat on the grass as he stared at the headstone. Ruby waited silently, although she didn't want to stay here much longer. When her legs grew tired, Ruby sat by Kalin.

"Why is your mom here?" Ruby carefully asked.

"Because she's dead," Kalin replied.

Ruby felt her blood rushing through her face. "I know… but…" Ruby began to trail off into a mumble. "Wasn't your mom a good person?" Ruby asked.

"Yeah, she was the best." Kalin looked at her as if she had offended him.

Ruby quickly looked away.

The two sat in silence, simply staring at the headstone. Frustration building up inside and unable to form her feelings into words, Ruby's emotions manifested physically as she tore the grass around her while tears started to drizzle down her face.

"What's…. wrong…?" Kalin asked, confused by the Witch's sudden burst of emotion.

"Why did your mom have to die?" Ruby asked.

"What?"

"She was a good person, right?"

"Yeah…"

"Killed by bad people. The world just seems to be filled with bad people." Ruby wiped off the tears with the palm of her hands. Her face was becoming a mess. "Why can't the world just be filled with good people? I don't like this world. If I could change it, I'd only make it filled with good things."

The Witch's naiveté startled Kalin.

"I don't think it's that simple, Ruby," Kalin said.

"Good is good. Bad is bad," Ruby said.

"Yeah, but what's good and what's bad? Sometimes what's good for someone can be bad for someone else, and someone who's bad could be good. Until I met you, I thought the Witch was bad." Kalin bit his lip for that last remark.

Ruby looked shaken.

"I'm sorry. I mean, what I'm trying to say is…" Kalin back paddled. "I guess in some way, I'm saying you're right."

Ruby tilted her head.

"The world isn't bad or good. It just is. Sometimes the world does seem like it's full of bad people. But we can't forget that what makes the world good is also its people."

Ruby's head remained tilted.

Kalin found himself confused by his own ramble. "My mom got killed, and that sucks. I'll forever hate those guys who killed her." Kalin gave it a second shot. "But I won't blame the world for it because… there are lot of bad people and bad things, and they're just part of the world just like the good things and good people. And those who are good can't give up or forget being good even during the worst times because then there'll be nothing good left."

Kalin studied Ruby's face to see if he had made any sense. "I might not know what I'm talking about," Kalin said with an embarrassed smile.

"I don't understand," Ruby said. "Maybe I will later."

"Maybe," Kalin chuckled. "And I'll probably learn a thing or two as time goes on. Maybe even from you."

"So if you had a chance to change the world, you wouldn't make it just full of good things?" Ruby asked.

"I wouldn't change anything, I guess," Kalin said after thinking about the question for a moment. "Because who would know what would be best for the entire world? I don't think mankind was meant to play god. Whether the world is good or bad just happens to be our responsibility."

Ruby seemed puzzled again by his answer.

"Let life just be. We'll deal with it as it comes," Kalin finished his answer.

"You're smart," Ruby said.

"Not really," Kalin said.

"And I think you're a good person."

"Not really."

Ruby frowned.

"You seem like a good person, too," Kalin said.

Ruby shook her head.

Kalin wasn't sure how to respond to her answer. Perhaps he wasn't sure yet if he actually knew enough to mean his words.

Kalin stood up and offered Ruby his hand. The sky was already orange with the day's end. She took his hand and stood up with him. It was a long walk through the rows of headstones out of the cemetery.

"Why do you think you're not a good person, Ruby?"

Kalin wondered if that was a dumb and obvious question.

Ruby didn't say anything.

"You hungry, Ruby?" Kalin changed the topic.

"Is it okay if I'm called something else?" Ruby stopped walking and looked at Kalin.

"What?"

"I want to be called something else. I don't like that name. Is that okay?"

"I guess. It's your name. You should be called whatever you want."

"What should I be called?"

"I don't know. What do you like?"

The nameless girl thought for a moment.

"I liked those flowers you got your mom a lot."

Kalin raised an eyebrow as the girl's eyes glittered and her lips stretched into smile.

"Is that bad? I'm sorry." Her face quickly turned back into a frown.

"No, I guess that's fine," Kalin said. "I guess your name's Lily starting today."

"I like it!" Lily said. "I'll be a good girl as a Lily!"

Kalin wasn't sure what Lily meant but smiled and nodded. "To celebrate, do you want to go get some of those donuts you like, Lily?"

"Yes!"

"Alright. After eating some real food first, though." Kalin began to guide Lily out of the cemetery again.

"I want to see the world. Maybe I'll understand what you said after I see the world," Lily said.

Kalin chuckled. "The world is a big place. I'm not sure how much we'll get to see of it searching for your parents, especially considering…" Kalin stopped himself. "But maybe seeing as much of it as we can isn't such a bad idea either."

Lily looked up at Kalin with a hopeful smile. It had been a long time since the last time she felt excited. "And I want to get taller," Lily said in Kalin's shadow.

"Yeah? Maybe you still can." Kalin decided if Lily didn't really have complaints, sandwiches would make a decent dinner. It'd be easier to feed her vegetables this way as well, he thought.

"I want to be as tall as you," Lily declared.

"Nope, I'm pretty sure that's impossible." Kalin didn't need to look at Lily to know that she was probably frowning.

Soon, the Witch and her friend were out of the cemetery and onto the main road. It was a quiet day, and the weather was fair. The orange sky felt warmer than it should to both Kalin and Lily. Kalin looked to his left and then to his right. Neither of them were entire sure where there journey would go and how the journey would be, but the two of them took the first step of it together.

Chapter 63
FOR BETTER DAYS

A fanfare-like jingle played as the segments of the previous episodes of *The Point* played across the screen in the opening sequence. After the big logo "*The Point with Brian O'Connor*" lingered on the screen for a bit, the program immediately cut to Brian, himself.

"Welcome back to The Point. I'm your host, Brian O'Connor."

The camera switched to one with a different angle, and Brian gently spun in his chair to face the audience.

"It's been a little more than a couple of weeks since that mysterious aurora-like tsunami encompassed the world, and the Light that puzzled us all disappeared."

The screen split as a panel appeared next to Mr. O'Connor. It was now two-thirds Mr. O'Connor, and one third text that listed the key points of what Mr. O'Connor had been talking about.

"Here's what we know—all we know—even after more than two weeks after the incident. We know that the Witch was involved. We have no idea how she was able to get through the barricade. We know she raised some sort of a temple from the leaked photos which is now in ruins and off-limits to the public. We have no idea of the impact of what she's done, assuming that the aurora incident was her cause. Let's see… we know it was Landris Jones, the brother of the famed Nancy Jones of the Silver Aegis, who apparently slayed the Witch and is now hailed as a hero. We don't know the details yet of how he was there in the first place and who, if anyone, was there with him."

Mr. O'Connor shrugged and made a face to capture the dumbfounded-ness he knew his audience was feeling towards the story and their government.

"Now, we obviously have a lot of questions that are unanswered not only by our government, but also by the rest of the world who seems to be in a pact to leave their citizens out of the loop. The leaked footage that everyone's seen of the battleship cannon fire supposedly being stopped by the Witch and the

crystal tower... thing... only raises more questions than answers. We have a guest today who we hope can shed some light into this story. Joining us now is Mr. Robert McKinley, the head of the McKinley Securities a company that was once in charge of our nation's security against the so called Gifted."

The screen bisected into two. Mr. O'Connor on the right and Mr. McKinley on the left. Mr. McKinley seemed to be either bothered by something or just had an angry resting face.

"Hello, *Brian*." Mr. McKinley wanted to assert his authority.

"Hello, Robert. So, what do you think about... about... this boy hero, Landris Jones; and on that note, where's his sister? Where's Nancy Jones? Why is this Yuri Ivanov currently in charge of the Silver Aegis?"

"Well, Brian, Yuri Ivanov's actually been a part of Silver Aegis since Nancy's father ran the company, so I'm not surprised he's taking over. Where Nancy is... I don't know. I can't say."

"You don't know, or you can't say?"

"Both."

"Your thoughts on the boy hero? Landris Jones?"

"I mean... I never met the boy, but if the stories are true, then sure! He's a hero. But I can't be the only one who thinks it's a bit odd that the Witch's body happened to conveniently disappear and with it whatever the hell was going on with that castle at the Light." Mr. McKinley's rationality suddenly grasped control over his bitter emotions. "But... yes... the boy's a hero. No doubt. He killed the Witch! Who knows what that thing could have done if she had been alive any longer."

"You don't seem sure, Robert."

"Boy's a hero, Brian."

"Alright, well, we got lots more to talk about, so I won't press further. But what happened that the government decided to switch companies regarding the security against the Gifted?"

"Well, Brian, that's just business. Our contract with the government expired, and we couldn't come to an agreement regarding its renewal. Maybe hiring the boy hero is good publicity for them. The McKinley Securities has been proud to serve this country, and we are all a bit disappointed that the deal fell through."

"Is that all that was, Robert?" Mr. O'Connor had a sly smile on his face.

"I'm sorry?" Mr. McKinley's raised an eyebrow as agitation slowly began to turn over to anger.

"Well, Robert, I must say I do have a little surprise for you here on The Point today."

"What is this?" Mr. McKinley was starting to lose his showmanship.

"We have another special guest who said he knew why you might have lost the government contract. Can we have Detective Fowler on the line, please. Detective Anthony Fowler, ladies and gentleman."

"Hello, this'll be quick," Detective Fowler's voice played in the background. "I was entrusted with a package from a former employee of yours, Mr. McKinley, who told me I should do with this whatever I wished. I figured for the sake of everyone involved, I'd let it loose on national television."

"What video? I wasn't told of this! What is this, Brian?!" Mr. McKinley gave everything he had to hold himself from screaming.

"Let's play the video," Mr. O'Connor said with a smug smile.

The screen showed Mr. O'Connor grinning and Mr. McKinley going through a museum of emotions as they both waited for the video to play.

"Where's the video?" Mr. O'Connor asked when it didn't appear.
Mr. McKinley looked a bit relieved.

"What do you mean there's a technical difficulty?" Mr. O'Connor was now the one who had to give everything he had from screaming at his staff.

Julian pressed a button on his remote to switch the channel.

Another news station.
"There has been more and more reports of people discovering that they may also be a 'gif—"

Switch channel.

"In just six weeks...."

Switch channel.

A man missing a tooth and hiding his long messy hair under a hat is being interviewed with the woods behind him.

"Well, I reckon it was a fairy or something. It was glowing, and it was real pretty..."

A gentle knock on the door made Julian turn off the TV.
Before Julian could give permission, Sarah poked her head inside.

"Oh my god," Sarah quickly walked into the room. "Julian... you're awake!"

Julian wanted to respond or smile back, but physically and mentally, he had never felt worse before in his life. His head felt like it was weighted down by an anchor, his muscles felt as if they were melting off his bones, and his insides felt like they were cluttered with gunk. It took more effort than he imagined simply turning his head on the pillow to look at Sarah.

Sarah's eyes glittered as she held back the tears. She closed the door behind her and pulled up a chair so she could sit by Julian's bed. Her warm hand caressed his hand. "I was worried that maybe you'd never wake up," Sarah said.

"Did..." Julian tried to speak, but his throat felt too weak. "Did they make it?"

The unexpected question caught Sarah off guard. "You mean..."

Sarah only had to look into Julian's eyes to understand who Julian was asking about.

"We..." Sarah paused for a moment. "We don't know, Julian. As far as we know, none of the bodies were found. Not even Ms. Jones. Because the entire plaza began to crack from the damage, some of us thought that maybe their bodies slipped into the ocean... but..." Sarah cleared her throat.

Julian simply stared at Sarah until tears poured from his eyes.

"Ever since I woke up..." Julian tried to strengthen his throat. "I just couldn't help but keep thinking over and over if I could have done something different."

Sarah couldn't say anything.

"Then I keep going backwards and backwards," Julian's voice shook. "How can so much happen, and how can so much change in just a few days? Was there a point to any of this? For us? For them?"

"Julian..."

"I could have done so much more, Sarah. I could have done so many things differently."

Another knock on the door.

"Bad time?" Emily poked her head in. Julian quickly covered his teary eyes with his hand.

"I'll come back later. Good to see you awake," Emily said as she pulled away from the room.

"Just come in!" Julian spoke as loudly as he could.

Emily looked to Sarah for permission. She nodded her in.

"What's she doing here?" Julian asked.

"I didn't know who we could turn to... so I called her for help," Sarah said.

"Unbelievably, you ended up appearing with her at the field of your old school. That's nearly a quarter ways around the world. Did you tell him yet?" Emily asked Sarah as she stood by her.

"Oh right. Julian, as far as the hospital is concerned, you are Emeril Peterson, and I'm Raina Green."

"Our parents' names?"

"Thought it wouldn't hurt to be careful," Emily said. "Though it turns out, it might have been unnecessary."

Julian waited for Sarah to give an explanation.

"The official story so far is that Landris, Lily, and Kalin were the only ones who were there at the temple," Sarah said. "Though there are strong rumors that others were with them, so they may change that story later. Especially when they answer people's questions regarding Director Jones. But for whatever reasons they're pushing Landris's story right now as the official story."

"Why would he do that?" Julian asked.

"To protect you guys seems the most logical explanation to me," Emily answered. "To give you to a chance to get away from it all. Or it's always possible that maybe he has other schemes up his sleeve."

"Whatever the case, you should really thank Emily, Julian. She's been very good to us. She kept us safe and is paying for all this," Sarah told Julian. Emily seemed uncomfortable with the praise.

"Thanks," Julian said. "Thank you."

"Don't mention it." Emily couldn't look at Julian directly. "Helping is what we do. I'll let your friends know that you've woke up. I'm sure they're dying to see you. We can probably arrange for you to meet up with your parents as well. I'll give the two of you some privacy now." Emily began heading for the door.

"Friends?" Julian asked before Emily could head out.

"Some of your friends we borrowed decided to go back. Some decided to go elsewhere completely. And some decided to stick around." Emily closed the door behind her.

"Who?" Julian asked Sarah.

"Gus, Maria, Howard, and Nada," Sarah smiled. "They all visited you while you were still asleep."

"I see." Julian turned his head and stared at the ceiling. "What do we do from here on now?"

"Live," Sarah said. "Just like before. We'll find our way to the better days."

"Wherever they are," Julian said after a pause. "I hope they're not running anymore. And… and I hope they're happy."

Sarah squeezed Julian's hand.

"I hope so, too," Sarah said.

"The sky outside…" Julian looked out the window next to his bed. The sky was clear and blue. "I never thought I'd ever see it again without the Light. I never thought it'd feel so empty without it."

Sarah looked out the window with Julian.

Emptiness.

Sarah wondered if that described what she'd been feeling for the last few days, hidden behind her dishonest smiles. She was already used to the Lightless sky, and whatever it was she was feeling, Sarah knew it wasn't the absence of the Light that caused it. It wasn't the Light that made her look up at the sky, nor would it be the Light that would make her keep looking up in the days ahead.

It wasn't the Witch and her friend that made her double-take anytime she heard a girl hum or caught a glimpse of something red walking past her, but it was out of the sincere and desperate hope that she may find her friends again. The ones she would never forget as the rest of the world had as the Witch and the Guardian.

Epilogue
a Recorder's New Task

"… If the legend of the magnificent powers of the Black Halo used by the Witch are true, then I wonder if it was mankind's defiance that let us survive the Great Calamity, or if it was simply that her intentions were not at all to end mankind. This tale that defines us, this story that was life for those who were part of that era, is nothing but legend and pages in history books now — and we're content with it.

But I believe there's more to the tale of the Witch and the Guardian. It's shortsighted for those who question the tale and yearn to dig further to be branded as loons and heretics. If not to simply learn of our origins, I think it's important for us to research further into the story behind the tale of the Witch and the Guardian to prevent something like the Great Calamity from happening ever again. This is why I humbly request that I may be given permission to take on this research.

Sincerely,
Mary Anna Candle."

Mary Anna felt something poke the back of her head. She looked behind her to find a paper crane on the ground.

"Was your trip successful, counselor?" Mary Anna turned around and expectedly found her mentor who had a penchant for folding paper cranes and harassing her (he said it was out of love).

Liam stood with a wide grin on his face in his black cloak of the Recorder. The large and defined collar of the cloak represented his status in the guild. He withdrew his hood and revealed his long dark hair. It was considered a bit rude to wear the hood within the guild halls.

"Very. I met fun new people and had a grand adventure getting to know them." Liam picked up the paper crane and stuffed it in his pocket. He'd probably fold another as soon as he had a chance, his apprentice figured.

Realizing something, Mary Anna shot a puzzled look at her mentor as he reached around and grabbed the parchment off her desk.

"That is not for you!" Mary Anna protested. "It is for the Master Raina!"

"Here a gift." Liam handed Mary a small, red paper pouch tied off by a blue bow as he began reading the parchment. She knew right away just from the bag what it was, and she eagerly opened it up to find the expected array of cookies. It was the final clue for Liam's misdeed.

"Though I am curious of your adventure and these new people you've met… and thankful that you got me these cookies," Mary spoke as she already worked on one of the cookies. "It does make me wonder if you actually did your assignment of investigating the sighting of the colossal beast at the Dead and Red Canyons—a task specifically given to you by Master Raina herself? A place where I'd be very surprised if you met anyone?"

"Yes, about that. I postponed it. That thing isn't going anywhere. I'll probably leave for him or her or whatever it is sometime the day after tomorrow." Liam grabbed one of the cookies for himself. Completely engrossed with the parchment, Liam didn't bother to look up or even say please and thank you.

"That's not very Arch-Recorder-like, counselor Liam." Mary grabbed her second cookie.

"My little apprentice," Liam chuckled. "It is because I am an Arch-Recorder that I can do such things." He popped the cookie into his mouth.

Mary Anna grumbled as she sent of her wooden golems by her feet to fetch the two of them some tea. The golems' wooden clogs of feet pattered on the wooden floor as they looked for the kettle.

"Well, I didn't think I'd see you for a while, so I intended that letter for Master Raina, herself. But since you are here… permission to start on a new assignment, sir," Mary said as her golems gently floated in the air with soft, fluttering wings of light. They bore cups of tea which they held above their heads with their little wooden arms. The two golems handed the tea to each of the Recorders.

"I remember you expressing interest in this old tale when you first arrived here, but I think you're still far too green to chase after an old tale that's barren in any clues and details." Liam set the cup on the table as he rolled up the parchment.

"An old tale of how the New World came to be." Mary saw Liam's eyes rise from the parchment to her. "And I think as a Recorder, as barren as it could be, it is our job and pride to try to find something that others couldn't have."

Liam gave a stern look as he held the parchment with one hand and grabbed for the tea with other. "Why are you so invested in this, dear Mary Anna?"

"I want to know the story—the *actual story* of the Witch."

Liam's look made Mary Anna nervous. Her nerves were calmed when her counselor's stern look washed away with a smile.

"I've lived long enough to know a stubborn girl when I see one."

Liam grabbed a ribbon from Mary Anna's desk and tied off the parchment.

"You don't look much older than me, Master Liam," Mary Anna said with a frown. "In fact, you don't look old enough to be allowed to say 'I've lived long enough.'"

"I'll take this up to the guild master myself and ask her for her thoughts. Mind you, she may decline your request based on the fact that many seasoned Recorders have tried before you and found it to be either a waste of time or a waste of effort." Liam put the parchment somewhere within the dark crimson insides of his cloak. He finished his tea and headed for the door.

Before he left, Liam turned around and placed the paper crane in Mary Anna's hand. "This new adventure I was just a part of," Liam said. "May shed some light to this old story."

END of Black Halo: the Witch & the Guardian

Acknowledgements

Raon-Jenna Aramiru
Bryce Betteridge
Anthony Claudio
Vinh Khanh Hoang
Hyun McMurray
James McMurray
William McMurray
Eri Nakatani
Chun Song
Jennifer Song
Jennifer Wee

Whatever success this project may find was made my possible by these people.

a Writer's Request

Best way for me to improve as a writer is to hear back from you, the readers, who've put up with my writing long enough to finish this novel.

Please leave me your comments, complaints, and even compliments at wherever you've purchased this novel.

And if you wish, for whatever reason, to keep up with my nonsense, follow me on Twitter (https://twitter.com/ASAramiru) and/or Facebook (http://www.facebook.com/ASAramiru).

You can also find more detailed ramblings of life and writing at http://www.Aramiru.com

Thank you for reading and hope to hear from you soon.

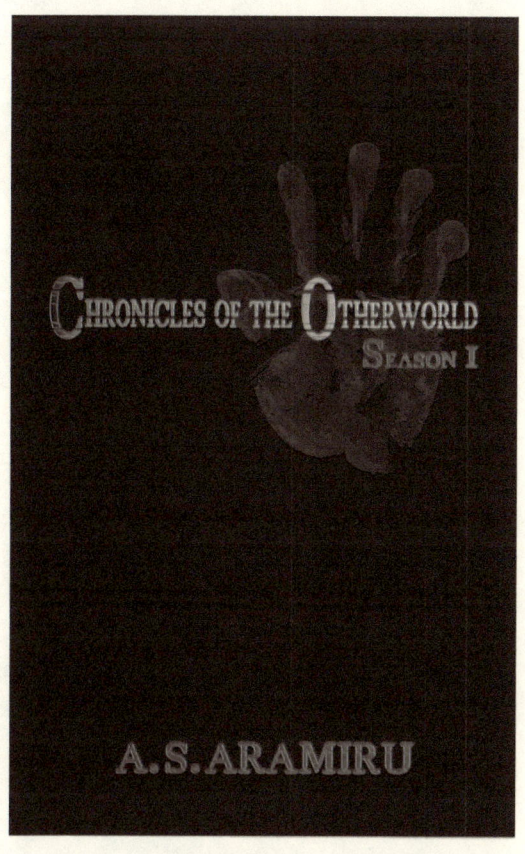

CHRONICLES OF THE OTHERWORLD:

SEASON 1

The world is for those who were born to conquer it.

They were just born elsewhere.

Neither this world's salvation or doom, nor protectors or foes, nevertheless their presence will irreversibly rewrite the fate of the Otherworld.

Season 1 of Chronicles of the Otherworld follows the tales of Tay, Camilla, and Robert.

Avaiable now on Amazon & Audiuble